EVERY ARM OUTSTRETCHED

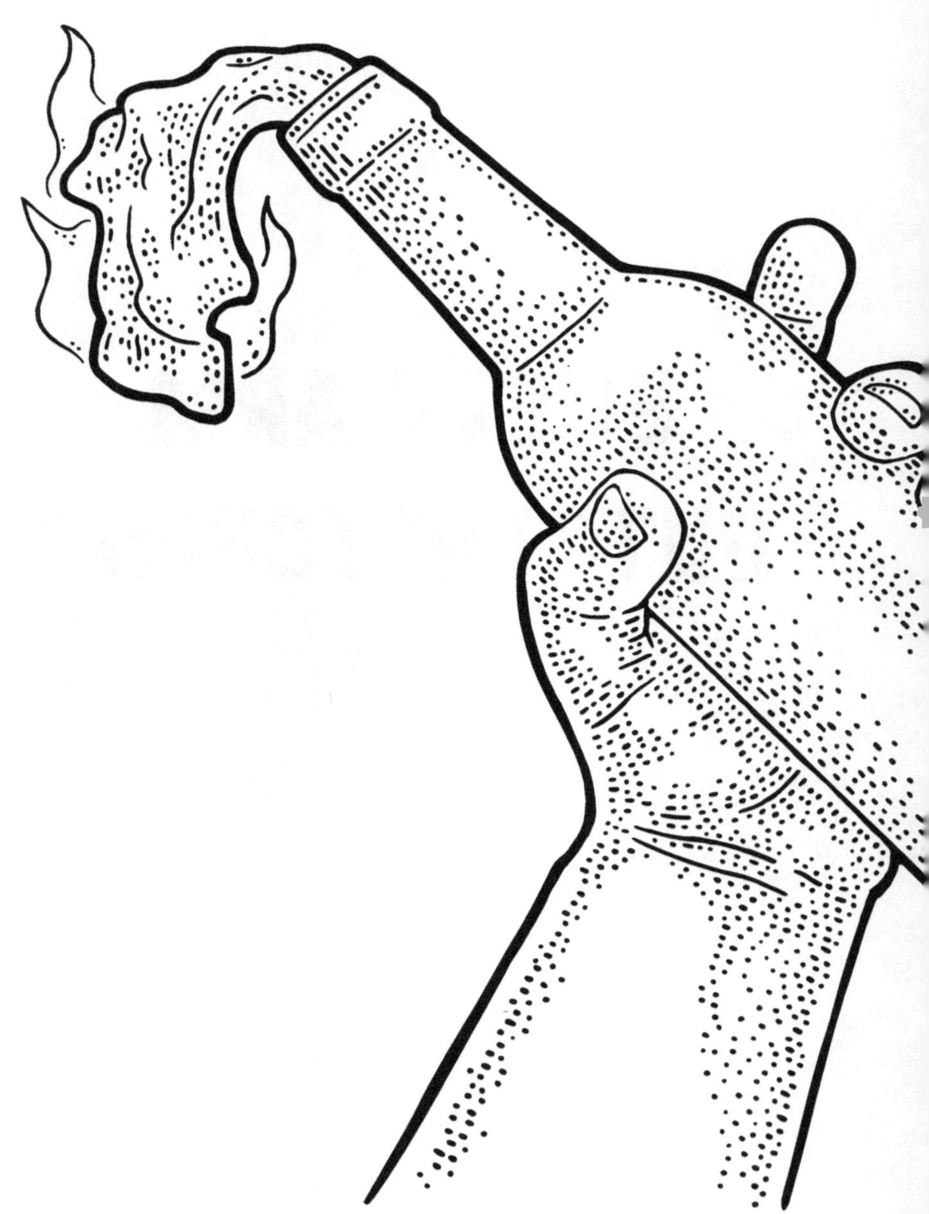

EVERY ARM OUTSTRETCHED

Phil Halton

Developmental Editor: Don Gillmor
Copy Editor: Lisa Meffe
Cover design: Paul Hewitt
Back matter photo taken by Dora María Téllez during the fighting in Leon, June 1979. Shown are Ma. Luisa Mendez (Miriancita) y Oscar Cortész.

Library and Archives Canada Cataloguing in Publication
Halton, Phil, author
Every Arm Outstretched / Phil Halton

First edition published 2020. Second edition 2023.

Issued in print and electronic formats.
ISBN: 978-1-990644-80-1 (hard cover)
ISBN: 978-1-990644-78-8 (soft cover)
ISBN: 978-1-990644-79-5 (e-book)

Molotov Books
Toronto, Canada

Para mis hijos.

1

IT WASN'T A PRISON, though some days it felt like one.

It shouldn't have mattered to me, I suppose, what colours the walls were, or that my room wasn't much bigger than my bed, or that the timing of meals, and everything else, was strictly enforced. I spent most of my time living inside my head, thinking of when I was young and strong and alive. I knew that I should've been happy that there was a roof over my head and that I never wondered when or if I would eat. But death stalked the hallways. Some days I felt his breath on the back of my neck, just as I had when I was in the mountains.

I put down the dog-eared copy of *Pedro Páramo* that I had been reading, sliding an old prayer card between the pages to mark my place. I maneuvered around the open door of my single room and rolled myself down the hall with the nicotine yellow walls. Most of the doors I passed had two neatly written cards mounted on them, each showing its residents' names. At the top of each card, written in block letters, was the resident's former rank. I glanced in each doorway as I passed until I reached the end of the ward,. I wasn't sure what I hoped to see beyond grey faces looking back at me.

It didn't take long for the orderly to see that I was at the doors, even though his attention was on a small television showing a protest that filled the streets somewhere. A young man in scrubs held the door open for me with one hand while giving my wheelchair a helpful push over the lip at the threshold with the other.

"Thank you," I croaked, without looking back. When my voice stuck in my throat, I realized that I had not spoken for several days outside of my thoughts and dreams.

Though I knew it was grey, the side of the building seemed to shine brightly in the sun. High up were metal letters discretely dripping rust. They read:

RESIDENCIA DE LOS ANCIANOS HÉROES

And peering down over the letters was a huge bearded face. Or, nothing more than an outline of a face, really, all the details of the man himself missing.

I turned away from the metal artwork and towards the sea, and let the sun warm my bones. I rolled down the concrete pad in front of the building, then stopped at the railing overlooking the malecón. I pulled the oxygen tubes from my nose, rubbing my itchy nostrils with my finger before replacing them again and settling back in my chair. I ignored the oil refinery squatting on the shoreline nearby, and instead looked out to sea. In the distance, just short of the horizon, I could see a collection of fishing boats huddled together, pushed by the waves. The sound of the water rhythmically hitting the stone of the malecón was constant and regular, and because of that, soothing.

"Comandante?"

I turned to look over my shoulder, and there was the orderly again. Standing with him was a young man who I immediately knew to be from the Party. His slacks and open-collared shirt were pressed and clean, and his chunky black glasses would have been fashionable in my youth. His only seeming pretention was a computer tablet that he held in his hands like a prayer book.

"My membership's paid up," I said, before turning back to the sea.

Out of the corner of my eye, I saw the Party functionary look at the orderly, who merely shrugged. "Mi Comandante, my name is Rubén Pacheco Losa. It is my absolute pleasure to meet you."

I merely nodded.

Rubén smiled at the orderly in the way that meant he wasn't needed anymore, and dragged a battered metal chair across the concrete to sit facing me. He tucked the tablet under his arm so that he could gesture with both hands, then leaned in toward me. "This year's commemoration of Liberation Day will be the largest since you and the others marched into Managua forty years ago." His earnestness was exhausting. I could see that he was trying to gauge how much I understood of what was going on around me. I looked much older than my years and had become used to the fact that every young person suspected I was becoming senile. More often than not, I was simply tired of listening to them.

"That is great news," I said, looking him in the eye so that he could see that I was lucid. "I will enjoy watching it. On television."

Rubén looked relieved for a moment, if only because he didn't have to convince a confused old man to do whatever he was here to convince me to do. "On this anniversary," he said, "all the living veterans of the Revolution will be included in the parade, leading representatives from every branch of the FTEN."[1]

I tapped the side of my wheelchair with the flat of my hand. "I am past marching in parades." I fiddled with the oxygen tubes again. They always made my voice sound too nasal to me. Even at my age, I could still be vain.

Before I finished speaking, Rubén pulled the tablet out from under his arm and swiped his finger back and forth on the screen. When he held it up for me, my eyes must have given away that I was surprised.

"This is a photo of you and some others in your jeep during the war." I gasped at the ghosts in the photo before he swiped the screen, and a new photo appeared. "And this is that original jeep today. The one that led the column as you arrived in Managua. The very same one that you drove during the war. It has been

---

[1] *Translator's note: Fuerzas Terrestres de la Ejército de Nicaragua / Nicaraguan Army Ground Forces*

fully restored, everything fixed except the bullet holes. In fact, it's probably better than new, and the Party would like you to ride in it with some of your comrades."

I swiped back to look at the old photo of the jeep for a few moments, at the faces I hadn't seen in decades who stared back at me. I mumbled their names under my breath, and he must have thought that I had said "yes," and so he began to talk about the arrangements to bring me from the residence in Puerto Sandino to the capital. I looked away from the photograph and into the young face of the man who reminded me, in his earnestness, of other young men I had known. I let out a long sigh, the air whistling through my nose a little, and tapped the armrest of my chair with one finger to punctuate my answer. "No," I said. "I am too tired to lead a parade, even if all I am to do is sit in my seat."

Rubén took off his glasses for a moment and rubbed his temples with the thumb and fingers of one hand. "Comandante," he said, "there are not so many excombatientes left from forty years ago. How many will be left at sixty years? It's important that you be together en masse. One day, it won't be possible anymore." He saw that his argument wasn't moving me. "It is important for the People to see the heroes who gave them their freedom."

I rolled my wheelchair backwards away from him, not looking as I told him a truth that I knew very well. "The only heroes died during the Revolution. And no one can be given their freedom. That's not how it works." I turned the chair as quickly as I could, aiming for the door again and looking through the glass to try to catch the orderly's eye so that he would open it. Rubén stuck out a foot and jammed the wheel of my chair. Without thinking, I stood and walked for the door. I totter around from time to time, so it was not a miracle, though you would think differently if you saw Rubén's expression. I kicked the chair so that it rolled into the railing, and the noise jarred him into action. In an instant, he was beside me, his arm supporting mine.

"No one will force you to do anything," he said. "I know that you are not as strong as you once were, but there is no need to run away."

I let him help me back into my chair. "Who are you with?" I asked, my voice sharper and more pointed than before. "The FTEN?"

"No," he smiled, "I am no soldier. I am a Deputy in the FNT for Managua. I work in the department that was run by Jamie Marroquín."[2]

I ignored the fact that the man he referenced had been dead for a decade because it was then that I understood why he had really come to speak to me.

"I am telling you that no one will force you to be in this parade," he said, holding his hands up plaintively. "But I am also telling you: you have to be there. You fought and won the Revolution once, but it needs to be won again every day. The People need to see that their freedom was paid for with flesh and blood. The Revolution must go forward, whatever the personal cost."

I saw it in his eyes. He was an idealist in the way that only the young and inexperienced can be. I sighed heavily again, looking at this young man who was not much older than I was when the Revolution ended. I reached out and grabbed his arm. Judging by his expression, he was as surprised as I was at my strength.

"I will attend the parade, but on one condition."

His face was a mask of concern, not knowing what I might demand of him.

"Between now and then, I want you to record my story. All of it, from before the Revolution until victory."

He smiled again, and I realized that it was a common defence that he used to rebuff people. "I am sure," he said, "that there are military historians who will do this for you."

I did not release my grip on his arm, even though my fingers ached at the effort. "I don't want some officer trained at a military school in Moscow trying to refight old battles with me. I want someone who will just listen."

"I can ask for a voice recorder to be given to you. My wife will tell you, it will listen more reliably than I can," he said, laughing a

<hr>

[2] *Translators note: Frente Nacional de los Trabajadores / National Workers Front.*

little at his own joke.

"I'm too old to sit and talk to a machine all day," I said. "You can record it electronically if you like, but I need a person, flesh and blood as you said, to talk to."

Rubén began to push me towards the entrance of the residence, hoping to end the discussion. "Comandante, it would be an honour to listen to your memories, but I am very busy on various committees, and it is far for me to come here to Puerto Sandino . . ." His voice trailed off. "I am sure that there is someone else who can be detailed by the Party for this important task."

He brought me to my room, glancing at the photos on my dresser, of me standing with men he knew primarily from history books. I seized my chance. "During the Revolution, we worked seven days a week, and only because we couldn't work eight. Don't tell me that you're too busy."

Rubén hesitated, but when he glanced up at the thin glass case on my wall that held the original pennant that had been reproduced for his restored jeep, I knew that I had him. "You can come on Sundays," I said. "Just for the afternoon."

He reached out to shake my hand, and I gripped his as firmly as I could. The veins stood out against the back of my gnarled hand, making his hand look impossibly smooth and soft as I squeezed it. "OK," he said, finally.

"And this is between you and me," I said. "Not Party business."

He shrugged, I'm sure because he didn't see what difference that made.

"And you have to bring me a cigar. The rough kind that campesinos smoke, nothing fancy."

Rubén pointed at the oxygen tank strapped to the back of my wheelchair. "I doubt that is a good idea, Comandante."

"Not for me," I said, "for you. You're going to smoke it, and I'm going to enjoy the smell."

His face set in an expression of submission. "Alright," he said. "Next Sunday, Comandante."

"And you have to call me what everyone called me then. Paco."

"Of course, Coman . . . Paco."

Rubén left before I could make any further demands of him, and although I knew that he didn't want to spend his Sunday afternoons with me, I also knew that he would be true to his word. I rolled myself back down the hall and out through the lobby to look out at the sea again. The smell of salt in the air seemed stronger now, and I could see that the wind was whipping up waves in the distance where the fishing boats had been clustered. With white caps and darkening clouds at their backs, they were scurrying back to shore, the storm growing behind them.

PAZ Y BIEN... TODO PARA BIEN!

LA CIUDAD

2

THE FIRST FEW MONTHS OF 1978 were the hottest I can remember.

That may seem like trivia now, but I think that it actually shaped history. The nights were so hot no one could sleep. The streets were full of people at all hours, just walking, or sitting at outdoor bars and cafés hoping for a breeze. Many old neighbourhoods were still just piles of rubble from the earthquake in '72, and if they couldn't afford to pay for drinks, people would just sit on the heaps of brick and stone. No one slept well that summer, except maybe the rich. It was as if there was twice as much time in a day. We talked more, laughed more, danced more, and in the end, that is what caused history to take the path it did.

Along with some of the boys I grew up with in my barrio, I worked as a musician. I wasn't the best guitar player, and there were lots of better singers than me out there, but I could always get a crowd to start dancing. Some people liked American music, even "disco," whatever that was, but we played local music, son nica, or sometimes cumbia. Sometimes we got paid to play in bars, but we mostly played for tips, around restaurant tables in the plaza or at parties. With the unreliable electricity in the city, the only music you could count on was live. It was at one of these parties that I met Ramón.

The parties we played at weren't in the richest houses, but they were still a world away from the barrio of my youth, or the rooming house where I lived. University professors, journalists, or sometimes even artists after they had made a big sale, were our best clients. The number of guests often outstripped the size of their houses, and so parties spilled out into the garden or street. I guess you'd say we were part of the leftist intellectual scene, but I didn't think of things that way back then. I knew them as the people who gave us a little extra on top of our tips and gave us bottles of beer so we could cool off as we played through the night. They were simply good people, who didn't see me as an uneducated youth living just a hair's breadth above the gutter.

It took more than an hour of walking to get to this particular party on the other side of Managua. Our band was Esteban, Miguel, Luis, Antonio, and me, and we all carried our own instruments. My guitar was easy enough to bring, and I had a piece of rope that I had made into a sling so it hung over one shoulder. Miguel played guitar as well, and with the lightest loads, the two of us were always hurrying the others along as they lagged behind. Esteban's small marimba fit in his lap, and he had nailed leather straps to the underside, so he carried it like a backpack. Luis carried the wooden box that he used for percussion in both hands and a few rattles and claves. Antonio's accordion had straps on it already, but he was always stopping to change how he carried it, and so, was perpetually bringing up the rear.

The streets were crowded at all times of day, and we walked single file between the traffic and the market stalls that filled up many sidewalks. We walked straight through the Plaza de la República, with the ruins of the old cathedral looming over one edge. The streets leading from the plaza were surrounded by crumbling colonial buildings that leaned inwards as if taking great interest in the happenings beneath them. We weaved around a loose group of protesters in the centre of the square. They were listening to a man standing on a box and shouting about freedom. This demonstration meant little to those of us who had to hustle for money if we wanted to eat. Sometimes we made up songs as we walked, picking up snatches of conversations or the shouts of vendors. I don't remember all the words anymore, but Esteban made up a whole song about two chicken vendors who shouted out prices to attract customers from where they stood across the street from each other. There was an energy to the streets that we fed off of as we walked to our gigs. In crossing the city, we saw how every neighbourhood lived, rich and poor. I learned more from playing music in all parts of the city than I ever did during my few years of school.

That evening, Miguel took a few wrong turns while leading the way. He admitted that he was following a young woman, selling tostones from a huge basket, and wasn't paying attention. It was one of those hot, hot nights when women sweat through their dresses so that they cling to them in a way that was flattering and not at the same time. We were playing in the garden of an old colonial house that had seen better times. It was a professor of medical science who lived there, with his wife and three young girls, and every time I looked up from where we were playing, I could see all three children peering down from a window on the upper story. The garden was lush and unkempt, like a jungle, full of students and professors and neighbours.

We had been playing for nearly two hours when I looked around at the other players and using nothing more than glances, we agreed to take a break. We brought the song we were playing, a raucous version of Besada por el mar, to a big ending. All the dancers stopped and clapped, we took a quick bow, and leaving my guitar leaning against a fruit tree, I walked straight over to a tub of ice to find a beer. The tub looked mostly empty, but I fished around the bottom until I pulled out a bottle of Victoria. I passed the first one back to my friends, and then another, and so on, until at last, I could keep one for myself. I held the crisp bottle against my forehead to cool off while I looked around for the bottle opener.

Hearing a commotion, I looked across the garden towards the house. The crowd parted to make way for a line of young women, all balancing trays of beer on their heads, led by a young man. He looked to be a little older than me and was dressed in the open-necked shirt and pleated slacks that were practically a uniform for students at the university, though his clothes were far more rumpled than was fashionable. His thick, dark hair was piled in waves atop his head, making him look a little younger than he probably was. He had his arm around a young woman in a polka dot dress as he sashayed towards the tub, eventually stopping to direct the giggling line of women to put the beer into the ice. Although his expression was generally playful, he had a piercing gaze that swept across the room like a searchlight, catching me in its glare for an uncomfortable moment. He extended his hand towards me, like a waiter offering to open the bottle.

He took the bottle from my hand rather than wait for me to pass it to him, and, while still grinning at me, put it in his mouth and pried the cap off with his teeth. He wiped the mouth of the bottle on the sleeve of his shirt and handed it back to me. The girl on his arm gave him an exasperated look and went off to talk to another group of students. He watched her go with a laugh and stuck his hand out for me to shake.

"Ramón Espinoza de la Fuente," he said.

"Paco," I replied. Even then, I didn't put much stock in my lineage. The other guys in the band had found the opener without me and had dispersed into the crowd to chat up the university girls.

"Where did you learn to play?" he asked.

The first answer that leapt to mind was that I had no idea. Before the earthquake, my earliest memories were of music in my house, my mother and father and uncles and everyone else playing and singing. That was all gone now. I shrugged. "Around, I guess."

He nodded, and we stood there for a moment in silence, both sipping our beer. I was going to say something else when I noticed that suddenly the party had become much quieter, even accounting for the lack of music. Everyone had turned to face a new arrival in the garden. He was past middle age, and though still tall and thick across the shoulders, he was preceded by a huge belly against which his shirt buttons strained. Even in the heat of that summer night, he wore a suit and tie. I recognized him from the newspapers, as

I'm sure everyone did. A leader in the UDEL, Jaime Marroquín had been a professor at the university and was often in the news for his newspaper editorials.[3] He stood at the edge of the garden, a diminutive woman clinging to his arm, waiting. A young man, with broad shoulders and a boxer's nose, stood just behind him, watching the crowd. The host shook his hand effusively and kissed the woman on both cheeks before offering them both a drink from the bar. I saw that Ramón was watching him. I was surprised when Marroquín walked up to us directly.

His voice was higher and a bit breathier than it seemed when I had heard him on the radio giving speeches. He looked back and forth between me and the stack of instruments on the other side of the garden. "It's time for you to play again, boy. We want to dance." He patted the woman's arm, entwined with his.

I still had almost half my beer left. I looked around quickly, but I couldn't see all of the other players. As I hesitated, a look of irritation flashed across Marroquín's face. "You are with the band? You're not some other kind of help?" The host called out to him from the bar, holding up two drinks. Marroquín led his date away from us, and I had still not spoken.

Ramón spat on the ground. "They say that you can't trust a skinny cook or a fat union leader."

"What was that?" asked the boxer, who was still nearby.

"Poor hearing must be a prerequisite to work for that ass," said Ramón.

The boxer took a half step forward, and without really thinking, I grabbed Ramón by the arm and pulled him away, and as I did, I began to sing. "El pueblo unido" wasn't the most popular song anymore, but most people still knew it, and when we played it, we did it with a cumbia rhythm that people could dance to. I could see that Marroquín recognized it and approved. No wonder, as it had begun as a protest song for striking workers. I sang the first verse a cappella, drawing it out a little and focusing on the suffering it

---

[3] *Translator's Note — The UDEL was a moderate opposition group, the Unión Democrática de Liberación / Democratic Union of Liberation.*

described so that the other band members had time to join me. I handed Ramón two claves, and he played along, although his sense of rhythm wasn't terrific.

The other players joined in as they reached their instruments, and so, the song began to build. In no time, people were singing and dancing along, including Marroquín and his date. When we brought the song to a crashing finish, I didn't pause to catch my breath or do anything that might have let the crowd out of the palm of my hand. I started straight into another leftist anthem, "El trabajador poderoso," also in the cumbia style, and people just kept dancing. Ramón kept banging away with his wooden blocks, more or less in time with the rest of us. Throughout both songs, he ignored the crowd and kept looking at me with an inscrutable expression.

After that, we just kept playing, sweating in the heat until our shirts were soaked. Eventually, Marroquín got tired of dancing and left with his date, though the bodyguard gave Ramón one last hard look before he followed them out. Finally, we finished our set and took a bow, anxious to cool off and have another drink. Ramón clapped me on the shoulder and laughed at what had just happened, and despite myself, I laughed too.

"Let's get out of here," he said. "I know another party where there are more girls."

The party here was still going strong, and I knew that they would want music for a few more hours. "I can't," I said. "I won't be paid until the end of the night." Ramón looked a little surprised, then walked over to the tub of beer, pulled one out by the neck, and gave me a little salute with the bottle. "Next time, maybe," and with that, he was gone.

I saw him again a few weeks later at another party, also at the house of a university professor. This time they had cleared out the largest of the rooms in the house as a dance floor and had flung open the windows to let air circulate. Still, the room was hot and got more so as it filled with dancers. We played with the windows to our back, and the cool breeze helped, but it still felt like it would be a long night.

I watched the crowd as we played, as I always did, trying to gauge what song would keep them on their feet. We found the rhythm of the party, and soon the room was so packed with dancers they could hardly move, slowly shuffling in a large circuit. Sitting in a windowsill off to my left was Ramón.

He had a short bottle of rum dangling in one hand, and he looked more dishevelled than usual. Other students passing him on the dance floor leaned in to speak to him, and more than one girl seemed to invite him to dance, but he waved them away with one hand, not bothering to look anyone in the eye. He looked like a sailor, shipwrecked on a tiny island.

We brought a popular dance number to an end, holding the last note and laying on the vibrato long enough for everyone to understand that we were done playing for the moment. There was no way we could move until the crowd thinned out, and so we shared a joke and eyed the girls in the crowd while we waited.

Esteban, who I had grown up with, and who played a small marimba, lit a cigarette and used it to point to Ramón. "See that guy sitting there?" he said. "I heard the craziest story about him earlier."

I took the cigarette from him, as I had none, and took a drag before passing it to one of the others.

"He's a medical student," said Esteban. "Or he was one. He got thrown out of the university for this prank he pulled."

Ramón caught my eye, and perhaps he could tell we were talking about him. He took another pull from his bottle and slunk off through the crowd. "They have a professor of anatomy," Esteban continued, "a Doctor Velásquez, who has been there for decades. Supposedly he looks in worse shape than even the cadavers. His lectures are as dry as a nun's panties, they say, and it's also the toughest class. And so, he came into the anatomical theatre this morning and started droning on about whatever it was, and then he went over to the dissection table to remove the sheet from the cadaver. When he got close, the cadaver sat up and grabbed his arm. Apparently, Doctor Velásquez passed right out and split his head open on the side of the table. And it was that guy who was under the sheet."

We all laughed and agreed that Velásquez should be able to take a joke and that expelling Ramón was a travesty, though none of us had ever even seen the inside of a university. After a while, I left the others to go find Ramón. There were tight knots of people, deep in conversation, jammed into every possible space, and the noise filled the house until the walls felt like they were buzzing. Standing halfway up a staircase, in an intense dialogue, I found Ramón.

I had seen the man he was talking with at other parties. He was dressed in the same shirt and pleated slacks as the students, but he was older than them and very clean cut. His greying hair was buzzed short, and he had thick glasses that made his eyes look larger than they were.

"I think that if you apologize and give it a little time, they will take you back," said the man in heavily accented Spanish. Ramón was not really looking at him but was nodding. I stood nearby, waiting for an opportunity to interrupt. When Ramón saw me, he smiled and pulled me by the hand up the stairs. "This is my friend," he said, an arm around my shoulders. "Paco."

The older man shook my hand with a firm grasp. "Alan Green," he said, with a strong American accent. "The Economics Department."

"Professor Green was just giving me some academic advice," said Ramón.

"I heard that you might need some," I replied.

Ramón's body stiffened, and he looked at me curiously. "News travels fast."

"If you'll excuse me," Green said suddenly. "It's hotter than hell in here, and I'm still getting used to it. I think that I'll be calling it a night."

"Thank you, professor," said Ramón.

"Let me know if I can be of help," he said as he left.

Ramón offered me his bottle of rum, and I took a quick pull from it. "You'll get back into school, I'm sure."

Ramón winced, still embarrassed that I knew of his problem.

"That's the least of my worries," he said. "Being kicked out of medical school in my last year is one thing. But I've also been kicked out of residence, and I haven't told my parents yet."

"Can you kill two birds with one stone and stay with them?" I asked.

Ramón shook his head. "They're in León, not here." He hesitated for a moment before sharing with me. "I think I'd rather die than tell them in person."

"Friends?" I said tentatively.

"I couldn't ask them. They're all at the university. Anyone who sneaks me in risks getting expelled themselves." He drank the rest of the bottle, setting it down on the stair between his feet. "So, in summary, I'm fucked," he said.

I'm not entirely sure why I wanted to help him, though I can see now that he inspired the same kind of feelings in almost everyone. "Well, there's an open bed in the house where I stay, and I'm sure that the landlady would rent it to you."

Ramón brightened up a little. "Where is it?"

"Barrio San Pablo," I said.

"Perfect," he said, though I suspected that he didn't really know where that was at all. "Let's find something more to drink." And like that, he was back to being the same person I had seen at the other party. He chided and cajoled people, made jokes and laughed with them, and in no time had a bottle of beer in one hand and a cigarette in another, surrounded by pretty girls and jealous boys.

I went back to work, but he danced until the party finally finished, and then grabbing one more beer for the walk, fell in behind the band clutching a battered suitcase that contained all his worldly possessions.

3

THE PENSIÓN WHERE I LIVED was in a crumbling colonial house whose grand rooms had been crudely divided and filled with bunks. The matron, Señora Botello, was an imposing woman who guarded the entrance from an overstuffed settee in the front room. She carried the huge key to the front door on a chain around her waist, and she was punctual down to the second when it came time to lock it at night. Watching from her perch, she knew every resident's comings and goings and was not too shy to judge their behaviour.

"You're an embarrassment to the mother whose pains brought you onto this earth," she would say to anyone whose shirt was not tucked in. Or, she might say, "Laziness is the greatest sin," to anyone who was not working on a day other than Sunday. But the rooms were clean enough, you could do your own laundry in the backyard, and the price was as low as you could find. No one stayed at the Pensión Botello for the food.

When I presented Ramón to Señora Botello as a potential resident, he quickly worked to charm her. He took her hand and kissed it, bowing formally. She laughed and smiled, but she was sizing him up. No one who is easily flattered could make a living with a pensión. "What is your name?" she asked.

"Ramón Espinoza de la Fuente."

"And what do you do for a living?

"I'm a doctor."

She laughed. "Staying here?"

"Nearly a doctor," he said. "I'm finishing my last year at the university." Even this was not exactly true anymore.

"And who will be paying your bills, then?"

"Myself or my father, Antonio Espinoza Larco." He said his father's name in a way that suggested it should be guarantee enough, but Señora Botello only snuffled in reply.

"Rent's due at the beginning of each week. Meal hours are posted on the wall. I lock the front door at eleven-thirty every night, whether you are here or not. Paco can show you to a bunk."

"Of course. However, as a doctor, sometimes I see patients late in the evening. I assume that, in these cases, an exception could be made?" When Señora Botello hesitated, he pressed her. "There is no schedule for sickness."

"Perhaps," she said, waving us away with her fan.

I showed Ramón to the room where I had a bunk and pointed to the vacant one. He looked around, taking in the peeling paint and the potholed plaster ceiling, but if it disturbed him, he said nothing about it. He quickly made himself comfortable, lying on the bed with his shoes on, either sleeping or meditating deeply.

Before long, he was up with a start and digging through his suitcase, pulling out suits and shirts that looked to be in much better condition than the shabby clothes he was wearing. He had a small pile of books, one of which I picked up and began to read: *Azul* by Rubén Darío. His poems were good, and I thought that I might be able to set them to music. Ramón looked over at what I was reading.

"My mother's favourite," he said. "But, to me, he seemed too quick to forget his home."

"Maybe his home looked like this," I said, gesturing at the shabby room.

Ramón shrugged. "His family had enough." He finished organizing his clothes and set aside a pair of trousers and one shirt on the bed. "There's more gold on his tomb in León than the conquistadores ever found." He bundled the rest of his clothes over one arm and picked up the remaining books.

"Come on," he said. "You can give that back to me when you've finished reading it."

"Come on, where?"

"To get some money so I can pay the rent."

I went with him, and he found the nearest shop where he could sell his spare clothing. He haggled to get the best price for his suits, ties, shirts, and even socks. When he had finished, he pocketed what was a fairly small wad of cash. Although my wallet was also mostly empty, I took Ramón to a local cervecería for a drink. Pretty soon, he was telling stories to the regulars and getting them to buy us both drinks.

To keep up the fiction that Ramón was a student and that I was employed in a respectable job, we left each morning as if we were going to work, and only came back in time for dinner. This meant we had long days to wander the city, although finding money was a constant concern. Once word had spread that a "doctor" was staying at the pensión, patients would sometimes seek Ramón out for treatment. He would accept their meagre payment in exchange for hearing their troubles and prescribing a small dose of something they could easily buy at any pharmacy.

The tips for musicians were best in the squares lined with restaurants, even the ones where the corners were still choked with rubble from the earthquake. Ramón would come and watch us play, but his sense of rhythm was bad, and we couldn't really even get him to shake a rattle in time with us. Instead, he solicited tips from the diners or tried to get passersby to stop and listen. What any of his patients would have thought had they seen their doctor busking in the street, I can't honestly say.

We soon fell into an easy rhythm, as if Ramón had always been part of the group. Even though we lived hand to mouth, I can't say it was unpleasant. Ramón seemed to have no interest in returning to the university, and I had no plans for anything beyond the next meal or the next day. So, our problems seemed small. But all of this was turned upside down when, one day, Ramón became obsessed.

We were in a small plaza in a good neighbourhood, playing under the shade of one of the trees lining its edges. Ramón was accosting everyone who walked by to stop and listen. He was so insistent that I could see that some people began to cut across the square to avoid having to refuse him. One of the people who gave him a wide berth was a young woman in a yellow dress. I didn't pay her much attention until I saw that Ramón had stopped talking and was staring at her. At second glance, I could see how he found her striking. She had jet black hair and full, red lips that were pursed as if she was about to speak.

When Ramón dashed across the square to follow her, he ran straight into one of the young shoeshine boys who also made a living in the plaza, knocking him down and sending his wooden box crashing across the cobblestones. The boy shouted as he was knocked over, and Ramón was quickly accosted by every other shoeshine boy within earshot. They pulled their compatriot to his feet and circled Ramón, threatening him with violence in words that would have made a longshoreman blush. In any case, by the time we had settled the matter, by Ramón apologizing profusely and each of us getting a shoeshine we couldn't afford, the girl was gone.

As we walked home empty-handed from the day's work, everyone's mood was sour except for Ramón's. It was as if he no longer walked on the ground like the rest of us. He was floating along, propelled by his feelings for this girl he'd never met.

To both avoid trouble with the shoeshine boys and try to find more lucrative places to play, we didn't go back to that plaza again for quite a while. Ramón still came with us to work the crowds, but on any day he could find the time, he took off by himself, and I could guess where he went. One morning, as we debated where we should try to busk that day, he grandly announced that he had found us a paying gig. We were all skeptical, but still hungry enough to listen. He had convinced a restaurant owner to pay us to play over the lunch and dinner hours, and, if Ramón wasn't exaggerating, the money was good.

"How did you find this job, exactly?" asked Esteban.

Ramón gave us all the hurt look he used when he felt a question was beneath his dignity. "Through a friend of a friend," he said with a shrug. "It doesn't pay to judge a gift too closely."

Standing outside playing all day in the sun was hard work, but playing inside wouldn't be nearly as bad. I thought there might even be some free drinks thrown in. If the taberna he took us to had a name, you wouldn't know. There was no sign. The windows were thick with grime, and the restaurant smelled musty. The only menu was written on a chalkboard that advertised a set lunch without describing its components. I assumed from all of this that its customers weren't particularly discerning. The only thing appealing about the place was how close it sat to the plaza where the girl of Ramón's dreams had disappeared.

The taberna owner was a short, fat man whose hands were always either slicking back his thinning hair or rubbing on his dirty apron. He looked at us in much the same way that we were looking at the taberna. He had expected a real band, and we had expected a real restaurant. The owner pulled Ramón aside and quickly renegotiated the deal. He would only take us for a day or two a week and offered less money but threw in a meal instead. Having no better option, we agreed.

Playing in the taberna actually turned out to be alright. We made as much money there as we did on an average day of tips, but the work was easier, and we seemed to pull in a few more customers for the restaurant than they normally got. Ramón stood outside the entrance, trying to hustle customers inside and scanning the crowds on the street. Everyone was happy.

We had been playing there for a couple of weeks, and although it was a good gig, I could tell that Ramón was getting restless. We were all standing outside the restaurant with the owner, smoking and chatting, as the night began to cool off. Esteban had a copy of La Prensa that someone had left behind, and was sitting apart from us, reading.

"What's so fascinating?" asked Miguel.

"This Pinochet bastard," said Esteban, "he's held a referendum to see if the country supports his 'defence of the dignity of Chile.'"

"And?" asked Miguel.

"Over 78 percent said yes," said Esteban, "to murdering and disappearing people!"

"What's he supposed to do? Tickle the violent revolutionaries into submission?" asked Luis with a snort.

"But what if the revolutionaries are right?" asked Miguel.

"If they were in charge, they'd be bastards just like Pinochet, only it'd be a different bunch getting murdered," said Luis. "It's the same thing here. If you think anyone else would be better than Somoza and his blood-sucking kids, you're wrong."

"What do you think, Ramón?" I asked. "You're the university man."

Ramón shrugged. "I can see the truth of the matter right here under my nose. I don't go looking for my opinion in the newspapers."

I was about to call him out on not answering the question when he suddenly perked up, eyes focused on a point over my shoulder and down the street. I turned to look, and there she was, the girl in the yellow dress. She was on the arm of a much older man. His suit looked well-worn but expensive, and whatever he was saying to her made her laugh. I thought for sure that Ramón would interrupt them, but he didn't. He just stood transfixed as they strolled by, the girl looking at her partner as if he was the only man in the world.

When they were a little farther down the street but still in sight, Ramón turned to me in a panic. "Give me my share of the money," he said, his hand thrust out towards me.

I held up the single bill the owner had paid us. "I don't have change," I said.

The taberna owner shrugged. "I need my small bills and coins," he said. "For the customers."

Ramón snatched the bill from my hand and ran off down the street to follow the girl. Without really thinking, I ran after him. I had introduced him to our little group and somehow felt responsible for safeguarding our pay.

I turned the corner at the end of the street at full gallop, and seeing him turn again at the next block, I ran faster. I skidded around the corner, my worn soles giving me little traction, and nearly ran straight into Ramón, who was looking at a nearly-empty dirty shop window. His chest was still heaving from his run, and his clothing and hair looked dishevelled from the effort. A short distance away, the man was buying the girl a flower from an old woman carrying a basket of them. She was making a show of breaking the stem and weaving it into her hair.

"What was that about?" I hissed at Ramón.

He looked at me with eyes that were filled with pain. "I'm good for the money," he said.

I nodded, knowing it was true. In a few minutes, the man and the girl were walking again, arm in arm, with Ramón and I following at what we thought was a discreet distance. She seemed to be leading the man as they walked along the street, turning, eventually, up a hill and into a small neighbourhood that I knew was called San Pascual.

The old stores and houses that made up the neighbourhood were built around a park whose grass had been worn away to dirt. The girl led a man up a set of metal stairs to one of the apartments that made up the building's second and third storeys. Judging by the number of doors along the exterior hallway, the apartments were tiny. They disappeared into one of them, a dim light showing through heavy curtains in its one narrow window.

"Satisfied now?" I asked.

"Not at all," said Ramón. "I'm going to wait."

"For what?" I asked.

He didn't answer. Underneath the apartments was a bodega with a few tables and chairs spread out on the sidewalk in front of it. The moon illuminated the tables well enough. There were still a few people sitting there, likely escaping the heat of their tiny apartments. Ramón nodded at them politely as he walked past, though, with his shabby clothes and wild hair, he looked like a madman and knocked on the door of the closed bodega. He rapped a few more times before the door was pulled open.

"A small bottle of rum," he said as if it were the most normal thing in the world.

When he came back, he had the bottle and two borrowed glasses, and we sat at one of the tables.

"He didn't grumble about giving you change?" I asked.

Ramón focused on pouring out two equal glasses. "He said he didn't have any, so I took store credit."

If he was embarrassed, he didn't show it, even though he had just tied up all of our wages in this out-of-the-way bodega.

"What has gotten into you?" I asked.

He looked at me seriously, taking a long drink from his glass of rum. When he set it down again, his throat sounded thick. "I'm . . . I can't get her out of my head."

"You don't even know her name," I said.

Ramón's eyes burned feverishly. "I do. It's Magdalena." I gave him a curious look, and he gave me a pleading one in return. "I was eavesdropping on them, and heard him call her that."

"And so now we wait here for morning?" I asked.

Ramón shook his head. "Sooner than that, I think." He took a long drink from his glass of rum and then refilled it. He was in no real mood to talk, and neither was I, given the circumstances. We sat in silence for a while, sipping our rum and listening to the faint sound of music on a radio in one of the apartments.

A middle-aged man in a dark suit stood beside a table next to us. He craned his neck to see something on the balcony above and then, disappointed, sat down heavily in one of the rickety cane chairs. He held his hat in both hands and worried the brim with his fingers, looking as if he might jump up and leave at any moment.

I was about to tell Ramón that I had had enough when a door opened above us, casting a long beam of light that caught our attention. Framed in the doorway, wearing a silk housecoat, was Magdalena. She gave the older man a short embrace and a peck on the cheek. As she pulled him close, she looked over his shoulder down at us in the park, though only for a brief moment. When he turned to leave, he pulled the brim of his hat down low and walked straight through the park with long strides, neither looking left or right.

Ramón seemed to be rehearsing something in his head, he seemed so focused and detached. He took his glass of rum, now only half full, and downed it in one long gulp. Then, he stood and, uncharacteristically, straightened his shirt and trousers and beat some of the dust off them. The middle-aged man was watching Ramón uncomfortably and stood as well.

The door above opened again, and Magdalena came outside, dressed in the yellow dress again. She walked quickly down the staircase and walked straight towards us. Ramón watched her approach, his eyes wide, managing only to choke out her name as she came near.

"Magdalena."

She gave him a curious look, pausing mid-stride. "I'm sorry, I don't think I know you," she said, then walked around him to greet the middle-aged man. They spoke in hushed tones for a moment, the man looking sheepish, before she took him by the hand and led him back up to her apartment. Ramón watched them go as if transfixed, not saying a word.

"Let's go," I said. "If it wasn't clear before, it is now. She's not the right type."

Ramón's expression crumbled, but only for a moment before he composed himself again. "Come on," he said, wobbling a little as let go of the chair. "I know just the place to go."

"Home?" I suggested, hopefully.

He gave me a look of disdain. "Señora Botello will never let us in at this hour. I've got a better idea."

He started walking fast across the little park and down the street, his eyes fixed on some distant point that I couldn't see. I strode faster to catch up, but he always seemed to be pulling away from me no matter how fast I went,. We went back to the main street and turned away from the crumbling neighbourhoods like San Pascual towards the city's wealthier part. I didn't know the streets here as well, but Ramón seemed to know exactly where he was going.

The street we were on joined with the Avenida des Ángels near a strip of fancy night clubs with marquees and neon signs. Ramón stopped at the corner to get his bearings, and I just gaped at the lights and the people. I'd never been in this part of the city before, and certainly not at night when Managuan society was out in full force. A couple of soldiers were manning a checkpoint nearby, leaning on their rifles and smoking. They paid us no attention.

As we stood on the corner, a polished saloon car pulled up by the curb, chauffeured by a soldier in dress uniform. The man who stepped out of the car was in a suit, but you could tell from his bearing that he was a General or something. Next out of the car was a woman in a sequined dress that clung to her like wet cloth. First, the driver saluted the General. Then, the soldiers and the checkpoint did the same, grinding out their cigarettes under their boots as they came to attention. He walked up the sidewalk and into a nightclub without so much as a glance at them or us.

This was when Ramón decided where we were going.

"Come on, let's get a drink," he said, waving his arm grandly at me. I didn't move, but as Ramón stepped forward, the soldiers suddenly noticed us.

"Get lost," said one of them, lifting his rifle to cradle it in his arms. "There's no soup kitchen here." The other soldier laughed.

Ramón smiled at him as if he enjoyed the joke as well, but he kept walking and brushed past the soldiers as he headed to the night club.

"I said stop," said the soldier angrily. Ramón ignored him and kept walking, and the soldier raised his rifle.

"Ramón!" I shouted, trying to get his attention, but just as he turned towards my voice, the second soldier stepped forward and hit him across the jaw with a wooden truncheon. Ramón dropped to the ground with a wet thump. I rushed forward towards him, but stopped, my hands held up in front of my face, when the two soldiers turned on me.

"Get this sack of shit out of here," said one of them, taking a moment to spit on Ramón's prone body. I scuttled forward quickly, in fear of being given the same treatment, getting one arm under him and lifting him up. When he was upright, he spat out blood and part of a tooth, and I backed away from the soldiers, bearing his weight on my shoulder.

We hobbled down the street together, and I didn't stop to take a look at him until I thought we would be safe. By then, Ramón was able to walk for himself, one hand rubbing his jaw. The last thing that I heard was one of the soldiers yelling up the street at us, "Get back to the garbage heap where you belong, hijos de puta." As I said, it was a part of the city that I had never seen before.

RAMÓN HAD TO HAVE A TOOTH PULLED after that night but couldn't pay the dentist in cash. Instead, he spent a week wearing a sandwich board advertising the dentist's business. Anyone else in their last year of medical school would have balked at doing that kind of work in public, but not Ramón. If it bothered him in the least, he didn't show it.

Money was getting tighter, it seemed, not just for us, but for the whole city. There was less food in the market, and the price of bread went up when the bakers had trouble buying grain. People were restless. Not so restless that they didn't entertain, with music and drinks, but our tips were getting smaller with every gig. And Ramón still hadn't solved the problem of our money being tied up as credit at the bodega. Its owner, confident knowing we weren't locals and that our money was captive, was charging exorbitant prices for everything.

One afternoon, I was lying in my bed, dreaming of ways to make money. At the top of my list were strategies to convince Ramón to get the money back from the bodega. Before I had devised a way to convince him, he came into the room, whistling happily. Under his arm was a large package wrapped in brown paper.

"Ramón, we need to talk about money."

"Your problem is solved," he said, scowling and shaking the

paper wrapper open to reveal a suit and a few shirts. "A gift from my Mamá," he said. He flipped open the letter attached to it and began to read:

. . . Your father and I want you to look respectable, and so we had these clothes made for you. If your measurements change, let us know. Have you decided where you will practice yet? I imagine that Managua is exciting, but León is not the same without you . . .

He smiled broadly and gestured at the room around him with the letter. "If they only knew."

"You really haven't told them?" I asked.

"Eventually," he said, "eventually."

"Maybe if you do, they'll send you money instead of clothes."

"There are more important things to discuss." He sat down on the bunk across from me, his expression very earnest. "I've organized an expedition," he said as if that explained everything.

I had seen him in these moods before, so I simply waited for him to continue.

"When I picked up my mail at the university, I got to talking with a classmate of mine, Mateo, about how no one in school really even knows our own country anymore. He has a car, and pretty soon, we'd agreed to address the problem."

I nodded, still not sure of exactly what he was talking about.

"And so: you, me, Mateo and some girls are going on an expedition tomorrow to see the ruins at León Viejo and have a picnic."

I wasn't sure what to think about this, exactly. He was already back on his feet and heading out again. "I'm going to go pawn these things, but you should think about getting some alcohol for the expedition." He was gone before I could reply.

The next morning, Mateo appeared in a massive American saloon car that had the top down. There were three girls seated in the back, all looking excited, though I don't remember any of their names. Ramón climbed over the front seat to squeeze in between the girls, and I sat in front beside Mateo. Ramón took a drink from a bottle of rum that he pulled from his pocket and then passed it to me.

"Driver, to León Viejo!" he roared. Mateo revved the engine a few times in response before lurching forward and down the street. It was slow-moving through the crowded streets, but Ramón was in high spirits and kept us all entertained with a steady banter about whatever he saw around us. He made up conversations with street vendors and speculated about the love life of forlorn-looking police officers directing traffic. He even spoke in character voices, pretending to be a donkey or dog or pigeon or whatever else he saw.

Eventually, we made it out of Managua's tight streets and onto the highway that ran along the southern shore of Lago Xolotlán, where a cool breeze blew off the lake. That breeze, along with the view, made that part of the journey extremely pleasant. Ramón's bottle of rum was finished quickly, and one of the girls produced a bottle of gin that we passed around. Mateo insisted that as the driver, he had to be responsible and keep both hands on the wheel, and so I held the bottle for him and poured it carefully between his lips. The condition of the road got worse the farther we drove from the capital. Still, Mateo didn't really slow down, weaving around the potholes he could see, and passing trucks carrying produce on either side as he saw fit.

The last part of the trip was along a narrow and winding road that was cut through the jungle, probably by hand, finding the path of least resistance. Mateo finally did have to slow down, taking each corner blindly and hoping that the road wasn't washed out or that there was no one coming the other way. When we reached the ruins of León Viejo, it was hot and sticky, the cool breeze of the highway driving long forgotten.

We all hopped out of the car and started to explore the ruins. Destroyed by an earthquake more than four hundred years ago, there was little left now. Low stone walls sat amid piles of rubble, some of which had been cleared by enterprising locals looking for building material. With a bit of imagination, you could see where the streets had been laid out. One of the girls found an area that must have been the central plaza. We all wandered together and chatted, half looking at the ruins and half flirting and having fun.

Mateo had brought a few bottles of beer with him and some glasses, and although it was warm and a little skunky, no one complained.

As we wandered, Ramón climbed on top of one of the remaining walls and told us about the site's history. How he knew all of this information, or if any of it was even true, I had no idea. Still, he had the manner of a professor, and soon the girls were raising their hands to ask him questions. With great detail, he described what life would have been like in the city when it was still a vibrant capital. He pointed out different buildings and deduced their use as he talked. We followed him through the site until the sun was getting high in the sky and it was too hot to keep going. Mateo found a shady spot with some large flat rocks that we could use for picnic benches, and we settled in to eat.

"What were these rocks used for, Professor?" asked one of the girls who had taken a shine to Ramón.

He appeared to consider the question with a great deal of concentration before pronouncing, "Undoubtedly, human sacrifice." A great groan rose up from everyone, but he maintained his serious demeanour. He would not admit that his opinion was anything but scholarly. We sat on the altars nonetheless, Mateo making a show of examining them for bloodstains before spreading out our blankets, and the girls passed out sandwiches that they had brought, as well as some fruit and more warm beer.

The conversation turned to the usual things that young people talked about—music, their families, and flirting. Mateo and the girls took turns arguing that they had the toughest professor or class, describing the workload or the essays or whatever. I just kept quiet and nodded, not really understanding what they were talking about. When Mateo did an impression of a particularly difficult professor, he had the others in stitches. Their laughter filled the air around us.

Suddenly, we were interrupted by what I first thought was a monkey, whooping from high up in the trees. Guarding what was left of my lunch with one hand, I shaded my eyes and tried to find the obnoxious creature lurking above us. The whooping continued from deep in the leaves of the canopy, and we all searched with our eyes until one of the girls pointed and shouted, "Ramón!"

While we had been talking, he must have gotten bored. He had climbed one of the trees until he was thirty or forty feet in the air. He had then shuffled out along one of its branches until he was perched high above us, looking down with an air of delight.

"Who's going to join me?" he asked.

"Come down! Before you get hurt," implored a chorus of girls.

"The fast way or the slow way?" joked Ramón, grabbing a branch and swinging back and forth, his feet kicking out far in front of him.

"I can't watch," said one of the girls, burying her head in my shoulder. I put an arm around her and cooed something reassuring.

We watched him goof around among the treetops for another fifteen minutes or so before he was tired of it and scampered down the trunk of the tree. When he presented himself to the girls again, his clothes were even dirtier and more dishevelled than before, but they still took turns hugging him in relief.

When they were done, he came over to where I had been sitting and finished the bottle of gin. The sandwiches were mostly gone, but he sat and proceeded to eat two apples, core and all, in less time than most people would take to cut them into slices.

Springing to his feet, he addressed Mateo, "Ready?"

Mateo looked at all of us to see if he was the butt of a joke. "For what?"

"To head back to the city," said Ramón.

"I suppose," said Mateo. "What does everyone else want to do?"

"Let's drive back along the highway and find a beach where we can swim," said Ramón.

"But no one brought clothes for swimming," I said.

Ramón waggled his thick eyebrows to imply what he was thinking, and the girls laughed.

"Only up to our knees," said the girl who had brought the gin.

"I would expect nothing less from a lady," said Ramón with a mock bow.

Although I still wanted to see some of the ruins that we had missed, we all piled into the car again and took off along the dirt track that led from León Viejo to the highway. Ramón had fixed his attention on one of the girls in particular, now sitting on his lap. The others in the seat with him were looking perturbed. Mateo was twisted around in his seat, trying to make conversation with them while he drove, and they were leaning forward to better ignore Ramón.

It was humid in the close air of the overgrown road, and I was anxious to get back onto the highway. As the road worsened, Mateo had to stop flirting to pay attention to the winding route. He was driving slowly, the big car taking up a lot of the roadway on each turn.

"Speed up," complained Ramón from the back seat. "We're sweating through the upholstery."

Mateo's face was flushed, from the heat or the alcohol, I wasn't sure, and he was very focused on driving. "It's too treacherous for that," he replied, wheeling the car in a wide arc through a tight turn.

"Come on," continued Ramón, "we want to get swimming before sundown."

Mateo didn't say anything, but he started driving faster, and the car began to feel more like a ride at an amusement park. We swayed back and forth as the car turned, the girls squealing as Ramón pretended to crush them. Mateo began to drive even faster, turning around to shout at Ramón: "Just don't start to complain of getting seasick!"

I caught sight of the donkey cart out of the corner of my eye. I shouted at Mateo to stop while fishing around with my own foot for the brake. We were slowing down as we hit it, but the cart was propelled forward, throwing its cargo of firewood and stones pulled from the ruins into the air. The car skidded sideways, its back fender hitting a tree at the edge of the road. There was a scream as the cart flipped over. Whether the sound was made by man or beast, I could not tell. No one moved or spoke for a moment as we sat in shock.

"Is everyone all right?" asked Ramón, the first of us to regain his senses.

Mateo sat frozen, clutching the steering wheel, eyes looking rigidly ahead into the trees. I checked myself over with both hands. I was bruised from striking my chest on the dash but not really hurt. The girls in the back seat were on top of each other, and in the pile of arms and legs and skirts and blouses was Ramón. He stood up, disentangling himself from the others, and climbed over the door of the car. I followed him, leaving Mateo still stunned.

The cart had collapsed under its load when it was hit, folding over the old man driving it, and lodging a long piece of wood into the donkey's side and pinning it to the ground. The man was conscious but breathing in long, ragged breaths. He had a cut on his head and a sheet of blood pouring across his face.

Ramón knelt over the man and looked into his eyes, saying gently, "I'm a doctor," then, turning to me, his manner was brusquer. "See what you can do for the donkey."

The donkey was conscious as well, and its legs were kicking in pain though it was held in place by the wood piercing its side. It looked as if part of the cart had been driven forward, catching the donkey just behind its ribs, and lodging somewhere in its chest. There was no way that I could move the donkey, and I wanted to stay clear of its legs in case they kicked me. I felt helpless. Ramón seemed to be examining the man with perfect knowledge of what to do, but I was lost. I finally settled near the donkey's head, trying to cradle it in my lap and soothe it during the final moments of its life. The donkey stopped kicking, though its eyes swivelled around wildly, and a bloody froth appeared at its lips.

"Mateo! Bring me a blanket," ordered Ramón, and Mateo, released from his state of shock, quickly brought one from the car's trunk. The man was still conscious, though barely, and was speaking in a whisper to Ramón. "Help me lift him onto the blanket," said Ramón, and together the they carefully moved him. "He's asked us to take him to his home," said Ramón, before directing the others to lift the man and place him in the back seat. The girls climbed out of the door on the other side, watching with tears in their eyes. Mateo unfolded the rumble seat for them, locking it open. When Ramón had organized everyone in a new seating arrangement, he turned his attention to me. "What are you doing?" he asked. Seated on the ground with the donkey's head on my lap, I could only shrug. Ramón's eyes shot daggers at me, and he quickly stepped around me to rummage in the cart's wreckage. He turned around, an old axe in both hands. "Well, get out of the way," he said, and I stood up. The donkey brayed loudly as I disturbed it, but Ramón swung the axe in a short arc and hit the donkey between the eyes. Blood sprayed up onto both of us, but the donkey stopped its noise abruptly, and I guessed that it was dead.

"It was suffering," said Ramón, before climbing into the back seat with the old man.

Mateo sat in the driver's seat, his hands on the steering wheel again, sweat pouring down his face. Ramón said nothing to reassure him, only ordering him to turn the car around and head back the way we came. The road was narrow enough that it took a few maneuvers for Mateo to get the car facing the other way.

"Take your time, this man is only dying," said Ramón.

No one spoke as we drove, cautiously now, back along the road. Ramón watched for some sort of landmark, while also keeping a close eye on his patient. He finally waved an arm and told Mateo to stop.

"Turn there, by that rock pile."

I saw then that there was a track leading off the road that we had missed entirely before. Overgrown and narrow, it was invisible when we were speeding along the road. The car bounced over its rutted surface, and the old man groaned softly. Ramón was focused on the old man, listening, with one ear pressed to his chest. The trees that loomed over the road opened up, and we pulled into a large clearing, filled with patchy cornfields that covered the hilly ground. Clustered beside the road were houses built from stone and thatched with palm leaves and sheet metal. As we pulled to a stop, a dog standing in a puddle began barking at us from the middle of the street. A few people looked at us from windows and doorways, but no one came outside. The faces I saw were dark, their features indigenous. I looked around and realized that I knew less about these people and their lives than I did about the lives of the girls at university that had seemed so foreign only a few hours before.

"We have a man with us who lives here," said Ramón, standing in the back of the car. When no one responded, he spoke again: "He's hurt. He wanted us to take him home." The dog was still barking, and two others had trotted in from somewhere to join it.

"I'll help you carry him," I said to Ramón. "Did he tell you which house was his?"

Ramón seemed to really look at our surroundings for the first time since we arrived, taking in the muddy path we drove in on, and the ramshackle buildings. He climbed over the car door and let himself down into the mud. The dogs began baying even more loudly. Ramón went to the first house, knocked on the door, and without waiting, opened it and stepped inside.

He was in there for what seemed an eternity, and when he returned, he was followed by two women. One had grey hair in two thick braids, and I assumed she was the old man's wife. The other could have been his daughter. They both wore homespun dresses and scarves to cover their hair. Ramón held the car door for them, and they climbed in over the old man. Neither uttered a word or betrayed any trace of emotion. They sat on the edge of the seat, the old man lying behind them, and stared fixedly ahead. Ramón went back to examining the old man. "Turn the car around," he said. "We're not leaving him here."

Mateo looked at me, uncertain of what to do. I shrugged, but asked Ramón, "But where are we taking him? Our pensión?"

Ramón looked up, his face furious. "The nearest hospital is in La Paz Centro."

Mateo began the laborious process of turning the car around again. The old man groaned more loudly now as the car lurched about. This time he drove faster, back out to the road, past the cart wreck, and onto the highway. We sped down the relatively smooth asphalt of the new highway and covered the dozen miles or so to La

Paz Centro in no time at all. The hospital was a large whitewashed building on the edge of town with a huge metal crucifix on the wall facing the highway. We pulled into the covered entranceway, and Ramón was on his feet and through the front doors before the car had even stopped.

The old man's relatives got out of the car as well and stood to one side, their eyes darting about and betraying their nervousness. Ramón burst through the doors again, this time leading two orderlies with a metal gurney.

"I'm telling you that I'm a doctor, and my assessment is that the man needs care immediately." The orderlies seemed overwhelmed by the torrent of direction Ramón was pouring out at them. Still, they found a way to lift the old man out of the car and onto the gurney. When they wheeled him inside, Ramón gestured to the two women to follow him into the hospital. They were gone for a long time.

Mateo sat clutching the steering wheel, sipping at a flask that had been in his pocket. The girls were talking quietly. I let out a heavy sigh and clapped Mateo on the shoulder.

"I don't know what I'm going to tell my father about the damage," Mateo said.

"I'm sure he'll understand," I said.

Mateo was non-committal, and so we waited without speaking.

When Ramón finally appeared again, he stopped and opened the hospital door to speak to someone inside. "And send the bill to me at the Faculty of Medicine. These people are not to pay a penny," he said, his voice heavy with authority.

He quickly rearranged all the passengers in the car, seating the girls with him in the back seat as it had been when we left the city. He rapped twice on the side of the car with his hand while taking a pull from the flask. Mateo swung the car back onto the highway to return to Managua.

We rode back to the city with the sun already low in the sky. After a while, I twisted around in my seat to say something to Ramón, but I stopped when I saw the expression on his face and the streaks of blood on the girls' dresses. By the time we arrived, Managua was dark, save for flickering specks of light. We'd grown used to the city's many power outages.

5

THE SUMMER NIGHTS SEEMED HOTTER and longer after that failed picnic, and so we tried to spend more of our time out in the streets rather than in the stifling rooms of the pensión. There was still some money to be made playing music, but Ramón hadn't received any packages from home for a while, other than some poetry books that we couldn't sell, so money was getting tight.

After we'd given up playing one night, Ramón and I were walking together in the streets, arguing.

"What's wrong is wrong, no matter what," I said.

"It's only the rich who think that stealing from them is wrong," said Ramón.

"Rich people have looked down at me for being poor my whole life," I said, "but that doesn't mean it's right for me to look down on them for the same reason in reverse."

"But you didn't get poor by oppressing anyone," said Ramón. He halted, mid-stride, his eyes wide.

I turned to look at what he saw. Off to our right, coming down a narrow, cobbled street that led from an old church, was a procession. A dozen men in white robes walked slowly towards us, their faces masked by heavy, pointed hoods. At their head, one of the hooded men carried a tall wooden cross. On the shoulders of four of the others was a massive gold painted platform on which rode a statue of Christ. Carved from wood, the statue's skin was pitch black. It was a colour made all the more prominent by the fresh white robes, trimmed in purple, that adorned it. Behind the men was a large group of people, shuffling along in silence.

We stood back as the procession passed and remained silent. The stares of the men at the head of the group made me very uncomfortable. Their faces unseen, their eyes gleamed as they turned their heads towards us. I had not seen the relic before, but I knew what it meant.

Ramón gripped my arm and whispered, "What the hell is this?"

"The Cristo Negro," I told him quickly, crossing myself. "Now shut up."

The common people who made up the procession shuffled by. They were a seedy-looking group, hardly what one might expect from a religious gathering, a mix of men in rough clothing, a few in flashy suits, and behind them, two groups of women. The first was younger women, heavily made up and brazen, who all seemed to stare at us. Behind them were older women, grey and stooped, many clutching rosaries in gnarled hands.

We waited until they had passed before beginning to walk again, though there was something malevolent about what we had seen that left me feeling shaken.

"How did you know what that was?" asked Ramón.

I crossed myself again. "Everyone in my neighbourhood knows about the Cristo Negro."

"I went to Mass every Sunday," said Ramón. "How is it that I've never heard of it?"

"This isn't exactly church the way the Pope imagines it," I said. "The statue was found fifty years ago in a cave used by smugglers. They brought it here, and now it's what this church is best known for. He looks like the one in El Sauce, but people treat this Negrito almost like a saint."

"The saint of what?"

"Criminals," I said.

"So, all those people?" asked Ramón.

"Mostly," I said. "Maybe some have family members in jail or in trouble. Probably a few cops too, and not just the dirty ones."

Ramón looked surprised.

"Cops and robbers," I said. "Two sides of the same coin."

"Come on," Ramón said, hurrying to catch up with the procession. I didn't know what to say, so I followed him. The men and women marched separately behind the statue, and we had to pass by the women to get to our place. We fell in behind three men in suits who looked like they were doing alright for themselves. We began to shuffle at the same slow pace as everyone else, though I had to elbow Ramón to get him to stop flirting with the women behind us.

The procession wound through the poorer neighbourhoods surrounding the church until eventually returning up the hill to where it had started. It was nearly midnight when the statue finally disappeared back inside the church, and the heavy wooden doors were closed behind it by the last of the hooded men. One by one, the crowd went up to the door, where a few young men were passing out prayer cards to the participants. I was ready to leave, but Ramón stayed in line. When he got to the front, one of the boys handed him a card.

"And for my friend?" asked Ramón.

I didn't want a card, but I took one anyway. "And could I have one for my mother, who dearly wanted to be here this evening?" asked Ramón.

The boy looked at him suspiciously but handed him another card.

"And my sister?"

A few of the men around us had turned to see who kept asking for more cards, and I could see that Ramón was going to push his luck. I grabbed him by the elbow and pulled him off to the side. Several men continued to watch him. "They're not going to put up with any of your nonsense," I said. "We need to leave."

Ramón stuck the cards in his pocket and took mine as well. Pointing off into the night, he said, "Let's go then." I expected that he would outline his criminal master plan as we walked, but for the rest of the night, he was silent, and when the doors of the pensión opened in the morning, we went to bed.

Sometimes, Ramón wandered by himself. When I was at loose ends, I would take my guitar and find a comfortable place outdoors to sit and play. Sometimes I would sit by a shop that had a radio playing, and by listening carefully and strumming along, I could learn new songs to teach the others. I had a good memory for the lyrics, and the rhythm mostly didn't change, or at least that's how I played. Whatever the song, I always made sure that it had a good rhythm so that people could dance to it.

Life was like that too. Whatever the tune, I kept on dancing, the rhythm of my days bleeding from one to the next. I suppose that is why it took me a few days to notice that I had not seen Ramón.

"Where's your friend?" demanded Señora Botello. "And his rent?"

I passed her my rent, a few bills that had been folded too many times and some dirty coins, before I answered. "I don't know."

She eyed the area around his bed space suspiciously, searching for clues as to whether she was being tricked. She pulled his valise from where it sat forlornly under his bed. Before I could protest, she popped the clasps and opened it, revealing nothing inside other than a torn silk liner.

She quickly turned on me, shoving a thick finger towards my face. "You brought him here," she said. "I'm holding you responsible for him." She adjusted her housecoat, straightening her back to achieve her full height before storming off. "And he's three weeks behind!"

I didn't put much stock in her threat to extract Ramón's rent from me, but I did not doubt that she could make my life miserable. The bigger issue for me was Ramón's disappearance. For the next few days, I checked the parts of the city that he and I used to visit together on our long walks. Scanning the faces in the crowds around me, I often thought I saw him. Sometimes, I'd even hurry to catch up with him before realizing that the person who I thought was my friend was someone else. I heard his voice in snatches of conversation in the market or the square, but every time I turned to look for him, it was someone else.

After having exhausted every possible place that I thought I might find him, I began to accept that he was gone. I assumed that he had gone back to school, or even gone home to his family, and I imagined all the reasons he might have done so without saying goodbye. I listed them out in my head, one by one, and ordered them according to how likely I thought it was that each was true.

"It's because he's an asshole," said Esteban. "That's why he skipped out."

"You don't know him as well as I do," I said. "There must be a reason."

I sat with my friends in the shade of a doorway on the side of the plaza, resting in between sets. Esteban drank from a bottle of beer before passing it to me.

"I'm sure that he just got tired of all of this luxury," said Esteban gesturing at the others, splayed out in the dirty doorway with their instruments on their laps, "and went back to his Mamá."

Everyone laughed, but I just smiled and said nothing.

It was hot enough that few people were still walking about, so with the prospect of tips so low, we stayed sheltered from the sun to pass the time until it began to cool off. Miguel had picked up a newspaper that had blown by in a swirl of dust.

"Son of a bitch!" said Miguel, turning the paper towards us so we could read the headline. In red, bold letters, it simply read:

"MURDERED!"

"Who?" asked Luis.

Miguel began reading. "Pedro Joaquin Chamorro, the most prominent critic of the Somoza dictatorship, was assassinated by unidentified gunmen in the capital."

"Skip to the gossip section," said Antonio. "You'll make my head hurt with all of that political stuff."

Luis tossed a piece of trash at him. "Let your head hurt, then.

This is important. Keep reading."

"The shooting occurred as Chamorro was on his way to the offices of this newspaper, which he has owned and directed since 1952. President Somoza has denounced the assassination and promised an exhaustive investigation."

"Sure!" said Luis. "That bastard probably did it!"

"No way," said Antonio. "What does he care about a nobody like Chamorro?"

"Somoza is like an octopus," said Luis, "with his tentacles wrapped around every bit of this country worth anything to anybody. Look around—the bastard even stole every penny that was supposed to rebuild Managua after the earthquake."

"That doesn't mean that he murdered Chamorro."

"Chamorro reminded people about all of this, in every issue," said Luis. "There's no one else who wanted to murder him more."

"And he found out what happens to the nail that sticks out from the board," said Esteban. "Did he think he could criticize Somoza forever?"

"Not just Somoza, all the latifundistas too," said Antonio.

"Someone has to call them out. It's a crime that farmland sits fallow while campesinos starve," replied Luis.

"But the government can't just start taking private property," said Antonio. "It's theft. Shouldn't we be worried about that, as well?"

"You're right, my friend," said Esteban. "I stay awake at night, worrying about the government stealing all of my riches." He pulled his empty pockets inside out to emphasize his point.

We finished reading most of the paper, and when the sun dipped behind the tall buildings on the far side of the square, we set up again and began to play. I sang some of the new songs I had heard on the radio, and the others followed along with a simple rhythm until they had heard the melody once, and then added more depth with their parts. A few people passing by threw pennies into the plate we left out for tips, but no one stopped to listen, and it was still too early for anyone to dance.

After a while, we took another break, this time using our tips to buy three empanadas that we had the lady cut carefully down the middle so that we could share them. I handed the half leftover to the lady and asked her to cut it five ways. She gave me a disdainful look and refused. Instead, we each took a more or less equal bite and handed it to each other until Esteban popped the last piece in his mouth. A television nearby that had been playing a Mexican telenovela was interrupted by a newscaster who reported that labour leaders and the UDEL had called for a general strike to oppose Chamorro's murder. Large crowds were gathering in front of the Palacio Nacional.

"We should go there," said Luis.

"There's no money to be made by protesting," said Antonio.

"Fuck the protest," said Esteban. "If we want to make money, that's the place to be tonight."

After we had finished eating, we picked up our instruments and began the long walk to the main square. Weaving through the crowded streets that led there, it quickly became clear that we were not the only ones with this idea. There were lots of normal people who seemed to be walking in the same direction, but there was also a long line of food vendors, shoeshine boys, and even a few other musicians, all hoping to make some money.

When we reached the square's edge, there were already a few thousand people gathered on one side, facing the Palacio Nacional. It didn't seem organized. There were no signs or people chanting or anyone making speeches, but everyone had gathered there to show their support for Chamorro. How could I tell they weren't there in support of the President? No one in that crowd looked like they were rich enough to be a Somocista. These people didn't have to worry about having anything taken away from them. Either they had already lost it, or they had never had it in the first place.

We headed straight for the front of the crowd, but couldn't push through and so settled for a spot on one side. We set ourselves up on the steps of the Catedral de Santiago, still in ruins since the earthquake. As soon as we got there, I started to sing, trying to find the right song to motivate the crowd. They looked bored, and a few people even moved away from us, maybe so that they could hear themselves speak. After three of our regular songs, I could tell that we were getting nowhere, and I only had to look down at our empty plate to prove it.

I looked back at the others, and their despondent expressions told me that they didn't have any better idea of what to do than I did. That's when I had a thought.

"We're going to play that new song, the one about the girl who keeps saying no," I said.

"No one wants to hear any of our stuff," said Luis.

"Just play it," I said, and I spun my finger around to show them that I wanted them to do the long introduction that we sometimes used to catch the crowd's attention. They started playing, and while they did, my mind was spinning. When it was time for me to start singing the verse, I had it figured out.

"The moment I saw her, I knew what I wanted . . ." I sang, turning a few heads in the crowd who recognized the popular song. As I continued, though, I started changing the lyrics, and soon it was clear to everyone that the man who lusted for the girl was the President, and the girl was everything in the country that he could steal. When people started to understand what I meant, laughter began to ripple through the crowd. I kept going, making up the lyrics as I sang, making it as rude and funny as I dared. When I finished, I took a bow, and I heard the pennies hitting the plate.

"What next?" asked Esteban. "Can you pull off another one like that?"

"Just follow me," I said, and I began to sing again before anyone wandered off. Next, I tried a song that people sang at protests, called Boca Roja, but I gave it a snappier beat. I sang the first verse a cappella so that my friends could hear what I was doing and join in. Sometimes it was easier just to show them what I wanted, rather than to explain it.

Soon there were a few people in the crowd singing along, and through no fault of mine, I could see that the crowd was really starting to grow. By then, there must have been over a thousand people in the square, though it was big enough to hold ten times that many. I kept making up songs or repurposing old ones, and our corner of the crowd stayed in a tight knot around us, listening and singing.

A few police officers ambled through the crowd in pairs. They had their hats in their hands and said little. I could see they were searching, though, trying to see who was leading the protest. As far as I could tell, there was no one doing that, but I didn't like the way one of them stopped and watched me sing, his thumbs hooked in his gun belt. I had no especial dislike of police, but I could tell nothing good would come from these.

Next, I sang Besame Mucho, always a favourite, and the crowd loved it, but I was getting tired. I looked at the others with that expression that meant would bring it all to an end, and we built up the noise and the tempo a little and then brought it all together in a crash. When we had stopped playing, the crowd clapped and cheered, and we took a bow. I leaned my guitar up against the wall and sat down on the ground. Someone in the crowd had handed Esteban a beer, and he took a few sips before passing it around. It was warm and a little stale, but it tasted like perfection after all the singing I had done.

The rumour had been going around for a few hours that Somoza was going to make a speech. The lights in the Palacio Nacional were off, and the curtains were drawn tight across every window. There was a balcony up high, but I doubted that anyone would be using it tonight.

Since I was sitting down, I couldn't see very far through the crowd. As I was chatting with Luis and the others and starting to think about doing another set, a noise rose up on the other side of the square. It was more like the roar of the surf coming in on a beach than a sound made by humans. I stood up on a piece of the stone façade to see above the heads of the crowd. A long line of military police, their white helmets shining brightly in the moonlight, had formed on the other side of the square. They were standing shoulder to shoulder and ran from one edge of the square to the other like a human wall. As their officers adjusted their alignment, that end of the crowd turned to confront them.

The soldiers began walking slowly forward, trying to push the crowd across the square towards us. At first, the crowd's weight held them back, and their thin line looked as if it would be unable to have any effect.

"They're trying to push us out of the square," I said.

"They can't be," said Luis. "We're not doing anything!"

"I'm just telling you what I see."

"Fuck them," said Esteban, "we outnumber them ten to one."

That was when I heard sharp whistle blasts from behind the soldiers. They surged forward into the crowd with a shout, and the noise changed into a cacophony of screams and yelling. I could see the truncheons hammering up and down, and the crowd melted back onto itself, creating a ripple that knocked me off my perch. Pouring over me, the crowd began to run, pushing everyone along with it.

Our plate was just within reach of where I lay. I snatched at it, and a boot stepped on my hand. The plate slid under the weight of the running man, and coins sprayed out of it. Esteban was beside me in seconds, trying to shield both me and the coins, while sticking as many as he could into his pockets. The crowd streamed over us, and I was getting knocked and bruised. I saw that my guitar had been knocked down, a hole now in its side. However many coins were left, we needed to move. I stood and pulled Esteban to his feet, grabbing my guitar by its neck with my free hand, and we began to run.

The crowd was streaming towards the corners of the square, where roads led away to safety. The torrent of people headed for the nearest side street carried us along, but I could see that just ahead of us was another line of military police, blocking the road. They stood with their truncheons in their hands and grim expressions on their faces. Anyone unlucky enough to get close was struck by two or three officers at once and pushed behind their line to be arrested by waiting soldiers. The forward edge of the crowd recoiled from them, pushing back against the wave of people following behind.

I thought for a moment that we would be crushed, but the crowd rolled forward again, and we suddenly had a little room to breathe. The thin line of policemen couldn't make arrests fast enough, and nothing they could do was enough to stop us.

The momentum of the column of people broke their line, pushing the policemen, still swinging their truncheons, aside. Esteban and I were separated as the crowd heaved and surged, and I panicked as I was carried right past the police and out into the wide street behind. One of them jabbed his club at my ribs, knocking me over, but I fell just out of his reach. I staggered to my feet and broke into a run.

I ran for blocks, not looking back until I was certain that I was safe. There were a few people on the street who, like me, were covered in sweat and wild-eyed from our escape. My chest was heaving as I struggled to breathe, my lungs burning. I forced myself to slow down and get my bearings again. Still fearful of being arrested, I tried to walk in a way that I thought looked respectable. I knew my broken guitar didn't help, but I was loath to throw it away. Even as I slowed down, my mind spun, thinking about what had just happened. As I turned a tight corner without really looking where I was going, my head twisted around to look behind me, I bumped into someone.

"Apologies," I said before looking up.

And there he was—Ramón. And standing behind him was the girl in the yellow dress. He smiled at me, and very casually said, "Paco, I want you to meet Magdalena."

And with that, he was back in my life again.

I QUICKLY REALIZED THAT WHEN RAMÓN had disappeared from the pensión, he had moved in with Magdalena. She was pretty but very thin, and this made her face seem angular and hard. Her shoulder bones jutted out where her frayed silk shawl had slipped down. She held out her hand.

"Paco, I've heard a lot about you."

It was odd shaking a woman's hand, and so I took it gently and released it quickly.

"The pleasure is mine," I said, sounding more formal than I intended.

She laughed at me, in a way that was thoroughly charming, and for an instant, I glimpsed exactly what Ramón saw in her. We walked together for a while, talking about the events in the Plaza de la República until we reached Barrio San Cristóbal, where our paths split.

"Take care," said Ramón.

"Will you come by the pensión?" I asked.

"As a doctor, I can say that I don't think that would be good for my health," said Ramón. "I'm allergic to Señora Botello."

"Or to paying your bills?"

Ramón looked hurt, and I regretted my words almost as soon as I said them. "She'll get what I owe," he said. "It's not that I was skipping out on her. Just that . . ." he looked at Magdalena and snaked an arm around her thin shoulders. "I have new priorities."

I hardly saw him after that, though one of the few nights when I wasn't singing at a party, I ran into him in the street. He was standing just outside the main entrance of a cathedral and had a little suitcase opened up on the street in front of him. As I got closer, I could see that he was selling little wooden icons. When he saw me, he cracked a wide smile.

"Come to save your soul?" he asked. He held up one of the icons. It consisted of a dark wooden frame, and inside was a prayer card of the Cristo Negro. Hanging from the back of the frame was an electrical cord.

"They light up," he said proudly.

"Where do you get these?" I asked.

"Magdalena and I make them. From scraps, mostly."

He handed me one of the icons, and when I looked at it more closely, I could see the paint was uneven, and glue had seeped out at the seams.

"Do people buy these things?" I asked.

Ramón took it out of my hands. "Of course, they do."

I never had a chance to witness a sale; Ramón announced that he was done for the day. I walked back with him to San Pascual. When we arrived in the little park beneath Magdalena's apartment, I could see that he was looking up at the window.

"Let's have a drink," he said.

"In your apartment?"

He shook his head. "Here in the park." He dusted off two chairs and disappeared into the bodega where he had lost our money the first time we had come here. He came back with a small bottle of rum and two glasses and poured a generous drink for each of us.

"Salud," he said, knocking his glass against mine. After draining half of his drink, he fished in his pockets and pulled out a handful of bills and coins. Spreading it on the table, he counted out the amount that had become credit at the bodega and pushed it across to me.

"Ramón Espinoza de la Fuente pays his debts," he said.

"Are you sure?" I asked. He nodded as he drank again, gesturing up at the apartment with his free hand. "We're doing fine."

I scraped the money into a pile and put it in my pocket. "Is Magdalena out?" I asked, regretting it almost immediately.

"See the red scarf hanging in the window?"

I nodded.

"That means she's working, and so I sit here and wait."

We didn't talk about her after that. I didn't know what to say. I told him about the latest gossip among our friends at the pensión, but he didn't seem that interested. We sat in silence with our drinks. After a while, Magdalena and an older man appeared at the door of the apartment. She gave him a peck on the cheek, and he smiled, then walked down the stairs and out of the little park without looking at anyone.

Ramón finished his drink and picked up the bottle. "My turn," he said a bit grimly, and he shook my hand and was gone. I wandered back home, thinking about his expression when we parted.

It was some time before I saw him again, this time at a party where we were playing. Professor Green had invited everyone he knew, it seemed, and his house was full beyond capacity. The party spilled out into the street, and still more people came. Normally, everyone would be dancing at these parties, but ever since Chamorro was killed, all anyone did was talk. We played our usual songs, but people hardly noticed. The only time I got a reaction from the crowd was when I played protest songs. The crowd would sing along or clap, but no one danced.

When we finished our set, I leaned my guitar up against the wall. I had patched the hole in the side with cardboard and tape, and it looked terrible. I tried to imagine how I'd get the money to buy a new one as I wandered into the crowd to find something to drink. I squeezed past the throngs of people, mostly students, but also some famous faces I recognized from the newspaper. No one paid much attention to me, which suited me fine. I didn't want to stop and chat. I just wanted to relax for a moment and cool off.

I found the bar, set up in an alcove of the front hallway, and was surprised to see Ramón leaning against it. Even more surprising was that Magdalena was at his side. The two of them were in deep conversation with the American professor.

"And so, you're not even interested in coming back to the university?" asked Green.

"I have enough education for what I need," said Ramón.

"And what is it that you 'need' this education for, exactly?"

Ramón launched into an argument that sounded rehearsed. "The first and foremost need of the People of this country, and by that I mean the campesinos who live far from the cities, is health care. If the government wants to begin a program of social improvement for them, agrarian reform is the first step. Still, it must be followed soon after by a program of sending doctors into every community."

"And where will you find these doctors willing to live in isolation?"

"It has to begin in the university, where those people who enter medical school understand that they are not just to become doctors, but to become the vanguard of modern civilization," said Ramón.

"Oh, is that all we're asking of them?" said Green, smiling.

Ramón was about to say something back when he saw me. "Paco, brother, I thought that was you singing."

I rubbed my throat with my fingers and croaked out a reply. "It was," I said, "but now . . ." I feigned distress, and Ramón got the hint. He pulled a bottle of beer out of a tub under the table, uncapped it and handed it to me. I took a long pull from the bottle. Other than at these parties where they had ice, I rarely ever drank anything so cold. I could feel the delicious coolness seeping through my whole body.

"What do you think?" asked Green. "Is the country ready for Ramón's revolutionary program?"

I looked around for a moment, thinking. "I'm not sure," I said. "It won't be easy to change things that have been one way for as long as anyone can remember."

Green smiled. "You're right, though it is easy to talk about change, whether the conditions are right or not."

"We could wait our whole lives for the conditions to be right," said Ramón.

"But this isn't just about us and our lives, is it?" offered Magdalena.

"We can make the conditions right," said Ramón. "Otherwise, while we wait for the moment, the People suffer."

"You sound like a communist," said Green.

"If I'm any 'ist' at all, I'm a humanist," said Ramón.

I suddenly realized the way that people in the room were looking at us. Or rather, how they weren't. Ramón evidently thought nothing of bringing Magdalena to the party, but in her flimsy dress and heavy makeup, it seemed that people knew what she was, and so, kept their distance. Even progressive, Leftist society had its limits, I suppose. It's one thing to argue for the rights of all people, and something else entirely to socialize with them. I supposed that Green wasn't astute enough to pick up on the social cues.

Two young men, probably students, came into the hallway carrying a heavy wooden-cased television. They set it down on the table that was doubling as the bar. One crawled under to plug it in while the other explained what they were doing.

"They're going to broadcast Violeta Chamorro giving a speech," he said.

More and more people crowded into the foyer, first listening to some kind of classical music that the station was playing over a static image of Mary and the Christ child. I liked the complexity of all the different instruments playing together in the symphony, but the music just seemed so slow. Nothing that would get your feet moving. When it stopped, there was a brief pause, and then a grainy image of two people seated at a table draped with the UDEL banner appeared. On one side sat Marroquín, looking sombre. Beside him was a woman who the announcer introduced as the widow of the martyr Pedro Chamorro. You could hear her clear her throat before she spoke.

"It is a primary function of the State to develop agricultural activities, and industry in general, toward the end that the fruits of labour shall preferentially benefit those who produce them and that the wealth shall reach the greatest number of inhabitants of the Republic. This government not only hoards wealth for itself, it murders those citizens, like my husband, who dare to criticize it."

She continued for another half an hour, explaining in detail how Somoza abused his power, ending with a call for a general strike across the country that would last until Somoza resigned. When she finished, she said the words I would hear so often again in the years to come.

"¡Viva Nicaragua, viva el pueblo, y vivan los trabajadores!"

One of the young men turned off the television, and everyone spread out around the house again to talk excitedly. Esteban appeared in the doorway, waving at me to come back to play. I shook Ramón's hand and kissed Magdalena on the cheek.

"Come by and hang out more often," I said.

"Sure, sure," said Ramón, not sounding like he meant it. "There is just so much to do right now."

I had no real idea what he meant, but I smiled and left him by the bar to go back to playing.

For the next two days, everything had come to a standstill. Across the country, there were protests and marches. I stayed up both nights, barely sleeping at all, playing at the parties and gatherings that followed the street protests. I was exhausted, but it was so hot that when I did get to bed, I just lay there, thinking. That was probably why I heard the rattle of the little window. It was set high in the wall and opened inward, but I could just see out of it standing on a chair. I craned my neck to look down through the opening, and a pebble hit me in the face.

"Fuck!"

Standing on the roof of the smaller building next door was Ramón.

"You need to leave. Now," he said.

I touched my face, and there was a drop of blood from a cut just under my eye. Still groggy, I had to steady myself to not fall off the chair. "Can't you use the door like everyone else?"

"Paco, there's no time. They're rounding everyone up from the parties."

"I'm not a communist," I said.

"They don't care," said Ramón. "They're arresting everyone associated with the Left. We need to go," said Ramón.

"I can't just leave," I said. "I owe rent, I . . ."

"They're going to break this strike the only way they know how. They're arresting students, professors, everybody. Chamorro's wife is in hiding. If you're not willing to go, now, I have to."

The look in his eyes told me how serious he was. I had to make a decision. I quickly pulled on a pair of pants and shoes, and with my shirt still open, I climbed up to the window again.

"And grab those books of poetry that my mother sent," he said.

"I thought this was an emergency?" I replied.

He looked sheepish. "There's money inside one of them that I missed."

I stepped down and went to where his things still sat. I shook the books one by one until a few bills fell out of one of them. Stuffing them in my pocket, I climbed up to the window and managed to wriggle through it, though I had to go head and arms first. I pulled myself out and onto a ledge that ran around the outside of the building.

Looking across at Ramón, ten feet away and below me, I knew that I couldn't make it over to him. And the ledge I was on was crumbling in spots. I wasn't sure I could trust it to hold my weight.

"Come on," said Ramón. "Jump!"

There was just no way I could. I tried to put my leg back inside the window, but I got tangled up and nearly lost my balance. "I'll find a way out on the main floor," I said.

"There's no time to think about it," said Ramón. "We need to go."

With my foot snarled in the window frame, all I knew was that I wanted off that ledge. I looked all the way down to the narrow alley between the buildings. I was about to make another excuse to Ramón when I heard a commotion at the front of the house. There was a pounding on the door, followed by a moment of silence. Then, the pounding started again, and someone shouted, "Policia!"

I looked at Ramón again, and he shouted at me, "Come on!"

I think I must have closed my eyes as I pushed off the building and leapt for the roof where he was standing. I crashed down onto Ramón, knocking both of us over, and hurting my knee, badly.

"Let's go," he said. He scampered down a drain pipe at the back of the building. I followed him, still not sure how we would escape.

There were police and soldiers at all the main intersections, stopping people and making arrests. We stuck to the alleyways as best we could, though more than once we had to backtrack to find a different route around a roadblock.

"The Mexican Embassy might be giving people shelter," said Ramón.

"What about Magdalena?" I asked.

"I don't know," said Ramón, not meeting my eye.

"You weren't with her?" I asked.

Ramón shook his head.

"You can't leave her," I said.

He stopped and gripped me by the shoulders. "Listen, I'm sure that they'll be looking for me, but maybe not for her. If I go to her apartment, I might just lead them there. She's safer without me."

"Is that what she thinks?" I asked.

"It's what I think," he said and began walking faster. I hobbled to keep up.

We were still blocks from the Mexican embassy when we saw that all the roads were blocked by soldiers. They were searching everyone who came close to the checkpoint and only allowed the passage of those who could prove they had business in the neighbourhood. I was nervous even standing within sight of them and tried to look as if we had a reason to be on the street.

"We can't stay here," I said.

Ramón grabbed me by the arm and pulled me towards a church, San Juan Bautista, whose door was ajar. The church's interior was dark, votive candles lighting the foot of a statue of the saint in a side alcove. As we stepped inside, an old woman turned to us from where she was kneeling at the front of the church.

"You can't hide here," she said.

"They're arresting everyone," I said.

"We need to make a call," said Ramón. "Is there a phone in the parish office?"

She hesitated for a moment and crossed herself. Standing up, she led us without a word to a side door in the chapel. The oiled wood gleamed dully in the dim light. She pushed it open and motioned for us to follow. Down a short hall was an office. She pointed to a phone on the desk.

"You'll have to pay for the call," she said.

Ramón placed a few coins down beside it, which she scooped up and placed in her pocket.

Ramón connected to the operator. "Yes, please connect me to Señor Jaime Marroquín."

"One moment," I could hear the operator say.

Both the old woman and I gave him an incredulous look. He covered the receiver with his free hand but didn't look at me. "My mother knows him from university."

"That number is not available," said the operator.

Ramón hung up the phone. He hesitated for a moment, and then connected to the operator again. This time he asked for a number in León. The old woman rapped on the table with her knuckles, and Ramón gave her a few more coins.

"Mother, I need something from you. Quickly, I don't have time."

I couldn't hear what she said in reply.

"They're arresting everyone. I need to contact Jaime Marroquín. Not at his home, wherever he would have gone."

There was a long silence, and then I heard his mother giving a muffled reply. Ramón plucked a pencil up from on the desk and wrote a number down on a slip of paper. He then quickly hung up and got the operator to connect him to the new number.

"I need to speak to Señor Marroquín," said Ramón.

"There's no one here by that name."

"Tell him that Pilar de la Fuente's son is calling. He grew up with her in León. I need his help. He can call me back." He read the phone's number off a piece of paper taped to the receiver and hung up.

We waited in that office for what seemed an eternity, but the phone didn't ring.

"You can't stay here," the old woman said.

"We won't be long," said Ramón

"How can you be sure that he's there? Or that he'll call?" I asked.

"He'll call," said Ramón.

I was about to ask why he was so certain when the phone rang. Ramón practically leapt to grab it.

"Señor Marroquín?" he said. No one replied. "This is Ramón, Pilar de la Fuente's son. I need to get out of the city." He looked at me briefly before averting his eyes. "Myself and one other."

I could hear that when the voice on the other end of the phone spoke, it was surprisingly warm.

"Are you asking to join with us?"

"If that's what it takes," said Ramón through gritted teeth.

"Then listen. You must do exactly as I say. There is no time to hesitate."

LAS SIERRAS

7

WE WERE SMUGGLED OUT OF THE CITY in the back of a delivery truck, along with dozens of others. The net had not yet been drawn tightly by the Guardia Nacional. The military was at first too concerned with the visible leaders of the opposition to be able to scoop us all up. As soon as they were able, though, every student, every professor, every person suspected of even the slightest tendency towards the Left was arrested, the details of their crimes to be determined at a later date. Almost everyone I knew was arrested, and some were never released or found again.

The President broadcast assurances that the dignity of the country and its people would be protected. But he and a tight circle of families were the ones who frequented the glitzy nightclubs and had privileges that no one else in the country enjoyed. I still wasn't political in those days, but it was clear to everyone who scrambled each day to survive that he was lying.

At first, I wondered if the opposition was doing us a favour by spiriting us out of the city, but it was soon clear that they were not. Many of us would pay for their gesture with blood. After driving through the night, the truck brought us to a large estancia on the western side of the mountains that made up the country's centre. The pastures around the main house were filled with men being hastily organized into groups. Some were armed, but most looked confused, tired and slow-moving like us. We were directed to stand together with another group of men. We gathered from their clothing and accents, that they were a mix of campesinos and Managuans, like Ramón and I. There were about fifty of us, shivering in the damp morning air, quietly talking as we guessed at what might happen next.

"How do we know this isn't a trap?" asked one man.

"A lot of work just to kill us," said another. "They could have done that hours ago."

"Maybe they wanted us somewhere out of the way first."

"Nothing bad will happen," said Ramón, "I'm sure of it."

I was glad that he was certain, but I looked around to see which direction we should run, just in case.

A short man with a bushy mustache and a rifle slung over his shoulder strode over to stand in front of us, fists on his hips. Behind him stood a loose line of four men, all carrying shotguns. He surveyed us critically, making sure we knew that we did not meet his standards without saying a word. He stood just looking at us until we were uncomfortable, men shuffling and staring at their feet.

"What is all this about?" asked Ramón, stepping to the front of the group.

The man's mustache twitched a little as he looked over at Ramón before deciding to ignore him and address the group. "My name is Braulio, commander of Column F. Welcome, new volunteers, to the Frente Sandinista de Liberación Nacional."[4] he said.

"Do we swear an oath or something?" asked one of the campesinos.

Braulio gave a short laugh like a bark. "Deeds, not words," said Braulio. He waved at his lieutenants, standing behind him. "Get them ready."

And with that, we were recruited.

There weren't enough guns to go around, and the ones we had were in poor condition. Other than Braulio's, a scoped hunting rifle, all the others were either shotguns donated by campesinos or

____

[4] *Translator's note: Frente Sandinista de Liberación Nacional (FSLN) / Sandinista National Liberation Front*

revolvers stolen from the police. In those days, maybe four men in ten had a gun. There were some odd bits of uniform for us to wear, but not enough for everyone. Ramón had questions for everyone who seemed to be in charge, but they all ignored him. When one of the guerrillas stationed at the estancia gave him a long pole with water jerry cans suspended on each end to carry, he lost his temper.

"I'm a physician," he spat at the man, with real venom. "The Revolution can make better use of men than as donkeys." Braulio was watching from a short distance away and intervened.

"You can be our medic, then," he said.

Ramón nodded, satisfied.

"And Señor Doctor," added Braulio, "we need you to carry the water jerry cans." Braulio walked away, leaving Ramón cursing at the guerrilla still standing in front of him, his mouth agape. Ramón regained his composure and asked the rest of the column for two volunteers who could carry a stretcher to be his assistants, and I volunteered. The other volunteer was a gangly ginger in a natty cowboy hat he said he had found on the ground near the estancia. He hadn't even told us his name before Ramón nicknamed him El Rubio.

Braulio led our column away from the estancia and onto the forest-covered mountain slopes not yet cleared for farming or ranching. There must have been three or four other columns like ours that set out from the estancia. Who knows how many others there were across the country, Braulio was tight-lipped. He wouldn't speak of how many columns there were in the FSLN, or who commanded it, or what he planned to do with us. I soon realized that Braulio wasn't even his name, just a nom de guerre chosen to conceal his identity. He encouraged all of us to adopt new names as well, and not to speak of our families, homes, or anything else from our past lives.

"We don't yet know if there are traitors in our midst, or what trouble they could cause if they were to report our identities to the Somocistas," he said. I stuck with Paco, as it was a nickname already, and I had no family to protect. Ramón had decided our new companion's name the moment he set eyes on him. Rubio was also quick-witted and gave him a name in return: Fósforo.[5] When I heard it, I laughed so hard that I had trouble breathing. Soon everyone around us was laughing as well—everyone except Ramón.

"I'd prefer to be called Doctor," he said huffily. The fact that he didn't see the humour in it, even standing caked in dirt, thin as a rake and with a head of bushy hair, meant that the nickname stuck.

Soon, Fósforo, Rubio and I were inseparable, marching just behind Braulio as he led us deeper into the mountains. We climbed through the forest, marching entirely at night, crossing over the mountains through a pass that Braulio said was called the "Ojo de la Cerradura." It was narrow and overgrown, fit more for goats and donkeys than for men. I was glad when we began to descend down the eastern side of the mountains.

"If you'd told me a month ago that I'd be living like this, I'd have said you were crazy," I said to Fósforo and Rubio as we struggled down a steep path, grasping at trees and slippery rocks.

"And just imagine what your future self will have to say to your present one," laughed Rubio. "We haven't yet seen what is in store for Column F."

"I'm not surprised at where we've ended up," said Fósforo seriously.

"Come on," I said, throwing a handful of grass at him that came loose as I grabbed it. "You can't tell me that you were planning to become a guerrilla."

"Not exactly," said Fósforo, "but the conditions that drove us here were plain for anyone to see. It was only a matter of time."

"Now you're just being too clever. If you saw this coming, why did we escape by the skin of our teeth?"

"Step by step, we were being pushed into this, along with everyone else. We were left with only two choices—intolerable suffering, or taking up arms."

"It seems to me that we've chosen to do both," said Rubio, his face such a mask of misery that both Fósforo and I burst out laughing. We marched onward.

---

[5] *Translator's note: Matchstick. Also, a short-tempered person.*

I later learned from Braulio that this part of the country was wetter than the west, the mountains trapping rains that blew in from the Caribbean. Whereas the western slopes were farmed extensively, the population on the eastern slopes was much more sparse, with little industry besides logging. The ground was eternally wet, and every day there was at least an hour of heavy rain.

We marched for over a week before arriving where Braulio intended to bring us, and the strain on the column had begun to show. Fósforo, myself, and some of the others were used to walking, and although the nights of marching were long and the terrain difficult, we had no trouble keeping up with Braulio. Some of the others began to straggle, worn out by the exertion, and Braulio kept two of his armed lieutenants at the rear to keep them with the group.

For our camp, Braulio chose a slope where the trees were well spaced, and where there was a stream that could be used for drinking water. He showed us how to build lean-to shelters from branches and fronds and divided us into four platoons, which he arranged in a wide circle around his own shelter. Braulio told us to set up our shelter close to his. Rubio and I built it while Fósforo conducted his rounds.

"Have you ever done this before?" asked Rubio, trying to break a fallen branch to the right length.

I laughed. "Not necessary where I'm from."

"Me either," said Rubio. "I suppose that someone built my parent's house, but we just lived in it."

"You suppose? It didn't just appear by magic?" I asked.

"I never paid any attention to that stuff," said Rubio. "I just worked in my father's pulpería and chased girls when I wasn't behind the counter."

When we'd partially finished, Rubio crawled into our shelter and pulled his hat down over his eyes. "We must be naturals at building shelters, I suppose. I think this will do just fine."

I looked at him through the many gaps in the shelter's roof and was not so sure. "This would be easier with a machete," I said, straining to break another branch over my knee.

Braulio, lounging nearby under a plastic tarp that he had strung between two trees, must have heard me. He stood up and gave me a disparaging look. "Soft hands from that easy city living, Paco?"

I merely smiled and focused on improving our shelter. I gave the soles of Rubio's shoes a kick, and he sat up, his head poking through the shelter roof. "Come on," I said. "It's going to rain again soon enough."

Fósforo reappeared, wiping a bloody penknife on his shirt. He saw that Braulio was looking over at us and held it up so that our leader could see it. "Nearly half of the men have blisters, many infected, and all I have to treat them is this." I saw that he had torn strips from the bottom of his filthy shirt to make bandages. He stuck the penknife in his pocket and held up his empty hands. "I can't be a medic without medical supplies," he said. The rain started falling, pelting the trees and the ground with large droplets that stung the skin when they hit.

Braulio smirked under his moustache. "The Revolution will provide," he said, ducking back under his tarp and out of sight.

Fósforo, Rubio and I huddled under our lean-to, rain pouring through the gaps in the roof, and tried to wait out the storm in good humour. As the rain continued, the gentle stream that ran through our camp became more of a torrent. Smaller streams appeared across the hillside. A rivulet of water raced through the centre of our shelter, growing stronger as the rain continued. Fósforo used his hands to make a channel in the soft earth that diverted it, keeping it from flooding us out entirely. Wiping his muddy hands on his pants, he lay back and closed his eyes. With only a bed of mud to lay down on, I sat upright.

"When this is over," said Rubio, "We can make a fire and brew up some tea."

"Who has tea?" I asked. Our rations had been meagre, to begin with, and were growing ever slimmer.

"Tea made from ocote needles," said Rubio. I looked at him doubtfully. "My grandmother used to drink it sometimes," he said. We sat huddled together for over an hour as the rain pelted the ground around us and rendered it sodden. The noise of the rain became so loud that conversation was impossible, so we all sat looking out into the trees in silence. After an hour or so, the rain slackened and then stopped. One by one, men appeared from their shelters.

It seemed that everyone had the same idea as Rubio, and soon several dozen plumes of smoke rose from our camp, as the wet wood burned. We had saved a tin can from one of our first meals, and along with a handful of ocote needles, Rubio began to brew his tea.

We sat sullenly in our wet clothes watching the small fire. Over time, the noise of men laughing and breaking branches resumed across the camp. We could have continued to work on our shelter, but none of us bothered. We had already become used to things being just good enough.

One of Braulio's lieutenants called Julio, a tall man with narrow eyes and a long mustache that hid his mouth, ducked under our leader's tarp. We couldn't hear everything they discussed, but we heard enough to understand that a platoon was being sent out on a patrol. Braulio clearly knew the territory well and seemed to describe in great detail the route to take, somewhere down the hill and along the road that ran below us.

When Julio left, Braulio climbed out of his shelter and stretched. He looked at us, and I suppose that I must have looked guilty for eavesdropping because he walked over to us. I didn't look up and instead watched the fire intently. He reached down and plucked our can out of the fire, holding it gingerly with his fingers by the edges. He sniffed it, wrinkling his nose, before taking a sip. He spat and tossed our tea aside. "Cat piss," he said, dropping the can.

Fósforo was always the boldest man I knew, and so he stood, gesturing to the tarp where the teniente had been briefed. "What was that all about?" he asked.

Braulio's face was a mask. "Why do you want to know?"

"I'm your doctor," said Fósforo. "I want to know what to expect. I don't have much to treat wounded men, but I'll do what I can."

"I'll tell you what you need to know when you need to know it," Braulio said. He turned away and walked back to his shelter.

Rubio gave a low whistle. "You sure are good at making friends," he said as he threw another handful of ocote needles into the can and began to make more tea.

The next morning, Fósforo took us both on his rounds of the camp, checking on people's feet and poking at the abscesses that had appeared where pack straps had rubbed men's skin raw. One of the platoons, led by Julio, had left before dawn, and their shelters stood empty. Although Braulio had not told us exactly where they were headed, it seemed that the platoon itself had talked, and everyone else knew. They were sent to "liberate" supplies from a hardware store that was a few miles away, along a road used by logging trucks and anyone else traversing the district.

"I wish I had gone to rob those rich bastards," said one man, with the deeply creased face of someone who had worked outside in the sun all his life. He took off his shoes when he saw Fósforo, revealing feet that were soft and raw after the long march to the camp.

Fósforo poked at the red soles of the man's feet, sniffing them for signs of infection, before wrapping them up again in the bandages he had made from his shirt. "I don't get the sense that anyone around here is likely to be very rich," he said. "Maybe the men who own the lumber mills, and sell the wood in the city, but that's about it."

"I know what the store owners are like around here," said the man. "They charge triple for everything they have, and no one has any choice but to buy from them. The ladinos are parasites, worse than the landowners because they come from the People."

"Maybe so," I said, "but if we rob the store owner, what will be left for everyone else?"

The man had no reply, and so once Fósforo had finished tying the bandages on his feet, we moved on, eventually coming back to our part of the camp. Seated around the cold remains of yesterday's fire, we didn't bother to light it again, having nothing but ocote tea to cook.

"Some of these men are not going to be able to walk out of here very easily until their feet heal," said Fósforo. "We need to make stretchers to be ready."

"Ready for what?" I asked.

Fósforo pointed with his chin towards Braulio. "For whatever he decides."

We found stout young trees that we could use to make simple wooden frames that could be used to carry injured men. We lashed them together with strips torn from men's shirts, which Fósforo collected from the platoons, convincing them that it would be in their best interest. We managed to build two of them before the rain started again. Although they would be uncomfortable, they would be better than the alternative.

Sitting inside our shelter, both Rubio and I looked for leaks in the roof and wove branches into the structure to fill in the holes. Once that was done, we waited. Our days had been reduced to tedium, half spent enduring the daily rainfall, and the other half spent drying out from it. Our meagre meals did little to add interest to the day, and although our rations kept getting slimmer and slimmer, only Braulio knew the real state of our supplies.

That evening, just as the light began to fade over the mountain tops behind us, we heard shots from the forest below. Three loud bangs in quick succession, then silence. Every man in the camp was soon standing in a crowded circle around Braulio's tarp.

"Get back to your positions," said Braulio, his rifle cradled across his chest. "We'll find out what those shots meant soon enough."

No one moved. Braulio kicked a man in the ass, hard, and the man ran a few steps before stopping again. He kicked another, and then another, and the circle widened, but no one returned to their shelters. As Braulio swirled around inside the crowd, men dodged him but did not leave.

We watched this all from our shelter, wondering how it might escalate. A shout went up from the far side of the crowd, and men surged past Braulio towards it. We got on our feet and followed, amazed at what we saw.

Julio's platoon had returned from their raid laden with goods. The shots we had heard were the lead men of the platoon shooting two wild pigs, both of which were laid at Braulio's feet like a bloody offering. Man after man from the platoon stepped forward and disgorged a load of supplies in front of him. Julio stood smiling, the pile of booty spread out like a carpet. Sacks of rice and flour, rolls of leather strapping, machetes, saws, hammers, nails, oil lanterns, boxes of candles, a half-dozen round metal canteens and a bundle of tarps. The last item to appear was a first aid kit in a metal toolbox, which Braulio immediately gave to Fósforo. The mood in the camp, which had been bleak, was suddenly carnival-like. The variability of men's hearts was plain to see, and what an hour before had felt like slow defeat felt now like victory. The two pigs were gutted and roasted on a fire of green wood in front of Braulio's shelter. He and the lieutenants carefully divided up the loot so that each got a fair share, though how the lieutenants divided it up amongst their platoons, we did not see. Braulio kept none of the tools for himself, nor did he save any for us, much to our disappointment. He did keep one of the oiled canvas tarps, which he used to make his accommodation larger. Even given the state of everyone else's shelters, no one complained.

The pigs were eaten to the last morsel, and even the bones were carted away. When the feast was over, there was no trace left to betray even where they had been slaughtered. There was a constant movement of men inside the camp throughout the night, which Fósforo reported was because of a rampant plague of diarrhea. Still, morale was high, and the men's confidence grew. In the morning, Braulio called a conference of his lieutenants. We stayed seated around our morning campfire, cooking some rice issued for breakfast. This time we could hear the leaders' discussion clearly.

"We will keep up the pressure on the capitalists of the district," said Braulio.

"There's nothing left there now, but we could rob the store again when they restock," said Julio.

Braulio waved his hand. "There's no water in a dry well." He stabbed his finger down the hill. "I want to start stopping traffic on the road. We'll levy a revolutionary tax on whoever passes by."

Julio snorted. "A tax of everything they have?"

"No," scowled Braulio, "not so much that they will stop using the road."

"There's a tight bend in the road near here. That's where we should set up," said Julio.

"You need to set up a mile or two down the road, not so close to our camp," said Braulio.

"This isn't the first time I've been a tax collector," said Julio.

Braulio scowled but didn't push his point.

The platoons took turns setting up checkpoints and collecting taxes, and we heard about it when we followed Fósforo on his rounds. Julio and a few of his men, we learned, had made a living before the Revolution as bandits. Robbing travellers and country stores, stealing farm animals, and living rough were familiar to them. They taught the others what they knew about avoiding the authorities and fleecing the unwary.

Every day a new platoon set up at the tight bend in the road, and each night they would bring the profits back to Braulio. Most often, it was small amounts of cash, a few chickens or a small pig. Braulio kept the money in a tin box in his tent, and the food he divided into five shares, one each for the platoons and one for himself. Sometimes, when he felt social, he invited the three of us to join him.

"Come and eat some of this soup," said Braulio one evening.

We walked over cautiously, to find him sitting bare-chested on a log in front of a fire on which a big tin can of soup bubbled away. He had crude blue tattoos on his chest and arms, like small smudges, and a fair number of scars that looked white against his dark skin. He had received a good portion of a chicken, and in the pot were a few pieces of vegetable and some meat. It smelled heavenly compared to the cornmeal that we had made into coarse tortillas for our dinner.

He dipped a tin mug into the can and pulled out some broth, which he handed to Fósforo, who thanked him and passed it on to Rubio.

"Not to your taste?" asked Braulio.

"I'll have some after these two have eaten," said Fósforo.

Braulio was suspicious that there was some criticism implied in this gesture, but he still took a larger mug and filled it for himself. Using a dirty finger, he carefully coaxed a few pieces of meat into it. Satisfied with his share, he blew on it and sipped it gingerly. "Aren't we keeping you busy enough, doctor? Not working up an appetite?"

Fósforo thought for a moment, choosing his words. "I'm just having trouble seeing where this is all going."

Braulio's face went red, and he put down his soup and picked up a stick. "You want to know where this is going?" I thought that he might lash out at Fósforo with it, but instead, he scratched a rough map on the ground.

"This is the district. Mountains in the west, swamps to the east." He scratched two circles in the dirt, connected by a line. "There is one major road through the district, with a small garrison of Guardia Nacional in town and a smaller one at this bridge." He gestured with the stick as he spoke. "We have to stay out of the way of the Guardia while building our strength." He scratched the road deeper into the earth with his stick. "And so we avoid the town and the bridge and focus on the road."

"Build our strength for what?" asked Fósforo. "How does this help the People?"

"Help the People," spat Braulio. "We help them by getting the authorities to take their foot off their necks, and we do that by getting stronger."

"But no matter how strong we are, we don't achieve anything unless we fight the government. Right now, we're just robbing regular people," said Fósforo.

"I bet you think we should just attack the Guardia head-on?" he said to Fósforo.

Fósforo was silent, studying the rough map.

"You think that you know what's best, but you don't," said Braulio. "We're a mosquito fighting an elephant," he said. "Little bites, little bites, each time sucking a little more blood. That's how we'll win this war."

"It seems like we're sucking the People's blood, not the government's," said Fósforo.

"We need to get stronger, and so we feed off who we can," said Braulio. "I have a plan for us to sabotage the factory in town."

"What kind of factory?" asked Fósforo.

"An imperialist one," said Braulio, "a soda bottling plant. Coca-Cola."

Fósforo gave a low whistle. "A real blow against the regime and the Yanquis," he said. "They'll write songs about that one."

Braulio wrapped his shirt around his hand and pulled the tin can of soup from the fire, carrying it and his cup into his shelter. He gave one last piece of advice as he left.

"Fósforo, you should learn when to shut the fuck up."

8

I WOKE TO THE SOUND OF GUNFIRE, shouts, and screams. Before I even sat up, Fósforo sprinted out of the tent, shirtless, with his medical bag in one hand. I followed him, shouting at Rubio to get moving as well.

The stretchers were leaning against a tree beside our shelter, and I cursed myself for putting them there, now seeing how obviously man-made they would look from a distance. I grabbed one and caught up with Fósforo in a crouched run, skidding to a stop and flattening myself beside him. The tarpaulin of Braulio's shelter made snapping noises as bullets cut through it. Rubio flopped down beside me, his t-shirt on backwards and inside out and already darkened with sweat.

Braulio was half-dressed and barefoot, clutching his rifle and looking around, still trying to make sense of the situation. Fósforo was beside him, watching. When Braulio didn't speak, Fósforo shook him by the shoulder.

"What's the plan?" he asked.

Braulio's voice was thick like his tongue was swollen. "We need to organize the platoons," he said. "A counter-attack."

Fósforo said nothing. The pace of the firing began to slacken. Based on the sound, I realized the shots were all incoming. No one within the camp seemed to be firing back. The shouts were those of men in agony, wounded and begging for help. I rolled over to look past Braulio to Fósforo.

"We need to help them," he said. The moans of the wounded sounded more like animals than men.

"This isn't combat," I replied, "this is murder. They don't need a medic. They need a leader to pull us out of this."

"We need to find Julio and his men," said Braulio. He gestured with the barrel of his rifle towards where that platoon was camped. Trying to move anywhere in that camp under fire seemed like madness to me, but Fósforo didn't think so. He shouldered his medical bag and dashed off towards Julio's platoon with Braulio on his heels.

I took a deep breath, then ran after them. Rubio followed me. An angry fusillade of bullets struck the tree trunks around us as we moved. They sounded like a madman hitting the trees with hammers. We hadn't gotten very far when Rubio and I dropped back down to the ground by instinct. The firing intensified as we lay there, showering us in leaves and small branches. I was frozen; my face pressed to the ground.

"Stop fucking around," called Fósforo, crouching behind a cluster of rocks a dozen yards ahead of me. Braulio was behind him, looking through his rifle's sight, though not firing. Those few yards between us seemed an impossible distance. I tried to imagine myself leaping up and dashing across the open ground towards them, but I couldn't. I was about to shout to them to leave us, to save themselves, when Rubio raced past me, moving on his knees and elbows and keeping low to the ground like a snake. I rolled over a little to cross myself, swallowing hard, and then I did the same, ignoring the roots and sharp rocks that tore at my sleeves. As I moved, I felt my fear start to subside. I was no longer just a target. I was doing something. I could hear the bullets whizzing by, some striking the tree trunks, but they all sounded as if they were going high. We covered the ground faster than I would have thought possible and crawled in beside the others.

"Ready?" asked Fósforo.

Without waiting for a response, he crawled forward, Braulio

close behind him. Rubio and I fell in behind Braulio, and Fósforo led us out of the centre of the encampment and towards its edge. It was easy to follow Fósforo's pale, naked torso in the morning light, and I was sure that the soldiers could see him as plainly as I did, but no shots ever came close to us as we made our way through the bush.

He avoided the trail that we had been using that connected Braulio's tent to the nearest platoon camped on this flank. Fósforo somehow found a gap where there were no guardsmen and following him, we all slid through their line unseen. There was still firing all around us, but it was no longer the long, concentrated volleys that had woken us. Every few minutes, a few shots rang out. When one guardsman fired, the others around him did too. I suspect that they were firing at nothing, but doing something kept their fear at bay, which I understood. As we slunk through the bushes, I saw the guardsmen hunkered behind every piece of cover they could find on the slope below us. Seeing them crouched there in a thick line of men, rather than truly all around us, and I realized that they must have come here by road.

We were moving slowly along the slope, threading between trees and rocks, and pausing to let Fósforo scout our next bound forward. In those moments, I wished that I had a gun, a machete, anything that would make me feel I could strike back. Instead, I felt like a rabbit amongst wolves. I eyed Braulio's rifle, slung across his back, and wondered why he was not firing it—not shooting to kill, even, just shooting like the guardsmen did so as not to feel so powerless.

We paused for a moment, huddled together under the low branches of a cypress tree. I was breathing heavily, and I took a moment to close my eyes and calm down. I heard a few more shots, but they were all behind us, and I hoped that we were outside the Guardia's positions around the camp. While we caught our breath, we heard a voice coming through a bullhorn.

"This is Captain Espina, of the Guardia Nacional! Surrender!"

I couldn't tell where the voice was coming from as it echoed off the trees. For a moment, there was silence all around.

"Fighting us is futile," he said. "Your leaders write letters to the newspapers saying that you are the protectors of the people. They sit comfortably somewhere safe, in hiding, while you are reduced to robbing travellers and slowly starving to death."

Espina was warming up to his speech, speaking as much to his men as to us. "Real men don't rob women and children. Real heroes protect them, as we do. We take no pleasure in hunting you down but hunt you down we will if that is what keeps our families safe at night. Your only hope is to surrender. You have my personal guarantee that you will not be harmed."

I saw a few of our men, farther along the slope, stand up from where they had been hiding and walk forwards with their hands up. They were half-dressed and dishevelled-looking. One man had a shotgun held over his head in both hands.

"We surrender," said the guerrilla. "Don't shoot."

When they were well in the open, we heard the bullhorn again. "Death to the traitors!"

A fusillade of shots rang out again, and the surrendering men were cut down where they stood. I could see the dirt around the fallen men torn up by bullets and see the men twitch as they were struck. "Enough!" shouted the voice through the bullhorn, and the shooting stopped. The forest was silent again, except for the dull moans of one or more of the guerrillas lying in the open.

A man stepped forward out of the woods, bullhorn in one hand and a pistol in the other. He was small and thin, with perfectly clean, well-tailored fatigues, his leather pistol belt shone dully, even from a distance. I watched him as he approached the fallen guerrillas, rolling them over disdainfully with his foot. The last man must have still been alive because he shot him twice. He holstered his pistol and picked up the shotgun. A guardsman dashed out from behind cover and took it from him. Captain Espina spat on the last corpse and walked away, wiping his hands on a handkerchief as if he had become sullied by his work.

Rubio had his fist clenched so tight that his fingers turned white. For a moment, he looked like he might run down the slope to where we had last seen the officer. "Give me the gun," he said, his eyes wild.

I pressed down on his shoulder. "It's too late for them."

"It's not too late for that Captain," said Rubio.

I was about to argue, but Fósforo started moving again, and I pulled on Rubio's arm to get him to follow. Fósforo pushed forward away from the execution, crawling quickly, and we were close behind. He led us further away from the camp and away from the guardsmen's dragnet. Sticking close to him, now loping in a low run, we threaded between trees and brush as quickly as we could without making too much noise. After a minute or two, we reached a jumble of fallen rocks that had lodged together in the roots of a tree. Peering over them, he froze, and then I saw his face relax. He turned and smiled at us, waving us forward and scrambled down past the rocks.

In a shallow cut made by rain and erosion were a group of men from our column. Julio sat on the ground, his moustache bushy and unkempt, almost hiding the lower half of his face. There were a dozen others with him, all young and frightened. At his feet lay a man shot in the chest, blood pooling under Julio's boots. No one bothered to help the man. I looked around at what remained of the column. Between us, we had Braulio's rifle, three shotguns and an enormous revolver that Julio had strapped to his leg.

Braulio made a show of hugging his teniente, trying to instill in the others the idea that he was not afraid. He took off his leather bandolier and made himself comfortable sitting on a rock. Julio was stiff, one hand bandaged and bloody, and he did not smile at the sight of our leader.

"Good work," said Braulio, "saving these men."

Julio nodded. Braulio had nothing more.

Fósforo approached and opened his medical bag. Julio waved him off with his injured hand, nudging the man at his feet with the toe of his boot.

"This one's dead," said Julio. "He made it here on his own, crashing through the bush like a wild boar, but then he just lay down and died."

"Your hand then?" asked Fósforo.

Julio shook his head, using his good hand to fish a cigarette and matches out of his pocket.

The men gathered around Braulio and Julio, anxious and wanting to know what to do. Julio took a long drag on his cigarette and then handed it to Braulio.

"There's no sense staying here to fight it out," he said.

Braulio nodded, sucking the life out of the cigarette in one long pull.

"Then let's get moving," said Julio. "I'll take us down to the highway. We can wait for the Guardia to leave and steal the next car or truck that drives by. From there, we can drive deeper towards the Caribbean coast."

Braulio considered this for a moment, looking around at the men to judge if they would follow. Fósforo was kneeling beside the man on the ground, and for a moment, I thought that maybe he was alive. That perhaps Fósforo would do something, and the man would sputter and gasp and heave a breath out of his chest. But the man lay still and waxen on the ground, and Fósforo manhandled him to remove his olive drab shirt, which he pulled on over his own bare torso. There was a neat hole in the man's chest, just an inch or so from his left nipple, and such a small wound did not look to me as if it should spell death.

"Maybe we should surrender," blurted one of the other men. A few others murmured their agreement.

"What did you say?" asked Braulio, unslinging his rifle and holding it both hands.

"Just that . . . maybe we should surrender."

"Even jail is better than that," said another, flicking his chin at the dead man.

"Does it sound like they are arresting people up there?" asked Braulio. The heavy gunfire had ended, but there were still shots from time to time. I suddenly realized what he meant.

"But I haven't done anything wrong," said one man. "I don't even have a gun."

"Tell that to them," said Rubio.

Julio stood up. "Stay and surrender if you wish. I am taking everyone who wants to go with me down to the highway and away from here."

Fósforo stood up, buttoning his new shirt, the bullet hole through the breast pocket obvious and bloody. "We can't go down to the highway," he said. "That's where this lot would have come from. They must have their trucks lined up on the road under guard."

"You don't know that," said Julio.

"I do," said Fósforo. "Our tax collecting attracted their attention. They came to put a stop to it and must have followed our men back to the camp this morning."

"So, you want to fight it out with them?" challenged Julio.

"No, just to survive long enough to fight them another day."

The men had split opinions. Some seemed to favour running down to the road, some said we should run up the mountain away from the road, and others thought we might still have a chance if we surrendered.

"We need to move up the mountain, and put some distance between us and the Guardia," said Fósforo. "They've got their victory. They won't run us down unless we make it easy for them."

"Go and starve up the mountain with the doctor if you want," said Julio to the assembled men. "But all the guns are coming with me. And once we steal a truck, we're going to find some . . ."

Julio's speech was cut short by a long burst of fire from just below us. Strung out in a loose line were a group of guardsmen, crouched behind bushes and firing wildly. An older man with a pistol stood at the end of their line, shouting: "Advance! Advance!" The guardsmen kept shooting but did not move.

Our group scattered as the gunfire struck the ground all around us. I crouched and dashed towards Fósforo, who was lying flat on his belly behind Braulio. Our leader lay crumpled on the ground at an odd angle, as if in a fitful sleep. His flat eyes stared past me, and I could tell he was dead before I even saw the top of his head—an open mess of gore that spread out behind him onto the forest floor.

I hesitated, transfixed by what I saw, staring. Fósforo grabbed me roughly by the belt and pulled me down beside him as a volley of shots hit the trees.

"Pay attention and stay down," Fósforo said, his eyes lit up as I had never seen them before. I was overcome by fear again and hugged the earth with my whole body. My fingers slid through the blood-soaked soil to find a grip on the ground, pulling me closer to it, making me smaller, doing anything I could do to avoid being shot.

Fósforo's face was close to mine, but knowing that he would sense my panic, I couldn't look him in the eye. I brushed my hair out of my eyes, smearing myself with blood and whatever else. When the smell on my hands hit my nostrils, I threw up, bile heaving out of my empty stomach.

"We're going to move," said Fósforo, tensing as he readied himself to run. We both leapt up, but Fósforo cried out and immediately tumbled to the ground, one leg kicking high out in front of him like a dancer. I saw this, but forgive me, I didn't stop to help him. I kept running, up and over the rockfall to a small area of shelter that overlooked our meeting place.

Bullets kicked up the dirt around Fósforo, but he didn't seem to notice. He rolled onto his knees, and I could see that one of the heels of his boots had been shot away, a nasty gash cutting across the shoe's now-exposed sole. In front of him were his medic bag and Braulio's rifle and ammunition. Without hesitation, he scooped up the rifle in one hand and the bandolier of ammunition in the other. Almost immediately, he was running past me with long strides.

He didn't say anything as he ran past, and he didn't need to. Some of the men came with us; others probably perished on the spot. I didn't know how many were with us and how many we left behind. I ran as hard as I could, keeping Fósforo just within view ahead of me until my lungs burned, my legs were numb, and my feet bled inside my shoes. We didn't stop until nightfall, and then we few survivors huddled together in a close circle, unsure of what might befall us next.

9

WHEN THE SUN BEGAN TO RISE the next morning, I was damp, cold, and covered in insect bites, but grateful to be alive. As miserable as I felt, I must have looked worse in the harsh light of the morning. Fósforo gripped my arm but said nothing. I looked him in the eye and simply nodded. Of the hundred or so men who Braulio had led, there were now only six of us.

The bandage on Julio's hand was soaked in blood and filth, but if it was painful, he didn't show it. He sat slightly apart from the rest of us, smoking and watching. Fósforo, Rubio and I had stayed close together ever since the raid on the camp and were miraculously unhurt. Fósforo had held onto Braulio's scoped rifle as we retreated and wore the leather bandolier across his chest. The remaining two members of our group were young brothers from one of the other platoons, Santiago and Juan, who had forgotten to use their noms de guerre and given their real names instead. They wore the straw hats typical of campesinos. Neither had carried anything with them when they ran.

"Does anyone have any food?" asked Fósforo.

Santiago spoke for his brother as well. "We have nothing, doctor."

I pulled my pant pockets inside out to show that they were empty, and Rubio did the same. We all turned to Julio, who was silent.

"And you, comrade?"

"I have nothing," he said, looking defiantly at Fósforo.

I thought that Fósforo might challenge him, but instead, he turned to the rest of us. "Well then, we need to keep our eyes open for anything to eat while we walk."

"Walk to where?" asked Julio. "Who are you to give the orders? Braulio made me a teniente, not you."

"His plans are as dead as he is," said Fósforo.

Julio's bandaged hand dropped to the handle of his holstered revolver, and he and Fósforo looked at each other in silence. Rubio and I shifted to stand on either side of Fósforo. Neither Santiago nor Juan moved, watching from the side. Julio's eyes flickered over each of us, then he crossed his arms over his chest. "For now," he said.

Fósforo didn't explain his plan, and only much later on did I realize that he probably didn't have one. Over many days he led our tiny band westward, back through the Ojo de la Cerradura and over the Serranías de Amerrisque. We walked down among the foothills above the plains that stretched hundreds of miles out to the Pacific. His gait was unsteady, limping because of his missing boot heel. He couldn't have known the route, none of us did, but his confidence instilled faith, and we followed him without question. We found nothing to eat as we walked, though we filled ourselves with water whenever we found a spring. This went on for days longer than any one of us would have guessed. Everyone's bellies groaned as we walked, and as we began to obsess about finding food, tempers flared.

One morning, Fósforo became convinced that Julio was chewing on some food he had hidden from us. When we took a break, he confronted him.

"What are you eating?" Fósforo asked bluntly.

"Just a wad of grass, fearless leader," he said. "You can have it to chew on when I'm done."

He stood and pushed Fósforo aside with one hand and began walking again. I could have sworn that I smelled garlic on his breath as he passed me. Fósforo started to walk after him, but I grabbed him by the arm.

"That bastard Julio is hiding food," he hissed.

"Did you see it?" I asked.

"No, but I could smell it on his breath. We should search him."

"His pistol might have something to say about that."

"I have a rifle, too."

"We're in no position to shoot each other over an imagined piece of sausage," I said.

"Imagined? I could smell it."

"Even if he does have a little bit of food, soon enough, he'll be like the rest of us."

When Fósforo saw that Santiago and Juan were watching him closely in silence, he turned red and started walking quickly to get ahead of Julio.

We continued like this for three more days, Fósforo never hesitating or backtracking as he led us forward. Mid-afternoon on the last day, Fósforo stopped our little column and gestured at the vista that stretched out far below us.

"We'll find a place that's easily defensible down there, in the foothills overlooking that river." The countryside below us was lush and green, with a slow wide river cutting a winding path through the canopy, and the regular shapes of cattle pastures just visible beyond it.

"I know this river," said Julio. "My shit heel father's people are from this part of the country." He snorted and spat, the phlegm striking a rock with an audible slap.

Fósforo stepped off, and we started marching again. Our pace grew a little faster as it felt like our journey was nearing the end. The countryside became lusher and more hospitable as we descended deeper into the verdant hills along the river.

I was beginning to think it was time to stop for the day and scanned the ground around us for somewhere that we could make camp. Our little column was strung out across an open field with waist-high grass, a large clearing in an otherwise thick wood. The sun was low and shining through the trees, and I had to shield my eyes from it. Behind me, there was a shout.

"What are you doing?" said Rubio loudly.

I turned around to see Santiago dashing off into the bushes that bordered the field.

After a moment's hesitation, Juan turned and ran after him, crashing through the underbrush on the other side. I shouted something unintelligible at them, but neither turned back.

I swivelled to look all around us, trying to see what had spooked them.

"Guardsmen?" Rubio asked.

"We'd be dead by now if it was," I said.

"They've more likely had enough of Fósforo's bullshit," said Julio, brandishing his pistol in his left hand.

Fósforo ignored this comment, though he had unslung the rifle and was holding it at the ready. I looked around, feeling naked without a gun, and settled for a fallen tree branch that was a little too long and heavy to really be of use.

"Come on," said Fósforo, leading us into the wood line where they had disappeared. We went a short distance before Fósforo halted again, cupping his hand to his ear.

We heard them returning, crashing through branches, before we ever saw them. When they broke through the underbrush, we were ready to fight, still not sure why they had run. As soon as I saw their faces, though, I understood. They were both covered in juice, their mouths too full to speak, and their arms filled with guanabana. They tossed one to each of us and dropped the rest on the ground, the spiny peel smarting as I caught it and broke it open with my bare hands. I tore into its white flesh with my teeth, ignoring the slightly acidic taste as I ripped it apart and ate as fast as I could.

"I saw the tree poking out above the others, and I knew what it was," said Santiago.

"There's more there once we've eaten these," added Juan.

"But mind you, don't eat the seeds, they're poisonous."

We stood without speaking, eating every morsel of fruit, grating the last of the flesh from inside each husk before discarding it and opening another. I ate three of the giant fruit before I stopped, and I think that some of the others may have eaten more. When I looked up from gorging on the guanabana, I saw that everyone was grinning madly, their beards matted and streaked with juice and seeds.

"We need to keep moving," said Fósforo, wiping his face on his sleeve.

"There is enough food here for weeks," said Santiago.

Fósforo shook his head. "It's too overgrown. We need to find a place where we can see the approaches. We don't want to make camp where we can be easily surprised."

"Listen to the General," said Julio dismissively. "What would happen if we took a vote? Would we stay where there's food or keeping marching to who knows where?"

"We'll collect enough food, and then find a safe spot to camp," I said, eyeing both Julio and Fósforo. Both men nodded.

We followed Juan and Santiago back to the guanabana tree and gathered as much fruit as we could carry, as well as some mangos and mamoncillo, using our shirts as makeshift bags. Bare-chested and laden down with fruit, Fósforo led us further towards the river.

The sun had nearly set when Fósforo dropped his fruit and sat down on the ground. I looked around at the spot he had chosen and immediately saw why. It was on a low rise, covered in trees and brush, but with good visibility in all directions. The river was still at least a few hours walk away, but the lush forests around us likely contained streams and more fruit trees.

"We'll build shelters tomorrow in the daylight," said Fósforo. "Everyone, leave your fruit here. Rubio, Paco—walk in that direction, not far, and see if there is any water or more fruit trees. Santiago, Juan—walk in the other direction, look for the same. Julio, follow our tracks back a hundred yards or so and do your best to erase them."

I thought that Julio might say something, but he simply walked off to complete his task. Rubio and I headed out in the direction Fósforo had indicated, looking for anything of interest.

The forest was thick here, tangles of roots covering rocks and rich soil, and it wasn't possible to move quickly. Soon we were panting with the exertion. Rubio stopped and leaned against a low branch, pushing his hat back on his head to wipe the sweat from his face. He smiled at me.

"Ever wonder how in hell you wound up here?" he asked.

"Bad life choices?"

"Should have gone to church more, perhaps," he said.

"You'd just be trading one mystery for another."

Rubio laughed. "At least in church, they tell you how the story ends. Here . . ." His voice trailed off. "Who knows?"

"I have faith in Fósforo," I said.

"Me too," said Rubio. "But aside from keeping us alive, what does he intend?"

"You might have to wait until Sunday to ask," I said.

"I'm not even sure that I care what it is," said Rubio. "I just want to know."

I laughed at him. "You sound like a philosopher."

"I think a philosopher would be doing better than this," he said.

When we returned to camp, the others were already back. We had found nothing but trees and rocks, but Santiago and his brother had found a small stream and more fruit. Julio gave Fósforo a withering glare when asked to report on what he had seen and done.

"I did what you asked," said Julio, refusing to elaborate further.

"Next time," said Fósforo, "we can't send the two city boys together into the woods. Not if we want to get any results."

Juan grinned proudly. "I'm sure that we can show them a few things, even if they are sure to be slow learners." Rubio threw a fresh guanabana rind at him, forcing him to duck.

"No fire tonight," continued Fósforo, ignoring our antics. "There's nothing to cook on it in any case, but we also need to keep a low profile."

"No fires ever?" challenged Julio.

"No fires for now," replied Fósforo.

When the light faded entirely, we all lay down and slept in a small circle, shirts draped over our heads to keep the insects out of our faces. The night was hot and sticky, more so than when we were in the mountains, but judging by the snoring that soon erupted all around me, no one had trouble sleeping. I lay awake awhile, looking from under my shirt at specks of light far past the river I guessed were coming from a small town before I too fell asleep.

The morning came quickly. Fósforo was up before anyone else and had divided the pile of fruit into daily rations and each daily ration into six parts. He passed the fruit to every one of us himself, and we all sat together in a circle, feet nearly touching, eating with our hands. As we ate, Fósforo talked.

"Today, we will work on shelters and dig a latrine," he said. "We'll also build a lookout post for a guard and begin a twenty-four-hour watch over the camp."

He paused to see if anyone would argue, but even Julio had nothing to say.

"Our first duty, the essential task of a guerrilla army," he said, "is to keep itself from being destroyed. As long as we exist, the government can't win."

Julio spat out a long string of spittle and seeds. "That's all well and good for the guerrilla army," he said, "but what about us? What if we have other ideas?"

"Such as?" asked Fósforo.

Santiago and Juan were watching Julio closely. He spoke directly to them. "You two understand me. You're not overawed by 'the doctor' like these other two. The guerrilla army is finished. We don't even have enough guns. And without those, we're nothing."

"And so, what do you propose we 'nothings' do, then?" asked Fósforo.

"Find someone weaker and richer than us, and take what they have. Build ourselves back up again. And then once we've done that, we can decide what's next."

"We're not criminals," I said to Julio.

"Oh, no?" he laughed. "Then why did the Guardia hunt us down and shoot every man they caught? Would you want to ask them whether or not you're a criminal?"

I didn't have an answer for that.

"If the authorities shoot you on sight, then you're a criminal," Julio said. "And so, you should start thinking like one, if you want to live."

"You said before that I was the leader," said Fósforo, "have you changed your mind?"

"It's not up to me," said Julio. "We should have a vote. Everyone gets a vote except you, Fósforo, since you're already the leader."

"Everyone votes means everyone," I said.

Fósforo waved my concern away with one hand. "As you wish, Julio. It is clear what a vote for you represents. My perspective is this: the difference between a bandit and a guerrilla is not how they are seen by the authorities; it is how they are seen by the People. A guerrilla is part of the People, and so can turn to them for help. A bandit cannot, and so, eventually, he will be run to ground by the government and killed."

"Fine words," said Julio, "but we can't eat words. Or do anything else with them either." He looked at Santiago and Juan, his eyes flashing. "If you vote with me, then we can all become rich men."

"Everyone who wishes to vote for Julio, raise your hand," said Fósforo. Julio put his arm up over his head, smiling. Santiago and Juan sat, staring at their feet.

"Rich men, I tell you," said Julio, nudging Santiago with his foot. "You'll be my second in command." Neither of the brothers said anything.

"And for me?" asked Fósforo.

Rubio and I raised our hands. Santiago and Juan still sat, staring at the ground. We waited for a moment, but when it was clear that they were abstaining, Fósforo ended the meeting. "Julio, use your experience to pick a spot for the lookout, preferably high up. Paco, take the others and work on a shelter. I'll find a spot to dig the latrine." And then he left to get on with his task.

Julio was furious and stormed off as well. I watched for a moment to make sure that he wasn't following Fósforo.

"What was that about?" said Rubio. "For the first time in your lives, you get a vote, and you sit there like statues?"

Juan paused for a moment before speaking, his lips pursed. "On the farm growing up, our father said that nothing worthwhile was ever achieved by a vote. The sun, the rain, the soil—these are the important things, and they change with the season no matter what we want."

"Farmers still make choices," said Rubio. "Crops don't fall from the skies."

"Everything in its time," said Santiago.

"And we're still reading the season," said Juan.

We started on the shelter without further discussion, and our small camp began to take shape. An axe or machete would have made the work faster, but we managed to use fallen branches or small trees that we could uproot entirely to build shelter for all of us, with smaller leafy branches woven to make them more or less waterproof. Fósforo, Rubio and I shared one lean-to while Julio and the brothers shared the other. I was a little worried by this arrangement, but equally didn't want to sleep with Julio. The entrances faced towards each other, and they were low to the ground. Fósforo stood thirty feet away, critiquing them, pointing out all the different parts that made them too obvious. When we were done, they were hard to distinguish from the surrounding brush.

Julio had found a pair of trees that had grown twisted together, making them easy to climb and giving him space to jam some branches to make a platform large enough to stand on. I clambered up to test it and saw that from the vantage point he built, one could see all the approaches to our camp. The trees were bushy enough that our sentry wouldn't be obvious to anyone until they were right on top of him. Fósforo climbed up as well and gave his approval, though, by that point, Julio looked disinterested.

The best part of our new camp, however, was the latrine. Having no shovel to dig with, I had wondered how Fósforo would do it. He had found a small cliff, perhaps twenty-five feet high, formed where rocks washed away from the hillside. At the top of the cliff, he lashed a small log between two trees using vines to make a seat. He then joined a second log higher up to create a backrest. Clean and comfortable, as long as one didn't look down, it was alright.

Once the camp was built, Fósforo kept us busy with other tasks. There was always one man in the lookout, day and night. Santiago taught us a bird call that he and his brother used when hunting that we adapted to signal someone was coming. We rotated the task every day of who would go and collect fruit for our larder. And Fósforo sent a pair of men each day on hikes, sometimes going himself, searching farther and farther out around the camp. Each day he questioned the pair when they returned, trying to understand the terrain around us and using the information to build a rough model out of stones and earth.

We found no signs of any other inhabitants, no trails or tracks, and no animals worth hunting. As we talked about what we saw, and sometimes walked the same ground as earlier pairs, we began to understand the surrounding countryside. We knew the easiest ways for the Guardia to approach the camp and the ways from which no one would come. We knew where we could be seen from far below, and where one man could hold up a hundred for as long as he had ammunition. We grew comfortable in our home, isolated from the world.

We passed several weeks like this, our bowels suffering a little from subsisting entirely on fruit, and our minds a little from being bored. I was repairing some loose roofing on our lean-to late one afternoon and singing softly to myself when I heard a bird call from the area of our lookout. One call meant a patrol was returning.

Then, I heard the call again. Two calls meant trouble.

I crouched down, taking cover behind the shelter, and looked around for the others. Julio had been resting, but was now on his feet, shirt unbuttoned but with his pistol in hand. He waved me forward, and together we approached the lookout. Santiago was up the tree, peering down the slope. Fósforo was leaning behind the tree, looking through the scope of his rifle.

"What is it?" asked Julio.

"Two men, but I can't tell if it's Juan and Rubio or not," said Santiago.

"Are they coming this way?" asked Julio.

"Yes."

"Then who else could it be?"

"They don't look right to me," said Santiago. "They're laden down by something."

"Army backpacks?" asked Julio.

"Maybe," said Santiago.

We strained our eyes to see them, but they were too far away. Fósforo braced the rifle against the tree and peered down at them through the scope.

After a moment, he handed the rifle to me. "It's them," said Fósforo.

Julio holstered his pistol and went back to his shelter. I looked through the scope, but it took a moment for me to focus and scan across the landscape to find them. They were still far enough off that it took the scope to see them clearly. They both carried heavy knapsacks and tools over their shoulder, though Rubio's tattered hat made it obvious to me who they were. Everyone except Julio waited by the lookout for them to arrive to see what they had found.

"Treasures!" exclaimed Rubio, clearly proud of himself.

"Just a little farther north than we had gone before," explained Juan, "we found an abandoned mine."

"A gold mine, I'm sure of it," said Rubio.

Juan shrugged. "Maybe. But abandoned."

"And look what we found," said Rubio. He laid out everything that they had taken: six filthy canvas and leather knapsacks that had been used to carry ore, a shovel with a bent blade, a pickaxe handle, a battered cook pot, and four tin cups.

"Quite the treasure," said Fósforo. "At least the knapsacks will be useful."

Rubio flourished his hands like a magician. "But you haven't seen the treasure yet." He reached into his pocket and pulled out a tube-like one for an expensive cigar, but red. Fósforo recognized it first and gave a low whistle.

"Dynamite," said Rubio.

Fósforo took it from him and examined it before passing it to me. I saw now that it had a fuse protruding from one end and taped to its side. I handed it back to Rubio. "Is it safe?" I asked.

Rubio shrugged. "Safe enough."

I knew nothing about such things, and so focused on picking out the best of the knapsacks, and then taking it over to the stream to wash it out. The others did the same, and Juan washed one out for himself and for Julio as well. When he took it to him and dropped it by his feet, Julio said nothing.

"I cleaned it for you," said Juan.

"Am I supposed to say, thanks for turning me into a pack mule?" asked Julio, rolling over to face away from the rest of us.

Santiago left his perch to come to get me for the next shift. So, for a moment, we were all together in the camp. Fósforo cleared his throat and put his hand on my shoulder to stop me from leaving.

"I've decided that tomorrow, we will walk to the town on the other side of the river, and see if we can get some food and information," he said.

"Are we going to take the food that we need?" asked Julio. "Or ask politely and hope that they will just give it to us?"

"We are going to ask," said Fósforo, tight-lipped.

"Let's hope that the revolutionary spirit is in full swing then," said Julio, "otherwise, we are going to have to keep shitting fruit all day."

"Do you really think that they will give us anything?" Rubio asked.

"The Revolution is not an apple that falls when it's ripe. We have to make it fall. No one in that town will lift a finger to help us unless we show them that we exist to help them. And as this will be our first action of note, we all need to begin to think and act like guerrillas. And when we return, we are going to redistribute our arms."

"What do you mean?" asked Santiago.

"Guns will be allocated based on merit, not merely on the fact of possession. The rifle and the pistol will go to those who most deserve them, and from now on, being armed will be a privilege that must be earned."

Julio spat on the ground and went back to lying down in the lean-to. Rubio and the others looked doubtful but said nothing.

"We'll leave just before dawn," said Fósforo.

I left camp and climbed up to stand on the platform in the lookout. Leaning against the trunk of one of the trees, I made myself as comfortable as I could. I scanned the terrain, but as the light faded, there was less and less that I could see, and I tried to listen instead. I might have dozed a little because I didn't hear Fósforo until he was tapping on the heel of my shoe with a stick.

"Hey, eagle eyes," he said. "Down here. Lucky for you, it's just me."

I dropped down from the lookout, wondering what orders Fósforo had for me. He had his pocket knife out and was whittling one end of a long stick.

"Are you the next shift?" I asked.

He shook his head, still working on the stick.

"Is everything OK?" I asked.

Fósforo pointed at the flickering lights of the little town with his stick. "Going there is a risk, but if we are going to fight for anything, it's for those people. We need to keep building our strength, and that starts with helping them."

"So that they give us food?" I asked.

"So that they see us as allies, not bandits, and let us operate here without turning us in," he said. "If we're the fishes, they're the ocean."

I rubbed my beard with both hands, the skin underneath dirty and a little raw, and thought for a moment. "I'm not the one you need to convince," I said.

"So, you understand?" he asked.

"I think so," I said. "But where are you getting all this philosophy?"

"Some books I read that Magdalena gave me," he said. "And some common sense."

This sudden reminder of our former life gave me a pang of nostalgia, but if he felt the same, he didn't show it. "So, when we ran from the Guardia and marched all the way here, how did you know where you were going?"

He jammed the point of the stick into the ground beside him, laughing softly. "I didn't know, Paco, I didn't know at all." He searched my face to see how I would react and clapped me on the shoulder. "But, the way is getting clearer."

10

WE WOUND THROUGH THE TREES towards the river, led by Fósforo and his unerring sense of direction. The countryside gradually became gentler the farther towards the river we went, and soon we passed overgrown stands of fruit trees that might have once been plantations.

"This is rich country," said Rubio. "I can't believe no one farms it."

"No one is allowed to," said Santiago. "A few families own all this land, and they use it for cattle. Even if they aren't using it, they won't let anyone else farm it. They keep it like this to inflate the prices of food and kill off any competitors."

"Truly?" asked Rubio. "To have bought this land and then never use it . . ."

Julio's laugh was more like a bark. "You're like a baby," he said. "Do you actually think they paid for this? The government stole it and gave it to them, and in exchange, they keep the campesinos in line. That's how they stay rich men."

"It's one thing to read about this in the newspapers, and something entirely to see it with your own eyes," I said.

We trudged in silence until we reached the river, which flowed sluggishly between wide, sandy banks. Fósforo took off his boots and tied the laces together. Hanging them around his neck, he slipped into the water. We all followed, crossing the river in single file. The water was cool and never reached past our waists. We took a break in a copse of trees on the far side to dry off while Fósforo searched the horizon for signs of the town.

"Do we know what this place is called?" I asked.

"I'm not sure," said Julio, "but it is of no account in any case. The only town with more than one street is San Jose Guachipilín, in the centre of the department."

"Which department?" asked Rubio.

"What am I? A school teacher?" asked Julio.

We resumed the march, though Fósforo moved slowly, watching carefully for signs of inhabitants. We avoided cultivated land as best we could, moving through the high brush that separated the fields and properties. A few cows stared balefully at us as we passed. We were careful not to come too close to any dwellings, mindful of waking any dogs that might betray us.

"These are big farms," said Rubio with a low whistle.

"Imbecile," said Julio. "These are just different pastures. This is probably all one farm, with one fat owner sitting in the middle, counting his money." Rubio flushed a little and said nothing more.

After an hour, I could see the outline of a church tower in the distance, starkly black against the still-starlit sky. Fósforo swung our path around to approach the town from the north. When dawn broke, we were settled in the brush along a low hill overlooking its one street.

There were a dozen buildings arrayed closely together. The most significant was the white-washed church with its square bell tower. Huddled beside it was a post office, a general store, and a cuartele that housed the Guardia Nacional.

The cuartele was a squat building made of brick reinforced with a thick layer of sandbags around its base. A line of laundry ran between the building and a tree. The windows were covered with iron shutters that a half-dressed guardsman was latching open. He went back inside, leaving his rifle leaning against the wall. The street was still; even the stray dogs were asleep in a pile by the church steps. A few roosters called out to each other without enthusiasm.

"The town will be awake soon," said Julio.

"If we didn't look so bedraggled, we could hide the guns and just walk through town," I said.

"People would notice new faces just as quickly as they'd notice the guns," said Santiago. "Campesinos don't like things that are new or different."

Fósforo eyed the buildings in front of us. "Those guardsmen are still half asleep," he said. "There is a rifle right there that is ripe to be stolen. And we might ambush them and seize more guns when they patrol outside the town."

"That seems like an awfully large risk," said Julio.

"Not if we go now," said Fósforo.

I looked at the others. They seemed frightened. Fósforo didn't wait for Julio to raise any further complaints, and when he started moving closer to the outpost, his rifle in both hands, I followed. I heard the rest rise hesitantly to their feet behind us.

The grey light of early morning was disappearing, though long shadows still obscured parts of the landscape. Trying to keep to these, we quietly covered the few hundred yards to the last piece of cover behind the outpost, settling in behind a collapsed wooden fence. There were perhaps thirty yards between us and the rifle. Fósforo gave me a meaningful glance, and I understood what he wanted. I rose to a crouch with my hands on the ground like a sprinter, trying to calculate what would be the right mix between moving quickly and moving quietly.

"I'll shoot anyone who comes out that door," said Fósforo, tucking the butt of his rifle into his shoulder and laying the fore stock across part of the fence. I was certain that he had never fired a rifle before, but his confidence was infectious.

I half-ran and half-crawled toward the guardsman's rifle, my vision narrowing to that short section of sandbagged wall where it stood. I was just over halfway there when I heard a shout from the doorway.

A guardsman, the same one as before, stood at the back door. He saw me running at him like some wild animal that had launched itself out of the bushes, and he froze in place. His shout was inarticulate, a garbled 'hey,' as he struggled to understand who or what I was. As he hesitated, I closed the distance between us.

A shot rang out from behind me, and a piece of the brick wall broke into dust and fragments a foot from the guardsman. This broke the spell, and he grabbed the rifle I was running for and disappeared back inside the building, slamming the heavy door behind him. There was a tremendous amount of shouting from inside. I knew that we had failed.

I crashed into the sandbagged wall and turned back to look at the cover I had just left, impossibly far away. The guardsmen inside began to fire from the open windows with wild rapid shots. One man leaned out of the window, part of his torso visible to me, to pull the iron shutter closed. Another shot from Fósforo's rifle, this time ricocheting off the shutter, caused him to pull himself back inside. I tried to make myself small, curled up against the wall away from the windows with my eyes closed tightly. I contemplated making the run back to cover. In my imagination, I was cut down by a half dozen bullets as soon as I began to move. The shooting from inside slackened a little, and neither Fósforo nor Julio fired back again. I was working up the courage to make the run back when I heard a sound that made me open my eyes.

It was an animal sound more than a yell, coming from the pit of Rubio's stomach, a long, drawn-out noise that terrified me. I saw him running with long strides across the open ground towards the outpost, the stick of dynamite held high over his head. It trailed a wisp of dark smoke behind him, making me think of some sort of insane locomotive.

As he got closer to the building, I thought he would throw the dynamite, but instead, he stepped on the sandbag wall and vaulted in through the window with a crash. His battered hat sailed through the air and hit the ground outside. The result was instantaneous.

Half a dozen guardsmen leapt out the windows, some only half-dressed and most without their rifles. I braced myself for the explosion, pushing my face into the nearest sandbag. I waited long seconds. The burlap sandbag was rough against my face, but I kept pressing, waiting.

There was more shouting behind me, and scuffling movement,

but I kept my body tense and as flat as possible. I wondered if I would even hear the explosion that killed me, or if I was already dead. I got lost in that moment of anticipation, my mind locked up tight.

A foot nudged my back. "Did you die of fright?" asked Julio.

I opened my eyes and looked back at the yard. Behind me, Julio stood over the confused guardsmen with his pistol drawn. Santiago and Juan stood over them as well, rifles in their hands, encouraging them with kicks and shouts to stay on the ground. Hanging down from the window to look at me was Rubio, grinning like a madman and waving the dynamite in one hand and the extinguished fuse in the other.

"Comrade, pass me my hat," he said, laughing.

I felt as dazed as the captured guardsmen. I tossed Rubio's hat through the window to him while still lying on the ground. I took a moment to gather myself before standing up, my legs feeling shaky and weak. By then, the guardsmen had been shoved into a line, all lying face down with their hands on their heads.

Fósforo stepped over the guardsmen to shake my hand. My grip felt weak, but I managed a smile.

"More target practice is in order," I said.

"And physical training, primarily the hundred-yard dash," he replied.

We both laughed, and Fósforo gripped my hand with both of his. "Thank you," he said quietly, before turning towards the back door of the outpost.

"Rubio! What have you found?" he called as he stepped inside. I followed him, curious as well.

The small building contained a single room with six wooden bunks. Equipment and clothing hung on pegs over each one. There was a desk covered in papers, a map on the wall, and sacks of rice and dry beans in one corner.

"It's a treasure trove!" said Rubio, holding up a rifle and a leather bandolier.

Fósforo walked over to study the map. "Paco, get the others

to come and take whatever they find that's useful." I nodded and stepped outside.

In the yard, Julio had taken charge, tying the six guardsmen's hands behind their backs with the laundry line and leaving them lying face down along the sandbag wall. Juan and Santiago had collected the rifles held by the guardsmen when they leapt out the windows—carbines sent to Nicaragua by the Yanquis—and were examining them with undisguised glee.

"Let's collect the rest of what's useful," I said, and we all began to loot the outpost. Soon there was a pile of military equipment—knapsacks, webbing, canteens and waterproof ponchos—stacked up in the yard. Santiago carried a wooden ammunition box with rope handles and set it down with the other equipment, and Juan came out carrying the two heavy sacks, one of rice and one of dried beans. Fósforo appeared with the wall map rolled up under his arm. The guardsmen watched with sour expressions as we looted their home.

"Look at this!" laughed Rubio, holding up a newspaper he'd found inside. "BANDITS DEFEATED!" he read. "According to Captain Menelao Espina Rodríguez, commander of the Compañías de Seguridad de la Guardia Nacional in San Jose Guachipilín, a decisive blow was struck against the bandits terrorizing travellers on the highway, all of whom have been killed or captured."

"Do we look killed or captured?" asked Santiago.

"That's the bastard from the original camp," I said. "I remember him saying his name when he promised that no one would be killed if they surrendered."

"Our appearance today makes a liar out of him," said Fósforo.

"Better if we make a corpse out of him instead," said Julio.

As if everyone had the same thought simultaneously, we all turned to look at the captured guardsmen.

"Do we look like bandits?" asked Juan, kicking the guardsman closest to him when he didn't answer.

"No," said the man, miserably.

"As pathetic as they are, we can't leave this lot alive," said Julio.

Juan and Santiago looked at each other without enthusiasm. "We can draw straws if you like."

The man closest to me began to mutter to himself, praying, his face in the dirt.

"Absolutely not," said Fósforo. "Bring them around to the church."

"So that we can pray for their souls and they for ours?" said Julio.

"To the church," repeated Fósforo. "And bring all of this material too."

I had no stomach to execute these men in the dirt, and neither did the others, except Julio. We did as Fósforo asked and gathered the material that we had looted, slinging our new rifles across our backs and pulling their web gear over our shoulders. Julio ignored us as we worked, focusing instead on the guardsmen.

"On your feet," he said, kicking the closest man in the ribs when he didn't move fast enough. They all struggled to get their legs under themselves with their hands tied, leaning on the sandbags or each other to keep their balance. Julio did nothing to help them.

Once they were on their feet, all tied together like dead fish on a line, he began to lead them away, jerking the rope so hard that it nearly pulled the first man off his feet. We carried everything else in our hands, keeping a close eye on the prisoners.

The street was deserted, but I could feel eyes watching us from behind every shutter. A pack of stray dogs trotted from the church to sniff at us and soon fell in to walk behind us. The town was small enough that it was less than two hundred yards from end to end, every building facing the central street. A small section in front of the church was paved with bricks, but the rest was dirt. We piled our goods on the dusty brick in front of the church, and Julio grabbed each of the guardsmen roughly and forced them into a straight line. One by one, he kicked out their legs from under them, until they were all kneeling. We unslung our new rifles and stood behind them, ready to shoot if any tried to run or fight, though, to be truthful, they were a pathetic looking lot. I saw now that most of them were crying. I might have done the same had the roles been reversed.

From inside the church came an old priest in a white cassock, misbuttoned in his haste. "There will be no more violence today," he said, looking pointedly at Julio.

"Padre," said Fósforo respectfully, "please gather the townsfolk for us."

"I will not bring honest people out of their homes to witness butchery," said the priest.

"Now," said Fósforo forcefully. "You have my word, no one who does as I ask will be harmed in any way."

The priest stood his ground, arms crossed, and did not move. Fósforo watched him for a moment to see if he would change his mind, and when he did not, he walked straight towards him. The priest flinched as Fósforo brushed past him and walked into the church. Within minutes, the bell in the tower was ringing.

"Padre, there's no reason to ignore us. The People are our concern as well," I said.

The priest looked down his nose at me, his fists clenched. "I'll not be ordered about by a filthy, mierde-skinned savage!" He turned on his heel and went back inside the church. It was a smart move, given that I was about to grab him by the collar and toss him down the steps.

Furious, I focused on the task at hand instead. Leaving Julio to guard the prisoners, the rest of us went house to house. The bell was the signal to gather together, and they began to crack open doors or windows to see better what was happening. As soon as they saw us, though, they disappeared back inside.

As I approached a small house that leaned against the side of the church, I could see a man inside, watching us. I rushed forward and caught the edge of a thick wooden shutter as he tried to close it. Rubio grabbed the other side, and together we pried it open. The man stood in front of his family at the back of the room. His arms spread backwards around them in a protective gesture.

"Señor, please, we're asking that everyone gather at the church," I said. He didn't answer me. One of his children, a boy of eight or nine, clutched at his pant leg and watched us with wide eyes. I tried it again. "The priest is asking that everyone come to the church. We will not rob or harm anyone, I swear."

We slowly coaxed them out and then moved on to the next house. We didn't have to point our guns at anyone or threaten them, but it was a slow process. You could almost smell their fear as we spoke to them. They huddled together around the priest, mothers clutched their children against their skirts, and families stood close together in tight knots. When we had gathered several dozen people, Fósforo pulled the wooden ammunition box we had taken from the outpost in front of the guardsmen.

"Is this everyone?" he asked me.

"Probably not," I said, "but we didn't search the houses or the cellars. These are the ones who we could get to come willingly, more or less."

He nodded, stepped up onto the ammunition box, and began to speak.

"You've been told by the Somocistas that we are bandits and that we are a threat to you and your livelihoods, but we stand before you today to share with you the truth. We are honest men and women, who have been obliged to take up arms by force of circumstance. We fight not for ourselves, but against the same oppressors who keep their boot heels on your neck. We fight to change the system that keeps our unarmed comrades chained in ignominy and misery. We fight for you."

"No one here asked you to fight for us," said the priest. A few people murmured their agreement in the crowd. "We're not your comrades."

"If you tremble with indignation at every injustice in the world, if you despair when cruel leaders are replaced only to have new leaders turn cruel, if you believe that every man and woman deserves to live on the fruits of their labours, then you are a comrade of mine and I of you."

"If you are fighting for us, to what end?" shouted a man from the crowd.

"To sow anarchy through which to profit," said the priest,

crossing himself. Many of the townspeople around him did the same.

"Nothing could be further from the truth," said Fósforo. "The first thing we want is to be masters of our destiny, a country free from foreign interference, a country that seeks out its own system of development. From an economic point of view, we want justice. The world is hungry but lacks the money to buy food, and paradoxically, here, in the world of the hungry, vast tracts of land are kept fallow by foreign owners to keep prices up. This is nothing more than a philosophy of plunder, which must cease to be the rule."

"Communist heresy," said the priest, crossing himself again.

Some of the townspeople did the same, but there were loud murmurs of agreement as well. "Our war is not with these men," said Fósforo, gesturing to the prostrated guardsmen. "It is with their leader, Somoza, and his cronies who hold power and riches at the expense of the masses."

"Then why have you brought us here to witness their murder?" asked the priest.

"Our quarrel is not with these men," repeated Fósforo, "but only with their corrupt leaders." He stepped down from the crate and began to untie the hands of the first guardsman.

"You are free to go," he said, "but not to stay here. Return to the garrison in San Jose Guachipilín, and tell them what happened here." One by one, he freed the prisoners, and as he did, they began to walk down the road towards the department's capital. The townspeople jeered at each one as he passed. As uncertain as the crowd was about us, the Guardia Nacional was universally disliked. When all six had trotted down the road, the crowd visibly relaxed.

"Is there a store where we can buy some supplies?" asked Fósforo.

"You can search the town for a store to rob yourself," said the priest.

"Not to rob," said Fósforo, "just to purchase some things."

"At the end of the street," said a dark-faced man in the crowd. "That bastard ran as soon as the shooting started, though."

"He's more of a robber than any bandit I've met," said another.

Fósforo spoke in Julio's ear. "Take Juan and Santiago, go to the store and take as much as we can carry. Dry goods, flashlights, anything else that you know we would need."

"And as for the payment?" asked Julio.

"Total up a fair payment for everything that you take, and leave a promissory note for the full amount, to be paid upon the success of the Revolution."

Julio laughed and gestured for the two men to follow him. "So that's how we 'buy' supplies, is it?" Rifles over their shoulders, they swaggered down the street behind him.

"One last thing, friends," said Fósforo, mounting the ammunition box again. "Our road will be long and full of difficulty, but it leads only to victory. Is there anyone who will volunteer to join us and fight the Somocistas?"

With the priest glaring at them, no one spoke up.

"We will be in front of the general store for another fifteen minutes," said Fósforo. "And so, for your hospitality, we thank the people of . . ."

"La Trinidad," said the priest. He walked into the church, followed by nearly all the townspeople, and barred the door from the inside.

When we rejoined Julio and the others, they had built a pile on the street of everything useful that they could find in the store—sacks of flour, tarps, ropes, hammocks, machetes, flashlights and some wide-brimmed hats. I held one up for Rubio.

"That thing you are wearing is more holes than hat. Take one of these."

Rubio gasped in mock astonishment. "Never!" he said. He took his hat off, pushed his finger through each hole as he found it. "This is my lucky hat," he said. "It and I are the only remaining survivors of the charge through the window this morning."

"Why didn't you just throw the dynamite?" asked Santiago.

"I meant to," he said, "but I was so excited I . . . forgot . . . ." His voice trailed off, and his face turned red.

"Forgot?" asked Santiago laughing.

"Lucky for those guardsmen that he did," I said.

Julio had arranged all of our material onto two tarps, which he was wrapping shut so that he could suspend the bundles from long poles pulled from the fence around the store's property. I went to help him, but he waved me away impatiently.

"It's faster to do this myself than to teach you how," Julio said.

Everyone stood back while Julio expertly laced a rope around the tarps, securing them like fat sausages. His hands moved so quickly that I had trouble keeping track of what he was doing. I saw that Fósforo was watching him intently, but I used the moment to ask him a question.

"That speech back there. Where did you learn all of that?"

Fósforo shrugged, still watching Julio. "Reading, back in the city. That book I showed you and some others that I left behind, that my mother sent me. But also, just thinking about it all."

I was going to press him further, but when Julio had finished, he looked around for Fósforo impatiently. "We don't have all day to stand around talking and waiting for the Guardia Nacional to come back."

"I agree," said Fósforo. "Let's move."

Rubio and I picked up one of the loads and braced the pole on our shoulders. Santiago and Juan picked up the other, and we began to move slowly away from the road and back into the bush. Fósforo took the lead, walking a little too quickly for us to keep up easily. I called out whenever I lost sight of him, only to find him waiting impatiently for us further down the trail.

We moved along the overgrown edge of a pasture, Fósforo out of sight again. I was thinking about singing, something that I could twist into a song about Rubio when there was a shout of alarm from the rear of our column.

"The Guardia!" said Rubio.

"The first we would have heard of them would have been shots," I replied.

We quickly dropped the pole and unslung our rifles. I ran in a crouch back toward Julio, who was in the rear, but Fósforo raced past me, rifle in his hands. Crashing through the brush, we nearly bowled Julio over when we found him.

Standing with him in a small clearing were six young men, all campesinos by their appearances. They all had sacks over their shoulders and were standing with their free hands raised in fear. Julio aimed his pistol at the one who had come the closest.

"We're volunteers," one of the young men said. "Don't shoot! We want to join your army."

"Get lost," said Julio. "I don't trust a single one of you."

I placed a hand on Julio's arm. "Lower your pistol," I said. "We can trust them enough to at least speak with them."

"Trust," sneered Julio, "will be the end of you."

Fósforo ignored us and instead looked each of them in the eye. All but one avoided his gaze, but in truth, they looked like solid young men.

"Do any of you have wives or children?" asked Fósforo.

The volunteers all shook their heads.

"Good," he said, "This country has enough widows."

The young men looked at each other nervously.

"What do you do here?" asked Fósforo.

One of the men, his skin very dark from a lifetime in the sun, spoke for the others. "Our families are all mozos jornaleros, jefe. We don't own anything, not even our own sweat." [6]

"And so, why join us?" asked Fósforo.

The same man spoke for them all again. "Our families have been abused by the Guardia for years. Without a bribe, they do nothing to help anyone, and even with one, they do little."

"So, revenge?" asked Fósforo.

"Justice," said the youth.

Fósforo lowered each man's arms and shook their hands. "In our band, those with rifles carry their rifles," said Fósforo. "Those without carry the rest, and must work to earn their rifles."

We were reorganizing ourselves and assigning the heavier loads to the new men when a young boy came crashing through the brush. He was barefoot and dressed in rags, with a filthy straw hat set on the back of his head.

---

[6] *Translator's note: day labourers.*

"No more recruits," said Julio. "Especially ones who aren't old enough to carry a rifle."

The boy blushed. "No, sir, I'm not a recruit."

"Then what do you want?" Fósforo asked, sounding kinder than Julio had been.

"I just wanted to know what you did with the lady?" he stammered.

"What lady?" demanded Julio.

"The Guardia Nacional arrested a lady and locked her up."

"In their little outpost?" I said.

"No, sir," replied the boy. "Under it."

"What did they arrest her for?" asked Julio.

"I don't know, sir."

"Who is she?"

"I don't know, sir. I heard them call her Esperanza."

"Well, she's no concern of ours," said Julio.

"She'll starve to death if we leave her there," I said. "We have to take some responsibility given what we've done."

"The guardsmen will be back to feed her soon enough," said Julio.

"Do you know that for a fact?" I asked.

"Julio, I want you to take everyone and start heading back to camp," said Fósforo. "Paco and I will go back and release this woman and then catch up."

"You're risking yourselves for nothing," said Julio. "But that's your own business. Alright, let's move."

The new men picked up the heavy loads, and Julio led them back towards our camp at a brisk pace. We watched them disappear into the undergrowth.

"Do you think that's wise to leave Julio in charge of them? Can he be trusted?" I asked.

"He can be trusted to save his own skin, which is what I need the rest of the column to do right now as well," said Fósforo.

We followed the boy back into town. The streets remained still. I assumed that everyone would stay indoors until they reckoned we were far away.

"Where are they keeping this woman?" I asked the boy.

"I'll show you," he said.

We went in through the front door of the outpost. The interior was a disaster, unwanted items strewn around inside where we had left them. The boy stood mutely, pointing at a heavy trap door under one of the beds that we had missed.

"Madre de Dios," I said. "This is what passes for a prison here."

"At least she's alive," said Fósforo.

"That remains to be seen."

I slid a deadbolt aside and grabbed the door's iron ring, pulling hard. Fósforo looped his hands through the ring as well, and together we managed to pull it open. I peered down into the black hole, almost fearful of what I might see.

Staring back up at me, blinking in the light, was Magdalena.

<h1 style="text-align:center">11</h1>

WE STOOD THERE IN SILENCE for what felt like ages as our minds spun.

Finally, I reached down past the trapdoor to grasp her arm, and Fósforo did the same. We lifted her out of the tiny cell as gently as we could. Her campesina blouse and skirt were filthy, and her hair was matted, but under the filth, it was clear that it was her.

"Ramón? Paco?" She blinked in the light, shading her eyes and gazing from one face to the other.

I still couldn't speak, but Fósforo leaned forward and kissed her on the lips. He held her for a moment before she broke his grasp and slapped him, hard. The sound seemed louder than any of the gunshots had been hours earlier. Then she pushed past him and began frantically searching the room.

"Magdalena," said Fósforo, hesitating.

"Don't call me that," she said.

"But how did you get here?" I asked.

"I suppose I should be asking you the same thing?" she said as she tossed abandoned equipment around the room in her search.

"Why were you arrested?" asked Fósforo.

She ignored us, trawling through the detritus covering the floor until she found what she was looking for. Cast aside by the sergeant's bunk was a leather-bound Bible, which we had missed or ignored. She flipped it open, checking something, before sliding it into a pocket in her skirt. Next, she picked up a long knife in a leather sheath that we had also missed. Ignoring us, she hiked up one side of her skirt, revealing her thigh, and strapped the knife around it. I turned away at the sight of her long, lean leg. My face felt flushed.

"Are you with the movement?" asked Fósforo. She ignored him and headed for the door, but Fósforo got ahead of her and blocked it with one arm. "Slow down," he said.

"I've got something I need to do," she said, trying to duck past him.

"They've arrested you once, they'll do it again," I said. "Come with us, and maybe the column can help you."

She stopped in her tracks and looked at me. It was if, for the first time, she registered our natty uniforms and the rifles hanging from our shoulders. "Which column?" she asked.

"Column F," I said.

"Where's Braulio?"

"Dead."

"Then who's the leader?" she asked.

"Me," said Fósforo.

She stood rooted to the spot, her eyes flicking towards the doorway, seeming to want to run. She wouldn't look at Fósforo, eventually staring, instead, at her feet. I wanted to reach out and touch her, to tell her that we would help, but I didn't know what to say that would convince her.

"Give us a minute," said Fósforo. He flicked his head, and I took the hint grudgingly. I walked outside to stand in the street. A stray dog came up and sniffed my pant leg before going back to lay in the shade.

My thoughts went back to the image of her as we pulled her from the cell. In my mind's eye, her face was perfectly framed by thick, black hair, but her features were dim¾all except her eyes. Her eyes burned with a deep-set fire that I hadn't recognized before.

After a few minutes, they both came outside. Neither of their faces betrayed any emotion, or what had been said or settled between them. They stood nearly an arms distance apart, and she clutched the Bible to her chest with both hands.

"Esperanza will travel with us," said Fósforo.

"Esperanza?"

"My *nom de guerre*," she said. "A new name for a new me."

I gave her a confused look, and she brushed past me impatiently. "It's not just men fighting this Revolution, Paco. Or do you have a new name too?" Fósforo followed her.

"I'm still just Paco," I said, falling in behind the two of them, cursing myself for being a tongue-tied fool.

We began to walk back down the road to the edge of town, Fósforo taking the lead. Once we reached the edge of the bush, Julio's tracks were easy to find, and we made good time as we tried to catch up to them. We halted when we reached a stream so that we could refill our newly-acquired canteens. Esperanza excused herself, disappearing into the brush, and I took the opportunity to grill Fósforo.

"What's going on?" I asked.

"I know, we shouldn't be taking her with us," he said.

"You heard her¾she's already one of us," I replied.

Fósforo nodded. "She said she was running a message to Column F when they arrested her. They never found the message but were holding her on account of her 'suspicious' nature."

"Then we have to bring her with us."

"This won't end well," he said morosely. "One woman and a dozen men?"

"We don't have much choice; she's the messenger that was sent to us. And at least tell me what the message is," I said.

"I don't know," said Fósforo. "It's still a little . . . complicated."

We reached Julio's group before they crossed the river and made it back to camp with them just before nightfall. Our shelters, which had seemed luxurious when we first built them, had been given to the new recruits. We "veterans" made use of hammocks and tarpaulins to make more comfortable places to sleep. The morning after our return to camp, we were in high spirits. Julio prepared a hot breakfast of beans and rice, the smell of which drew everyone from their sleep without the need for a reveille.

As we sat together, spooning the hot food into our mouths from tin plates, Fósforo rearranged us into a circle around himself. He waved away a plate of food, set down, steaming, on the ground behind him.

"It is important that I take a moment to explain the rules by which Column F will be regulated, and to describe what is expected of each of you clearly," he said.

I saw that the word "rules" caught Julio's attention, and he stood up from our circle, leaning instead against a tree and chewing thoughtfully.

"We are not just a small band of men, armed to fight the government. We are the vanguard of a great popular force of people—landless, dispossessed, and ill-used—who would join us if they could. In fact, they will join us in time if we set an example for them. In truth, the People only have two choices—to suffer or to fight. It is obvious which they should choose."

I scanned everyone's faces to see how they were receiving Fósforo's speech. Apart from Julio, who wore the dour expression that he had whenever Fósforo spoke, everyone seemed riveted.

"Our discipline is unlike that in the army or Guardia Nacional. It is a discipline that comes from here," said Fósforo, touching his heart, close to the bullet hole in his shirt. "To the stoicism imposed by the difficult conditions that we face, we must also add rigid self-control and austerity. It will be hard. Some days, like today, we will feast. Other days, we will starve. We must each work to our utmost to prevent a single excess, a single slip, whatever the circumstances. We must be both warriors and ascetics if we are to be successful."

He let this sink in for a moment before walking through the group, separating us into two halves. "In order to aid you in achieving this goal, I have decided to divide the column into two platoons and appoint a leader for each. We have amongst us men who have much to teach, by their example as much as by their word." Julio shifted position nervously.

He turned to the first group, which included Santiago and Juan. "You are now First Platoon, and you will be led by an experienced guerrilla, Teniente Julio."

They all turned to look at Julio, who said nothing in response.

"And you will be Second Platoon," said Fósforo to the other half, "led by a brave and honest guerrilla, Teniente Paco." Rubio slapped me on the back, and my cheeks turned red.

"And what of me?" asked Esperanza. "Which group of 'men' includes me?"

"You're proof that guerrillas aren't necessarily men," said Fósforo, "but your role is to be discussed." She did not look satisfied with that answer.

"And when will this 'armed vanguard' of the People actually all be armed?" interrupted Julio, gesturing at his new men.

Fósforo seemed oblivious to the venom in Julio's tone. "Our next operations will be to seize more arms, though I can't say that we will always have enough for every guerrilla. To carry a weapon is a privilege, not a right. There is much necessary work to be done by those without guns, and when we have new weapons to distribute, they will go to those who have demonstrated the greatest zeal. If your job is nothing more complex than to carry supplies, then see that you carry the most, the fastest, in the best way possible, and you will earn the privilege of being armed."

Fósforo looked at each of us, in turn, to see if there would be any complaint. The men continued to hang off his every word.

"If we are honest, we must admit that some of us will die during this struggle. It is inevitable. We must be ready to fall in battle, knowing that by our example, we will inspire another to take up arms and carry on. The duty of every guerrilla, whenever a companion falls, is to recover immediately these extremely precious things: arms and ammunition."

Fósforo began to pace as he spoke, stopping beside Rubio, placing his hand on his shoulder. "Comrade, I have something for you," he said.

Rubio's eyes shone. "Yes, Fósforo?"

Fósforo unslung his scoped rifle and his ammo bandolier and held them out in both hands. "These are for you." Rubio took them from him uncertainly. "With our bravest fighters carrying our best weapons," said Fósforo to the rest of us, "how can we lose?"

Rubio slipped the bandolier over his head and pulled Fósforo into a tight embrace. The two men clung to each other for a moment, and we all clapped and whistled. Fósforo was right. How could we lose?

"If you want lessons on how to use that thing," said Julio, "come and see me. I'll give you a tip for now—you don't have to run up and hit them with it."

We laughed along with Julio, and the meeting ended. Fósforo scooped up his meal from the ground, which had stopped steaming long before. He gestured with his chin, mouth full of cold rice, for Julio and I to follow him. He walked over to where his hammock was strung between two trees and sat down, spreading out the map taken from the Guardia Nacional. We were each sitting next to him, ready to discuss our plans, when Esperanza joined us.

"So, let's discuss," she said, pulling up her long skirt and sitting cross-legged. I saw a flash of the tip of the dagger that she had strapped to her leg.

Fósforo looked uncomfortable and glanced at Julio and me to see if we would intervene. When we were silent, he pulled at his beard and began to mumble an answer. "It's in your own interest that I am thinking . . ."

Esperanza cut him off swiftly. "I've seen how well you look out for my interests," she said savagely. "I'm a member of this group, the same as you, and I won't be treated any differently than the others. On the one hand, you speak of difficulty and sacrifice, and on the other, you blather on about looking out for my interests."

"Magdalena, I . . ."

"Esperanza," she hissed. "It's clear that this column needs help with certain things. You need an intelligence officer, for one."

"If I could whistle one up," began Fósforo before Esperanza cut him off.

"Me, you idiot," she said. "To begin with, I'm the only one who can keep you in touch with the central leadership."

She pulled her Bible out of a side pocket and handed it to Fósforo. "Do you know how a book cipher works?" she asked. We all stared blankly. "This is how they communicate with all of the columns. They sent me to bring this Bible to Braulio, along with a message."

"What's the message?" asked Fósforo.

"I didn't decode it yet," said Esperanza, pulling a piece of folded paper from her pocket and smoothing it. It was a typed list of passages that formed a course of Bible study, heavily annotated in pencil. She pointed out the markings to us and explained the code. "Each of these refers to a chapter, verse, and word. Together they form sentences. In future, they'll just send series of numbers— chapter, verse and word—for you to decode. Every other column has the same version of the Bible, and so you can communicate with them as well."

Fósforo picked up the paper and began flipping through the Bible's thin pages, carefully finding each word of the message. He chewed on a pencil stub while he worked.

"How did you escape Managua?" I asked.

"One of my gentleman friends," she said, glancing at Fósforo. "Though I spent hours looking for him first."

"And you were working with the opposition even then?"

"My friend is a senior member of the UDEL. He introduced me to people in the Sandinista movement. He wanted me to stay with him in the capital, but I told him that I couldn't. I wanted to fight."

"So, where are these leaders holed up?" asked Julio.

Esperanza shook her head. "I'm sure that they've moved by now, but the less we all know, the better."

"If they've moved," I asked, "how were you going to get back to them?"

"I wasn't," she said. "I got my wish—to join one of the columns."

"But if you were to stay with us, how would messages get back and forth?"

"Through a dead drop," she said. "I was arrested there, so we'll have to establish a new one, but it's possible."

Fósforo had been writing out the message on the back of the Bible reading slip, and finally closed the Bible and looked up. He read us the message. "Fight . . . Roman . . . rule . . . however . . . possible . . . assistance . . . forthcoming."

"Assistance forthcoming?" I asked. We all looked at Esperanza.

"Everyone is short of resources," she said evasively.

"This is meaningless," said Fósforo, "We have to assume that we're on our own."

"Only for now," said Esperanza.

"For some length of time between now and forever," said Julio, leaning back to spit against a tree behind me.

"If Braulio is an example of what these Sandinista leaders are like," said Fósforo, "we don't need their help. We can stand up to the Guardia on our own."

"Are you crazy?" asked Esperanza. "You think you can take on the world on your own?"

"You said yourself that the dead drop was compromised," he replied. "Why should we trust them when they are riddled with spies and have nothing to offer us in any case?"

"You're still an idiot," she said, fists clenched. "Who was the column's intelligence officer before?"

Fósforo stared at his boots, his lips tight against his teeth. I looked at Julio, who shrugged. "I don't think we had one," I said.

"And look how that's turned out," said Esperanza. "We'll need someone to start thinking about the enemy and what they plan. How else will we stay a step ahead of them?"

"I will be our intelligence officer," said Fósforo.

"If you're going to be the commander, then you need to

command. Your job is to rebuild the column," said Esperanza.

"Sounds like you're building an army," said Julio sarcastically. "Next you'll have us marching and saluting."

"Don't be stupid," said Esperanza, "that's not what I'm suggesting . . ."

"Enough," said Fósforo. He set the Bible aside and turned the map around so we could read it. "I don't want to talk about bureaucracy; I want to talk about winning."

The map lacked much detail about the terrain, although it showed the roads, rail lines and towns. I scanned it carefully, not knowing this part of the country at all. The department, filled with cattle ranches and farmland, stretched between two rivers in the north and south. The main town, San Jose Guachipilín, sat in the centre, with roads crisscrossing through it to join together the farming communities.

"The 'brain' of the department is obvious," said Fósforo, pointing at the San Jose Guachipilín, "as well as its nervous system." His finger traced the roads. "But we're not yet ready to strike at the centre."

"Oh," said Julio, "not ready to march on Rome with twelve men and seven rifles?"

Fósforo ignored him. "Instead, we're going to nibble around the edges. We want to draw the Guardia Nacional into little fights. Close to these towns." He pressed his face down to read the names: "La Trinidad, Chacimo, Palmitos, Hacienda Inocentes, Agua Dulce, San Luis, Guatachague, Patatapa. Close enough that the People will know the government is lying when they try to censor the news."

"We're not ready for a stand-up fight against organized soldiers," said Julio.

"Not on their terms," said Fósforo. "What we must do, every time and without fail is to destroy their vanguard. Every guardsman must know in his heart that to be in the vanguard in an advance is a death sentence."

"And so, we'll ambush the vanguard," said Julio hesitatingly.

"Yes," said Fósforo enthusiastically, "and soon, after a few attacks, there won't be a guardsman left in the department willing to be in the lead. They will fall over themselves to be in the rear. And their columns will stumble blindly through the fields and the jungle looking for us."

"And then we'll . . ." I said, unsure.

"And then we'll switch to attacking the rear. Always the rear, and always killing them to the last man," said Fósforo.

"Psychological warfare," said Julio, nodding sagely. "And every guardsman we kill must be stripped of everything of value."

"Exactly," said Fósforo. "Every weapon, every bullet we acquire, makes us stronger."

"And everything else of value," repeated Julio.

"We need to capture more resources than we expend in capturing them," said Fósforo, speaking over Julio. "We will be nothing but the angel of death to the soldiers in the field, and nothing but the angel of love to the common people."

Julio looked doubtful again. "Love?"

Fósforo's face split into a broad smile, and he put an arm around Julio. "Every true revolutionary is guided by a great feeling of love," he said. "It is impossible to think of a genuine revolutionary lacking this quality."

As I walked back to gather my men, I couldn't help but smile at the thought of Julio explaining this theory of love to his platoon.

The platoons reorganized our sleeping areas into the two sides of the camp, situated so that they were well camouflaged and could turn into a fighting position in an instant. We improved the lookout post in the tree, building a new platform set nearly six feet higher than the old one, and adding more branches to conceal the sentry. One of our old shelters became a makeshift headquarters and cookhouse, and the other was given to Esperanza for her use.

The new volunteers were good men, accustomed to hard work,

and they vied against one another to show the greatest revolutionary zeal in the hope of winning the privilege of carrying a rifle. I took my small group on a training march, carrying packs loaded with equipment, down the paths leading towards the river and across the base of the foothills. We stopped whenever there was a piece of ground that I thought we could use to our advantage, and we talked about how we would place ourselves to ambush any soldiers heading towards our camp. By the time we returned, it was night time, and although we had covered a lot of ground, there were no complaints. When Rubio removed his boots, I saw that there were spots of blood on his socks, but he said nothing about it.

The following day we did a second march, this time following the paths that led away from the camp in the other direction, and again, stopped to discuss tactics whenever I saw a place that we could turn to our advantage. I had Rubio take a position behind a jumble of rocks that gave him a long view down the hillside, and the rest of us played the role of soldiers trying to reach him unseen. Every time he spotted one of us, he called out our name, and the person caught returned to the bottom of the hill. No one got within a hundred yards of him, and after about an hour, I called an end to our game.

"Playing soldier is well and good," said Rubio, "but we should be practicing with our weapons." He scanned the forest below with his rifle scope while he talked. "I've never even fired this thing, and I want to see what it can do."

"We don't have enough ammunition to waste on practice," I said. "We'll get practice enough when we go on patrol for real."

"Then let's go," said Rubio. "We can show these kids how it's done."

We walked quickly enough on the way back to camp that we were all out of breath, and there was little banter. I could tell the men were restless. I knew that we needed to feel that we were achieving something beyond mere survival, and I resolved to take it up with Fósforo. We were greeted by a bird call from the sentry position as we reached the camp, which Rubio returned. Santiago waved at us as we marched beneath his perch. I wasn't sure what Julio had been doing with his platoon, but they didn't seem to venture far from their side of the camp. Perhaps he already knew more about training men for combat—I was training myself at the same time.

I took off my boots and socks and lay in my hammock, examining my sore feet for blisters. I had resolved to take the time to bathe tonight and try to wash my clothes when I was interrupted by one of the volunteers. He was younger and slighter than the others and had been confused when we told him not to use his real name. He stood transfixed as he tried to think of a new name, and so the others gave him one: Helado.[7] He stammered something about wanting a real name, but no one listened, and it stuck.

Helado held his straw hat in his hands, gripping it tightly enough to twist the brim. He didn't look at me when he mumbled his request. "Teniente Paco, I wish to go home for a few days." He tensed up as if expecting a blow.

I swung my legs off the hammock and sat facing him. "Has all of this marching been too much?" I asked.

"No, no," he said, "It's just that . . ."

I looked at him expectantly.

". . . I did not have the chance to say goodbye to my mother. I just need a day or two, and then I will be back," he finally said.

I didn't think much of this reason, but I tried to be even-handed. "I'll raise the issue with Fósforo in the morning." Helado nodded and gave a little bow before returning to sit with the others. I lay back in my hammock, brooding.

That night I slept fitfully, thinking about Helado and worried he would be the first of many desertions. That is how I saw it, desertion, despite his promise to return. He'd asked to leave—the next guerrilla might not bother to ask.

And so, when I heard someone rustling through the undergrowth nearby, I nearly leapt out of my hammock to catch them before they ran off. Instead, I found myself face to face with

------

[7] Translator's note: "Ice Cream" or "Frozen."

Esperanza.

She no longer wore the long dress and blouse of a campesina but was dressed like the rest of us in a mix of regular clothes and ill-fitting fatigues taken from the Guardia. Her hair was tied back and tucked under a scarf, and in her arms was a bundled tarp.

"Is everything alright?" I whispered.

"Fine," she said curtly. "I am going to sleep here tonight."

"But you have a shelter all to yourself," I said.

"It's safer to be with others than alone in that shelter," she said, not looking me in the eye.

I was angry when I heard this, and was ready for a fight. "Just tell me who," I said.

"Your glorious leader seems to have forgotten that we're not in San Pascual anymore."

I wasn't sure what to say, and she didn't speak of it again. She lay on the ground near my hammock and wrapped the tarp around her. I stood over her for a while, but she ignored me until I felt self-conscious and went back to lay in my hammock again. Sleep did not come easily to me that night, my mind spinning endlessly.

★ ★ ★

In the morning, I pulled my boots on and slung my carbine and webbing over my shoulders. It was a short walk to the old shelters where I could usually find Fósforo. Esperanza was still asleep near my hammock, cocooned in her tarp.

He was sitting cross-legged with a pipe jammed between his teeth, writing in a journal. When he saw me, he blew three perfect smoke rings that floated past my head.

"Thankfully Julio added tobacco to our bill at the general store," he said.

"He's a practical man."

"He is, indeed. And how is your band of weary guerrillas holding up?"

"Well enough," I said. "The training is going well, all things considered."

"Good. I need to speak to you and Julio about an operation I have in mind. An ambush that should net us some more guns."

"Sure," I said. "But there are two things first."

"Mmm." Fósforo worked to relight his pipe, only half listening.

"One of the new men, the one they call Helado, wants to go home for a few days. To see his mother, he says."

Fósforo puffed furiously to restart his pipe. He quickly pulled it out of his mouth to speak. "And what do you think?"

"I would say no. He should have thought of that before he volunteered. The Revolution isn't a part-time job."

"You've gotten very serious since becoming a teniente," said Fósforo.

"If the men think that they can leave as soon as it gets tough, soon we won't have anyone left," I said.

"Let him take his leave for two days after he guarantees that he will return. Make him swear to it in front of the rest of the platoon. This isn't the kind of army that flogs men for desertion—we all volunteer each day anew. If his heart is truly not in it, then we have no use for him anyway. And it will be to his everlasting shame that he squandered the opportunity to be in the vanguard of the victory of the People."

"Alright," I said, "but I'm going to repeat everything you just said in front of the others so that his shame begins today. After I'm done giving him permission to leave, there won't be a man in the platoon who will admit that he's ever even thought of it."

Fósforo clapped me on the shoulder. "Good. What else?"

I was suddenly hesitant, unsure exactly what to say. "Esperanza came to sleep with the platoon last night . . ." I left the rest hanging. Fósforo's face drained of colour.

"You know how it was between us. I just wanted to talk to her," he explained. "But she got emotional . . ."

"Perhaps it's for the best if she stays with my platoon for now. The men will get used to having her around." I hesitated for a moment. "And you can, too."

"That would be for the best," said Fósforo, suddenly serious. He stood and embraced me. "Men like you are the rocks on which this Revolution will be built."

12

IT WAS NO LONGER EARLY IN THE DAY, and the morning mist had nearly all been burned away by the sun. The green hillsides around us were visible for a great distance, as were the mountains above us. We had all gathered in the small clearing around the main shelter to eat a communal meal, though, by this time, we had finished. The joy with which we had initially greeted the beans and rice had faded and been replaced by a feeling of monotony. Each day passed much the same as the one before it.

What made this day stand out in my memory was the commotion that ensued when Juan walked through our platoon's area with a dark object slung over his shoulder.

"What did you find?" called Rubio from his hammock. "A girlfriend in the trees?"

"Not for me," said Juan, "but you might like her." He pitched a carcass off his shoulder onto the ground beside a low fire we had burning. It was a giant rodent he'd snared, that must have weighed twenty pounds and was covered in brown fur with light spots. Its dead mouth lay open, long teeth protruding.

"What in the Christ is that?" said Rubio.

Juan lifted its head to look at us. "A tepezcuintle," he said.

"Please don't tell me that you're going to . . ."

"Eat it?" said Juan. "Once you smell it cooking, you're going to beg me for a piece."

Rubio looked green. "We don't eat rats where I come from."

Juan picked up the carcass. "Neither do we," he said. "But we do eat tepezcuintle." He disappeared with his prize, back to where the rest of his platoon was camped.

Fósforo had been discussing a plan of attack with Julio and me for several days, and the details were nearly all worked out. I expected that he would make a decision soon that we could share with the whole group. I kept my platoon busy training every day, but their desire to strike a blow was clear. The tension that this desire to do something meaningful created was almost palpable.

"No sign yet of Helado?" asked Fósforo.

"He's only two days overdue," I said, trying not to sound concerned.

"You expect a boy with that name to move quickly?" asked Rubio, and there were a few laughs. Even still, I knew that the men were concerned, and watching closely to see how Fósforo and I reacted. I didn't betray my worries.

Even though we all stood together, Julio heard it first. He swore at those nearest to him to be quiet, cupping a hand to one ear. I began to listen as well, straining to hear what had alarmed him. After a moment, I thought I heard it too: a low buzzing noise to the east. We all stood still, in absolute silence, until everyone picked up the sound. No one knew what it was until a small plane flew low overhead.

Our camp was well camouflaged, but where we stood, we could be seen from the air. The plane circled back in a long, lazy arc, tilting its wings to turn the cockpit window towards us as it made a second pass. It didn't look like a military plane and was unarmed, but it kept flying a wide, slow circle around us.

"I'm not waiting around to see what happens next," said Julio.

His platoon gathered in close around him, but no one knew what to do. When he noticed them staring at him, he kicked the nearest guerrilla in the ass.

"What are you waiting for? Idiots! Pack your gear. We leave whatever we can't carry easily. Get ready to move. Now!"

I looked at Fósforo, who nodded.

"Rubio, have the men collect all our gear. Get ready to move in five minutes," I said.

"To where?" he asked.

"I'll let you know."

Everyone scrambled off except Julio and I, who approached Fósforo.

"Well, they've found us," said Fósforo.

"It was that bastard Helado," said Julio. "He shouldn't have been allowed to leave."

"We don't know that's true," said Fósforo.

"He betrayed us or was arrested and talked, how else could they find us?" spat Julio.

"It doesn't matter now," I said. "But there must be soldiers close behind that plane, and we need a plan."

"And we need more men if we're going to haul all this equipment any farther up the mountain at anything less than a crawl," said Julio.

Fósforo took a moment to relight his pipe, puffing hard on it. He took it out of his mouth and used it as a pointer. "Julio, you'll take your men and all the supplies, as well as Esperanza and one more of Paco's men. Head north to the next ridgeline, and then follow its edge as you move east."

"We'll be crawling along with that heavy gear," said Julio.

Fósforo nodded. "And so, Paco, do you know a place where you could hold up the Guardia for an hour or two, at least?"

I thought for a moment, hesitating enough that Fósforo scowled in irritation. "There's a place where most of the trails from the south converge. If they haven't already got past that point, we could."

"Good," said Fósforo. "I'll come with you."

I raced back to where I had left my hammock and found that Rubio had already taken it down and packed it into my knapsack. He and the others were standing in a loose line, their kit at their feet, waiting for my instructions. Despite the looming danger, my heart swelled with pride in them.

"We're going to hold the Guardia off while Julio's platoon carts the majority of our supplies away. We can give everything we won't use to fight to them." The men looked doubtful. "Only for an hour or so, and then we'll follow them." They brightened a little when I said, "Fósforo will be coming with us."

The airplane was still buzzing around the clearing where we were spotted. We avoided the open ground as we marched in single file southwards. I led the platoon towards the point where the trails that accessed our camp converged. Fósforo joined us, a captured rifle slung over his back, falling in at the rear. We moved quickly, helped by the fact that we had covered the same ground during training in recent days. In half an hour, we reached a thick stand of trees on the edge of a grassy field. All the routes from the south met here.

"Spread out," I said, moving around to adjust the position of each man in the platoon. I kept the newcomer who had joined with Helado close by. "When we kill the vanguard, you'll have your chance to get a gun," I told him. He looked frightened but gave a small nod in reply.

We waited. Every sound, whether the wind or a mouse moving through the grass, had us on edge. As the minutes turned into an hour, the sense of immediate danger wore off. Men rolled over on their backs to ease aching muscles. I walked in a crouch up and down our small line of men to try to keep order. I made sure each man was facing the open field and ready to fire, but I knew that they went back to being comfortable as soon as I passed.

"Maybe they went another way?" asked Rubio. "Maybe they're behind us already?"

I thought about the various tracks that we had hiked along in all directions from the camp. "This is the only route that makes sense," I said, "unless they were coming over the mountain."

"Maybe we should just leave?" he asked. "Julio's platoon has had lots of time to get away."

I was thinking about asking Fósforo to give the order to leave when I saw something move on the other side of the field. I lowered myself flat on the ground beside Rubio, and he turned to look in the direction in which I was staring.

First, one man came into view, walking slowly up a trail that cut through the grassy field. Dressed in fatigues and with a rifle, he was, without a doubt, a guardsman. Rubio aimed at him with his rifle, but I gently pushed it down.

"Wait," I said.

Two more men appeared behind the first, walking slowly as well. They stopped to kneel whenever they caught up with the man in the lead and scanned the area in front of them whenever they stopped.

"Let's kill them," said Rubio in a whisper.

"Not yet," I said.

When the three guardsmen were halfway across the field, six more men appeared behind them in a tight group. One of them, the leader, I guessed, carried a huge walkie-talkie slung over his shoulder.

"Aim for the one with the radio," I told Rubio, taking aim myself at the nearest man.

I shouted the signal for the ambush to begin. "Fire!"

I heard Fósforo shout from somewhere nearby: "Patria o muerte!"

When Rubio fired, so did I, and less than a second later, the others followed suit. As soon as we fired, all the guardsmen dropped to the ground and disappeared in the long grass. We fired as fast as we could while still taking aim, trying to make ourselves seem bigger and fiercer than we were. They soon started to fire back, though I don't think that they could tell where we were. I could hear the rounds flying overhead, but none of them felt threatening.

It was the first real battle that I had been in, or, at least, the first where I felt like I was actively taking part. It was hard to tell what was happening, and with nothing clear to shoot at, the firing slackened.

Rubio turned to me. "I can't see any of them."

"Keep looking," I told him, scanning the ground ahead of me

as best I could without raising my head too far. The silence didn't last long, perhaps thirty seconds, and then one of the guardsmen who had been in the lead stood up and ran back towards the far end of the field. Close behind him were the other two men who had been with him, zig-zagging back and forth as they ran. I fired at them all as they fled, and so did Fósforo and Rubio. At the far edge of the field, the men tumbled back into the grass and skidded out of sight, though whether it was because we'd hit any of them or not, I didn't know.

Rubio began to speak, but I gestured for him to be silent and used pantomime to show him that we would watch and wait for another of the guardsmen to move. In the back of my mind, I knew that bastard Espina was somewhere farther back in the column. I hoped he would show himself and that one of us would shoot him down.

As we lay watching, Fósforo crawled over to lay beside me. "The vanguard must have slunk away," he said.

"Then let's ambush them again," I whispered. "We need to kill the vanguard every time, no?"

"It's too risky to wait," said Fósforo. "We've given Julio time to get away. The rest of them will be on top of us in minutes, and we may not be able to hold them off so easily."

"We haven't even wounded one of them," I said. "This is no way to win a war."

"Sometimes winning is just surviving," said Fósforo.

I didn't agree with him, but arguing seemed pointless. "We'll take whatever gear those soldiers dropped first," I said. Before Fósforo could argue, I put my rifle down beside him and told Rubio to do the same. I wasn't yet willing to risk standing up, and so crawled forward towards the middle of the field, Rubio following close behind.

The grass was thick and coarse, and the edges cut at my hands as I pulled myself forward through it. There was no path for me to follow, so I could only guess where the soldiers had been when we first started firing at them. I headed in the general direction that I thought best, and soon found an area with flattened grass.

Discarded nearby were three heavy army packs, some web gear, and two rifles. One of the soldiers must have had the presence of mind to hold onto this weapon. Rubio began to open one of the packs to see what was inside, but I stopped him.

"This isn't the place for that," I said.

We heaved the packs onto our backs, Rubio taking two, and we each grabbed a rifle. There was no way that we could crawl back with them, and so we ran back, trying to stay low to the ground. My back ached at the pack's weight, which was so much heavier than the ones that we carried.

Just as we reached our side of the field again, shots rang out behind us. We slid to a stop in the grass, landing in a heap, pulled over by the weight of the packs.

"Let's go! Everyone! Move!" shouted Fósforo, and he took off at a run. The other men of the platoon were close behind him. The firing continued behind us. There was no time to redistribute the loads, and so Rubio and I grabbed our own weapons and followed him as quickly as we could. Deeper into the bush, Fósforo led the platoon at a run in a single file. Weighed down with the soldiers' equipment, we struggled to keep up with him.

I was last, and Rubio was just ahead of me, three rifles and two canvas packs slung over his back. I was having trouble keeping pace, but to me, it seemed as if Rubio moved as swiftly as if he carried nothing at all. We came to the bottom of a long draw that the others had already scrambled up. Rubio stopped and dropped the equipment off his back and crouched down behind a dense thicket.

"Keep going," he said. "I'll hold them up for five minutes or so, and make them think twice about chasing us very quickly."

I didn't say anything, just clapped him on the shoulder as I began to climb. Just as I reached the top, I heard him start firing slow deliberate shots that stood in contrast to the frightened volleys fired by the soldiers. I didn't turn around to see what he was firing at but just kept moving. Everything that I was carrying made it too hard for me to run any farther. I pushed myself as hard as I could to keep up, moving along the same narrow trail we had used to descend from the camp earlier. When we reached the small clearing where we had built our shelters, Fósforo was there, waiting. I quickly checked that everyone was there, dropped the pack and gave the spare rifle to one of the others.

"Quickly, open this pack and break up the load of anything useful," I said.

The straps were parade ground tight, and we had to work hard to get the pack open. Fósforo pulled me aside and asked quietly: "Where's Rubio?"

"He stayed behind to delay them a little longer. He should be a few minutes behind me."

"You didn't stay with him?"

"I can't lead from the rear," I said. "I stayed with the bulk of my men."

Fósforo looked at me disapprovingly and seemed as if he was about to say something when we were interrupted.

"Paco, is this a joke?"

They had open the guardsman's pack, and after they took a change of clothes out, it became apparent why it was so heavy. The pack was filled nearly to the top with rocks.

"What the fuck?" I said.

Fósforo gave a low whistle. "Looks like you scared off a defaulter."

"A what?"

"That's a field punishment. My grandfather used to threaten us with it when I was a kid. He must have been in trouble for something," said Fósforo.

"Madre de Dios," I swore, my back ache now meaningless. Years later, we all laughed about that bag of rocks, but I was fuming in the moment.

"We leave in five minutes," said Fósforo, giving me a look that meant with or without Rubio. He wandered off a short distance and stood by himself, looking in the direction that Julio had led the others.

The next few minutes passed slowly, everyone anxious to keep moving before the Guardia reached the camp. Fósforo checked his watch incessantly, and the moment that it said that five minutes had passed, he turned to me.

"We're leaving," he said.

"I'll go back and look for Rubio," I said. "If I don't find him soon, I'll double back around and follow your trail."

Fósforo said nothing; he just turned and began to march eastward after Julio. The new guerrillas, though confident from their first fight, hesitated.

"Go with him," I said to my platoon. "Rubio and I will be with you again in no time."

"Patria o muerte," said one of them as he turned to follow Fósforo.

I started back down the hill again, moving more slowly now. I didn't know how far the soldiers had climbed behind us, or where Rubio might be. I kept my rifle at the ready, planning on firing a few quick shots and then running should I see any of them. I heard a crashing sound below me, as if a dozen men were rushing through the underbrush, and froze. I aimed in the direction of the noise and slipped the safety off, ready to fire the moment I had a target.

The first thing that I saw, moving through the trees, was Rubio's tattered hat. I briefly wondered if it had been taken from him, but when I saw the shock of red hair sticking out from under it, I lowered my rifle. He was struggling to walk, holding himself upright by using his free hand to grab at every tree and branch that he could. He had dropped the captured rifle and packs and was using his scoped rifle to lean on. When he saw me, he broke into a wide grin.

"I thought you'd be gone," he said.

"The others left, but I decided to wait."

"Couldn't face the idea of living without me? With no one for company but those farm boys?"

I saw then that his pant leg, just over his calf, was dark and torn. I stopped him and tore the pant leg open. He stood gingerly on his good leg while I poured water on his calf to see the wound.

"How close are they?" I asked.

"They're expecting us to jump out from behind every tree." he said, "And so I think they've stopped, for now. But they'll get brave again soon enough."

His leg didn't look as bad as I thought it might be, just an angry red graze across his calf, the skin around it torn and ragged. I pulled one of the bandages Fósforo had made from shirttails out of my pocket and quickly wrapped it around Rubio's leg, tying it off on the outside. I slung both of our rifles over my back and let him support himself with his arm over my shoulders. We took off as fast as we could muster as if we were in some sort of mad three-legged race. We didn't stop when we reached the camp again, following the trail made by the others.

"This trail is pretty easy to follow," said Rubio.

I was too winded to do anything but grunt in reply.

"Easy for the Guardia, too," he said.

The thought had crossed my mind as well, but I tried to ignore it.

"Fósforo will think of something," I wheezed.

Before long, the path cut across a shallow stream, strewn with rocks that had tumbled down from higher up the slope. Waiting for us there was Santiago.

"I wasn't going to wait much longer for you two," he said.

"I'm thankful that you did."

He looked doubtfully at Rubio's leg.

"Paco, if you take his gear, I'll carry him for now," said Santiago.

I was too tired to argue, and so let Santiago pick him up on his back, briefly checking the bandage on Rubio's leg. Santiago carefully walked down the stream, avoiding the slippery rocks and the shallower edges where his footprints might be seen.

"This was Julio's idea," said Santiago. "To throw the Guardia off our tracks."

We travelled several hundred yards through the water until we reached a stony beach. Concealed in the bushes overlooking the stream, I saw the rest of the guerrillas. Santiago lay Rubio down on the ground beside the water, his face sheeted in sweat. I took off my gear and lay down beside him, exhausted.

Esperanza brought me a canteen of water, which I waved over to Rubio first. She looked concerned when she saw his leg.

"Fósforo should look at that," she said.

"Only if we have time," said Rubio.

I passed a set of newly-acquired webbing to her and took the captured rifle back from the man carrying it. "These are for you," I said to Esperanza, "on condition that I never have to carry any of it ever again."

She smiled as she took the rifle. In her baggy clothes, the rifle stock thicker than her arms, she might have looked comical if not for her expression.

Fósforo appeared on the beach, his shirt filthy and crusted in salt.

"We need to keep moving," he said. "Julio, your men will take the lead again. But without the supplies."

Julio's men were refreshed after their wait for us. They dumped their heavy packs and the bundle hanging from the pole on the beach and disappeared into the jungle. I sighed deeply, looking for a reserve of strength for this next leg of the journey.

Fósforo watched as Julio led his men further eastward, breaking a trail where there hadn't been one before. He then turned to me and was about to say something when he stopped.

"How many rifles did you take from the ambush?"

I didn't need to count to know. "One," I said.

"But weren't there more?" he demanded.

I was trying to prepare a succinct explanation for what had happened when Rubio spoke up.

"I had one, but I dropped it, and the other equipment, when I was hit in the leg."

Fósforo stood over us, his fists clenched, saying nothing. His face was a tight knot.

"If I didn't drop them," said Rubio, "I would never have got away."

"We still have his rifle with the scope," I said. As soon as the words were out of my mouth, I regretted them.

Fósforo snatched the rifle up off the ground.

"His rifle? This rifle belongs to the Revolution, and in the hands of a guerrilla who knows how to use it."

Rubio was about to speak up again when I put a hand on his chest to stay him.

"We have men without rifles who were counting on you to give them the means to fight. You had those means in your hands, but you left them for the enemy. And then you say that at least you kept your rifle. Selfish bastard," spat Fósforo.

"Rubio saved our skins," I said, "and was wounded for his trouble."

"If you had been leading your platoon properly, this would never have happened," he raged.

Esperanza and the other guerrillas were standing by, meekly listening to Fósforo rant. He turned on them. "Pick up these supplies and get moving." They scrambled to grab everything that Julio's men had left behind.

Fósforo held the scoped rifle out towards Rubio, though just out of reach. "I am going to give this to Santiago, a man who proved himself today. And until you prove me wrong, Rubio, you will carry nothing more dangerous than a pack full of supplies." Before any of us were ready to leave, he plunged into the trees ahead of us.

Rubio turned his face away from me, tears forming in his eyes. I got to my feet and offered him a hand to pull himself up.

"You won't be carrying anything until that leg heals," I said.

He embraced me tightly, and I felt his tears on my cheek.

"You'll prove yourself again," I said.

"Patria o muerte."

13

THE FOREST WAS THICK ENOUGH that we had to hack a path for ourselves through it, avoiding anything that might have passed for a trail. I knew why we were doing it, but still cursed every vine or bit of brush that had to be defeated.

We found some respite as we moved along a rocky draw, the maddening nature of the clinging underbrush traded for loose river rocks instead. I was looking down, watching my footing, when I saw something move out of the corner of my eye and looked up.

On a short rise that overlooked the draw were two young women with broad, dark faces framed by thickly braided hair. They were squatting with a mottled dog between them. What struck me the most about them, though, was that they shared a pair of tall rubber boots, each wearing one. They stared at us in silence as we trudged by.

I slipped on a loose rock, landing on my backside and rucksack, stuck for a moment like an upended turtle until I could loose one arm from under the strap. When I rolled over to look back at the rise, the women were gone.

"Are you hurt?" asked Rubio.

"No, no, I'm fine," I stammered.

"Drink some more water," he said, offering his canteen. I took a pull from it and rubbed my eyes before we marched on.

We walked for two more days before we found a new site for a camp that suited Fósforo. Nestled in the foothills of the Serranías, it was thickly wooded and easily defensible. A stream ran through it, the water cool and sweet. Some of the men plunged their heads into it as soon as we arrived.

"First Platoon will build their shelters there," said Fósforo, gesturing to the west, "and Second Platoon will build them there," gesturing to the east. His voice was quiet, his shoulders slumped.

I nodded, eyeing the ground he had assigned me.

"Once that's done, I want you to each build a watchtower that your platoon will man," he continued.

"Will we divide up this material first?" I asked Julio. He ignored me, his expression dark.

"Comrade Fósforo," he began, "before we begin to do your bidding, I'm wondering if you will share your thoughts with us."

Everyone was still.

"Thoughts on what, Julio?"

"On the future of the Revolution?" asked Julio. "Or your plans to develop this campsite?" He was warming up to the subject, looking to his men for support. "Or perhaps on the fucking disaster of the last few days?"

None of the other men looked at Julio or Fósforo. Even Esperanza seemed unwilling to get involved. Fósforo and Julio faced off against each other as if alone.

"And what disaster would that be?" asked Fósforo wearily.

Julio counted off each item on his outstretched fingers. "That bastard Helado's betrayal. The discovery of our camp. Rubio's injury. Getting chased halfway across this mountain by the Guardia. Take your pick."

Fósforo sounded calm when he replied, but I could see the tension in his neck and hands. He was barely holding himself together.

"Construction can wait," said Fósforo. "Everyone gather around and take a seat."

We all shuffled closer to him, sitting on our packs or leaning against trees. We were bone tired and sore, but still willing to obey.

"Who else agrees with Julio that we have suffered a disaster?" asked Fósforo. "Don't be afraid—you can speak your minds."

Everyone was silent. Fósforo looked at each man as if to encourage them to speak. Finally, Juan broke the silence.

"Fósforo, I don't know what else to call it. We've been kicked like a stray dogs, running with our tails between our legs. I don't know what we're doing or why we're doing it anymore."

"Anyone else?" asked Fósforo.

"My brother's right," said Santiago. A few more men, including ones from my platoon, murmured in agreement, but no one else spoke up clearly. Julio looked triumphant, his eyes gleaming.

"What we need," said Julio, "is a change in leadership."

"Let's set that aside for the moment," said Fósforo. "I'd like to hear what Paco thinks."

I wasn't sure what to say. "It didn't feel like a victory," I finally said.

Julio slapped his hand on his leg. "See? He agrees."

Fósforo began to speak, his voice quiet enough that we had to strain to hear him. Even the sounds of the forest around us became quieter as we listened.

"There are many different things that I have wanted to say to everyone. Paco is right—the last few days have not felt like a victory. But I would ask you to rethink what we mean by the word. It is not just the kind of victory that we read in storybooks. It is not just defeating the enemy."

Julio snorted. "This is some kind of trickery that you learned in university."

"No trickery," said Fósforo. "The Guardia killed nearly every man in the column when Braulio led us and said so to the world. But we survived to humiliate them in La Trinidad. They destroyed our camp and will likely crow about their victory again. But we've survived once more. And we'll humiliate them once more. Victory for them is fleeting. Victory for us is merely surviving to fight again and prove that the Guardia cannot win. Every time they claim to defeat us, only to have us reappear, we win a victory in the People's hearts."

"So, retreating through the jungle for two days is a victory?" said Julio, trying to encourage the others to ridicule Fósforo.

"Fósforo's right," I said. "The government can't claim victory as long as we continue to fight."

"But make no mistake," said Fósforo, "these are difficult times. Maybe the most difficult of our lives. Many people have made mistakes over the past few weeks, including me. I can see now what the biggest one was. But in this process, like in a crucible, we are becoming something important. I've realized that a guerrilla, a true guerrilla, is the highest stage of human development. We are humans willing to give everything, even our lives, for the betterment of others. In moral and political terms, we are nearly a different species than who we were before."

I sat and thought about Fósforo's words for a few moments. He was right. As hard as my life had been before, this was harder. But, now I was working towards something greater than myself.

"Fine words," said Julio, "but a man cannot eat fine words, nor can he hide behind them when the bullets begin to fly." He acted this out, getting a laugh from his platoon. "We've all come from hard lives, and we all know the deck is stacked against us. I've been called a bandit, but it's the people in the highest positions who are the biggest thieves. There is no higher purpose than getting as happy as you can, as rich as you can and as drunk as you can. I'm not here to fight the government to gain nothing. I want to take back some of what they've stolen from the People, and enjoy life while I can."

"What are you proposing?" asked Fósforo.

"That we forget about the Revolution, avoid the Guardia at all costs, and start looking out for ourselves," said Julio, ticking each item off on his fingers.

"You'll be run to ground eventually, my friend," said Fósforo.

Rather than let Julio convince anyone any further, I decided to put an end to this. I stood up and spoke loudly. I realized that I still had faith. "I'm with Fósforo."

Rubio stood as well, though he wouldn't look at Fósforo. "Patria o muerte."

Esperanza stood next. Then Santiago and Juan together. Swayed by our numbers, the newer recruits stood as well.

"Fucking fools," swore Julio. "The only patria you should care about is the land under your own two feet. And death is coming for us all, in quick time just for standing up to the government." He stormed off into the bush. Fósforo watched him leave, then turned to us.

"Let him go," he said. "I'll tell him of our plan once he's cooled down." Fósforo took a stick and began to scratch out a diagram in the dirt. "We won't be setting up a permanent camp again that the Guardia can locate and attack. That was my mistake. We're going to keep moving. And even though the Guardia thinks they've won a battle, we're going to go on the offensive."

"We can't attack them head-on," I said.

"No," said Fósforo, "but we can hit them where they don't expect it." He drew a long line to represent the river with an 'X' at the far end. "This is the town of Chacimo. It is unremarkable and unimportant except for the fact that there is a small factory there. We're going to move down to the river at first light tomorrow and find a place to cross. We'll observe Chacimo overnight and determine where the garrison is located if there is one. Then we'll attack and destroy it and the factory."

"The message that we were destroyed will be overridden by news of our attack," I said.

"Exactly," said Fósforo.

"If it gets into the national news, the organization will hear of it as well," said Esperanza.

"With luck, the whole country will hear of it," said Fósforo.

"And when the Guardia counter-attacks?" I asked.

"We'll be long gone," said Fósforo.

No one objected, and so the platoons broke off to prepare for the night. I stayed behind, as did Fósforo.

Before I could speak, he stood close to me and spoke in a murmur. "Brother, I've made many mistakes." He looked me right in the eye. "I realize that I need to harden my heart, and not let my emotions get the better of me."

I realized that his words applied to me too. My mind swirled with the things I had been thinking the last two days, all the accusations and angry words that had filled my head. But, as I looked at him, they washed away. This was no time for emotions. I just nodded.

"Patria o muerte," he said.

We were on the move again before dawn. Leaving our heaviest supplies buried in a shallow pit near the waterfall, we could move quickly. Rubio led the column through the heavy undergrowth, carving a path for the rest of us with a machete. He volunteered for every work party, every task, for anything that might let him win back the right to be armed. So far, Fósforo was blind to him, and I suspected willfully so. I resolved to take it up with him after the raid on the factory.

Julio's platoon followed us a short distance behind, close enough to hear if we were discovered by the Guardia, but not so close that they would be found as well. Julio listened grudgingly to Fósforo when he gave instructions, his expression full of resentment. Fósforo seemed blind to this as well, treating Julio no differently than before. His equanimity only served to make Julio more resentful.

After an hour, I called a short halt and posted a sentry. Rubio lay on his back and pulled his tattered hat over his eyes. Esperanza sat next to me, her fatigue shirt hanging loosely off her boney shoulders. She clutched her rifle across her lap, never complaining about carrying it. As everyone busied themselves with their own concerns, we had a moment to ourselves.

"I've never really said how sorry I feel about what happened in Managua," I began.

"I understand," she said slowly. "Those early hours and days of arrests were chaotic. I didn't search for Fósforo for very long before I realized that I needed to plan my own escape."

"Have you spoken to him about it?" I asked.

She shook her head. "I don't want to complicate things. And, if I'm being honest, I was angry that I didn't know what had happened to him more than anything else."

We sat in silence for a moment, listening to the growing sounds of wildlife in the forest.

"I can show you how to patch those holes in your shirt if you want," she said.

I hadn't really noticed them before, but suddenly felt self-conscious when I looked at the ragged state of my apparel. "Perhaps we'll find new clothes in Chacimo," I said.

"My mother would have been so angry to hear about people throwing away clothes rather than patching them. Though she was a seamstress, so I suppose she had a vested interest."

"Did she teach you to sew?" I asked.

"I was a seamstress as well until she died. And then it just didn't bring in enough money to survive on." Her voice trailed off as she became lost in thought.

I gave her shoulder a squeeze. "And now we all know what it feels like to do whatever's necessary to survive."

The march to Chacimo was long and uneventful, although I scanned the forest fruitlessly as we walked. Although the river here was often deep and fast, we found a gentle place to cross where the water did not go past our knees. I waited to watch as my platoon crossed, first stopping to take off their boots and roll up their pant legs. Julio's men caught up with us, and soon there was some good-natured splashing between the platoons as they waded across.

Julio and I shared a log to sit on as we pulled off our boots.

"Tell me, Paco, was there a wooden or a dirt floor in the house where you were born?" he asked.

"I don't know where I was born, but it could have been either," I replied.

"There were only dirt floors in my village," said Julio. "And if I asked Fósforo, what do you think he would say?"

"I imagine he was born in a hospital, but what difference does it make?"

We stepped into the water as we talked. The river bed was soft, and my feet sunk through a thick layer of mud. I walked slowly, worried that I would lose my footing.

"Men like you and I knew what it meant to be hungry before the Revolution. The injustices that Fósforo gives speeches about are ones that we know in our bones."

"Fósforo has suffered alongside the rest of us from the very start," I said.

"From the start of the Revolution, but not from the very start, like you and me."

"And what of it?" Julio's lips barely moved as he spoke, hidden behind the bulk of his moustache.

"Open your eyes, Paco. The man is just playing at being a revolutionary, but you and these others follow him because he uses honeyed words. If we topple the government, what do you think will happen then? A new set of people will go and live in the palaces, and the rest of us will go back to our dirt floors."

Julio started walking faster, sure-footed, leaving me to struggle through the river on my own. On the other side, I quickly washed my feet and pushed myself to catch up with my platoon. Julio and his men waited for me to leave, saying nothing.

When we reached the outskirts of Chacimo, the sun had started to set, leaving just enough light to make out its features. The town was sprawled along the southern bank of the river. Many of its buildings had elaborate balconies that hung out over the water's edge, propped up by wooden poles. In its centre was the usual cluster of buildings dedicated to church and state and a dock for the small boats that people used on the river. Close to the dock was a low building with a metal roof that I assumed was the factory. The road from San Jose Guachipilìn was little more than a rough track which ended at the eastern edge of town.

"A depressing shithole if I ever saw one," said Julio.

"An important one for the regime," said Fósforo. "That factory belongs to a wealthy family, who line the pockets of government ministers for the privilege of exploiting the local population and selling the food that should feed the People."

"The factory doesn't look like it's guarded," I said, straining my eyes in the dying light. "What kind of business is it?"

"An exploitative one," said Fósforo. "More importantly, the Guardia still think that we're somewhere near La Trinidad, not out here," said Fósforo. "When we destroy that factory, they'll wonder if we've moved or if there are two columns in the department."

"And what of the workers who feed their families by working at that factory?" asked Julio. "What of them once we put them out of work?"

"Your sudden concern for the common man is surprising," said Fósforo.

"I, at least, know what a common man looks like," said Julio.

"And I know what a military target looks like, and that factory is one," said Fósforo.

"Are you saying that I don't?" Julio's face was flushed. Fósforo merely shrugged.

"We've been over this before," I said. "Hitting this factory will get their attention, and remind the government that there is nowhere they are safe. The workers will either join us or suffer. They have the same choices to make that we did."

"More grist for the mill of the Revolution," said Julio, his voice dripping with contempt. "I suppose they'll just have to subsist on revolutionary love."

I ignored him. "Let's plan this attack," I said. "It looks like it will be a piece of cake."

Fósforo shook his head. "We need to find the Guardia's location in town first," he said, "and if reinforcements come from San Jose

Guachipilín, I'd rather fight them in daylight."

"Or even better, not at all," said Julio.

"Agreed," said Fósforo, "if we have the choice."

We made camp in a small gully well outside of town and prepared to pass an uncomfortable night. We didn't light fires, and so had nothing but cold rice that we had cooked in the morning for our dinner. The insects who rose from the wet ground were ferocious and bloodthirsty.

Fósforo asked for one of the platoons to determine which building was being used by the Guardia. Julio immediately volunteered his men.

"I'd rather get shot than stay here and be bled dry by these mosquitos," he said.

I had placed my men in their position for the night, sleeping in a long row so that they would be ready to fight immediately upon waking up if needed. I saw Fósforo sitting by himself, and not yet ready for sleep, so I sat next to him.

"I doubt that we'll have any visitors tonight," said Fósforo, crushing a mosquito that had landed on his throat.

"You're right, no guardsman would be mad enough to subject himself to this willingly." We both laughed while swatting at our tormentors.

"Not everyone is as willing to follow as you," said Fósforo a little ruefully.

"You mean Julio?"

"Who else?"

"Don't mistake his words or manner for his actions," I said. "He's never failed to do what was needed."

"It's hard enough to keep everyone's spirits up," said Fósforo, "without being questioned at every turn."

"I disagree. The more questions asked the better everyone understands what we are doing, and the more committed they will become. This is what we're trying to build together."

"Words have a power that even actions don't sometimes," he said. "I just don't know what he'll do next."

"Don't convict the man for crimes he hasn't committed," I said. "Worry about the problems we have, not the ones that we might."

Fósforo gave my arm a squeeze. "Maybe you're right," he said. "We have problems enough as it is."

Fósforo was quiet, thinking about what we had said. After a few minutes, I bid him goodnight. I walked back to where my platoon was lying and looked for a suitable spot for myself. I could see one snoring guerrilla wrapped in a hammock, nothing sticking out but their tiny boots. Recognizing Esperanza, I lay down beside her.

I wrapped my tarp tightly around myself in hopes of keeping the insects at bay and tried to sleep, though I couldn't block out the incessant buzzing. It felt like I was awake all night, but I must have fallen asleep for a few hours because the next thing I recalled was someone shaking me awake roughly.

"Get up. There's a vehicle coming this way," said Rubio, whispering into my ear.

"Coming here?" I asked.

Rubio was already waking the next man, but he looked back at me and pointed in the direction of the vehicle. I could hear it, though not see it. Its lights were off, and it sounded as if it was having a tough time navigating over the broken ground. I called out quietly to the platoon:

"No one fires unless I do."

Esperanza looked groggy as if arisen from a very deep sleep.

"Are you alright?" I asked.

"I was having the most wonderful dream," she said, rubbing her eyes with her free hand while clutching her rifle with the other.

"You'll have to tell me about it later," I said, straining to look out in the darkness. I could make out some of their shadows against the night sky, but that was all. I continued to listen to the vehicle approach, slowly winding its way towards us. Looking down the sights of my rifle, I couldn't make out anything other than a vague silhouette in the darkness.

Fósforo dropped down beside me. "Why wasn't I woken sooner?" he asked.

"You're upper management now," I said. "This is still getting dealt with on the shop floor."

When he smiled, I could see the whites of his teeth.

Out in the darkness, the vehicle stopped and flashed its headlights twice.

"That can't be the Guardia," said Fósforo.

"Who else?" I asked.

"Who will volunteer to go out and see?" asked Fósforo.

I didn't respond. Before Fósforo asked again, Julio's voice came out of the darkness. "Stop shitting your pants and come see what I've found."

Fósforo and I walked toward Julio's voice. As we got closer, we could make out the shape of a jeep stopped on the rough ground ahead of us. It had men in every possible seat, including on the hood. Julio walked out to greet us.

"In troubled waters, fishermen prosper," said Julio. "Come and inspect my catch."

His platoon was seated on every conceivable part of the back of the open-top jeep. Sitting in their midst were two sullen guardsmen with their hands tied behind them. Julio's men had smiles so wide that they might have cracked their faces open.

"We caught them by the side of the road, taking a piss," said Julio.

"Good," laughed Fósforo. "Heading into or out of town?"

"Into town," said Julio, "with these." He handed a leather folder to Fósforo. "Orders from Captain Espina, indicating that the 'bandits' had been defeated but to remain vigilant."

Fósforo leafed through the typed letters in the folder, most of which were routine administration and of no interest.

"The best prize of all," said Julio, "is this." He gestured to his men, who clambered off the back of the jeep and brought forward a wooden crate forward on which they had been sitting. Julio opened the latch and flipped the lid open. Sitting inside the crate was an American-made rocket launcher. Fósforo lifted it and hefted it onto his shoulder.

"There's only a few rockets for it, but still," said Julio. "There's also a box of grenades and a few crates of rifle ammunition." I gave a low whistle.

Fósforo put the bazooka down and went to examine the prisoners. One was a young guardsman, evidently the driver, who had been trussed up and thrown in with the guerrillas in the back. In the passenger seat was a fat man in the dress uniform of a lieutenant. He had sweat through his shirt and looked as if he might be sick.

"Filthy bandits," he said.

"Please," said the young guardsman, "I have a family. A son."

"Shut up," said the fat lieutenant.

"Both of you shut up," said Julio.

"Don't worry," said Fósforo, clapping the officer on the shoulder. "We're not bandits, we're revolutionaries. You're both safe, but as prisoners arrested for crimes against the People."

The remaining colour drained from the officer's face.

14

PEOPLE HAD ALREADY BEGUN to move about on the main street in Chacimo, and stevedores were loading a flat-bottomed riverboat when we released the fat lieutenant and his driver. Clad only in their underwear, they hurried toward the Guardia outpost despite our admonishment to walk slowly. The townspeople stopped to watch and laugh at them as they passed.

The lieutenant waved his arms angrily at the townspeople, gesturing back toward the hill from where we were watching him. I imagined that he warned them of an impending bandit attack.

The little cuarteles that housed the Guardia was stuccoed, with a small garden out front. The national flag hung limply from a pole at its centre. When the humiliated guardsmen reached the outpost, they raced in the door and slammed it shut behind them.

"Do you think they'll keep their word?" I asked Fósforo.

"What makes you think they'd start now?" said Julio.

"Even better than making them look weak is to make them look foolish," said Fósforo. "This does both." He looked at his watch. "We told them they had fifteen minutes to convince the others to surrender. Let's see."

After a few minutes, the iron shutters began to slam shut over the building's windows. The lieutenant reappeared, dressed in his fatigues and wearing a helmet. He shouted at the townspeople who had begun to gather curiously in the street, waving his arms emphatically. As he grew more frantic, the crowd dispersed, hiding in their shops and homes. The stevedores stopped their work. The half-loaded riverboat slipped its mooring and motored over to the other side of the river, where it waited.

"I think that answers our question," said Julio. "I should have killed them when I had the chance." He gave a low whistle to his men, who were concealed in the brush to our left. They raised themselves onto their knees to see him. "It's going to be a fight after all," he said, drawing his finger across his throat. His platoon looked eager.

"We'll see about that," said Fósforo. "I have one more thing in mind."

Fósforo went back to the jeep and took the bazooka from its crate. He slung the canvas ammunition bag that held three rockets over his shoulder. There was a diagram showing how to load and fire it glued inside the lid of the crate. He studied it for a moment before rejoining us.

"Do you know how to fire that thing?" I asked.

"It can't be hard," said Fósforo. "Soldiers do it." He leaned the bazooka against his leg and pulled a rocket from its cardboard tube in the bag. He looked at it for a moment before pulling the safety pin off and sliding it into the back of the bazooka.

"I'll watch from over here," said Julio, striding off to join his platoon in the brush.

Fósforo walked forward until he was on the exposed edge of the hill and put the bazooka on his shoulder. He aimed at the Guardia building, the muzzle of the weapon waving unsteadily. I stood nearby, fingers in my ears, not knowing what to expect. When he pulled the trigger, there was a tremendous rush of noise as the rocket motor ignited. A cloud of dust and leaves blossomed behind him, rolling quickly away from us. The rocket streaked out towards the outpost and then suddenly fell short, ploughing into the street well less than halfway to the target. It exploded with a deafening crack.

"Shit," muttered Fósforo as he loaded another rocket. "I don't really get how this sight works."

"I won't tell anyone," I said.

"I think they can tell," he said.

"Let's move closer. With the shutters closed, they're not dangerous."

Fósforo put the bazooka over his shoulder and called out to Julio: "We're going to advance."

"We have to advance just because you're cross-eyed?" shouted Julio in return.

"Do you want me to hit the building or not?" said Fósforo.

Julio stood up and brought his men over to stand with us. I waved at my platoon, and they did the same.

"Just to the edge of town," said Fósforo, taking the lead.

"After you," said Julio mockingly.

I fell in behind Fósforo, and my platoon followed. Soon the whole column of guerrillas streamed down the hill like a line of ants to where the first buildings sat astride the town's single street.

Fósforo walked to the middle of the street and stood with his legs apart, bracing himself as best he could. Each platoon huddle behind the nearest building on either side of the street, watching him intently. He took aim, staring through the sight for what seemed a long time before firing. There was a whir, a crack, and a cloud of dust that rolled back down the street behind him. I couldn't see what had resulted but heard an impact and the sound of something clattering against the metal rooftops of the houses near the outpost. When the dust cleared, we could see that he had struck the top corner of the building, carving a piece off but not causing serious damage.

"Let me try," I said, but Fósforo ignored me. "Perhaps we need to get closer still." He ignored me, carefully loading the bazooka with the last round, and hefting it onto his shoulder again.

I heard Julio speak quietly to his platoon. "If he misses, the attack is over. We've lost the element of surprise, and we won't pry those guardsmen out of their hiding place with a crowbar."

"We'll have rattled them enough that we can negotiate their surrender," I called over to him.

"You think you can you negotiate a turtle out of its shell?" asked Julio.

I looked back at Fósforo. He stood perfectly still, bracing the bazooka into his shoulder so tightly that I could see the veins in his hand standing out. Again, when he pulled the trigger, there was a whir, a crack, a cloud of dust, and on the other end, there was a terrible sound. I rushed forward of the dust cloud to better see what had happened, and my platoon came with me. It was immediately obvious what had happened.

His third round had hit one of the iron shutters directly and staved it in, carrying on into the building itself. The damaged window frame was jagged and raw like an empty eye socket. Dust swirled about the base of the building, and smoke poured out of every crack in the building's stonework.

Fósforo set one end of the bazooka down and leaned on it, watching the building.

"Do you want us to . . ." I began, but Fósforo held up a finger to gesture for me to wait. After a minute, one of the other shutters opened, and someone hung a limp white sheet over the windowsill.

"They're giving up," said Fósforo. A few guardsmen staggered out of the building with their hands up, looking for someone to whom they could surrender.

A shout went up from everyone at once: "Patria o muerte!"

No one else moved in the street as we advanced. The townspeople remained hidden and fearful. We quickly took control of the three guardsmen standing in the street, forcing them to lie down with their hands on their heads. Their faces and bodies covered in cuts from flying bits of stone. The dust was beginning to settle inside the outpost, and I led my platoon inside to pull out the remaining guardsmen.

As I stepped through the door, the air was so thick with dust I started coughing. Rubio and Esperanza were right behind me, and they too started choking. I tried to control myself as I searched the room, but my chest was wracked with coughs no matter what I did. I threw open all the shutters that were not already blown open to try to clear the air. Rubio began by looking in the back of the room, where there was a heavy metal bunk. With a shout, he pulled a man out from under it, and I saw it was the fat lieutenant, stunned but otherwise uninjured.

I saw a pair of boots sticking out from under the bunk closest to me, and I grabbed them to drag the guardsman out of his hiding place. He was heavy, and Esperanza grabbed hold of one leg as well, and together we hauled him across the floor.

When he was halfway out from under the bunk, I realized that he must be dead or unconscious. As his shoulders cleared the bunk, I turned away. His face had been smashed by something large, perhaps a chunk of stone from the wall or a piece of the shutter, leaving little of him remaining from the nose up. A trail of gore spread out behind him where we had dragged him across the floor. I looked at Esperanza and saw that she was staring at the man, looking at what I had turned away from. I decided to look as well, and not shy away from the results of our actions.

"We can't be soft," she said quietly to me, "not if we are going to do what needs to be done."

I knew what she meant, and the longer I looked at the man's head, the harder it was to look away. My eyes searched the blood and bone and hair at the top of his head, trying to make sense of it until Rubio grabbed me by the arm and gave me a shake.

"Just leave him. There's one other that we're not carrying outside without a shovel, but we can drag the rest of them out and the wounded too."

In all, there were five dead guardsmen in the building and three others who were badly wounded. We carried all but two out into the street and laid them in a row beside those we had captured. I took coarse wool blankets I found inside the cuarteles and lay them over the faces of the dead men. I kept the lieutenant on his feet, knowing that Fósforo would want to speak to him.

Fósforo saw him and approached, glancing only briefly at the dead men.

"Do you have bandages for the wounded?" he asked the lieutenant.

"We don't have any supplies," he said.

"You'll have to rip up your shirts, then," said Fósforo. "You know, you could have spared the lives of these men if you had surrendered when you had the chance."

"Better to die fighting than to be murdered in the street." The fat officer's bravado was unconvincing.

"Paco, have your men search the building carefully and take anything of value. Julio, take your platoon, search the town for any other guardsmen and round up all the townspeople. And, lieutenant, for the second time today, I am telling you to strip to your underwear and have your uninjured men do the same."

Julio led his platoon back to the entrance to the town so that they could go building by building. I tasked Esperanza and Rubio to help bandage the wounded, while the rest of us searched the outpost. The dust had settled enough that I didn't start coughing again, and the first thing I did was to throw blankets over the two dead men we had left inside. I saw that the bazooka round had drilled a hole right through the edge of the stuccoed wall by the shutter and sent pieces of it flying into the room in a deadly shower. Furniture was gouged and shattered, and there were pools of blood on the floor. "Collect the ammunition, weapons, food, personal equipment, maps, and documents," I said, listing the items of interest. We combed through the wreckage, tossing whatever we could salvage out the front door into a heap.

It was a meagre haul. Much of what could have been of value was ruined in the explosion.

"Two damaged rifles, eight working ones, a pistol, a few hundred rounds of ammunition and a sack of rice," I rhymed off to Fósforo.

"Hardly worth it," he said.

"True, but cheaply won."

"And cheap has a quality all its own," he replied. "Let's examine this factory while Julio's men finish their work."

He and I left my platoon guarding the prisoners and walked around the corner towards the factory. It was a large metal-roofed building behind a chain-link fence that sat close to the river.

"Let's hope that there is something useful . . ."

Fósforo had stopped walking, so I did too. I followed his gaze to the end of the street, but it took me a moment to notice what had caught his eye.

Hanging from a tree by the river was the body of a young man, painfully thin. His face was purple and swollen, and the rope around his neck looked thicker than his arms. A piece of paper was pinned to his shirt: "Matias Cabrero is a THIEF."

"Madre de Dios," I said.

"Bastards," said Fósforo.

"Feeding yourself when you're starving isn't theft," I said.

"The theft is sending the food grown here to be sold in the capital while people here starve."

We approached the corpse slowly, and as we did, I realized that he was not a young man but a boy. Fósforo pulled himself up into the tree and took out his pocket knife.

"Hold him up while I cut the rope," he said.

I grabbed the boy around the waist, lifting him a bit, and realizing how little he weighed. Fósforo took ages to saw through the rope, and I stood with my arms around the boy, my eyes closed, not thinking about what we were doing. My nose filled with a sweet scent, ripe, that I told myself was from the factory.

When we finally cut the rope, I thought that the boy would flop over my shoulder, but he stayed upright, rigid and cold. I carefully lay him down in the middle of the street and pulled his shirt over his face. Exposing his emaciated chest and sunken belly seemed even more undignified than leaving his face uncovered, but I left him like that.

"We can bury him with the others," said Fósforo.

"Unless he has family who will claim him," I said.

"Maybe," said Fósforo, before turning his attention to the factory. It was built of heavy mud bricks with a fenced-in yard on either side that stank like nothing I'd smelled before. I walked up slowly until I could push open the side doors of the building with the muzzle of my rifle and peer inside.

It was not large. Hooks hung from the ceiling in long rows. The walls and floor were spattered with blood, the room filled with flies. A line of tin cans snaked through a huge steam-powered canning machine in the centre of the room. From there, they were crated by hand. A bloody hopper on top of the machine smelled sickeningly sweet in the close, hot air of the building. I gagged as I looked around.

"Surrender!" I called out, scanning the dark corners of the room. No one answered. We slowly swept through the dark room, and I regretted not bringing some of the others with us. Moving carefully, we peered behind crates and piles of material until we were certain that we were alone.

"This hardly qualifies as a factory," said Fósforo. "Other than this thing that cans the beef, it looks like all the work is done by hand."

"In our country, people are cheaper than machines," I said, holding my hand over my nose.

"And easier to replace if they break down," said Fósforo.

He opened a door on the far side of the building and peered outside, shading his face against the sun. "There are at least twenty cans of gasoline here for the generator," he said. "Enough to finish this place off."

"Those and a few hand grenades in the machinery, and one for the generator," I said thoughtfully.

"Use as few as you think you can get away with," said Fósforo. "I want to save what we can for the Guardia." I nodded, and he clapped me on the shoulder. "We'll light this up as we leave town."

When we arrived back on the main street, there was a crowd facing the Guardia outpost. Julio's men were nowhere to be seen. Esperanza was deep in conversation with a tall man in a broad-brimmed hat, whose impeccable clothes made him look like a model of respectability.

"I can assure you," said Esperanza, "that these men are safe in our care."

"Recent events would suggest otherwise," said the man, gesturing at the row of the dead.

"If you won't take my word, perhaps you should speak to our Comandante," she said.

Fósforo approached the man with his hand outstretched. "I'm Fósforo, of the People's Revolution," he said. You could not imagine a bigger contrast between two creatures of the same species. Fósforo was filthy, his pant legs ragged, and his beard matted, with a rakish look. The tall man looked at him with a degree of horror.

"Do you mock me?" the man asked, refusing to shake hands. "Do you not even have a Christian name?"

"It's our custom to use nicknames," said Fósforo, "to keep our families safe."

The tall man was hesitant before finally shaking Fósforo's hand. "Fernando Ruiz Paiz."

"Are you the Mayor?" asked Fósforo.

Fernando shook his head. "I'm the manager here."

"Ah, the rancher's man," said Fósforo.

"You say that as if it is a curse, rather than a boon," said Fernando. Their conversation had attracted the crowd, which gathered in closer.

"The streets here aren't exactly paved in gold," said Fósforo. "Why does a country where people go hungry send meat to a rich country that pays almost nothing for it?"

"We pay a fair wage to the ranch hands and workers."

"But paid nothing but bribes for the pastures where they graze, and the land that it keeps fallow. And this 'fair wage' is barely enough to put food on the table, much less children in school or shoes on their feet."

"You think on too small a scale," said Fernando. "Nicaragua operates in the global marketplace, and canneries like ours have helped it stake out a place there. We've brought modern jobs and machinery to this department. I came from a poor family myself. My father worked himself to death on a family farm, but look where I am today. You would have us go backwards in time, to subsistence farming, which is no solution."

"And what of the boy who was hanged by the factory?" asked Fósforo.

"A thief," said Fernando, "But there was a magistrate and a trial."

"What did he steal?" asked Fósforo.

Fernando hesitated before muttering his answer. "A can of corned beef."

Fósforo turned from Fernando and addressed the crowd instead. "This man drips honey in your ears. But you don't need me to tell you that ranch owners put only enough in your bellies to keep you coming back each day for more work. It is a crime of historical proportions that in a country as rich in good soil as ours, that people go hungry. That people have to resort to stealing back the very food that they produced. The rich would keep you poor while promising you the potential to be rich. They're selling false dreams, nothing more."

"I warn you that if you damage company property, you'll do nothing but hurt its employees here in town," said Fernando.

"I don't intend to hurt anyone," said Fósforo, "though breaking their shackles might bring a momentary sense of pain. They're no more free as your 'employees' than common serfs."

"Whatever you say about us, you've shown that you lack the common morals of honest people. Look at these dead men—you will answer for this on Judgement Day." People in the crowd crossed themselves as he spoke.

"You don't think that the ranchers have blood on their hands?" asked Fósforo.

"That may be," said Fernando, "but I don't, nor does anyone else here except for you and your guerrillas. We will never condone violence as a tool to solve economic or political problems."

Rather than rebut him, Fósforo instead let out a long, loud laugh. "That only seems hilarious to someone who has embraced violence," sniffed Fernando.

Fósforo straightened up, deadly serious. "I'm laughing at how you view the world. You say that you do not condone violence to solve political problems. But you clearly condone it to maintain political systems. Why accept the government's use of violence against the People, while rejecting the People's use of it against the government? It's so illogical that it's laughable!"

Fósforo faced the crowd, turning his back to Fernando.

"This government is not afraid to use violence to keep you in line. These Guardia were not here for your protection; they were here to suppress you. While the Somocistas get fat and rich in Managua, your children are barefoot. Hungry men, whose labour grows the fruit that makes them rich, are hanged in the street for wanting enough to eat. Men like Señor Ruiz preach against violence while managing a system that is based on it."

"So, what should we do?" asked a man in the crowd.

"Join us," said Fósforo, "and together, we'll rebuild society."

"What you preach is anarchy," said Fernando angrily.

"What I preach is justice," said Fósforo.

Fernando elected to turn and leave rather than argue further. The crowd began to disperse, few wishing to linger by the corpses of the soldiers.

"I'll have these guardsmen dig graves for their comrades, and the hanged boy as well if no one claims him," I said. Fósforo agreed.

He walked over to where the lieutenant sat, apart from his men and looking miserable. "Tell me about Matias Cabrero."

The lieutenant looked back and forth at us, confused. "I don't know who you mean," he stammered.

"Think," said Fósforo.

When the lieutenant didn't say anything, Fósforo grabbed a roll of fat at the back of his neck and dragged him down the street toward the factory. As we turned the corner, the lieutenant realized where we were going.

"There was a trial!" he said. "The boy was caught red-handed!"

Fósforo dropped him in the dust.

"What did he steal?" asked Fósforo.

"Corned beef," said the lieutenant.

Fósforo pushed him over with his foot, and the officer lay in the dusty street like a fat grub fallen from a leaf. "Is a can of beef worth a man's life?"

"Stealing is a crime," said the lieutenant, who had begun to cry. "Captain Espina even said that he had no choice but to punish the boy because if everyone stole something, the country would collapse."

"Espina was the magistrate?" I asked. "What kind of court is that?"

"A military court," said the lieutenant. "There's an emergency. All the courts are military ones. I had no choice . . ."

I looked at Fósforo. "If justice was hard to find before . . ." I began.

". . . it's impossible to find now," he finished. "And what would you have us do with you?"

"What do you mean?" said the lieutenant.

"Perhaps a military tribunal of our own?"

The lieutenant looked back and forth between us, perhaps looking for sympathy. I imagine that our stony faces gave him no comfort. "But I haven't committed any crime!"

Fósforo kicked the man in the belly, and his grotesque body shook, shock waves rolling out to his sides. "Your crimes are so enormous that you can't even see them," he said.

I put a hand on Fósforo's shoulder and spoke to him quietly. "We're better than this," I said. "We can't be seen beating people up in the street, no matter what he's done."

"Then get this worm out of my sight," he said before turning and walking away.

I pulled the crying man to his feet and pushed him back towards where my platoon guarded the other prisoners. I think that some of the guerrillas were surprised to see him return, but no one said anything. "On your feet," I said to the other prisoners. "Get over there behind the outpost."

They moved warily, shaken perhaps by the sight of their officer in tears. I asked Esperanza to ask at the nearest houses for shovels, and she came back with several, as well as a watermelon that had been cut into thick slices and wrapped in a cloth.

"The people here have no love for the Guardia," she said.

"Frankly, I think that they're disappointed that we didn't kill more of them."

I took one of the slices and began to eat, the soft flesh quenching my thirst. I made sure that the rest of the platoon had slices as well, but gave none to the prisoners.

"The woman who lives in that house," she said, pointing to an adobe building at the edge of town, "said that this lot collected "taxes," regularly snatching anything they could stick in their pot. She started keeping her chickens inside just to stop them from stealing them. The stench nearly knocked me over when she opened the door."

One of the prisoners said, "The lieutenant sold every morsel of rations he could steal from us. We were starving half the time."

"You had a choice," I said. "You're either with the People or against them."

I gave the shovels to the prisoners and put them to work in the overgrown patch of ground behind their home. We sat in the shade of a nearby tree, while the three guardsmen dug graves for their comrades.

An hour later, the dead were buried, and the surviving soldiers were sent marching in their underwear to San Jose Guachipilín, carrying their wounded on makeshift stretchers. Fernando tried to dissuade us as we prepared the factory for destruction, but quickly disappeared when he realized that we would burn it down around his ears if we had to. We used some fuel for the generator to torch the Guardia outpost, black smoke pouring out its windows as the wooden furniture inside burned. We set the captured jeep on fire as well, though I was sorry to lose it. Julio's men had made a very thorough search of the town and arrived triumphantly as we finished our work and were nearly ready to leave.

"We've found a prize that makes this battle worth having fought," he said grandly.

"More ammunition?" I asked.

"Even better—cold beer." He waved to one of his men, and they deposited a wooden case at his feet, half full of bottles. "There is a little bar in the house with the large balcony over the river," he said.

"How long has your platoon spent drinking?" asked Fósforo.

Julio ignored the question. "We grilled the woman who runs the bar as well," said Julio. "She knows a lot about the comings and goings around here." Julio pulled a bottle from the crate and held it out to Fósforo. "But there is always time for small pleasures."

Fósforo pushed the bottle away. "There is no time for pleasures big or small when you've been given a task to complete," he said.

"We did that too," said Julio. "We found nothing else of interest." His platoon, many of whom looked drunk, were crowded around him.

I could tell Fósforo was furious, but he held his temper. "Return these bottles to the woman who runs the bar, and pay her for whatever you've drunk. In cash, not a promissory note. And get your platoon down to the dock, now. We're leaving."

I looked at him for direction for my platoon, but he turned on his heel and left without another word.

"The bastard isn't human," said Julio under his breath.

"He's trying to be superhuman," I said, "but he doesn't ask anything of us that he doesn't demand of himself as well."

Julio held the beer bottle out to me, but I waved it away.

"Are you superhuman now, too?"

"No, just trying to keep my wits about me in case the Guardia come back."

"The more we let him get away with this kind of nonsense, the more he's going to insist on it. We're soldiers, not monks. You should know better."

Julio spat on the ground in the direction Fósforo had gone, and then he and his men left. I saw the expressions on my platoon's faces and realized they had been looking hungrily at the beer. In truth, I would have drained one of the bottles dry in seconds, after having paid for it. But once Fósforo had weighed in, there was no way that I would undermine him.

"Take these supplies and move down to the dock," I said to my platoon, breaking their reverie. I left Rubio at the factory, ready to pull the pins on the grenades with a long piece of cable that he had found.

While we worked, Fósforo enticed the riverboat to return to the dock, where it was now tied up. Local cargo of all sorts sat beside it in untidy rows, ready to be loaded by hand. Sitting nearby were over two dozen men from the town, all hoping to join us.

"The Guardia in this town have been the best recruiters we could ask for," said Fósforo.

"Although we're back to the problem of not having enough guns," I said.

"This is a good problem to have. It will keep them hungry to prove themselves."

"And as for Rubio?" I asked.

"Not yet," said Fósforo, ending the conversation.

The boat captain, a toothless man whose speech was hard to understand, said he would take us upriver, though he could not go very far. Rapids above the town prevented boats from reaching the interior of the department, though any distance he could carry us was welcome. We had the new men carry some crates of corned beef from the dock onto the boat, and then we clambered aboard. Julio's platoon, surly and still a little drunk, gathered together near the bow. I waited for Fósforo's signal that we were ready and then shouted to Rubio. After a moment, I saw him come running down the street, legs and arms pumping furiously. Behind him, two explosions ripped through the factory, destroying the machinery and setting the fuel supplies on fire. A column of thick black smoke rose into the sky.

I saw that my platoon was as comfortable as possible on the barge, seated in the shade of a stack of crates and feasting on fresh fruit given to us by the townspeople. Rubio offered me a papaya that he had sliced in half, which I took.

"I swear this is the best fruit I've ever tasted," he said.

"The taste of liberty," I said with a smile, before finding a spot near barge's stern where I could sit with my thoughts. I draped my hammock between two crates and rested my back on another, in a way that kept me shaded while letting me watch the overgrown shoreline drift past. I used my pocketknife to cut slices off the fruit, washed it down with cool water, and felt myself start to relax.

I had not been sitting long when Esperanza lifted the edge of the hammock to look at me.

"I thought you might be asleep," she said.

"Not until I finish the best fruit Rubio's ever eaten," I said, holding up a slice of papaya to her.

She sat down and ate the slice, chewing thoughtfully. "A little overripe."

"Like Rubio and the rest of us."

She laughed and flapped her shirt as if to air herself out.

We sat quietly for a moment as I passed her slices of fruit. When she spoke, it was very quietly.

"I've been thinking about Chacimo," she said.

"And?"

"And how things could have gone very differently if we hadn't captured the lieutenant and the bazooka."

"What of it?" I asked. "We could second guess ourselves into surrendering if we followed that train of thought too far. We were successful, the Revolution continues another day, that is all."

"We were lucky," she said, "very lucky, and it is only a matter of time before our luck runs out."

"Do you want to leave?" I asked, "to go back to the organization, or Managua even?"

"No," she said a little angrily, "but I do want us to be smarter."

"How?"

"We need to stop stumbling blindly around the department because once the Guardia starts to hunt us in earnest, it won't be so easy. We need to start to gather intelligence and build a network. I said I would take on this responsibility. I could be a shield for us if only Fósforo would listen." she said, the words all tumbling out.

"You say you've spoken to Fósforo?"

"I've tried, but he won't listen. If I'm going to do this, I need some resources. Some people. I thought that you might try to talk to him."

"I'm not sure he'll listen to me about this either. It's hard to argue against success."

She squeezed my hand. "If he'll listen to anyone, it's you. Would you?"

I nodded, chewing on a big slice of papaya. With the way that she looked at me, there was no way I could say no.

"Thank you," she said, ducking out from under the hammock. "I'll leave you to your nap."

I put down the fruit and tried to get comfortable with my pack behind my head. I quickly dozed off as we chugged slowly upriver. In my mind, I imagined that the cloud of black smoke hanging over Chacimo spread across the rest of the sky until we were blanketed in darkness.

15

THERE WERE TOO MANY CANS aboard the barge for us to carry easily, so we unloaded them onto the northern shore of the river and concealed them in a thick stand of brush. We no longer tried to build a permanent camp. Instead, we moved every few days to a new location that we had scouted out beforehand. This meant that our life was a constant burden of marching, carrying, and hiding, but our spirits were high.

The newcomers who joined us in Chacimo were a mixed bag. Most were malnourished and illiterate. None were very political, although they all knew in their bellies that something was wrong with the country. When Fósforo spoke to them, he gave them the words to express how they had felt for years.

"No country with soil as rich as ours should have a single citizen who goes hungry. Our first aim is to put all land to use to feed the population. And more specifically, for every campesino to have enough land to feed their family," explained Fósforo as he inculcated the new guerrillas. He seemed to know instinctively that the aspiration of every campesino was not for riches or power, but simply to own land. From the soil grew hope.

"I'm not willing to merely die to defend my ideas, but I am willing if that is what it takes to make them a reality. And I ask the same from you," he said.

Fósforo divided the new guerrillas equally between the two platoons, and I did my best to train those assigned to me. As I did before, I began by organizing marches in the areas around our camps. Those with rifles were assigned several men without. They understood that if the armed man was wounded, they were to take up his weapon immediately. This arrangement ensured that the newest recruits were constantly trying to out-do each other to earn a rifle. In truth, I wished that there were enough arms to go around. I remembered what it felt like to be unarmed in battle, and didn't wish that feeling on anyone.

I was kept busy planning this training regime, but my mind would wander during the long marches. There was a continuous buzz within the platoon about our success at Chacimo and about how weak the Guardia seemed in comparison. The new men told us stories of corruption in the town and how Somoza's canning company had exploited generations of their families. One night I asked them why they had never stood up to the company before we arrived. There was a long silence before one of them spoke for the rest.

"Paco, we just never imagined it could be done," said one of the men.

I thought quite often about this lack of imagination and what it meant for the town and its people. The Guardia were sure to return and likely in bigger numbers. Their corruption had not been erased. And with the factory destroyed, I doubted that the company would pay any wages, leaving more hungry mouths than there had been before. Had the townspeople merely exchanged one form of suffering for another? And for those lacking the imagination of those who joined us, what would they do?

I imagined that Fósforo would see it in black and white—they could join the Revolution and survive with us, or stay where they were, even though we had temporarily broken their shackles. I wasn't sure what was right, or what I thought we should do. I kept my thoughts to myself and did my best to make sure that my platoon would be ready to fight when the time came again.

Fósforo met with me and Julio regularly, and one morning after breakfast, he called both of us over to his hammock. He was balanced precariously as he reached down to fish his tobacco pouch out of his knapsack, one dirty foot held up in the air as a counterweight. After he had jammed a pinch of tobacco into his pipe, he tossed me the pouch, and I did the same with my own.

"We need to send a patrol down to the cache of cans again," said Julio. "We'll be out of food in another day or so."

"Your enthusiasm recommends you for the job," said Fósforo from behind a veil of smoke.

"Hardly," said Julio. "It's Paco's turn this time."

"They've done their share," said Fósforo dismissively. "I have two things to discuss. Firstly, I've decided to promote you both to capitán. You need to appoint three lieutenants in your platoons, each to lead a section."

"Does that mean we get a raise?" asked Julio.

"Secondly," continued Fósforo, ignoring him, "I've decided to set up a third platoon. It will be smaller than the other two. They'll be a group I can use as my reserve, and for difficult jobs. All experienced or promising guerrillas."

"Who will lead it?" I asked.

"Who indeed," said Fósforo. "Who do you propose?"

"I would vouch for Rubio," I said, cringing at Fósforo's expression as he heard the words come out of my mouth.

"He's neither experienced nor promising," said Fósforo. "What about First Platoon?"

"My best man is Santiago," said Julio. "But he'd want to take his brother as well, which would leave me with a bunch of babies."

"They'll grow up fast," said Fósforo. Spotting Santiago nearby, he waved him over to join us. "Santi, I have a proposal for you."

"Yes, Comandante?"

"I've decided to set up a third platoon, smaller than the rest. I will only use this platoon for the most dangerous jobs—when the other platoons have already failed, or when asking them to undertake the task would be to ask too much."

"You'd have to be suicidal to sign up for that," said Julio.

Santiago ignored him. "I'd like to join this platoon," he said.

"Actually, I was hoping that you would lead this 'suicide' platoon," said Fósforo.

Santiago smiled. "Can I pick my own men?"

"You can have anyone except your brother," said Fósforo, "and no more than four men from each platoon."

Santiago wasted no time organizing his platoon, asking four of my men, who all agreed to volunteer. When Rubio heard about Santiago's platoon, he came to me, holding his tattered hat in both hands.

"Paco, please let me join this new group," he said.

"Fósforo has said that every man in the platoon has to carry a rifle, and so you can't just yet." Rubio was crestfallen.

"I want to fight," he said. "Fósforo won't speak to me, and I know that you've asked on my behalf."

I felt truly sorry for Rubio. "I'll ask him again."

Rubio shook my hand. "Thank you, brother." He went and sat by himself, as usual, not talking with anyone else in the platoon but me.

I walked back over to where Fósforo was lying in his hammock, scribbling in his journal. I sat down by his hammock and waited for him to finish his train of thought. After a few minutes, he closed his book and slipped it into his breast pocket, the flap of which was missing.

"Plans for our future?" I asked.

"A poem," he said. "I haven't written them since I was in grade school, but lately, they have been appearing in my mind unbidden."

"I have a recommendation for you," I began, not quite sure where to start.

Fósforo used his foot to sway his hammock gently, listening as he stretched in the canvas, nearly touching the trees with his head and feet. "About what?" he asked.

"Two things. We are not using Rubio to his potential . . ."

"I don't want to talk about Rubio," said Fósforo abruptly. "He needs to pay for his grave error."

"Certainly," I said, "but for how long?"

"Until the lesson is learned," said Fósforo.

"Then we are past that point."

"Learned by everyone. He is an example to those who might fail in the future."

"You are robbing the Revolution of the efforts of a good man," I said, my voice carrying a little farther than I would have wished. Two men cooking a pot of rice over the fire looked over at us, but when I returned their look, they turned away.

"What is the other thing?" asked Fósforo.

"Esperanza. She has seen how they do things in the FSLN. Amongst the leadership. We should be using that knowledge and trying harder to gather intelligence about what is going on in the district."

"Is she getting tired of the life in a guerrilla platoon?" asked Fósforo. "I thought that was what she wanted."

"This is not about her wants or needs, or Rubio's, but about what is best for the column. I'm not here to criticize you or to complain, but simply to suggest what I think we should do."

"Have we done so poorly that you need to intervene?" asked Fósforo.

"Not at all," I said, suddenly defensive, "but I worry that we could do better."

Fósforo rolled over in his hammock away from me. "Trust me, Paco. It can only get better from here."

★ ★ ★

We began to send small patrols across the river as far as Palmitos, to lay ambushes and make contact with the campesinos. Slowly, our presence was being felt across the department. Sometimes the patrol would come back with new volunteers, eager to join us. At Julio's urging, we always led them to our camp blindfolded, to be certain that they could not easily desert and betray us.

Santiago began calling his platoon the "Novios de la Muerte,"[8] and they wore black funerary armbands. As macabre as this sounds, it only made everyone else clamber even more to join them. They didn't do any of the routine tasks that the rest of us did, and they lived apart from the other platoons. I only had a dim idea of what tasks Fósforo might assign to them, and Santiago would say nothing about their comings and goings. The first time they were away from camp, they brought back a treasure trove of weapons and ammunition when they returned. When I asked him where these weapons had come from, Santiago just put his finger to his lips and shook his head.

I had named Esperanza as one of my lieutenants within my platoon, and none of the men complained. Although she was still one of the few women in the column, or perhaps because of it, she was treated no differently than the men.

One morning, she and I sat together, spearing pieces of corned beef out of a can with sharpened sticks. At first, eating so much meat had been delightful. After a few weeks, everyone was sick of it.

"It's our turn to pick up supplies at the cache," I said, wiping juice from my mouth with my sleeve.

She gave a mock grimace. "How many more crates are left?"

"Too many, I'm sure."

We ate in silence for a while, until the can was empty. I let her finish it, which she did in loud slurps. When she saw that I was watching her, she was embarrassed.

"I don't know where my appetite comes from," she said.

I could see that her time with us had been good for her. No longer did her shoulder bones stick out through her skin. She was tanned and rounder, and although she never complained before, I could see that the burden of guerrilla life was becoming easier to bear.

I organized the platoon for the journey the next day, leaving all but our essential equipment in camp. Everyone carried an empty

---

[8] *Translators note: "Bridegrooms of Death."*

knapsack to carry food back to the main body. Everyone entitled to a rifle carried one and at least a belt with ammunition pouches as well. We hoped to make the return journey in one long day.

Sitting in my hammock with my rifle across my lap, I waited for my three lieutenants to confirm that they were ready. Fósforo came by, smoking his pipe. When he saw me, he blew smoke rings that drifted up into the trees.

"Almost ready to leave?" he asked.

"Almost."

"I'll come with you today." When he noticed my quizzical look, he clapped me on the shoulder. "Don't worry; I know that you don't need me. Truth is, I'm a little bored," he said.

"Did you bring an empty knapsack?" I asked, "Or are you coming just to supervise?"

He held up one of the filthy canvas bags we had found many weeks ago in the abandoned mine. "Of course," he said, speaking loudly enough for everyone to hear. "Every man is equal when it comes to labour."

We set out in single file, passing the sentry from Julio's platoon at the edge of our encampment. I could smell tobacco, and knew that he had been smoking, which was against our sentry rules. I stopped and accosted him.

"What's your name?" I asked.

"Pelón," he said. He flicked his hand behind his back, and I knew that he had been cupping a cigarette or cigar in it.

"When I come back, I'm going to report you to Julio for smoking on sentry," I said.

He flicked his chin at me. "See what he says to you when you do."

Fósforo had caught up to me. "And what do you think that will be?" he asked.

"I don't know, Comandante," stammered Pelón.

Fósforo kept marching past him, and I followed. "Find that cigarette butt before it starts a fire," I said over my shoulder to Pelón.

When we were out of earshot, Fósforo looked back over his shoulder at me. "Julio's platoon needs more discipline," he said.

"He has his own way to lead them," I replied.

"But is it the right way?" said Fósforo before going back to walking in silence.

The platoon wended its way through the forest, slowly descending. We stayed within the shelter of the trees whenever we could, concealed from view. My plan was to descend to the river and then follow it east until we reached the cache. I wasn't sure of a more direct route and thought this was the best way to avoid getting lost. Julio's platoon had recently spent a day walking in circles looking for the cache. It would have been funny if it hadn't meant a cut to our rations when they came back empty-handed.

It was before midday when we stopped just short of the river and turned east. We crossed a few streams that came down from the mountains to join the river, but none came past our knees. When I saw the rapids that had prevented the boat from carrying on farther up the river, I knew that I could pinpoint the cache. We were making good time as we marched, and before I expected it, the signal came back from the front of the platoon that we had arrived.

Esperanza's section had been in the lead, and she came back to crouch beside me. She spoke in a whisper. "We can see the trees where the cache is. I'll take my whole section and scout ahead." I simply nodded, and she disappeared.

I spread the rest of the platoon out in a line, ready to fight in case Esperanza's section spotted guardsmen or was ambushed. We lay in the brush for a long time before I saw one of her men walk back towards us, waving his hat in one hand to signal that it was clear.

We followed him to where we hid the cache. Esperanza's men had split open several crates and were already loading their backpacks. Looking at what was left, I guessed that there was enough for perhaps one more load after this one.

"We'll need to find another supply to supplement our food," I said to Fósforo.

"Thankfully, there are no more isolated slaughterhouses to raid," he said.

"I couldn't bear another month of corned beef," I agreed.

"Perhaps a chocolate factory next, then."

We both laughed.

We rested near the cache for half an hour, sending a party down to the river to refill our canteens. As I lay on my back, relaxing, I watched clouds gathering against the mountains to our north. They were dark and malevolent looking and sat like crowns of thorns around the distant peaks. I pointed them out to Fósforo, lying next to me with his eyes closed. He blinked and shielded his eyes with his hand.

"It doesn't rain until July in this part of the country," he said.

"Tell that to the clouds."

I got back to my feet and warned my platoon that we would leave in five minutes. They quickly finished eating, put socks and boots back on sore feet, and finished adjusting the loads in their knapsacks. One by one, the tenientes told me that they were ready, and then we started the return journey to camp.

We marched more slowly now, everyone weighed down by as much as they could carry. Fósforo and I stood watching as each section marched past. Rubio struggled with a pack that was so heavy that it looked as if the seams might burst. He kept his head down as he walked in front of us. I was about to speak about him when Fósforo read my thoughts and cut me off.

"Another time," he said, falling in behind the last man in line. I gave up trying to convince him at that moment and instead walked as fast as my own load would allow. I passed man after man as I made my way towards the front of the platoon. I stopped when I was behind Esperanza and fell into line.

I heard the first raindrop strike the trail in front of me, leaving a wet spot in the dirt like a tiny crater. It was followed by another, and then another until the rain was nearly deafening. I could see the rain was even heavier in the hazy sky above the upper slopes, like a grey sheet thrown over the mountain tops. I counted our blessings that we were lower down, where mudslides weren't as much of a problem and hoped that our camp was not being washed away at that very moment.

The path became slippery, and the thick mud clung to our boots, making them heavier than they already were. Even though the rain only last twenty minutes or so, by the end, everyone in the platoon was thoroughly sodden and miserable.

We came to the first of the small streams that we had easily crossed on the way to the cache. Unlike when we had last seen it, the stream was now a torrent, rushing down from the high ground in a churning fury. The head of the platoon stopped at the water's edge, and we began to bunch up along the top of its deep bank. Though only forty feet across, it looked impenetrable.

"We'll wait," I said to those within earshot. "It's the rains. It can't last for long." Everyone took off their packs and found relatively dry places to sit and wait it out. I sent a sentry back along the trail, and a second one down the slope towards the river, and then made myself comfortable as well. Sitting on the knapsack of cans seemed preferable to the wet grass, though others lay down on the ground happily. I took off my wet shirt and tried to wring it out, and some of the others did the same.

When Fósforo reached us, I admit that the platoon looked like hell. Half-dressed and bunched up in a small area, it was more like a summer camp than a military operation. I knew that I had made a mistake, and so tried to take responsibility right away.

"Fósforo, I ordered the halt while we waited for the water to subside."

I could see that he was furious and was barely able to keep himself from yelling. He leaned in close to me and growled an order: "Get this pack of amateurs on their feet and moving again."

I decided to put my shirt back on first before giving orders to the platoon, who had mostly all heard Fósforo's direction anyway. While I was thinking of the right words to say to my men, I heard a loud grunt.

Rubio had lifted four knapsacks, two over each shoulder, and was standing by the water's edge. His back was hunched over as if he might snap in half. He had cut a walking stick for himself while we rested at the cache, and he used it to steady himself as he stepped into the torrent.

"No, Rubio, wait!" I said, but he ignored me.

The water frothed and churned around his hips as he slowly walked forward, carefully keeping his balance with the stick. No one moved to help him, overawed at his willingness to step into the water that had cowed the rest of us. Step by step, he inched forward, grunting and breathing heavily through his nose. The other side of the stream had a steep bank, forcing him to stop when he reached it. He dropped two of the knapsacks onto the top of the bank and then pivoted to look back at us. I could see him smile and look over at Fósforo, and several of the men gave a cheer.

And then, as if by magic, he was gone.

16

IT WAS QUICK. I couldn't be sure what had happened. Rubio must have lost his footing as he pivoted, or been off-balance with the knapsacks over one shoulder, and the rushing water pulled him under in an instant. The cheer at his crossing died on the men's lips, and we all just stared at where he had been.

A primal howl broke the silence. Fósforo pushed past me, plunging into the water and thrashing across the stream to the other side, while we were rooted in place, still stunned. I had one of the men tie a rope to my waist before splashing in after him, cursing myself for not having Rubio do the same. Fósforo held onto the bank and ducked his head underwater, but I was sure that he couldn't see anything. I put my arms around his waist when I reached him to make sure that the current didn't pull him under as well. He emerged from the stream gasping for air before plunging his head under again. I tried to coax him out of the water, but he was inconsolable.

"He's gone," I said, shouting in Fósforo's ear over the noise of the water.

"He can't be," said Fósforo.

Fósforo eventually threw himself onto the far bank, and I climbed out after him. I untied the rope from my waist and tied it to a tree instead. My platoon stood hesitantly on the other bank, unsure of whether to follow me or not.

"We'll wait for the water to subside," I shouted. The platoon watched me sullenly.

When the torrent of water began to slacken, I took several guerrillas downstream towards the river. Fósforo followed us. Partway down, we found the two knapsacks that Rubio had been carrying, wedged in between rocks. The wet canvas was heavy and uncomfortable looking, but Fósforo shouldered both knapsacks without a word. Farther down, we found Rubio's hat caught in a tree branch that touched the water, but we found no sign of Rubio himself. Fósforo took the hat as well and sat down with his back against a tree.

We kept looking for another half an hour, working farther down the slope, but there was no other sign of Rubio. I had the guerrillas follow me back up and take the knapsacks from Fósforo. I sent them back up to join the others and sat down beside Fósforo.

He was turning the hat around in his hands, his fingers finding every hole and tear in it. I saw his face smeared with dirt from where he had wiped away tears, and thought, for a moment, about what to say. Finding nothing that would console him, I kept it simple.

"We have to go."

He nodded miserably.

The platoon finished the hike back to camp very slowly, and in utter silence.

The mood that evening was sullen. Fósforo was nowhere to be found, and I lay in my hammock, neither sleeping nor truly awake. I'm not sure how long I had lain there when I heard the sentry give the whistle that meant a patrol was coming in. I didn't bother to get up—it was on the side of the camp covered by Julio's platoon.

Esperanza walked by but did not look at me. I wanted to speak to her but was unsure what to say, and so let her go in silence. After a few moments, there was a commotion in the centre of the camp, and so I got up. It seemed that everyone was gathering there, though, for what, I could not imagine. I staggered towards the cooking area between the platoons, my legs stiff and sore. Gathered around the small fire were most of the column and two civilian women.

A young woman, in tears, was being held up by an older woman. I didn't recognize either of them. They spoke to Esperanza in hushed tones, and she listened intently, their heads close together.

"Who let these two into camp?" I asked.

"Our patrol went to the farms near Chacimo. We brought them from there," said Tembo, one of Julio's lieutenants.

"But why?" I asked.

"The old woman said she wanted to report a crime, but wouldn't give any more details until she saw our leader," said Tembo.

"A crime by who?" I asked.

Tembo blushed. "They wouldn't say."

"For all you know, these women work for the Guardia," I said angrily.

"We blindfolded them on the way here," replied Tembo.

"Enough, Paco," said Esperanza. "These women are afraid, but still brought their complaint to us, not the Guardia."

"A complaint about what?" I asked.

"About us," she said. "And with good reason. One of them says she was raped."

The older woman stood up straight, keeping her arm around the younger one. She spoke loudly enough for everyone in the column to hear her. "My name is Marina," she said, "and I run the bar in Chacimo. She works for me, and when your men were drinking all my beer, one of them raped her."

"This is Somocista propaganda," said Julio.

"What's your name?" I asked the young woman.

"We've come for justice," said the older woman.

I repeated myself. "Your name?"

"Candelaria, señor," she said, composing herself.

"You are safe here, Candelaria. Do you see the man who attacked you?"

Without hesitation, she looked up and pointed at Julio.

"She lies!" he thundered, taking a step towards her. I put an arm out to stop him.

"Doña, did you see him as well?" asked Esperanza.

"Yes," she said, "It was him." She only glanced at Julio before looking away and crossing herself.

Julio stood fuming in front of the women, seemingly unsure of what to do. I saw that he had his pistol in his hand, held down at his side. With everyone looking at her intensely, Candelaria burst into fresh tears and buried her head in the older woman's shoulder. For a moment, everyone was still.

"And Doña Marina, tell us what exactly she does at the bar," demanded Julio.

Doña Marina straightened up as she spoke. "She's a hostess."

"She's a whore," said Julio, jabbing a finger at the women.

The crowd had gathered in a circle around the women, ringing Julio in as well. He turned to face the rest of us, his pistol still in his hand. "There are half a dozen men here who will swear that I committed no crime."

No one spoke up, and the sound of Candelaria's sobbing had everyone on edge.

"Is this what your justice looks like?" asked Marina. She practically spat her last words, making us even more uncomfortable.

To our surprise, Fósforo appeared behind us. "Place him under arrest," he said, pushing through the crowd. Under the brim of Rubio's hat, which he wore, his eyes burned brightly. The Novios, mixed throughout the crowd, leapt into action as one and grabbed Julio, pulling his pistol from his grasp, and pinning his arms to his sides.

"This accusation is nothing but lies," spat Julio.

"We shall see," said Fósforo, stalking back off into the woods to be alone. A pall hung over the camp as we waited for what would happen next.

When Fósforo ordered us to relocate again, there was none of the light-hearted banter that often preceded a move. I sat with Fósforo, who swung in his hammock, Rubio's hat pulled down over his eyes.

"There has to be a trial," I said. "With a jury, and not just of guerrillas. We should have ordinary campesinos too. To show them what justice looks like."

"Justice would have been shooting him on the spot. Do you doubt the women's story?" said Fósforo.

"Of course, I don't. But shooting a man in cold blood doesn't look like justice. Let the process take its course."

"For who's sake? Yours? So that you can feel better about it all?"

"For the sake of the men in his platoon, who trusted Julio. If he's guilty, they need to see that he was wrong and that you don't have the power to have men shot out of hand," I said.

Fósforo swung in silence for a moment. When he sat up, his eyes were cloudy and dark. "Are you so sure that I don't?

We sat staring at each other for a long moment as I chose my words. I hadn't yet decided how to convince him that he was wrong when he looked away and spoke again.

"I leave it to you to organize this. But quickly."

"Of course," I said. "I'll set it up at our next campsite, and we'll bring in the locals to see justice served."

Fósforo nodded.

"But don't be surprised if the jury doesn't act the way you want them to. They may not ask for a death sentence. It's not easy to look a man in the eye and condemn him to death on the spot."

"It's easy to lose sight of what we are doing," said Fósforo. He slipped down off his hammock and slung his rifle over his shoulder. It had become his habit to go for long walks during the day, to exactly where I didn't know. He strode off into the woods again without another word.

We quickly organized the move to the new camp. Juan acted as the commander of the First Platoon in Julio's absence, though he was careful to emphasize that it was temporary. Julio had his hands tied behind his back and a rope around his neck. He was led by one of the Novios, with the remainder in a tight group around him. Santiago had ordered him gagged after he complained long and bitterly about his treatment, causing some of the First Platoon men to start griping as well. Although he could no longer speak, Julio's eyes flashed with anger when they led him past me.

The new camp was in a good location, at what had once been a farm. There were lots of trees for cover, a spring nearby, and the ruins of a stone farmhouse that we cleaned out to use as a shelter. When Fósforo saw it, he was quick to tell us what to use it for.

"This will be the jail for Julio."

The walls were sturdy enough, and we could guard the one entrance. It saved us the hassle of the platoons fighting over who might use it as well. And I suppose that it made holding one of our own as a prisoner seem more official, somehow more civilized, in a way that tying him to a tree did not.

I spoke with Juan and my own lieutenants about the need to identify any campesinos within a half-day march who we could bring to be the jury and witness the trial. We organized ourselves so that, over the course of a few days, short patrols went out in every direction to find them. And with every patrol that returned came more recruits.

The loss of the factory in Chacimo had caused nearly every plantation in the area to stop hiring mozos jornaleros, creating a mass of landless and hungry men. Some of them left the department to find work elsewhere, others scraped by as best they could, but a sizeable portion of them had begun to seek us out. Unrest throughout the countryside continued to grow, and so our numbers swelled. By the time that we were well-established at the farm, the column numbered close to a hundred men and women. The two women from Chacimo had elected to stay with us as well.

With our swollen numbers, it became more of an effort to organize ourselves, and the section leaders in each platoon were very busy. I was doing my rounds, checking on each of them, when Esperanza pulled me aside.

"Fósforo has made a decision," she said.

"About what?"

"That the column needs an intelligence officer."

"Of course, it does," I said. "We've both told him that."

"He finally sees the need to have someone other than himself to collect all the patrol reports and make sense of them."

"And so, he picked you for the job?"

"Do you object?"

I hesitated. Picking Esperanza made sense to me, but I liked having her in the platoon. "If you want the job, then, of course, I won't object."

"Then I'll take that as enthusiastic support," she replied.

My other two lieutenants were not as experienced as Esperanza, but they were still very capable. One was a guerrilla who had joined us outside of La Trinidad, a youth with boundless energy who had quickly been named Huracán. The other, a mozo jornalero who had joined us in Chacimo, had a weathered face that made him seem decades older than he likely was. He had a long white plastic rosary that he wore around his neck, yellowed from ground-in dirt. The others began calling him Papi before we'd even thought to give him a nickname, and it stuck.

"You should pick Iván to replace me," she said.

"He's only been with us for a few weeks. Will the more experienced men follow him?"

"They already look to him when I'm not there. I think they would choose him themselves if they could," she said.

I called Iván over to speak with me. He was also a mozo jornalero, but much younger than Papi. He was lanky and spoke slowly, but he also exuded confidence in a way I couldn't put my finger on.

"I need to replace Esperanza in your section," I said. "Will you take the job?"

He looked briefly back and forth between us. "She shouldn't be replaced," he said.

"I have another job that the column needs me to do," said Esperanza.

"In that case, yes," he said. He waited for a moment to see if I had any further instructions for him. When I didn't say anything, he nodded and walked back to where the section was bivouacked.

"Big talker," I said.

"When he does speak, the others listen," said Esperanza.

"I'll keep that in mind."

She had already packed her things, and with the leadership of her section assured, she carried her knapsack to the other side of the camp, setting up close to Fósforo.

That night, I gathered my three lieutenants and worked out a patrolling plan that everyone agreed was fair. With that out of the way, I could concentrate on trying to organize the trial. Never having seen one before, it was left to my imagination to determine how it would run. In lieu of a code of laws, I had to try to determine the universal values against which Julio had trespassed. It seemed easy enough until I tried to write it down, and my thoughts became muddy. I was scratching some ideas into my notebook when Juan appeared with several of his men.

"Comrade Paco, we come bearing gifts," said Juan.

I was a little wary, unsure how the First Platoon men felt about Julio's incarceration, but still managed a smile.

"What can you buy for a man who has everything?" I asked, gesturing at my hammock and knapsack.

"Everything but one of these," said Juan as one of his men brought out a guitar from behind his back. I was speechless. "Honestly, we found it, and immediately thought of you."

I sat up and took the guitar in my hands, giving it a few experimental strums. It was out of tune, and pretty beat up, but it would play. It felt like the body of a familiar lover in my hands.

"Thank you, comrades," I said, slipping off my hammock to embrace them one by one. "This is what my spirit needed."

17

I ORGANIZED THE TRIAL to the best of my ability, at least on paper. We had fixed its start date to a few days in the future. I was no longer comfortable staying in one place for that long, but it seemed necessary to stage-manage all the details. Fósforo was disinterested in what he saw as minutiae, not even wanting me to tell him about it.

"Just tell me when it's finished," he said dismissively.

After the trial was done, I planned to send the jurors home again and break camp immediately. We'd move during the night, running no greater risk of the Guardia finding us than necessary. Everyone agreed that it was best not to stay here longer than we had to once the location was widely known.

"What if they find him guilty but want to imprison him?" asked Santiago. "What then?"

"We'll cross that bridge when we come to it," I said, "but I can't see us running a jail."

"Those women don't have any doubt that it was him," said Esperanza.

"Let's wait for the process to take its course," I said.

It had become fairly commonplace for patrols to return with volunteers in tow, blindfolded and often holding onto a knotted rope that they started to take with them for just that purpose. A patrol came in while we were all speaking, bringing with them a new string of volunteers. We were surprised that amongst the typical campesinos, they were also leading a tall blond man with a heavy satchel.

"Come with me, and I shall make you *fishers of men*," joked Juan as he led the man towards us. "There is someone you should meet."

Juan pulled the blindfold off the man's face. He stood blinking and shading his eyes.

"This is Paco, the man you need to speak to," said Juan.

The blond man held out his hand. "I'm a journalist with Radio France Internationale," he said affably. "Jean-François Passereau."

His Spanish was a bit odd but understandable. For the moment, I ignored him and pulled Juan aside. "Where did you find him?" I asked.

"We heard about him from some farmers outside of La Trinidad. He had been asking around, trying to arrange an interview with a 'guerrilla.' We found him on the road in a hired car and brought him here through the usual route."

"How do you know that he's not working for the government?"

"He had this," said Juan, handing me a letter. It was typed on thin paper and had smudged in the humid air. It was a letter of introduction to any members of the opposition, signed by Jaime Marroquín.

"That seems a bit much," I said. "Just the kind of thing a government spy would fake."

Juan shrugged. "He seems legitimate to me."

"How did you get this?" I asked Passereau, holding the letter in front of him.

"My editor is a member of the Party in France," he said. "I don't know exactly how the letter made it to us, but it was given to me in France to carry here."

"If you could manage to get this letter, why couldn't you manage to set up a meeting before you came as well?"

Passereau looked embarrassed. "It was set up, but the meet-up never took place. Maybe the contact was arrested," he said. "Or I might have misunderstood the details."

I waved the letter at him. "And how do I know it's not a fake?" I asked.

"I can't convince you of that," he said, "but imagine for a moment what it would have meant for me if they caught me with that letter. I've taken a great risk coming here."

That was true, though it didn't make the letter more real.

"Wait here," I said, leaving the Frenchman standing alone.

I walked across the camp to where Fósforo had set up his hammock. I saw that Esperanza had set her hammock up using one of the same trees he had. With a small fire in between them, it made this part of the camp seem homier than the others. Fósforo was lying in his hammock, reading. He sat up when he saw me.

"Have you ever read this?" he asked, holding up a copy of *Don Quixote*.

"Never," I said. "What's it about?"

"A man whose ideals are so strong that he tries to make the world conform to them."

"That doesn't sound like light reading."

"It's very funny. I'll give it to you when I'm done. I've read it a dozen times, at least, starting when I was a kid," he said.

I crooked my thumb back towards the middle of the camp. "Juan has brought in a journalist here who wants an interview with our leader. He's from France."

"A long way from Paris," said Fósforo.

I handed the letter of introduction to Fósforo, who scanned it before folding it up and handing it to Esperanza.

"Does he speak Spanish?" asked Fósforo.

"More or less," I said, "though it sounds like he's talking out of his nose."

"This I have to see for myself," said Fósforo, climbing off his hammock.

"Are you sure it's a good idea? We could give him anyone to interview, and he'd be none the wiser."

"If he can get our message out to the world, it's important that

I speak to him."

Esperanza held up the letter. "I want to speak to him as well," she said.

We walked together to where Passereau was waiting. He stood up as we approached.

"Jean-François? I'm Fósforo." The two shook hands. "And this is Esperanza."

He gently shook her hand. "Enchanté." He turned back to Fósforo. "Are you the leader?" he asked.

"I lead this column," said Fósforo.

"And how many men is that?" asked Passereau.

"No more questions like that," I said. "Nothing that the government could use against us."

"Of course," said Passereau, though I could tell that he was disappointed. "Can I interview you about the Revolution in general?"

"Of course," said Fósforo, leading him away to the shade of a nearby bunch of trees. Once they were out of earshot, I grabbed Juan by the arm. "Did you search him? Thoroughly?"

"Of course," said Juan. "I wouldn't bring just anyone into . . ."

"Get a few of your men to watch over him while he speaks with Fósforo. Armed," I said.

"Of course," said Juan as he went to find a few men to put onto the task.

"His wandering here is a stroke of luck," said Esperanza.

"How so?"

"He can get a message out for us, straight back to Managua."

"Should we trust him with that?"

"He won't be able to make any more sense of the code than you can," she said, laughing.

"I'll make sure that you can speak to him before he leaves," I said. Esperanza squeezed my arm and went back to where her hammock was hanging. I walked over to where Fósforo and Passereau were sitting and found a spot nearby where I could both see and hear them.

Passereau had pulled a tape recorder out of his bag and had plugged a microphone into it. He sat cross-legged in front of Fósforo, the tape recorder on his lap. He turned it on and began to speak. "This is Jean-François Passereau, deep in the countryside of Nicaragua, for Radio France Internationale. I am speaking with one of the leaders of the guerrilla movement engaged in a struggle with the government, Comandante 'Fósforo.'"

Passereau shifted position to get the microphone between himself and Fósforo.

"First, let me ask, what was your profession before the Revolution?" asked Passereau.

"I'm a medical doctor," said Fósforo.

"You've come a long way, then," said Passereau.

"As must every citizen who longs for justice."

Passereau paused for a moment as he adjusted the settings on his tape recorder. "To begin with, what is the purpose of your uprising?"

"That's simple," said Fósforo. "We want a country free from foreign influence, that can develop in a manner that is best for its own people. We want a country where every person is free from worry about where they will find their next meal or whether they can afford the medical treatment they need. A country where every person is free to develop to their highest potential."

"I've been told that you have a man under arrest in this camp awaiting trial. Are you building a new legal system as well?"

Fósforo glanced at me as he spoke. "There is a man, one of our own, accused of crimes. He will be tried by a jury of the People. But this is not about legal reform. Everything I have spoken about, at its most basic level, is about justice. In one word, that is what we are fighting for."

"That sounds like a high ideal. So why not seek it through the ballot box? Or don't you believe in peaceful political change?"

"As to whether armed resistance is the only answer to the condition of the People of this country, we have no other path. And we think that, in the majority of Latin American countries, there is no choice other than armed struggle. It seems to be the same situation in many other countries in Asia and Africa as well."

"Why is that?" asked Passereau.

"Imperialism counts on the fact that by joining with the oligarchy in every country, using every means possible, they can prevent the democratic triumph of the Revolution. Imperialism is hanging the common people with a rope of their own making that can only be cut by armed struggle. We didn't choose the armed struggle as the best path; it's the path that the oppressors imposed on us."

"And have the People chosen to join you, or are you fighting for them on your own?"

"The public has two choices—to suffer or to fight. More and more, they are deciding to fight," said Fósforo.

"But the government forces seem to have every advantage, and they have requested that the United States send advisors as well as arms and munitions," said Passereau.

"It's true that our enemy has massive economic and technological resources at their disposal. Whereas we have only the resources of the terrain we live on, and most importantly, the social resources of the People themselves, to overcome these advantages. Exploited people, both workers and campesinos, motivated by a just cause and strong moral considerations, can endure privations and live in the most difficult conditions. That is what we are doing, in order to walk the only path to victory."

"But assuming that you defeat the current government and install a new one, what then?"

"Our goals are simple. To fill the mountains with roads, to provide proper living conditions for every citizen, to eradicate ignorance, to let every person benefit from the fruits of their own labour, to advance as a society in every field. We will no longer live as a vassals to foreign oligarchs. And to prepare to defend what we build."

"And so how long have you been a Sandinista?"

Fósforo looked indignant. "I'm not part of any party."

"Does this not put you, in practical terms, in the communist camp?"

"That's your label, not mine," said Fósforo, "I'm a humanist.

For Nicaragua or any other country to allow latifundismo to flourish is madness. Allowing the majority of our country's arable land to be owned and misused by a small group of families is a kind of colonialism that sucks the life from society and prevents it from developing in any positive direction. As we move forward, we will work along two fronts. There is the creative impulse to carry out the Revolution to its logical conclusions, and the defensive one to ensure the continuation of what we build, in the face of any aggression we might face."

"And if you are victorious, do you intend to export the Revolution to other countries?"

"I don't believe that revolutions are exportable: revolutions are created by oppressive conditions which Latin American governments, aided by the imperialists, exercise against their peoples. From this comes rebellion, just as we see here in Nicaragua. We are not the ones who create revolutions. It is the imperialist system and its allies, internal allies, who create revolution."

"So, you only intend to liberate the People of Nicaragua, and nothing more?" asked Passereau.

"I am not a liberator," said Fósforo. "Liberators do not exist. The People liberate themselves."

"The government has called you, and other guerrilla leaders, 'bandits, opportunists, and adventurers.' How would you respond?"

"I am none of those things," said Fósforo. "I might accept being called an adventurer, only one of a different sort: one who risks his skin to prove his platitudes."

Passereau clicked the tape recorder off and looked at Fósforo with a smile. "Thank you for that, Comandante, there is a lot of good material there." The two men shook hands.

"Get our message out to the world," said Fósforo as he walked back to his hammock.

Passereau wanted to remain to witness the trial as well, but I insisted that he leave.

"To get the interview into the news," I said to him, though I had my own reasons as well. Juan's platoon prepared to send out another patrol, intending to leave right away. I told them to escort Passereau back to the main road south of the river near where they had found him. I made sure that Esperanza had time to speak with him privately, and I saw that she passed him a slip of paper. I hope he understood that being found with that paper, decipherable or not, would be a death sentence. Before he left, he was allowed to take a few group photos of some of us. Everyone covered their faces so that they couldn't be identified.

Fósforo and I stood together as the patrol left, Passereau stopping to shake our hands as they passed.

"Bon voyage," said Fósforo.

"Patria o muerte," replied Passereau.

We watched them walk into the forest for a moment before we spoke.

"You've been reading a lot," I said.

"How so?" asked Fósforo.

"Did you listen to yourself during that interview? You sounded like a professor, not a guerrilla."

Fósforo stiffened a little. "Everything I said is true."

"You used so many words I couldn't even tell," I said. When I saw his face tighten again, I clapped him on the shoulder. "I'm just pulling your leg."

"It's just that I've been thinking," he said. "About everything that we've seen, about where this all goes."

"Well, someone needs to be thinking," I said. "It might as well be you."

He laughed and ran his hand through his matted hair. "I'm sorry, Paco. I'm not myself," he said.

"Why? What have you got to worry about?" I said laughingly. "But I know I, for one, didn't want him watching this trial."

"It's true. There's no need to broadcast the fact that there was looting and rape," he said.

"Seeing that there was a trial wouldn't have been a bad story,"

I said. "But I was more worried about him witnessing the results."

"Do you mean an acquittal?"

"I mean an execution," I said. "If things don't run smoothly, if it looks like a kangaroo court, then we don't want him to witness an unjust punishment."

"There is no way that punishing Julio could be unjust," said Fósforo.

"He hasn't even been convicted yet," I said.

"Are you saying he didn't do it?" asked Fósforo.

"I'm saying we haven't heard the evidence, for and against. There's a process."

"Justice needn't be as rigid as you think it should be," said Fósforo, before walking away.

That evening, I was restless and walked over to the ruined farmhouse. It was dark, and the man guarding Julio did not have a fire. He stood up as I approached, and I recognized him as one of the newer recruits.

"Capitán," he said awkwardly.

"Relax," I told him. "I'm just here to check on the prisoner."

He pointed into the ruin with a tilt of his head and retook his seat against the outside of the stone wall. I walked through the empty doorway to find Julio sitting against a shattered supporting pole. His elbows were tied together behind his back, and he was tethered to the pole by a short rope that ended in a loop around his neck.

"Forgive me if I don't stand," said Julio.

I squatted down beside him, my face level with his. He looked rough, like he hadn't slept in days, maybe longer. He looked worse than he had the morning after we had escaped the ambush that killed Braulio. He must have seen how I was looking at him because he turned his face away.

"Come to gloat?" he asked.

"Just come to check in," I said.

"I'm tied up well enough if that's what you mean."

"Of course, that's not what I mean," I said, sitting down.

"Listen, just fuck off," he said. "I don't want your sympathy, either."

I sighed heavily. "I don't know if you're guilty or not, but you have my word that you'll get a fair trial," I said.

Julio looked up at me suddenly, his eyes red under his scraggly hair, and he laughed. "I've always known that Fósforo was a fool, but I thought that you knew better."

"Knew better how?"

"That you knew what was getting built by this movement."

"A just society," I said. "One that doesn't hang people in the streets."

Julio shook his head. "Can't you see it already? You're speaking like the underdog, crying for justice. But every little bit of power that Fósforo gains corrupts him. If the Revolution is ever successful, you'll be no better than the men you depose. The mighty rivers of milk and honey that the Revolution promises are just false advertising." He went back to looking at the dirt at his feet, tugging on the ropes that bound him. I realized that it was humiliating for me to see him like this, so I stood to leave.

"There will be a fair trial," I said with conviction.

"No such thing," said Julio. "A rey muerto, rey puesto."[9]

As I walked out of the ruin, the guard leapt to his feet. I waved at the guard to sit down again and went back to where my platoon was camped. They were sitting together around a low fire, chatting and joking around. I ignored them and climbed into my hammock. They saw me pass, and their chatter quietened down for a few minutes until one of them approached me.

"Paco?"

"Yes?" I didn't move from where I lay.

"Is it true that the Novios brought you a guitar?"

"Yes."

"Would you play for us?" he asked.

"Not tonight," I said.

The man hesitated, swallowing his disappointment. "Of course." He went back to sit with the others around the fire.

---

[9] *Translator's note: "A king dies, and is replaced by another."*

I lay in my hammock for a while, listening to their voices. It was hard to tell who everyone was, but then I heard Esperanza's laugh. I swung out of the hammock and took the guitar from under the tarp that I had used to wrap it carefully. I gave it a few gentle strums, my fingers instantly finding their position on the neck. I walked towards my platoon, singing and playing softly so that I was almost on top of them before they heard me. I had thought of playing a revolutionary song for them but instead began by playing an old favourite.

"Besame, besame mucho, como si fuera ésta noche . . ."

18

THE COLUMN WAS REORGANIZED, with more guerrillas assigned to join the Novios, and a few to work for Esperanza as what she called her escopeteros.[10] Santiago chose young, enthusiastic men who had distinguished themselves in some way to join his platoon, and it remained the most coveted position in the column. Esperanza's criteria were harder to discern, all of her recruits seeming unremarkable, including men and women, young and old.

When I asked her about her thinking, she laughed at me. "I try to pick the guerrillas who look least like guerrillas," she said, "the ones best able to survive on their own, and the ones least likely to try to be heroes."

However she chose them, it was clear she knew what she was doing. In a short period of time, information began to flow to us from all directions. The column suddenly seemed less isolated. She dutifully questioned every escopetero when they returned to camp, keeping track of their answers in a children's notebook she had found somewhere. She'd then transcribe their answers onto another sheet where she tried to piece together a picture of the situation in the department. Waiting for her to brief us one day, Fósforo and I both hung over her shoulders.

---

[10] *Translator's note: a lightly-armed scout.*

"Don't you have something better to do?" she asked.

"Truthfully, I don't," said Fósforo, fingering the holes in Rubio's hat.

"What have you figured out?" I asked.

She put down the stub of her pencil and closed her book. "That we need to send out more scouts," she said. "There's too much we don't know."

"You must have learned something," I said.

"Only bits of this and that. But they're doing the best they can," said Esperanza.

"In war," said Fósforo, "one's best often isn't good enough." He stormed off into the bush for one of his long walks.

"We're getting good information from your escopeteros, even if you can't patch it together into a bigger picture yet. It's important that we have eyes all around," I said.

"As hard as it is for those eyes to see what they see."

We heard a lot of stories about the mistreatment of civilians at the hand of the Guardia. All across the department, and indeed, the country, young men and women suspected of rebel sympathies were being arrested, or simply disappearing. In one instance, we found some youths who had been arrested—shot in the head, their bodies pitched into a ravine.

Even with the disappearances aside, food was getting more scarce and life more difficult for the campesinos. Sometimes, Esperanza's reports made my blood boil, and it was all I could do to remain still and listen. We all agreed that we had to do more than just fight—we needed to take social action, even with our limited resources.

The first initiative was Esperanza's idea, and it was a popular one. She convinced Fósforo to start coming with some patrols again, not as our leader, but as a doctor. Many of the campesinos in the small villages we visited had never seen a doctor, much less one that was free.

We would arrive unannounced and set up a clinic under a tree or in someone's home. Nearly the whole village would line up to see him, all with ailments from imaginary to serious. He still wore Rubio's hat, a ragged and almost ridiculous thing to be truthful, but no one ever said anything. What the campesinos thought, I could only guess, but even the poorest of them would not present themselves in public with such a hat, I'm sure.

I watched Fósforo work, and I realized why they wanted to see him more than anything: he listened. No matter who they were, he listened to them with such serious intent that they seemed to grow in stature as I watched. We distributed what little medicine we had when needed, but the real power of those visits was in showing that we cared. Fósforo, however, was still his difficult self.

"You're like Christ himself," croaked an ancient woman who Fósforo had treated.

"I'm not a Christ," he replied while bandaging a weeping sore on her arm. "On the contrary, I fight for the things I believe in, with all the weapons at my disposal. I then try to leave the other man dead so that I don't get nailed to a cross or anything else for that matter." She quickly crossed herself, stunned into silence.

On one such visit, in a village so insignificant that it didn't appear on our map at all, it was mid-day, and Fósforo was only about half-way through the line of patients. The rest of the patrol were spread around outside the village to provide security. I kept a few men inside the village as well, though I didn't expect any trouble.

One of the newer tenientes, Papi, was with me. I gestured at the mud-brick and thatch-roofed homes around us. "Is this what it's like where you're from?"

"Pretty much," he said, "though I think this village is nicer."

"How so?"

"They've got pigs," he said. I hadn't really paid attention, but he was right. Nearly every house had a pig in a pen or tied up outside. "We mostly just had chickens."

We were still waiting in the shade of one of the houses when one of the village's older women approached us. She wore a long skirt and loose blouse that was typical in the region, her thick grey hair tied up with a scarf. Holding onto her hand was a young boy of maybe six or seven. One of our bandages was wrapped tightly around his head, covering one eye.

"Señor," she said nervously.

"Yes, Doña, what more can we do for you?"

She spoke very quietly so that I had to lean in to hear what she was saying. Her eyes shifted back and forth as she spoke, looking to see who was watching.

"Señor, a week ago, a very bad man came to the village. A stranger."

I waited for her to continue, but she had stopped. "How is it that he is a bad man?" I asked.

"He was not dressed like a soldier, but he worked for the Guardia. A chivato," she hissed.[11]

"And what did he want?"

"He was asking about your men and looking for volunteers to act as guides."

"And what was he told?"

"Nothing, Señor, nothing," she said hastily. "But I think that later, one of the men of the village may have seen him more privately." She lowered her voice even farther. "They say he was willing to pay with coins of silver." She crossed herself at the implication.

"And who was it?" I asked her.

"His house is not in the village, exactly," she said, "but is a little farther away." She indicated the general direction with a crooked finger. "Most everyone here knows, flies can't enter a closed mouth. But not him."

Fósforo was still busy with his patients, so I did not disturb him. I took Papi and another man with me and followed a faint track from the village in the direction the woman had indicated. We walked for about ten minutes before coming upon a ramshackle hut, made entirely of wood cut from the forest.

"Hello!" I said, standing a respectful distance from the door. We

---

[11] *Translator's note: an informer.*

heard scraping noises from inside, and then the door was pushed open by an old campesino wearing nothing but filthy pants held up by a rope belt.

"What do you want?" he said, one hand still on the door.

"We are running a clinic nearby, and we wanted to be sure that you knew," I said. "It's free, and we have some medicine to share as well."

"I'm not sick." The man turned and started to close the door behind him.

"A question," I said, stepping quickly forward to grasp the door before it closed. "Have you seen any Guardia patrols near here in the past few weeks?"

I saw then that one of his eyes was milky and nearly opaque. The other stared at me, malevolently. "What did they say in the village?" he asked.

"Whatever they've said, I want to know for sure." I waved the other two men forward, and they pushed past the campesino and into his home.

"Thieves!" he shouted.

"We aren't going to steal anything," I said. "We're just looking."

"For what? An army hiding under my bed?" he spat.

There wasn't much in the filthy house, so it did not take us long to search it thoroughly. The campesino watched us as we worked, and I watched him to see if he would betray himself. His face was a mask, marked by profound distaste. I was sure that there was nothing to be found when Papi began digging into the dirt floor by the base of one of the shack's support poles. The campesino lunged at him when he saw what he was doing, though I yanked him back by grabbing the rope around his waist.

"As I thought," shouted the campesino. "Thieves!"

Only a few inches down, Papi found a rough leather bag, from which he poured a stream of silver córdobas. I let the campesino go, and he fell to the ground to collect them.

"That's the same place my father used to hide his money," explained Papi.

"And how would a man such as you come to have that kind of money?" I asked.

The campesino looked up guiltily. "I don't have to explain anything to you. Rob me or keep to your word, but in either case, get out!"

"He is a chivato," said Papi. "That's the only way he could have gotten that money."

"I'm no such thing," said the campesino defiantly.

I nodded at Papi, who didn't move. "Encourage him to remember," I said pointedly. When Papi hesitated again, I kicked the man myself. "He's a chivato, a worm."

Papi kicked the man in the stomach, harder than I had, his rosary swinging around wildly. The old man rolled over onto his back with his arms around his knees.

"Fuck you both!" howled the campesino in pain.

I nodded at Papi, and he kicked the chivato again in the ribs. The old man tried to roll out of the way, but there wasn't enough room in his shack to do so. As Papi kicked him again, he moaned like a wounded animal.

"Lift him up," I said, and Papi placed his rifle under the man's chin and hauled him to his knees, choking him. The man looked frightened now.

"They made me talk. I didn't want to," he sputtered.

"Talk about what?" I asked.

The campesino's face was turning purple, and he couldn't seem to force any more words out of his mouth. I gave a signal, and Papi let him drop to the floor. He lay there, his hands grasping his neck and gasping for air.

"About . . . you," he said. "About . . . your camp . . . what routes you take."

"And how would you know anything about that?" I asked. "Have you been watching us?"

"No!" he said quickly. "Everyone knows some things. I know where the fords in the river are that can be used by a man, and which by a horse. Things like that."

"And what did you tell them?"

"Nothing!" he said.

Papi picked up a coin off the floor. "This is a lot of silver for nothing."

"They threatened me. And I told them I could lead them across the river to your camp. God help me, I didn't want to." Tears streamed down his face.

I didn't feel any sympathy for this man, who gave in to threats and the temptation of money when so many others had not—watching him cry didn't improve my opinion of him.

"Death to traitors," said Papi, looking at me for approval. The old campesino still lay on the ground and had curled around Papi's feet, begging for his life.

"Not today," I said. "Not today," a little louder so that the man could hear me. Papi gave him another kick, and he rolled over towards me. I crouched down to speak to him. "When are you leading the Guardia across the river?"

"In two days," he said. "But I won't! I'll run away instead."

"No, my friend," I said, "you will do exactly as you promised. Where are you going to have them cross?"

"At the Vadito," he said.

"I've never heard of it."

"It's close. Everyone calls it the Vadito," he said.

"You're going to tell me where it is," I said.

"I will, I will."

I bent down to look right in the man's eye. "And you are going to do as you promised them, without mentioning this conversation, or we'll show you what happens to traitors."

I chose not to mention anything to Fósforo until we had left the village and were marching back to our camp. When the old man explained in greater detail the ford he planned to use with the Guardia, I knew which one he meant. We often used a more difficult ford that was better-concealed, but I had the man leading our group take us across the Vadito instead.

"Why the change of direction?" asked Fósforo.

"There is a traitor in the village, who has agreed to guide the Guardia across the river to our camp," I said.

Fósforo stopped and grabbed me by the collar. "And he lives?"

I clapped him on the shoulder playfully, but he didn't let go. "How else would he be able to lead them into a trap?"

Fósforo's eyes flickered with comprehension, and he let go of me. "Why didn't you tell me when we were in the village?"

"I didn't want any of the villagers to overhear. And besides, Doctor Fósforo was busy."

"Even when I'm working as a doctor, I'm still a Comandante."

"I've never said you weren't. You didn't need to know then, and I'm telling you now."

"Next time, I'll decide whether and when I need to know," he said petulantly. "Understand?"

"Understood."

We walked on for a while before he spoke again. "So, tell me what you're thinking."

As we marched, I told him what we should do. By crossing at the Vadito today, I hoped to leave tracks that would give the impression that the Guardia had found one of our routes. We could ambush them there and use the river to split their forces. We'd draw the vanguard across the river, where we would hit them alternately from all sides. Whenever they advanced, we would withdraw and strike them from an unexpected direction.

"It will be like they are a bull trying to fight flies," I concluded.

"We'll have them dancing a minuet," agreed Fósforo. "When will they come?"

"The day after tomorrow."

Fósforo gave a low whistle. "Not much time."

"Thankfully, we don't need much."

"What about the trial?" asked Fósforo.

For a moment, I was surprised that he was interested. "We'll just have to postpone it," I said. "We can't risk getting ourselves trapped here by the Guardia."

"We can do the trial tonight, and then it's over with," said Fósforo.

"It's not justice unless it's seen to be done," I said. "We need to bring in a jury and witnesses from the villages."

"There's no time for that," said Fósforo.

"There is if we postpone it."

Fósforo said nothing more about the trial, and instead, we marched the rest of the way back in silence.

When we arrived at camp that night, Fósforo called a meeting of all the leaders in the column. We gathered by his hammock and sipped on weak tea made on a low fire built for the meeting. Word on the purpose of the meeting had already spread throughout the column. Everyone was apprehensive.

When we were all seated facing Fósforo, he began to speak: "Twice now the Guardia has attacked and destroyed our camp," he said, immediately putting into words what was most worrisome. "The first time, when our leader was Braulio, was a disaster. Nearly a hundred men died."

He let his last words sink in, his countenance grave.

"The second time we had evacuated everything of value before they reached our camp, but it was a close-run thing. This time," he said, "it will be different." He nodded at me.

"The chivato is going to lead the Guardia across the river at the ford the locals call the Vadito," I said. "We don't know how large the enemy will be or exactly what equipment he will bring, but to cross there, he'll have to be on foot or horseback."

"Are we going to keep him from crossing?" asked Juan.

"Not exactly," I said. "Once roughly half of their force is across, my platoon will hit their lead elements, and keep up a healthy fire on the river itself to discourage the remainder from trying to cross. Once they start pushing, though, we won't be able to stop them, and so we'll fall back."

"And what about my platoon?" asked Juan.

"You are going to wait for Paco's group to withdraw, and as

the Guardia starts to pursue, you are going to attack them from the flank," said Fósforo. "And as soon as they turn to focus on you, then you must withdraw as well."

"And then the Novios attack?" asked Santiago.

"Exactly, you'll attack them from behind, and then it will be our turn again, over and over again until they can't tell up from down."

"And so, when does it end?" asked Juan.

"If we haven't defeated them by sunset, everyone withdraws. We will move west and link up by the river again," said Fósforo.

Everyone took a moment to digest this plan. There were nods all around as the idea sunk in.

"We've learned a lot since the last time they tried to destroy our camp. This time, the hunter becomes the prey," said Fósforo. "Tomorrow night, we will move into position and wait."

The meeting broke up, and the other leaders returned to their platoons. Esperanza had been silent throughout the discussion, listening from just outside the circle of light around the fire. She joined Fósforo and me when the others had left.

"Are you sure about this plan?" she asked us.

"I'm sure that it's better than letting them chase us off again," said Fósforo.

"Do you have any information from your network about how large a force the Guardia will put together?" I asked.

"No," she said, "this is all a surprise to me, and we don't have time to collect much new information. I'm going to send two escopeteros to try to watch the Guardia advance, but they won't be able to give more than an hour or two of advance notice."

"This intelligence network of yours needs work," said Fósforo.

"It needs to know more about your plans earlier than the day before," said Esperanza.

"We know what we need to know for now," I said, giving Esperanza's arm a squeeze. "There's no sense putting anyone at risk for this information."

"Everyone's at risk all the time," said Esperanza.

"You know what I mean," I said.

"I need to brief my people," said Esperanza as she walked off into the darkness of the camp.

I wanted to go after her, but Fósforo held me back, ploughing on with business.

"There's one other thing we need to discuss," he said. "The trial."

I had momentarily forgotten about Julio. "We've already discussed this. It can wait until we make a new camp," I said. "It's too late to do anything about it now."

"Why not conduct it in the morning, with guerrillas as the jury?"

"We've talked about this. Just as important as the fact that we will dispense justice, we have to be seen to dispense justice. The word will spread amongst all the campesinos if we have a representative jury, though not as quickly as it will spread if we execute a man without a fair trial. We need to do this the right way."

"You ignore that, while we wait, there is no justice for anyone," said Fósforo. "We can spread the word after the fact, but we need to act. This has gone on for too long."

"I know that you're frustrated by how long this has taken, but I am only trying to do it right," I said.

"A decision delivered by a jury of his peers now is a hundred times better than a decision delivered by a jury of the People a month from now," said Fósforo. "The People have no patience for justice to be done."

"When we next make camp," I said. "The jury will be the nearest campesinos we can find, and we'll spread word of the result ourselves immediately afterwards. We can devise a script for the patrols to read out at every village they enter."

"No later than the day we next make camp," said Fósforo.

"I'll make sure of it," I said.

"Justice cannot wait," said Fósforo.

19

I HAD ALREADY WALKED the platoon lines three times and got up to piss twice. Rather than get up again, I lay in my hammock and looked up at the leafy canopy above me. For the first time, I had begun to wear a watch, and it came with a new feeing. I felt like a slave to time. I had taken it from the fat lieutenant in Chacimo before we sent him into town in his underwear, knowing that it would be useful. I couldn't tell if it was cheap or expensive, but the tips of each hand on the watch glowed faintly in the night. I could see that there were only fifteen minutes before it was time for the platoon to prepare to move. Already, I had watched hours creep by as I waited.

With five minutes still to go, I finally slid out of my hammock. As I packed it into my rucksack, I could hear that everyone around me began to do the same. No one could sleep that night, expectation gnawing at our stomachs.

The whole platoon, less the sentries, were soon gathered in a loose circle around where my hammock had been hanging. They waited in silence for my direction. Their faces were only dimly visible in the dark, but I took the time to look at each of them intently. It was in the hours before something like this that I felt the weight of leadership most heavily.

I led the platoon to the edge of the camp, near our sentry post, and found the second platoon already there. Juan shook my hand

and clapped me on the shoulder. I could tell from his face that he hadn't slept either.

"This will go our way," he said, giving my shoulder another squeeze. I didn't say anything. I just smiled in return.

"Where's Fósforo?" I asked.

"He's coming," said Juan.

I walked down the line of men and women in my platoon, speaking briefly to each of them. Their faces were drawn and haggard, like mine, I was sure. Even still, no one complained or admitted to feeling anything but ready. When I reached Huracán, he chided me a little.

"Jefe, I've already checked them myself. Twice."

"That's what I expect you to do," I said, "but when I check them, I am actually checking you." He smiled, his teeth suddenly visible in the dark. I had learned to distract myself by inspecting things to avoid feeling anxious, and I suspect that Huracán did the same. I pitied the others who had nothing to do but wait.

I had reached the end of my platoon when Fósforo appeared out of the darkness. He chewed on the unlit stub of a rough cigar, the type that campesinos might make for themselves. Around him were four young guerrillas, new recruits, who he had asked for as his bodyguards. They were just teenagers, little more than kids, and they hung off his every word. After he sent the first one who goofed off to Juan's platoon, unarmed, the remainder worked twice as hard as anyone else in the column. The boldest of these boys was nicknamed Siki. He had a vinegar tongue for everything and everyone except Fósforo.

Fósforo smiled when he saw me, switching his rifle to one hand so that he could quickly embrace me.

"Ready?" he asked.

"The platoon is ready," I replied.

"I was asking about you," he said.

"As ready as ever."

From further out in the darkness, I saw the last of Fósforo's bodyguards appear. Behind him, with a rope loosely tied around his neck, was Julio. His hands were bound tightly in front of him, and he staggered when he walked. The boy leading him jerked on the rope, and Julio stumbled. When he saw me, Julio dug in his feet to stop.

"Paco, reason with these kids. Give me a gun and let me fight. No man should be treated like this," he said.

I looked at Fósforo, who was pretending not to hear any of this. "Another fighter wouldn't hurt," I said to him. "He can stay with me."

"Will you vouch that he won't escape?" asked Fósforo with a touch of acid.

"I won't," said Julio.

"I trust him to keep his word," I said.

"If you wanted him back in the column, you should have organized his trial by now," said Fósforo. "I won't do anything until the matter is settled. Justice needs to be seen to be served."

"There won't be any justice tomorrow if we don't survive today," I replied.

"Then win," said Fósforo, before turning away and walking noisily through the brush. Siki and the other boys followed, pulling their prisoner behind them.

Julio turned to me as he was led away. "Remember, Paco, that earnest men always get fucked in the end." He choked out these last words as Siki yanked hard on the rope around his neck.

For a moment, I considered following them but knew that instead, I had to focus on the matter at hand. When I looked at my guerrillas standing close by, watching me for assurances that everything was alright, I pushed my doubts aside.

"We're moving out," I said, before walking back to the head of the column. I started walking, and my platoon fell in silently behind me. The brush was thick in places, but I was able to weave around the worst of it. We didn't have time to hack an easy path through it all, and I'm sure that my path looked like that of a drunk. I could hear quiet swearing behind me as the platoon traced my steps, but I kept up a quick pace. I headed to the ford that we had crossed yesterday.

I could see the break in the trees over the river, like a wound through the forest, before I could see the water. There was a half-moon, but it was bright, and there were few clouds to obscure its light. I stopped the platoon here and had them drop their knapsacks and pile them within a thicket. I tried to look at each guerrilla in the eye as they deposited their belongings and give them a confident look. Some returned it to me; others, I could tell, were raw with the emotion that comes when you are waiting for a fight. There was little I could do for them other than tell them that, for better or worse, it would be over soon. I kept that thought to myself, and once everyone was ready again, I led them farther forward. I walked more slowly as we approached the river, looking for the landmarks I had tried to memorize before. There was a large oak tree, with smaller saplings at its base, off to one edge of the ford. I scanned for it as we approached, hoping that I had led us to the right place.

When I was close enough to see the edge of the water, I also found the tree. It was hard in the light to tell if this was the Vadito or not. As we approached, a guerrilla stood and waved at me from where they had been concealed. They must have been one of the escopeteros sent to watch this area, and so I knew that we had found the crossing.

I turned to Papi, who was the next man in the file. I had him take his section to the west and then told Iván to take his to the east. I kept Huracán's section in the centre with me and told him how I wanted the guerrillas deployed.

"Just as we've practiced a hundred times already," he said. I took the hint and let him get on with his job.

The guerrilla who had been waiting for us came over to me. I only recognized her when she got close.

"I was starting to get worried that you'd never show up," said Esperanza.

"What are you doing here?" I asked, realizing too late that I sounded like a concerned older brother.

"Where else would I be?" she said. "The escopeteros are all

across the river, waiting to see the Guardia start moving. I'm here to get their reports as they fall back."

"Of course," I said, "I didn't mean . . ."

She waved away my concern. "It's a few hours yet until dawn, but I don't know if the Guardia will try to cross the river in darkness or wait until sunrise."

"If they think they will surprise us, they might try to reach our camp before dawn. Or they might assume that attacking us will be a surprise all of its own, and not risk a night approach."

"We'll know soon enough," said Esperanza.

"Not soon enough for me," I said quietly, wondering if she felt the same anxiousness I did.

When she didn't respond, I left to check on my guerrillas. I started in the west and crept up slowly, stopping and listening as I went. I wanted to gauge how well-concealed and quiet the section was. More than once, I had come upon my men seemingly out of the shadows, catching them unawares. This time, though, I was immediately joined by Papi, who stood up from within a patch of tall grass, smiling.

"Did you hear me coming?" I asked.

"I didn't, but I knew you were coming, so I just waited for you," he said. "I would have been worried if you didn't check on us."

He led me along the loose line formed by his section, swollen to over a dozen men, but with just more than half as many rifles. We still paired each armed guerrilla with an unarmed one, but now nearly all of the unarmed ones carried machetes. As we checked on each pair, I saw that Papi had done a good job of positioning them. When we finished, I offered him my hand, and he took it in a vice grip.

"Your section's well placed," I said.

"Well, what did you expect?" he asked. "Do you think I've been paying no attention on these marches of yours?"

I smiled at him, thinking of how much I liked this man, who had no reason to follow me.

"Good hunting," I said as I turned to leave. "Make sure your men fall back when I give the signal."

"Yes, Capitán," he replied, and I walked to find the edge of Huracán's section.

I hadn't gone more than a dozen paces before I saw him sitting against a tree, waiting for me.

"Am I this predictable?" I asked.

"Ask Iván when he pounces on you next," he said.

His section was also well laid out, and my check was more cursory than before. Iván was waiting for me with Huracán's last pair of men, laughing when I expressed surprise to see him.

"The only question was whether you would start with Papi or me," he said.

Iván was harder on his section than the other two, and as we moved along his position, he corrected faults that I didn't see. He rarely spoke, but when he did, his voice was harsh and clipped. In times like these, every little fault could get one killed, and so no one complained when he told them what to do to improve. They knew that they were in good hands with him in charge.

We had finished inspecting the last of his pairs when there was a rustle in the trees beyond his position. We both heard it simultaneously, and dropped to the ground, our rifles instantly at the shoulder. After a moment of silence, there was a rustle again.

I held my breath, straining to see through the brush.

We waited, and I began to crawl forward when Iván put a hand on my shoulder to stop me. In front of us, there was a scream.

A capuchin monkey leapt from a low branch to a higher one, stopping to look at us again. This time when it howled at us, I could see its yellowed teeth.

"That thing looks fiercer than the Guardia," said Iván.

"Let's hope," I replied. The monkey scampered off, and the night was again silent.

Having checked on everything that I could think of, I resolved to settle into my own position and simply wait. My platoon looked to me to know that it would be alright, and I didn't want my checking to transmit my anxiety to them. I went back to where I had first seen Esperanza. She was chewing on a rolled-up tortilla, resting with her back against a tree. I sat down beside her, and she tore off half of the tortilla and handed it to me. It was stale and as tough as leather. I chewed thoughtfully.

"Who knew our lives would become so grand?" I said.

"Don't forget, I saw how grandly you used to live," she replied.

"It's true. This is not the worst tortilla I've ever tasted."

"No?" she asked. "This might be quite the story, then, as I can't imagine one that's much worse." She had a twinkle in her eye that I could see even in the darkness.

I started to make up a funny story to tell her about the worst tortilla in the world when we were interrupted by the sound of splashing in the river. We both turned around to see a young woman in peasant dress struggling through the water, her skirt held up high around her waist. Esperanza rose to greet her as she stepped onto the shore.

"Are they close?" she asked.

"Very," said the woman, whom I recognized as Candelaria. "At least four companies, led by the old chivato."

"Any heavy weapons?" I asked.

"I saw machine guns, strapped on pack animals, that's all," she said.

"That's enough," I replied. "How long?"

"Fifteen minutes, maybe less."

Esperanza handed Candelaria a canvas bag. "Good work. You can change once we've found Juan's platoon." She gave me a quick hug and a peck on the cheek. "Your turn, now, Paco."

They hurried away from the river and to the flank where Juan's guerrillas were waiting to take on the Guardia. I wanted to walk the line one more time and give one last word of encouragement, but I realized it was too late.

I hissed until the guerrillas next to me popped up their heads. I used both hands to signal ten minutes, and they passed it on in both directions. We would be ready when the Guardia arrived.

The first indication we had that they had reached the river was when we saw two guardsmen and a man in a peasant shirt standing by the water's edge on the far side. They were too far away for me to know whether the man was the chivato or not. They spoke for a moment, the campesino gesturing widely with his arms. He seemed to be encouraging the guardsmen to cross, but they argued with him. I saw other movement in the forest along the river, and for a moment, caught a flash of three guardsmen spreading out through the edge of the trees.

Whatever had been said, it became clear that the campesino had lost the argument. The guardsmen disappeared back into the trees, and the campesino began to trudge across the river alone. The water never went past his waist, and here it moved slowly enough that it wasn't dangerous. As the man got closer, I could tell that he was the traitor from the village. He crossed the river as if expecting to be shot at any moment, but we held our fire.

When he reached the near bank, I could tell for certain it was the old chivato from the village. He turned and waved at the guardsmen, and then pulled off his pants to wring them out. He spread them across the branches of a bush to finish drying, and stood with his skinny legs under his dirty shirt, looking back towards the far bank. After a few minutes, we saw the first guardsmen start to cross as well.

They came in two long lines, like ants, stretching out from a point deeper in the trees that I could not see. The lines stretched across the river and onto the near bank, and still, the guardsmen came. I knew we were out-numbered, even if our whole column was concentrated together, but seeing so many guardsmen at once still caused my stomach to drop. I knew the others would feel the same, perhaps worse, and knew what to do to banish that feeling.

There were perhaps three or four dozen men visible on our side of the river, clustered together as they reorganized when I began to fire. As soon as I did, the rest of the platoon joined in, and guardsmen started to drop. Men were killed close to us on the near bank and in the river. They scrambled to find cover where they could. I insisted that my guerrilla's fire only carefully-aimed shots. We couldn't afford to waste ammunition, but with so many targets clustered together, we could hardly miss. Anything that moved along the river was fired upon, again and again until it stopped.

The noise level increased when the Guardia brought machine guns forward on the far bank and raked the thick bush concealing us with fire. I pressed myself to the ground as tightly as I could, dirt in my mouth, as I heard branches getting snapped off by bullets around me. Whenever I was sure the fire had passed over me to somewhere else, I lifted my rifle and fired. I aimed at where I thought the machine guns were hidden, but that just drew their fire again, forcing me to take cover. A squad of Guardia tried to rush across the river, running comically slow through the water. Enough of us could still fire back that we cut them down before they reached the midpoint, and they didn't try it again.

We had reached a stalemate of sorts, and I realized that I had failed. The Guardia weren't pushing forward, nor were there enough of them across the river for us to toy with them in the way we had planned. The minuet I had envisioned, with each of the platoons attacking them from the flanks in rolling succession, was dead before it began. I was certain that Fósforo would appear at any moment and that I would stammer through an explanation. The only thing that I could think of doing was to attack across the river ourselves. Against those machine guns, it would be suicidal, but in the moment, that seemed easier than explaining how we had failed.

I realized that my eyes were closed, and perhaps had been for a long time when I heard the first distant crump. I strained my ears to hear what the noise meant and rolled over onto my knees to look up as the first mortar bomb exploded in the riverbed. A plume of water rose into the sky and dropped back down with a slap. There was another crump, and I braced myself for the next round. It dropped well behind us, shattering trees with a crack that echoed through the forest. The next round dropped off to my left, just in front of the tree line where we were hidden. Someone screamed, I don't know who. I heard four more crumps and tried to flatten myself against the ground again, and I heard a roar of yelling from the other side of the river that meant they must be trying to rush us.

Suddenly it seemed like our plan to draw the Guardia across the river was working, although I was certain that I would never live to see it succeed. I decided to do my best to pull my platoon back.

20

I HAD A WHISTLE that we had agreed would be the signal, and I blew three long blasts from where I was lying. The mortar rounds kept crashing into the trees around us, shattering the tops of them into splinters. I heard screams on my left and right, but I blew the whistle three more times and then began to scramble backwards away from the river. I could see movement all around me as I went, guerrillas travelling along on their bellies and pulling themselves with their hands. When the next salvo landed, I got up into a low crawl, and then into a run. Soon we were all running pell-mell deeper into the cover of the forest.

Huracán caught up to run beside me, an angry gash across one arm.

"I waited too long," I said between breaths.

"You made them believe they are winning," he said.

"I think I believe it too."

He laughed and ran past me, leaving a speckled trail of blood as he went.

I reached the place where we had hidden our knapsacks, panting with the exertion of running through the woods. Huracán had beat me there, along with two others. As I leaned over, hands on my knees, trying to catch my breath, more guerrillas arrived. I saw a young campesino who had started the battle unarmed standing with a rifle in his hands.

"Your partner?" I asked.

"Dead," he said, looking at the ground.

After five minutes, all but two members of the platoon had made it to the rendezvous. Several were injured, but none badly, and I posted sentries and took time to bind their wounds. Huracán was wrapping a bandage around his arm by himself and tied the knot with his teeth.

"We gave them a shellacking, jefe."

"I thought we were done for," I admitted.

He looked at me incredulously. "Are you kidding? They must have lost forty men in the first few minutes, and now they are charging headlong into an ambush."

As if on cue, there was a sudden noise of intense firing off to the west of us, where Juan's platoon was waiting. It got louder as the Guardia fired back. I heard the sound of grenades exploding mixed in with the rifle fire.

I was thirsty as hell and drained my canteen in one long guzzling drink. When I finished, my throat still felt parched. When I called my section commanders over to me, my voice was so hoarse I could barely make myself heard.

"Save some for me," said Papi as he handed me his canteen. I took a small sip, not wanting to drink his share, but neither would he let me hand it back to him right away. "I'd be pissing all day if I drank that whole thing," he said.

"Who are we missing?" I asked.

"My section is all here," said Papi, kissing his rosary.

"One of the new kids said he saw Iván get killed by the mortars," said Huracán. "And Yeti was hit in the head while we were running back."

"Wounded?" asked Papi.

Huracán shook his head.

"So, who should replace Iván?" I asked.

Papi rubbed his belly thoughtfully. "The next most capable person in that section is Loba," he said.

Huracán nodded. "She's the one you want."

I saw her standing with other members of Iván's section, speaking quietly to them. While they looked rattled, she just looked fierce. I called her over.

"Jefe?"

"Do you know what happened to Iván?" I asked.

She nodded but didn't elaborate.

"I want you to take over his section."

"Jefe."

"Big talkers, you lot are," said Huracán. She just glowered at him.

"How many wounded in your section?" I asked her.

"Two dead, one wounded," she said.

"We should count ourselves lucky," I said.

"Lucky that you were leading us," said Huracán. "You played them like a fiddle."

"More like a guitar," said Papi, and the three of them laughed.

They didn't know how close we had come to disaster, and although I couldn't bring myself to tell them, I was angry. "This isn't a game," I said, and the three of them were silent.

"We know that, jefe," said Huracán. "It's just . . ."

"Just nothing. Make sure your sections' wounds are bandaged, ammunition redistributed, and that they are ready to move again. After the Novios draw them back east, we are going to hit them again. You two can explain the plan to Loba."

I walked away before they said anything more, and none of them tried to stop me. I found a spot by myself and sat down, my back against a rock, and wiped down my carbine with an oily rag. It was already clean enough, but I wanted something to occupy my mind. I polished the rifle barrel furiously, worried about what I knew came next. If we had radios, it would have been easier to coordinate all of this. As it was, we could only rely on the sounds of battle and our instincts. I knew if we attacked again too early, the enemy would turn on us in an instant. And if we attacked too late, the Novios would be overrun. My head was spinning with all the factors that affected the one simple decision I had to make.

I was still furiously rubbing my rifle when Fósforo leaned down from behind me. He was smiling like a madman and holding Rubio's hat in place with one hand.

"It's working," he said.

"I'll feel better when we can say that it worked."

"We can't lose," he said.

"Someone needs to tell them," I said, jerking my thumb toward the river. "This isn't over yet."

"Paco, even if both of us fall, as long as two more guerrillas pick up our rifles and continue the fight, we can count this as a success." I almost laughed at this, but I could tell that he was serious.

"I'll make those bastards die for their cause before I die for ours," I said.

He looked stunned when I spat my response at him, and he stalked off without another word. I looked around at my platoon. No one was close enough to hear what we had said, though our body language spoke volumes.

The sound of firing had died off again. I climbed up on the rock and strained my ears to hear what was happening to our south. When I could hear the fighting, it was as if I knew where the enemy was and that we were safe. Silence meant that they were loose, and it gnawed at my stomach.

"Maybe they're retreating?" said Papi.

"It can't be that our platoon was overrun," said Loba.

"Then what do you think is happening?" said Papi, his fingers straying absent-mindedly to his rosary.

I was about to tell them both to shut up when there was an intense fusillade of gunfire just southeast of us. The sharp crack of rifle fire nearly drowned out the intermittent thumping of the Guardia's machine guns. The sound echoed off the trees, making it hard to pinpoint the direction from which it was coming. After a few minutes, the fighting started to roll eastward.

"Now," I said, looking at my section commanders. "Huracán's section in the lead."

I'd barely finished speaking before Huracán was leading his guerrillas back through the bush towards the sound of the guns.

They were spread out in a loose line, and I followed close behind them, with the remainder of the platoon in single file behind me. We were moving too quickly through the trees, and so I dashed forward to grab Huracán by the sleeve.

"Slow down," I said. "We need to find the Guardia without rolling over them."

"But we will roll over them," he said. "They're probably ready to break."

"Don't be so sure."

Huracán did slow down, but even still, it was hard to keep pace. The undergrowth was thick and spread out as we were, it wasn't possible to pick the best path through it all. Before long, I was out of breath, but I kept moving quickly to keep up.

We had advanced a few hundred yards when I saw Huracán stop abruptly and wave his arms at the guerrillas on both sides to get them to do the same. I moved forward to kneel beside him, leaning against a tree as I strained to lift my head a little higher to see.

"Right down there," said Huracán, gesturing with his rifle.

It was then that I saw the cluster of guardsmen. They were facing towards the Novios, unaware that we were watching them. Five men were sheltered behind a jumble of rocks, none firing their weapons or making any effort to advance. The weight of fire from the Novios was farther to the south, and these men were out of the fight.

"Give the word, jefe, and we'll roll them up, right to the river," said Huracán.

I ignored him while I scanned deeper into the forest, looking for more Guardia. The underbrush was thick, and I couldn't see any. The fight seemed one-sided, with the Novios holding the upper hand.

"They'll be dead before they even know we're here," said Huracán. I could see that his guerrillas closest to us were listening to see what I would say. The seemed ready to dash forward and pounce on the unsuspecting guardsmen below. I admit that I nearly gave the word for them to charge ahead, but the longer I looked, the more it felt wrong.

"Jefe! We can do this," said Huracán.

"You'll stay here, and fire when I say." I waved Loba and Papi forward and sent their sections to either side of Huracán's. "Extend the line in both directions, fire when I start to fire, and withdraw on the signal."

They dashed off in each direction wordlessly, waving their sections forward with them. After what I guessed was enough time to get in position, I put my rifle to my shoulder and looked to the others around me to do the same. I found the prone figure of the guardsman closest to me and steadied my rifle against the tree. Fractions of a second after I fired, rifles started cracking all along our line, and in moments, all five of the guardsmen were dead. It was more murder than combat, but I put that aside for the moment to focus on what needed to happen next.

"We'll get their rifles, at least," said Huracán, and I could tell that he felt hurt at not being allowed a bigger victory. I was going to tell him to start to move forward. Before the words came out of my mouth, a sound like a sawmill ripped through the forest just above my head. Huracán and I and everyone nearby dropped to the ground.

Branches and leaves fell on my head as I tried to scurry back on my belly behind the tree on which I had been leaning. Wood chips and pieces of bark carved from the tries around us flew through the air, and the wood cracked as it was struck by bullets. The air around us seemed thick with them, and it seemed that if I lifted my head even an inch off the ground, one would hit me.

Huracán was lying on the ground in front of me, his eyes wide and his hands over his ears. I couldn't hear him speak, but I could read his lips: "Santa Madre de Dios!"

Unseen behind the men we killed, there must have been more of them. They swept a machine gun back and forth across the trees where we were hiding in a way that would be catastrophic if they hadn't been aiming so high. I gritted my teeth and rolled over so that I could edge forward to see again. My chin touched the ground as I peered around the tree, and I couldn't see anything but grass.

I turned my face sideways and blew my whistle with three long blasts that I hoped would be heard over the din, and began to crawl away from the gunfire. Huracán was close beside me, and I could see long lines of guerrillas in both directions starting to crawl back as well. We had made it perhaps twenty or thirty yards when the machine gun fire stopped.

"Hold up here!" I shouted, getting up onto my knees to better see the platoon. I couldn't see to either end of the platoon, but I didn't dare run to check either. Satisfied that the bulk of the platoon had stopped, I lay back down and found some cover in a dip in the ground. With my rifle up to my shoulder, I waited.

There was an animal yell, low and guttural, and I knew that the guardsmen had rallied and were trying to rush us. Their shout wasn't triumphant as much as it was primordial, men rushing to avoid certain death in our trap.

"Get ready," I shouted, and there was a flash of olive drab ahead of me, and I began to fire. There was a ragged volley from across the platoon, screams from wounded men, and the sound of trees struck by bullets. Our fire picked up, and there were no more targets, and so seizing the chance, I blew my whistle again.

"Back, back," I shouted, not wanting to be outflanked or overrun, and we began to scamper back to the next place I thought we could hold. That terrible shout began again, and I heard wild firing off on my left. As I turned to look behind me, I saw that another wave of guardsmen was rushing forward.

Huracán was close by and began to shout back at them, and I stopped where I was and fired as quickly as I could at the charging figures. A man dropped, and then another, but then I pulled the trigger on an empty chamber. I saw men running past me in my peripheral vision, and I realized that we were being overrun. I pulled out a magazine to reload but didn't have time and swung the rifle instead by the barrel and hit a guardsman running towards me in the side of the head with a crack. Teeth burst out of his cheek, and he dropped on the spot as if he had been struck by the hand of God. I went to swing again at another man, but he was too close, and I hit him in the ribs. I was sure that it hurt, but he rammed into me all the same, and we both dropped to the ground.

He was on top of me, his hands snaked up around my throat, and the more I tossed at him, the tighter he gripped me. I could smell onions on his breath, his face almost touching mine as he tried to pin my arms with his elbows, and my vision blurred. I punched at his ribs and tried to knee him and roll out from under him, but he had me pinned. I clenched my hands in frustration, desperately trying to breathe, my mind white and empty and loud when my hand wrapped around the handle of a machete on the man's belt.

I pulled it from the sheath, cutting my hand as I did, and hit him in the back of the legs with it. He howled and squirmed, but I couldn't hit him hard enough to break his grip. I turned the machete in my hand, and with all I had left, I drew the blade down along his leg like the women in the market cut the meat from a drumstick, and I felt that machete scrape bone. The man rolled off, clutching his leg, and before I had even opened my eyes I had hit him three times in the face with the blade, cutting his cheeks open and causing one of his eyes to spew gore.

I got back on my feet and swung the machete at the man nearest to me, hitting him in the shoulder. Huracán grabbed him and pulled him off balance, and I hit him again across the back of the head, and he dropped. There was a melee all around me, and I stepped into it, hacking and slashing at every guardsman I saw, cutting into bark and flesh and wood and bone and everything in my path. I fought until my arm was numb, and my throat was hoarse, and only when I looked around and there were no more guardsmen standing did I realize I had been shouting. Huracán grabbed me in an embrace and then leaned back, his face smeared in blood. I don't know how long it had been going on, but there was firing on both sides of us, and I knew that the other platoons were attacking and not retreating anymore.

"Now," he said, "forward," and I waved that bloody machete in the air, and my platoon followed me at a run.

We pushed the guardsmen back in disorder, any pretense of modern warfare discarded. Whenever we caught up with one of them, they were shot or hacked or driven down to the earth with our hands without a second thought. We pushed them back across the ground we had fought over that day, stepping over the corpses of the slain, until I could see the river again, stretching flat and dark to the other bank.

As the guardsmen tried to escape and struggled across the water, we poured fire into them without mercy. The surface of the water looked like there was a monsoon striking it. The conclusion of the battle did not last long. Perhaps thirty seconds, maybe not even that. At that time, all the soldiers were down, and no one fired back at us. I stopped to listen to make sure it was over.

We all moved forward to the river's edge, stopping at each fallen guardsman to strip off their equipment. Some men waded in to drag the bodies ashore that had not already washed away. Some were wounded, but we neither finished them off nor helped them. One of the men I had seen go down by the water's edge had only been struck in the shoulder. He was bleeding badly and writhed in pain when I touched him. I tried not to look at his face as I wrestled his bandolier and waist belt off and slung his rifle over the same shoulder on which I carried my own.

"Help me," he moaned piteously, but I ignored him and stalked across to the next man.

This one had sergeant's stripes on his arm and was using his hands to try to crawl away. His right side was covered in blood, and I saw that the bullet had hit him in the hip, leaving a gaping wound on the opposite side. I kicked his rifle farther away from him and rolled him over onto his back with my foot. His breathing was heavy, but he managed to focus his eyes on me.

"How many are you?" I asked. When he didn't answer, I put my foot on his wounded hip and pressed.

"Over four hundred," he gasped.

"And who's in charge?" I pressed again with my foot.

"Lieutenant-Colonel Espina."

"Lieutenant-Colonel?" I said with a low whistle. "He's making quite a career out of losing to us." The man closed his eyes and didn't respond.

I searched his pockets for anything of interest but found only a bit of money, which I left, and cigarettes, which I took. He moaned as I pulled his cartridge belt out from under him and slung it over my shoulder, and pulled a bayonet out of its sheath on his belt. His hand reached out and grabbed my pant leg, and he motioned me to lean down. He was speaking, but I couldn't understand the words. Pinning his arm to the ground with my knee, I got close enough to hear what he was saying.

"You'll get what you deserve. Just like the bandits in the Serranías," he rasped.

I didn't think for more than a second, and I didn't cast my mind back to the day Braulio and so many others were killed. I had his bayonet in my hand, but I dropped it out of his reach and picked up his rifle, stuck the barrel under his chin and pulled the trigger. Warm blood splattered up my arms and on my face and the sound of the shot echoed across the river. I looked around at men clutching their rifles with tense faces. All eyes were on me.

Fósforo had seen what I'd done, and in a few quick strides, was standing beside me. He swept the rifle from my hands and gave me a shove.

"What the fuck are you doing?" he said.

"He told me that there were more than four hundred men here, led by our friend Lieutenant-Colonel Espina."

"Before or after you shot him?"

"Shot him again, you mean? This is a war, you know."

Fósforo was furious, practically sputtering as he spoke. "This is not how we treat captured soldiers! Our quarrel is with the government, not those it coerces to fight for it."

"We've been killing them all day. You didn't hear what he said."

"I don't give a fuck what he said," said Fósforo savagely.

Around a dozen guardsmen who had been captured unhurt were seated together in a tight clump, under guard. They had drawn their knees up to their chins, looking steadfastly away from the guerrillas towering over them. Fósforo took a canteen from one of the guerrillas and handed it to a guardsman.

"Drink," he said, "it's no less hot for you than for us."

The guardsman drank a few swallows and then passed it to the man next to him.

"They'll need more than one canteen," said Fósforo. "Have you forgotten they're humans?"

Two other guerrillas handed their canteens to the prisoners, and a prisoner held up a pack of cigarettes. Our men refused it.

"We'll collect enough cigarettes off the dead," said one of the guerrillas.

Fósforo rounded on him immediately.

"Are you threatening these prisoners?" he asked.

"No, jefe, just stating a fact," said the guerrilla. I recognized him as one of the former factory workers from Chacimo, though I didn't remember his name.

"Setting us against each other plays into the government's hands," said Fósforo. "If every person who had ever toiled under the government's yoke rose up as one, this regime wouldn't last an hour. These men are victims too."

"They didn't seem like victims when they were shooting back an hour ago," said the guerrilla.

"You're not looking at this like a revolutionary," said Fósforo.

"Tell them that," said the guerrilla, pointing over to where our dead and wounded were being collected. A dozen guerrillas lay dead in a line. A dozen more, in various states of agony, were being treated with what little medical supplies we had.

"Our men will get the same medical treatment as the wounded guardsmen. We mustn't lose our humanity," said Fósforo, walking away before the guerrilla could reply.

We continued to collect up all the equipment we could scavenge and herd the prisoners into one central place. I knew that Fósforo would lecture them and then make them an offer—they could join with us and earn the right to carry a gun, or they could leave. At the moment, Fósforo stood alone, not speaking to anyone. After the fight today, I suspected that there was little stomach for the kind of mercy he practiced.

When I spoke to him again, I could see he was deep in his thoughts.

"I haven't forgotten about the trial," I said. "I'll arrange it for tomorrow morning, with whatever civilians we can find."

"That won't be necessary," said Fósforo.

"You think I can't do it?" I asked. Everyone around us had stopped and was listening.

"Julio ran when the fighting started. But at least we didn't arm him, as you suggested."

"If he was still tied up, he won't have gotten far. We still have time to recapture him."

"That won't be necessary," said Fósforo. "He's dead. He was shot trying to escape. Siki is burying him as we speak."

I felt the eyes of everyone in the column on me but said nothing.

"It was justice," he said.

I turned to him, finally realizing what he had been thinking. "You're still mad about the sausage, aren't you?"

He knew exactly what I meant. Fósforo whirled towards me, a dirty finger in my face. "He was dishonest and untrustworthy from the very start," he spat.

I wasn't sure what more to say. Those days when we crossed the Ojo de la Cerradura to this side of the mountains seemed a lifetime ago. After another moment, Fósforo walked away, lighting the stub of his cigar as he went.

21

NEWS OF THE BATTLE at the Vadito spread like wildfire. Although I was glad for it, I also worried that it might make the Somocistas work that much harder to destroy us.

We had set up camp again just north of the river, roughly halfway between Chacimo and La Trinidad. Deserting guardsmen had more than made up our losses during the ambush, and campesinos from farther and farther away started making their way into the department to join us. Even though our numbers had swelled, we no longer had trouble arming ourselves.

Fósforo had called for a meeting of all the leaders in the column, not just Santiago, Juan and I. Why exactly he wanted to see us all, I couldn't guess.

"Maybe more news from the organization?" asked Loba.

"They might have settled on a design for uniform buttons," joked Huracán.

"I heard two men say that they had heard we were retreating north over the mountains," said Papi.

"Retreating?" said Huracán.

"Moving," said Papi. "To keep the Guardia guessing."

"We'll know once we hear from Fósforo," I said, disliking the gossip.

We made our way through the camp to the area where Fósforo

had his headquarters. A canvas tent captured from the Guardia was set up, with hammocks strung every which way around it. A small fire was burning, and a skinny, dishevelled guerrilla was boiling a large tin can of coffee on it. Crouched over the fire, his hair a matted mess, the man looked almost prehistoric. He lifted the tin out of the fire by threading a stick through its makeshift handle, then turned around to carry the coffee back to the tent. When he saw us, he smiled, and his eyes lit up. It was Fósforo.

"This is only the third time I've boiled these grounds. It should still be good and strong," said Fósforo.

I'm not sure why I suddenly saw him differently than before, but I did. We were all filthy and thin, wearing torn clothes, but it hadn't bothered me. Seeing him, I wondered what we were becoming. Whether we were the future of mankind or it's past. I shook off the feeling and followed Fósforo into the tent.

Juan and Santiago were already there, each seated on rough benches with their three section commanders. We squeezed in along the back wall, sitting shoulder to shoulder. We had all started wearing red armbands, sewn from rags, blankets or anything else we could find. I thought it was pointless, but Fósforo insisted. I brightened a little when Esperanza sat across from me and gave me a smile.

Fósforo set the tin can down on the ground, and Siki carefully poured coffee from it into cracked cups. There weren't enough to go around, and so Siki gave them to the capitáns first. I handed my cup to Esperanza, which she took without complaint.

"This is a bigger meeting than normal," said Fósforo, "and for good reason." He made a point of looking every one of us in the eye. "There is tremendous news from the capital."

This caught our attention.

"Led by 'Comandante Cero,' the FSLN took control of the Palacio Nacional while it was in session, capturing two thousand hostages. He ransomed them back for a half-million dollars, the release of political prisoners and safe passage to Cuba."

Papi let out a low whistle. "Who is that guy?"

"Cero leads the FSLN's southern front," said Esperanza. The

crowd buzzed with excitement.

Fósforo waved his hands for us to settle down. "Although not as spectacular, our successes have stacked up one atop another until we are nearly unrecognizable. Our column is over four hundred strong."

There were nods around the room.

"We began with two platoons, and then three. But we're like a lobster, that must shed its shell to grow."

I had no idea how lobsters grew, and I wasn't sure I understood where this was going.

"And so, I have made a decision. While the Novios will stay the same, the other two platoons will each split into three. The new platoon leaders are Loba, Huracán, Flaco and Calixto."

I looked at my former tenientes, and they smiled back at me. Papi clapped them both on the back and shook their hands, but wouldn't meet my eye. Fósforo waited a moment before pressing on.

"And for this new structure, I have news. We will be breaking camp in the morning," he said.

"Back over the mountains?" asked Papi.

"The opposite," said Fósforo. "Our target is San Jose Guachipilín." We were all stunned into silence.

"Do you mean to start targeting Guardia patrols outside of the town?" asked Juan.

"We could also start to sabotage the infrastructure," said Santiago. "There are a few small factories there, and a power plant."

"We will do no such thing," said Fósforo. "I want the factories, and especially the power plant, intact." He turned to Juan. "And we're done pecking at the edges. I want to capture the whole town."

I could see the uneasy side glances that passed between everyone, but no one questioned him. The elation of two minutes ago had dissipated. After a moment of silence, I spoke up.

"How big is the garrison?"

"A large security company, maybe more. People are saying that there are reinforcements from the capital. From the Batallón de Combate General Somoza," said Esperanza.

"Less those lost at the Vadito. Less deserters. Less those out on patrol. Less those who will refuse to fight," said Fósforo.

"We don't know if any of those factors are significant," I said. "We should make sure we know what we're up against . . ."

Fósforo cut me off. "Their numbers don't matter," he said. "They're a hollow shell. After the fight at the Vadito, they don't believe they can beat us. Now is the time to strike, before they regain their nerve. We strike, or we get struck."

"The Vadito was one thing; this is attacking a town. With a fort," I said. "They'll fight like cornered animals."

"They are cornered animals, and it's time to finish them," said Fósforo. "We leave in the morning."

He stood up and walked a short distance away, the meeting over. We sat in silence around the fire for a moment, until Esperanza broke the spell.

"Once you get your platoons organized, I can assign an escopetero to most platoons to lead you into town. Only a few of my people know the place well, so see if you have anyone who's already been there."

Huracán finished his coffee with a flick of his wrist and stood up. "Jefe, Loba and I can get things reorganized and then get your approval," he said.

I nodded. "Talk to Papi. If he's satisfied, so am I."

The leaders hurriedly went back to their encampments, and Esperanza disappeared as well. I saw that Fósforo was lying in his hammock, turned away from me. He must have been furiously puffing on his pipe, as I could see a plume of smoke rising above him.

"Ramón," I said.

He spun off his hammock in a flash to face me.

"Don't call me that," he said.

"Why not? There's no one else here."

"This column's success rests on one thing," he said. "Discipline."

And before I could say another word, he walked away.

As Fósforo wished, the column reorganized that night and set out southward in the morning. Without maps, we relied on Esperanza, and some guerrillas who knew the town, to sketch it out in the dirt. We didn't know enough about the town to assign firm targets to every platoon. But we did know that there was an old fort on a hill that people called "El Grano," and two police stations. The rest we would have to discover.

"Why don't we wait until the escopeteros can tell us more?" I asked Fósforo.

"Now is the time," he said. "We've rocked them back on their heels. We can't give them time to recover."

"Or us either," I said under my breath.

We suspended the captured machine guns from poles that two men could carry. When Fósforo offered one to my platoon, I declined.

"They're too cumbersome," I said. "We won't be making the Guardia dance like before lugging those things around."

"You won't have to," said Fósforo, "You can mow them down instead."

"I'll stick to what I know," I replied, and "our" machine gun went to Loba instead.

The column spread itself out, with each of the platoons assigned to approach San Jose Guachipilín from a different direction. We planned for it to take us three days to get into position. This plan gave the platoon that had the farthest to travel enough time to make it to their destination. On the morning of the fourth day, we entered the town, with Papi as our guide.

The road we were assigned was a diagonal called Calle el Arsenal that cut straight to the small Plaza de Armas. The road started at the edge of a farmer's field, marked by a plaster statue of Christ as a babe in arms. The plaster statue had been painted many times and was chipped and worn. I crossed myself as we walked past it, as did most of the platoon. I had never seen San Jose Guachipilín before, but I wasn't impressed.

"This is the department's capital?" I asked. "The roads aren't even paved."

"Farther into the town, they are," said Papi. "I've been here once or twice. This is Barrio Divino Niño."

"So, you know where we're going?" I said.

"We just follow this," he shrugged.

Near the start of the road were the ruins of an old building. It was nothing more than a foundation someone had long-since looted of everything useful, even the stones from its walls. There was a horse tied up beside it, its ribs showing against its skin. It watched us pass while chewing on a clump of high grass.

We followed the street through the outskirts of the town. My platoon was spread out in a staggered line on both sides of the road, watching carefully. Everything around us was perfectly still, except the stray dogs who fell in with the column, hoping for scraps. Although people must have known we were there, they kept their doors locked, and their windows shuttered.

The silence was broken by the sound of church bells up ahead and more on the other side of town. They rang urgently, without any discernable pattern, no doubt as a warning of our attack. Then, a long, drawn-out burst of fire echoed across town, answered by shots from a dozen rifles or more.

"So much for a surprise," said Papi, marching nearby, at the head of his section.

"I'm still surprised that we're here," I muttered to myself. Papi didn't hear me but must have seen my expression.

"Think of it: maybe tonight you'll sleep in a bed. An actual bed."

"I don't think any of us are going to be sleeping tonight," I replied, before turning around to look at the rest of the platoon. We had shrunk dramatically with the reorganization, but in truth, that made the platoon easier to handle. I pushed the worries about the new section commanders out of my mind and focused on the task at hand.

"I wish we'd been assigned one of the escopeteros," I said to Papi.

He waved for his section to keep walking and stopped at the first building on the street, a pulpería, and banged on the wooden shutter. I stopped to stand with him.

"Señor! Señora! Come out, please."

We could hear shuffling inside, but the shutter didn't open.

"We just have some questions," said Papi.

"Go ahead," replied a woman from inside.

Papi looked at me, but I shook my head.

"We want to know what to expect between here and the Plaza de Armas."

"What to expect?"

Papi looked exasperated. "Guardia Nacional, police stations, anything like that," he said.

"The Guardia come and go from the El Grano, but we don't see them here," said the woman.

"I also want to buy some eggs," said Papi, pulling some small bills from his pocket. I was about to lay into him, but he raised his hands in mock surrender.

We heard the sound of a bolt being drawn, and the shutter opened a crack.

"How many?" said the woman inside.

"Three?" said Papi.

The woman's hand reached out and pulled the bills from Papi's fingers. "For that, two," she said.

She handed the eggs out to Papi, who held them gingerly in one hand. The woman inside was old, and behind her, I could see three children huddled in a back corner. We must have looked like wild men, with our long hair and dirty clothes, but I tried to reassure her.

"We're not here to hurt anyone," I said, immediately feeling ridiculous, given the gunfire that still echoed across town.

Whatever she thought of that, she didn't reply.

"How many guardsmen are there here?" asked Papi.

"At least a thousand," she said. I shuddered, but Papi gave a huge sigh of relief.

"Gracias a Dios," he said. "With jefes like ours, that few will be no trouble."

She looked at him incredulously before closing the shutter.

I worried as we marched that I was leading my platoon to their deaths, but their spirits were high. One of Papi's men, Tomás, even began to sing before I cut him off.

"This isn't a picnic," I said harshly.

We trudged up the street in silence, and I strained to see what lay ahead. The town was bathed in grey light as morning came. Other than a few trucks parked far ahead on the curb, I couldn't see anything else on the street between the centre of town and us.

We passed a railyard that was empty and then the main market. It was a large open-air building with a tin roof. It would normally be bustling. Other than a few stray dogs who wandered between the stalls and barked at us, it was empty.

The buildings along the diagonal became more closely packed. Some were two stories tall, and all made of cinder blocks, covered in stucco, with red-tiled roofs. We kept moving along the edges of the street. The church bells kept ringing, getting louder as we closed in on the main square.

I was about to shout to Papi that we needed to slow down when tracer rounds started streaking down the middle of the street. I pressed myself into the nearest heavy wooden doorway, crushed by three others who did the same. One of the newer men, Rafa, lay dead on the street, his face in the gutter.

"Shoot, goddamn it, shoot," I shouted, leaning just around the edge of the doorway to fire my carbine. I felt stupid at getting caught like this, underestimating the Guardia.

"It's those trucks up ahead," shouted Papi from across the street. "They've sandbagged themselves into the cargo beds." I glanced around the edge of the doorway again to look, ducking back when I saw the muzzle flash coming from one of the trucks.

"Back!" I shouted, "Back!" and began firing again. One by one, guerrillas dashed out from under cover to an alleyway a few houses behind us. The firing from the trucks was inaccurate, but in the narrow street, ricochets shot off in all directions.

I'd emptied my rifle, but rather than reload, I turned and ran, not trying to duck or dodge but just running straight back to the alley. The machine gun began firing again, knocking chips off the wall above me. I dove around the corner and skidded to a halt in a pile of refuse. The rest of the platoon, less three guerrillas left out on the street, were crowded there with me.

Papi looked at me, and I could tell he wanted to go back for the wounded.

I shook my head. "We're going to press forward again," I said as I stood up.

"Of course," said Papi, but his eyes betrayed his fear. He kissed his rosary.

Behind the houses were a tangle of gardens and outhouses, each plot surrounded by low walls made of wood and odd sheets of metal. I waved one section forward, and they began to move forward in a crouch, tearing apart the fences where they couldn't easily go over them.

I fell in behind them, and the rest of the platoon behind me. We moved quickly through the gardens, causing a commotion amongst the pigs and chickens kept by many. I began to worry that we might run into another strongpoint, with nowhere to escape. The machine gun that had fired down the street at us was still shooting, though, at what, I couldn't guess. Soon we were nearly abreast with it, though separated by the buildings that lined the street.

The gardens ended in a tight corner where Calle el Arsenal met the highway. There was nowhere to go but through the back of one of the buildings. I picked what looked like a bar or restaurant, a two-story building that I hoped would look out towards the plaza.

Six men picked up a heavy wooden bench and swung it like a battering ram against the back door of the bar. After four swings, the door crumpled, and one of the men kicked it in. We poured inside.

"All the way to the roof if you can," I said to Papi as he passed by.

When I got inside, I saw that one section had remained on the ground floor, flipping over tables and pushing them towards the front of what was a bar. Wooden shutters covered the windows.

They were ready to throw them open on my word.

"Just wait," I said, taking a narrow set of stairs up to the second floor.

The first things I saw were their eyes. A woman clutched a young child to her chest, and, beside her, was a young man clutching a crucifix fallen from the wall. They were huddled in a corner, wide-eyed and afraid.

"Stay low," I said to them, trying to sound gentle.

"I've sent two men onto the roof," said Papi as the rest of his guerrillas pushed furniture into a makeshift barricade by the windows.

A head appeared from the trap door that led to the roof. "The trucks are just below the windows and a little to the left."

"What are they doing?" I asked.

"They've stopped firing, and an officer is craning his neck down the street to see where we went," said the guerrilla, with a wicked grin.

I got Papi's attention but spoke so the guerrillas downstairs could hear me as well. "On my word, we throw open the shutters and pour everything we have onto the trucks off to the left."

I gave them a moment to pass on the order, and then when they both looked back at me, I shouted: "Patria o muerte!"

The wooden shutters crashed open, and the sound of the firing inside the bar was deafening. There was a shout from below that was cut off mid-sentence, animal moans, and then silence. I crossed the room and looked out the open window. The officer lay dead on the street in a streak of gore, and heaps of men were in the sandbagged cargo beds of the two trucks—the bodies clustered around the heavy machine guns that had driven us off the street.

"Bring those up to the window," shouted Papi, and he sent four guerrillas scampering out the front door. They hadn't made it three steps before there was firing from the colonial-era Alcaldía across the street. We dropped down on the floor and scuttled for cover. The stone building was studded with high windows and seemed to be bristling with guardsmen.

Papi was dragging a table over to give more cover by the window, blood on the side of his face from a cut or wound I couldn't see. I dashed to the back of the room and down the stairs in time to see the body of a wounded guerrilla get dragged in the front door, which another man pushed shut with his foot. The sound of bullets ricocheting off the cinderblock walls or burying themselves in the wooden door and window frames was so loud as to be maddening.

I pressed my head against the wall and closed my eyes for a moment to collect myself. I had half formulated a plan when my train of thought was derailed by a man shouting in my ear.

"There's a police car headed this way!" The man gestured towards the street we'd been driven off of.

I quickly ducked my head out the window, obscured from the view of the Alcaldía, and saw the police car roaring up the middle of the street. I tapped the men nearest to me on the shoulder to get them ready to fire on it. As it got closer, I saw Siki stick his head out the window and wave an arm at us, and we relaxed. They stopped short of the dead officer lying on the street, out of view of the Alcaldía.

The side of the car was riddled in bullet holes, and inside was Fósforo and his pack of young bodyguards. Two of them sat in the open trunk, a stray dog perched between them. I dashed out to speak with him, beckoning him to shelter with me in a deep doorway.

"One of the police stations has already fallen, and the Novios have the last one surrounded," he said as he climbed out of the back of the car.

"That's good."

"The only hold up is here," he said. "When will you reach El Grano?"

"We can't even get to the plaza. We need to take the Alcaldía, and then tighten our grip on it."

"And so?" said Fósforo.

"And so, it will take time," I said.

"We need to take the fort," said Fósforo, "and the longer we wait, the worse it will get. A quick stroke and they'll surrender."

"The locals think there are a thousand men holed up in there, and every time one of us shows themselves on the street, there's a hail of bullets. Let's use the whole column to tighten the noose, starve them out. There's no need for men to die to take it quickly."

"There can't be that many. The longer we wait, the worse this will get," insisted Fósforo.

"Just give me time to do this right, and you'll get what you want," I said.

I could tell that Fósforo wasn't listening, but he took a moment to fill his pipe and light it without offering me any tobacco. "What would you do if one of your men disobeyed your orders?" he asked.

"I'd explain to him why it was important that he do that thing."

"And if he still refused?" asked Fósforo.

"I'm not refusing," I said.

"If someone in your platoon outright refused an order?"

"I'd take away his rifle and put him on trial," I finally said.

Fósforo stood just looking at me in silence.

I held out my rifle to him, but he didn't even glance at it before getting back in the police car. His bodyguards jumped in after him. I saw that Siki had Julio's pistol strapped to his leg as he turned and got behind the wheel. I felt a pang of feeling when I saw it, though I didn't know what it meant.

"Just give me El Grano," he said as they peeled off back the way from which they came.

Papi had been standing nearby, listening, and clapped me on the back.

"This is madness," I said.

"We'll get him his fort. Patria o muerte," said Papi.

I thought for a moment before going back inside the bar and calling the other tenientes over to me. The firing had died down, with only the occasional shots traded between the upper floor and the Alcaldía. Picking up a fragment of wood blown off of somewhere, I began to scratch a map out in the dirt at my feet.

"El Grano is here, and we're here," I said, orienting them to my drawing. "We need to coordinate with the other platoons and draw a circle around the fort." I put X's where I thought the other platoons would be. "Papi, you know the town the best. I want you to brief four runners to go and find the other platoons, and get them to link up around the fort."

He nodded, looking worried, which was exactly the reason I picked him for the job.

"And tell them not to take stupid risks when they do it," I finished. "Do you understand?"

He nodded and then went back upstairs to pick the four guerrillas.

"I want you to take part of your two sections back down the street out of view of the Alcaldía, and to spread out and around it, if you can. Stay behind the houses in the gardens, or on the covered slope of the roof. I don't want you to do anything other than see if you can find an unguarded side of the building, and then report back."

Everyone was busy with the tasks I had set, and no one was looking to me for direction. I took advantage of that moment to sit down on the floor behind the bar and rest. My heart was racing, but I was exhausted, and I think that if I let myself, I could have laid down and slept on the floor for a day, at least. Just as I closed my eyes, I heard my name.

"Paco, what are you doing?"

Esperanza was standing over me, a bloody bandage tied around her forearm.

"What happened?" I asked.

"Nothing," she said. "Come on. There is something you have to hear."

"What is it? Tell me," I said.

She shook her head. "You need to hear it for yourself. It's not far."

I knew from her look to take her seriously. I shouted for Papi, and he came back downstairs, the four runners in tow.

"Keep the pressure on here while we wait for these four to come back, but don't do anything stupid," I said to Papi, who nodded. "I'll be back quickly."

I followed Esperanza out the back and along one of the small streets out of sight of the Alcaldía. She ran ahead without a word, and I struggled to keep up. The road was cobbled here and slippery, and I cursed as my feet slid out from under me.

"Wait up," I said. "We need to be careful we don't run right into their sights."

"This is a short cut," she said. We ran down a side street that we had ignored as we advanced up the diagonal. We paused at the corner of a house whose wall was scarred with bullet holes. The stucco had been painted pink, and the gashes across it looked like torn flesh.

I stumbled as I looked at the wall and came to a stop pressed up against Esperanza. As soon as she felt me behind her, she dashed into the street.

"This way," she shouted as she ran.

She veered off out of sight around the corner. At that moment, the street in front of me was torn up by gunfire. The long rip of a machine gun firing made me cringe, and I dropped down onto my haunches, my chest suddenly tight with fear.

An that moment, I had no idea whether Esperanza had made it across the street—whether she had lived or died.

I didn't dare look to see. I could already imagine her sprawled out on the cobblestones, and I pushed the vision from my mind.

It should have been obvious before, but it was then I realized that I loved her.

22

I CLOSED MY EYES AS I RACED around the corner and across the street. I was halfway there when I heard the firing again, and dove onto the cobblestones, skinning my elbows and knees, and rolling into cover. I lay still for a moment, every muscle tensed, before looking up. Esperanza was nearly at the end of the street ahead of me.

I jogged to catch up with her, and she turned to look at me and laughed.

"What?" I said, the heat rising in my face.

"Your expression," she said. "You love this, don't you?"

I didn't know what to say. I hated "this," the chaos and blood and fear, even though I knew it was necessary. My tongue was thick with worry at what she might say back. I wanted to force the words past my teeth, to make them real by saying them.

"It's just, I . . ." She had already turned up a path between the houses before I had finished my sentence. I swallowed my words.

Sitting in the garden behind one of the houses was a man with a thick moustache. He wore nothing but uniform trousers, and someone had tied his hands behind his back. He had a black eye and a bloody nose, but stared up at me defiantly from his seat on the floor, knees drawn to his chest. Behind him were two of Esperanza's scouts.

"We caught this officer as he tried to run. He'd spent the night with his mistress," said Esperanza.

"Running is what you will do soon enough," he said. "I was reporting for duty in El Grano."

"Tell him what you told me," said Esperanza.

"Tell him yourself," said the officer.

Esperanza gave him a swift kick with the point of her toe just below the ribs. The man collapsed for a moment, retching onto his trousers.

"I am an officer of the Guardia Nacional! I will not be treated this way."

Esperanza kicked him again, this time mid-thigh, and the man rolled away from her onto his side.

"You'll be treated how I decide you'll be treated. Now tell him what you told me."

His voice was thick with pain. "You'll all be dead or running soon enough when the reinforcements arrive."

"When? How?" I asked. When he hesitated, Esperanza drew back her foot.

"You'll know soon enough," he said. She kicked him again, but he didn't say anything more.

I gestured to Esperanza, and we stepped aside. "He's a stuck-up shit, but I believe him," she said quietly.

"Have you heard about this from anyone else?"

"We haven't captured any other officers, but there has been a rumour spreading through town for days."

"And what's the rumour?"

"An armoured column has been sent from the capital. From the Primero Batallón Blindado. Some are even saying they're due to arrive tonight."

"The reinforcements that you'd heard about?"

"Maybe," she said.

"Is there someone who works at the railyard who might know for certain?"

"We're already trying to find someone like that."

"Have you told Fósforo?"

"Not yet. We're not sure where he is."

"He was rolling around in a police car when I saw him last."

"Then maybe he'll find us. But we need to come up with a plan for this train."

I ran my hand through my thick hair and rubbed my eyes for a moment. "Besides withdrawing? There are already too many of them."

She gave my arm a squeeze. "We can figure it out."

My cheeks flushed when she touched me, but I didn't think she noticed. I left her with the prisoner and ran back to where I had left my platoon. I took a longer route this time, avoiding the street where we had been fired upon, and making my way back to the yards that led to the back of the bar. Up ahead, towering over the roofs of the buildings, was a thick plume of dark grey smoke. I couldn't see where it was coming from exactly and started moving faster, tripping over the wreckage of the fences over which we had already crossed.

There was still gunfire from all around the city, but it was less intense than before. The church bells had stopped ringing, and in the moments when the city was silent, I could hear a droning noise that was out of place. I stopped for a moment, thinking perhaps the sound was in my head. My eyes closed, I heard it clearly, getting louder, and looked up towards where I thought it was coming from. Low in the sky, approaching the far side of town, were two planes flying one behind the other. For a moment, I thought that they might drop parachutists, but then I saw a short stream of black dots fall from their bellies. A line of fire and smoke cut across the silhouette of the buildings closest to me, all I could see of the destruction left by the bombers. I felt the explosions in my chest and my ears, the rippling sound filling my head.

The planes flew out of sight, and I kept moving forward, up to the back of the bar, which stank like wood smoke. I crouched as I entered the back to find Papi standing behind the bar, the floor awash with blood and covered with wounded guerrillas. Their wounds were being bandaged with what few supplies we had. There was the sporadic sound of shooting outside, but no one in the bar seemed concerned.

"What's happening?" I said.

"We took the Alcaldía," said Papi with pride.

I started to get angry. "But at what cost? Didn't I say . . ."

"Come look," said Papi, and he led me upstairs.

The second floor was empty, the family that had been sheltering there gone. Papi went and stood in front of the open windows, gesturing grandly outside. I stood beside him and looked out.

The smoke I had seen was pouring out every window of the Alcaldía, and the wall nearest to us was scarred and blackened.

"We used these," said Papi, lifting a liquor bottle from amongst a cluster of them on the floor. It stank of gasoline and had a rag stuffed down the neck. "The first few through the windows got them to think about something other than shooting, and when they started pouring out the doors like rats from a sinking ship, we were ready."

"How many?" I asked.

"Rats? Maybe fifty or more."

"No," I said, "ours."

"Perhaps ten, including the ones downstairs."

"We won't win at those odds," I said to Papi, trying not to shame him but just to make him understand.

"We won't win by retreating either," he said. "Patria o muerte."

As we stood by the window, I heard the droning sound of the bombers again in the distance. I grabbed Papi by the collar and dragged him down to the floor. He shouted in surprise and pushed me away as I pulled him off his feet.

"Just wait," I said.

He looked at me like I was mad, but I touched my ear with my finger, and he listened.

The planes must have unleashed another stream of bombs, and a quick series of explosions ripped through the street below us. A ball of dust rolled in through the window.

Papi's eyes were wide. "They'll destroy the city to save it."

I beat some of the dust off my shirt and trousers and helped Papi to his feet. At that moment, I knew what needed to be done.

"Where's the rest of the platoon?"

"Along the rooftops overlooking the plaza and el Grano."

"And did you link up with the others?"

"With Loba, Huracán and Juan. We're still hunting for the rest."

"Bring them here. We need to draw a tight circle around the fort, but not press it too hard."

"Why not press hard and finish them?"

"I'll explain in a moment, but we've got bigger problems."

"Bigger than the fort?"

My expression must have been enough because Papi stopped asking questions and went back to organizing the platoon. He sent a runner to bring each of the other platoon commanders to the bar. While I waited, I dragged a dozen mismatched chairs out the back door. I set them in a circle in the garden behind the bar, protected by the houses clustered all around us. I kept listening for the droning sound of the planes, but they seemed to have flown back from whence they came.

I took off my webbing and collapsed on one of the chairs. It had been a long night of marching before we entered the town, but I was used to those. It felt as if I had been awake for a week, and I suddenly wanted nothing more than to lie down and sleep. I stood up again, not willing to be asleep when the others arrived. I paced the short length of the garden to stay awake.

Loba and Huracán came first. Loba shook my hand, grinning, but her face was a mask of exhaustion. Huracán hugged me instead, slapping my back until we were enveloped in a cloud of dust.

"They didn't know what hit them!" said Huracán.

Papi had wandered out of the bar. "We had them on the run like rats!" he said.

I tried not to dampen their enthusiasm, but my look must have betrayed my feelings.

"What's wrong?" asked Loba. "It's not Fósforo . . ."

"No," I said, "not that I know. Just wait, wait until everyone is here."

We waited in the garden, and one of the men in the platoon

brought out cafécitos from inside. I drank mine in one short gulp and passed the glass right back to him.

Flaco, Calixto, and Juan arrived together, and we all embraced them, one by one.

"Where's Santi?" I asked, regretting the words as soon as I saw Juan's expression.

"The Novios took the police station," he said, "but . . ."

The word hung in mid-air, and I'm sure that we all finished it differently in our minds.

We all sat grim-faced on the odd chairs while the news sank in. By the time Esperanza arrived, we must have looked miserable. My stomach did a little flip when I saw her.

"Fósforo?" she asked quietly.

"I'm sure he's fine," I said, though I knew no more than she did. "He'll show up."

I called for more coffee and stood up to address the group. "We have an unexpected problem and an opportunity as well." I gestured to Esperanza.

"We captured an officer as he climbed over the garden fence of his mistress' house this morning," she said.

"I admire a man whose priorities are clear," snickered Huracán. His laughter broke the tension, and everyone laughed. Even I managed a smile at the officer's bad fortune.

"He's told us that there are reinforcements coming to the town. Rumour has it they have tanks."

"Can he be trusted?" asked Flaco, a tall man with a reedy voice. "Is he trying to scare us?"

"We've confirmed it since," said Esperanza. "A guy who drives a delivery truck told us that the Guardia was collecting all the diesel and oil they could find in town. One of the guardsmen let slip it was for armoured vehicles."

"When will they be here?" asked Huracán.

"Maybe tonight," she said.

"Then it's simple. We need to take El Grano before then."

"Simple? If we do that, there won't be any of us left to fight the tanks," said Loba. "Stop thinking like an idiot."

"Patria o muerte," replied Huracán.

"There needs to be something left of the country, and of us, in the end," snapped Loba.

"Listen to me," I said. "We need to be smart about this. El Grano is surrounded. We'll keep it that way while we get ready for the train."

"We can't fight them on two sides," said Calixto. "There's not enough room to make them dance like at the Vadito."

"I'm not thinking about fighting them," I said, "I'm thinking about killing them. Quickly."

"A column of tanks? Are you mad?" said Loba.

"Are you a coward?" countered Flaco.

The group erupted into an argument, voices and tempers raised, until I stepped into the middle of the circle. "Enough. There's no shame in being smart about this. We're not Spanish knights looking to joust; we're fighting for our lives and our country."

I took a broken piece of fence and quickly sketched the fort and the rail line in the dirt. "The majority of the column will keep the Guardia encircled in El Grano. We just need to keep enough pressure on them that they don't think of trying to break out. My platoon will move to the market adjacent to where the main road enters town and next to the railyard. When the train carrying the tanks pulls in, we'll block the road behind them with whatever we can muster and pelt it with Papi's special cocktails from all sides. If they stay inside their tanks, we'll cook them alive. If they do escape, we'll shoot them down. In either case, we'll have them."

No one looked at me. Instead, they studied the dirt at my feet.

"Starting tomorrow, we'll strangle El Grano. And this will be simpler without the spectre of reinforcements at our back. Step by step, we are marching to victory."

"But . . . tanks," said Loba.

"Patria o muerte," replied Huracán.

"Patria o muerte," repeated everyone else in the circle.

The meeting over, each of the platoon commanders went back

to pass my instructions to their people. Esperanza waited until we were alone. "I'll stay with you," she said.

My tongue was thick again, and I felt as if I could hardly speak. "No. I don't know if this plan of mine will work."

"It will work," she said.

"I need you and your scouts to do something else for us."

"What's more important than the train?"

"I need you to find Fósforo."

I wasn't confident that we could hold the streets around El Grano if they tried to break out, but I was certain that the tanks were the bigger threat. We'd found all the buildings that overlooked the main road as it reached the edge of town, and I'd placed a handful of guerrillas in each of them. I'd sent Papi house-to-house to ask for bottles, and we'd drained most of the gasoline from the two trucks that we'd ambushed in the street below the bar. There was just enough left for them to be driven into place to block the road behind the tanks. Everything was ready to be set in motion once the tanks arrived. Even worse than combat was the waiting.

I sat with Papi and a young guerrilla who we'd named Abelito on the roof of a pulpería from where I could see all the other occupied houses. A flimsy billboard for Victoria beer hid us from view. Our bottles were stacked in a cluster near the edge of the roof, ready to be launched when the time came. There was still firing throughout the town, but it came in short spurts. I had no idea what any of it meant, if anything, but neither could I worry about it for long. My focus was on the problem at hand.

"I've never seen a tank before," said Abelito.

"You won't have much of a chance to see these, either," said Papi. "They'll be heaps of smoking metal before long."

Abelito didn't look convinced.

"Say what's on your mind," I said to him.

"It's only that . . ." He looked back and forth between Papi and

I. His lower lip trembled a little. "Why are they sending these tanks if we are going to defeat them so easily."

Papi cuffed him across the back of the head good-naturedly. "They don't know what we have up our sleeves," he said. "if they did, the whole lot of them would put down their guns and walk away. The war would be over."

Abelito said nothing further, sitting sullenly against the billboard.

"Listen to me, boy, when we're done with these tanks, that fortress will crack like a rotten egg," said Papi.

"We have a good plan," I said, "and no matter what happens today, we'll win in the end."

Papi opened his mouth, and I saw Abelito cringe a little, but he was cut off by a sudden crash of gunfire from across town. The noise built and built as more guns joined in, echoing down the streets towards us.

"Is that the fortress? Are they breaking out?"

I stood up and strained my ears to listen. "I can't tell." Papi leaned out beside me, his hands cupped around his ears. "It's in town, at least."

We listened to the noise for a few minutes more. Four explosions, in rapid succession, sent a cloud of smoke up from near El Grano.

"Something big is happening," said Papi.

"Take Abelito and go and see what's happening," I told him.

"What about the tanks?"

"I'll throw bottles with both hands," I said.

He smiled at my weak joke. "Come on, boy," said Papi. He swung his leg over a rickety ladder that led to the ground and clambered down. I passed his rifle down to him and did the same for Abelito when he followed him.

"We'll be quick," said Papi. He dashed across the street and disappeared into an alleyway.

The noise of firing continued, but I strained to listen for the sound of the train instead. The wind whistled through the gaps in the billboard, and aside from the fighting in town, it was all I could hear. I kept listening to the ebb and flow of the battle raging blocks away, almost missing the sound of someone climbing up the ladder. I swung my carbine around, shoving it in the face that appeared at the edge of the roof.

"It's just me," said Loba, pushing it away. "What's happening in town?"

She climbed up and stood next to me, looking over the rooftops towards the fort.

"I've sent Papi . . ." I said, when she interrupted me with a shout.

"Look!" She stretched out her arm to point towards the centre of town. I pushed myself up to my feet with my rifle. Over the top of El Grano fluttered a yellowed bed sheet that had been hoisted up the flag pole.

"The bastards quit!" she said, before kissing me on both cheeks. I didn't know how to respond.

She practically slid back down the ladder and shouted at her platoon. "They've quit! Look!" One by one, her guerrillas appeared in windows and on rooftops to gaze out at the bedsheet rippling gently in the wind.

The bells in the church towers began to ring again, not the slow and steady beat of this morning, but wild pealing as if madmen pulled their ropes. More of my guerrillas came out of hiding, standing in the open and looking towards the centre of town.

"Get back where I put you," I shouted, waving at them. "This isn't over yet!"

Loba was about to say something, but I gave her a look, and she trotted across the road. "Back to your posts," she shouted.

I could see a police car racing down a street from the centre of town, and I climbed down from the roof to meet it. It was the same car Fósforo had been in this morning, and it pulled up at the edge of town. I could see Fósforo sitting in the front seat, furiously smoking a cigar. As I stepped closer, I noticed that his arm was in a sling, a bloody bandage wrapped around his forearm.

"How's your arm?" I asked.

"It's nothing," he said, waving his cigar at me with his good hand.

"Where have you been?"

"Where you should have been, fighting these bastards. What are you doing hiding here?"

I was stunned at the venom in his voice and didn't answer.

"Are you deaf," said Siki, leaning over Fósforo to glare at me from the driver's seat.

"Esperanza captured an officer this morning. There is a column of tanks coming . . ." My voice trailed off as I saw that Fósforo's expression remained unchanged.

"Just rumours," he said. "We captured the radio room in El Grano. Although they've asked for reinforcements, all they've received back was encouragement and thinly-veiled threats not to surrender."

"Do we know for sure?" I asked, confused.

"You can look through the logs for yourself," said Fósforo. "We'll need your men to help handle the prisoners we captured in El Grano."

He turned away from me and clapped Siki on the shoulder. The car slipped into gear with a thunk and drove off, turning too quickly up the next street that led to the town's centre. As the car passed, my platoon cheered from their vantage points, and Fósforo waved at them, the cigar clenched in his fingers.

I rubbed my face with both hands, alone on the street. When I opened my eyes, Loba was standing in front of me, her face a knot of concern.

"Should we abandon the ambush?" she asked.

"There are no tanks coming," I said, my throat suddenly dry. "Gather everyone together, and we'll march up to El Grano."

She turned away and began shouting at the platoon. The church bells were still ringing, and I could see that people were beginning to venture out of their houses and onto the street. They kept a wary distance from us, and I was in no mood to try to convince them of our good intentions. When the platoon had gathered together, we marched in a loose column up towards the Plaza de Armas.

More and more people began to fill the street, and it felt like we were swimming upstream as we marched. People began to bring us food and drink, and it was only with a great deal of shouting that Loba, Huracán and I were able to keep the platoon together.

Out of the crowd ahead appeared Papi and Abelito. Between them, they were dragging a civilian, Papi holding him by the scruff of his neck. The man's feet dragged across the cobblestones as he stumbled and was half-carried forward. A small crowd followed them as they brought him towards us.

"Keep walking," said Papi, backhanding the man across the face. He dropped the wretch at my feet, and the man collapsed into a heap.

"Who's this?" I said.

"The King Rat," said Papi.

"Who?"

Papi grabbed him roughly under the jaw and lifted his face. I recognized him in an instant. He seemed smaller than he was in my memory, his hair thinner and with more grey showing. "He looked shifty, and so I grabbed him. Some of the townspeople recognized him. The bastard took off his uniform and was trying to sneak away and left his men to surrender."

I cleared my throat. "Lieutenant Colonel Espina, is it?"

If he recognized me, he didn't show it. He stood up and straightened his shirt with both hands. He didn't look comfortable in civilian clothes, but he looked me in the eye when he spoke. "I wish to speak to one of your officers," he said.

"Our Capitán isn't enough of an officer for you?" asked Papi.

Espina eyed me with disgust but said nothing further.

"We'll bring him to the Comandante," I said. At this, Espina brightened slightly. "He has wanted to meet Matias Cabrero's murderer for quite some time."

The colour drained from Espina's face as Papi grabbed him by the collar again.

"We don't hang men on a whim," I said. "There'll be a fair trial."

Espina laughed. "You're a bigger fool than I thought."

Papi cuffed him across the back of the head. A thousand things vied for my attention, but Espina looked at me with contempt.

"I'm not afraid of your justice," he said. "Patria o muerte."

23

THE GARRISON OF EL GRANO was a pathetic lot, seated in long rows inside the walls of the fort. They'd been stripped of their uniforms and were shivering in the early night air. Nearly four hundred of them had surrendered in the end. Their dead lay in a heap nearby, beside an even larger stack of abandoned weapons and clothing.

My platoon had been tasked to search the fort for every useable piece of equipment we could find. We busted open the lock on the door of one of the storerooms built into the fort's outer walls.

"Madre de Dios," huffed Papi under his breath.

The room was stacked with boxes of ammunition of all types. It was so full that only one of us could fit inside at a time.

"Move all of this outside and give me a count of what there is," I told him.

Papi rubbed his belly thoughtfully. "There's too much here to carry," he said.

"Stack it by the Guardia's trucks," I said. "We're not going to be able to go back to how things were."

Papi swung his long rosary around his back and grabbed the first box from the stack by its rope handles, and carried it out of the storeroom. I lifted one as well and followed him across the interior of the fort.

"It would be best if we just took what we can carry and destroyed the rest," said Papi. "We could melt back into the hills, where even an armoured train couldn't touch us."

"And what about the townspeople? Do they all come with us?"

"They either join us, or they go back to their lives," said Papi.

"Easier said than done. There will be a reckoning when the Guardia come back."

Papi laughed as he set the box down. "Maybe they never come back."

"Wishful thinking," I replied.

We kept up a steady flow of boxes from all the storerooms, like ants raiding a rival colony. A mountain of equipment began to form, with the lines of prisoners prostrate at its foot.

The Novios had been tasked with tracking down any police or government officials hiding in plainclothes in town. A posse of eager locals helped identify them and point out where they could be hiding. As we continued our labour, I saw the Novios march in through the gate of the fortress in two loose lines, a half dozen sullen civilians, hands tied behind their backs, walking in their midst. Behind all of them marched Fósforo.

"Strip them and line them up with the others," he said, strutting across the open space to stand at the head of the lines of prisoners. None of them looked up at him, trapped in their own dark thoughts and worries.

"If the tables were turned, and fate reversed our roles," said Fósforo loudly, "there is no question what you would have done to any of us you had captured." Not one of the prisoners looked up as he addressed them. The column closed up around the prisoners instinctively, leaning in to listen to Fósforo.

"But we know that you are not all criminals, but rather are victims like us. The same oppressive regime that saps the blood of the People spills yours to keep itself fat and wealthy."

He paused for a moment. The column was listening in rapt attention.

"And so, we will give you a choice. Join us, and fight towards victory and a better country for everyone. Or crawl back to your masters in a regime that will continue to exploit you as it goes down in defeat."

A low murmur swept across the rows of guardsmen, but none of them got to their feet or indicated that they would defect. Fósforo waited, maybe hoping that if one of them chose to join us, others would follow. After a few long minutes, he signalled to the Novios, who prodded the prisoners back to their feet and towards the gate. Fósforo turned his back on them and walked towards me, his head down.

"You can't shame them and embrace them at the same time," I said to him.

He looked up at me in surprise, not having seen me until that moment. "I'm just telling them the truth."

"The truth is something you can't be told; you have to see it for yourself."

The prisoners were herded out the gate, which hung askew on its hinges. In the plaza, we could see a large crowd had gathered. They jeered at the guardsmen as they filed out. Fósforo and I watched them march in silence, their tanned faces and thin, pale bodies giving them a ridiculous look, like an army of matchsticks trudging out into the streets.

"Releasing this many at once feels risky," I said.

"There aren't enough jail cells in the country to hold them all."

"There's at least room for a man like Espina. I'll organize a trial in the morning."

Fósforo kept watching the prisoners filing out. "We already had the trial," he said. "Guilty."

"What do you mean?"

"Justice was seen to be done, just as you've said. He's in the heap with the others." He was coolly watching the last of the guardsmen marching out the gate, but I could see that his jaw was clenched. I said nothing.

Papi walked up to us, followed by Loba and Huracán. All three of them were holding a mortar round in each hand like maracas.

"We found new instruments for the orchestra to play when we next meet the Guardia," said Papi, shaking his hips and the mortar rounds in unison. At any other time, I would have convulsed with laughter, but at that moment, my face was a mask of anger.

"Does the maestro have the means to make those maracas heard?" asked Fósforo.

"Three tubes," said Huracán. "Maybe the same ones from the Vadito."

The three guerrillas had come to joke around and celebrate with us, but they quickly realized that we were in no mood.

"Make sure those are crated carefully and stacked beside the trucks," I said.

"Of course, jefe," said Huracán, and the three of them departed.

We stood in silence again for a long moment until I found the right words.

"Our justice has to be different from their justice," I said.

Fósforo relented a little, his shoulders slumped. "You're not wrong," he said, "but sometimes justice must be swift."

"But only if it's still justice."

"Do you see the heap of dead men there?" he said, pointing. "That doesn't even include our own. What's one more, whether Espina or you or me. The war goes on."

He started to walk away but stopped and retraced his steps to look me in the eye. "If those tanks had arrived, you would have saved us, you know," said Fósforo quietly.

"But how did you know it was just a rumour?" I asked.

"I didn't," he said. "Not until we captured the radio room here and saw the log where it showed the request for reinforcements was denied."

He gave me a smile, the one I recognized from the other times that he'd muddled his way through things by luck. He clapped me on both shoulders and then wandered off to where the police car was parked, his bodyguards lounging on the seats or asleep on the hood.

It was hard to stay angry at Fósforo, and I wandered back into the crowds of guerrillas and townsfolk who filled the inside of the fort. A band was starting to play, a funny old song I remembered that always got people dancing. A young boy sat on a wooden box, hammering out a beat with his hands, while three guitarists strummed the melody in unison. "When the farmer and his wife go to bed at night,/ Two by two, the animals get up and dance . . ."

Pairs of dancers flooded the area around the band. Guerrillas mixed with townspeople in a swirling, laughing mass. Across the dance floor, I could see Esperanza watching the crowd, smiling. A guerrilla from Juan's platoon grabbed her hand and tried to get her to dance, but she turned him down, and he grabbed an older woman standing nearby instead.

I knew that I wanted to speak to her, to dance with her, but seeing her send that guerrilla away made me suddenly nervous.

On the other edge of the dance floor, I saw Papi and another guerrilla carrying a metal washtub and setting it down. He pulled a bottle of beer from it and held it up for me to see. Esperanza seemed entranced by the dancers, and so I left her where she was and walked over to Papi.

"Donations from the townsfolk," he said. I raised an eyebrow. "Freely given," he added.

"In that case, I'll take three," I said. I took the first one he handed me and upended it, pouring the cool beer down my throat as quickly as I could. It warmed my belly a little, and I felt a bit flushed.

"Take it easy," said Papi, "we have all night."

"Not for what I want to do," I said, taking the other two bottles from him.

I walked back to Esperanza with a bottle in each hand. Esperanza's face was illuminated by the light of a dozen lanterns set up around the band. Her hair was tied back in a thick braid that hung down her back. Even in her baggy clothes, I could see the outline of her lean, hard body. The light danced in her eyes, and when she turned to look at me, my stomach flipped. Before I could speak, she wrapped her arms around me.

"Paco, we did it."

I suddenly didn't know what to say.

She leaned back, her hands sliding across my shoulders. "Are you alright? Did you speak with Fósforo?" she asked.

"He spoke to me," I said.

"It's not as bad as all that," she replied.

"The strain of leading this," I said, gesturing at the guerrilla column around us, "is getting to all of us."

"Even Fósforo is feeling it," she said.

"Especially Fósforo."

She shook her head. "Of all of us, his is the vision that has never wavered, never been clouded by doubt—even when the rest of us are discouraged. That's what he brings to the Revolution. Unquenchable zeal."

"You're an optimist, too," I said. "You've never let anything stop you."

She smiled at me, her face alight. "I love you, Paco," she said.

I was stunned. "I love you, too," I replied, pulling her close to me.

"You're like the brother I've always wished for," she whispered in my ear.

I held her stiffly before taking my arms from around her, a weak smile plastered on my face. If she noticed, she said nothing, and we went back to listening to the music and watching the dancers. My gaze wandered over to Fósforo.

He still sat apart from the column, silent and brooding, his young bodyguards all around him. Siki was telling a joke or a story, waving his arms emphatically, and eliciting laughter. Fósforo was unmoved.

Esperanza saw who I was looking at and squeezed my arm. "I'll talk to him," she said. "He gets like this sometimes." She took the beer bottles from the ground and held them in one hand as she wrapped her other arm around me. "Maybe these will help," she said.

I watched as she walked over to Fósforo and held the beer out to him. He waved it away, but she sat down beside him and took a sip herself. She called Siki over to her, and soon he was telling another story. Fósforo smiled and took a sip from Esperanza's beer. I kept watching, trying to read her lips, to hear what she was saying to him.

"Capitán, you have to play for us."

The interruption derailed my train of thought. Loba held out a guitar for me. More of my platoon stood behind her, their faces alight.

"I'm out of practice," I said.

"Then practice," she said, "for us."

I heard the band stop playing, and they looked over expectantly at me. Behind them, the moon looked small and dim, hanging low in the sky.

"How do I know if it's even in tune?"

"Nonsense," said Loba. "Try it, and if it is isn't to your liking, you can tune it."

With a sigh, I took the guitar from her and strummed my hand across the strings. The sound was fine, though my fingers felt soft. Walking towards the band, I began to play. The dancers parted in front of me, watching expectantly. My heart felt heavy. As I walked, I began to sing, making the lyrics up as I went:

"A lantern shines in a high window, burning brightly, out of reach, / Below I sit in darkness, the tower's walls I cannot breach."

EL VOLCÁN

24

THAT MORNING WE DID NOT KNOW what the day would hold, and so the date was not yet etched in our consciousness. After daybreak, we started burying the dead. We buried our comrades in a park behind El Grano and the guardsmen in a long trench dug by bulldozer in a disused lot on the edge of town. I helped Juan dig a grave for his brother, one of many burying a friend or relation.

We could not find either of the town's priests to say a Mass for our dead, and so it was left to Fósforo to speak. People thronged the park, and it seemed that nearly every person in town came to pay their respects.

I don't remember what Fósforo said exactly, although as I recall it was more about the future than the past, and more about the lives of the townspeople than the lives of the dead guerrillas laid out beside their graves. I remember that we sang a song, "Hasta Siempre," and that when that was done, Juan and I twisted up the ends of the blanket wrapped around Santi so that we would have a tighter grip and lowered him into the ground. The silence afterwards was only interrupted by the sounds of sobbing and shovels.

Fósforo had agreed not to linger in town any longer than we had to, for fear of the bombers returning. We spread the tattered map we had captured in La Trinidad across the hood of his police car. When we looked at the department, it was obvious what we had to do.

"If we hold the bridge just south of Hacienda Inocentes, we control the route between here and the capital. I sent two escopeteros by car this morning to scout the village and the bridge," he said. "They'll meet our column with word on whether there are any Guardia."

I nodded. "And from there?"

"One step at a time," he said.

I didn't know if he didn't trust me or if he was just unsure of the future, but I left it at that. I'd taken his admission that I was right about the tanks as an apology and didn't expect to get much more. For the moment, I was focused on the problems right under my nose.

The column's size had swelled again as over a hundred men and women from the town volunteered to join us. There weren't enough trucks and other vehicles in El Grano to carry the entire column and our supplies, and so I took Papi with me in a jeep to drive around town to find trucks or buses we could commandeer. There was no shortage of people who were willing to donate to the cause.

"If only the townsfolk were as free with their daughters as they are with their trucks," said Papi as we drove to the corner of town where the factories were.

I laughed at the forlorn look on his face as he spoke. "Don't you have someone waiting for you at home?" I asked.

"Neither a sweetheart at home nor a home for her to wait at," he said.

"How so?" I asked.

"I haven't been back to my village for many years. I left to seek my fame and fortune," he said.

"Well, why not go back?" I asked.

"Maybe once the Revolution is over, and I can show up in my uniform," he said. "That'd make the women notice me."

"I didn't know you had so much trouble," I said.

"Well, we're not all as lucky as you, having a piece of ass like Esperanza hanging off your every word," he said. The words died on his lips as he spoke them, my expression cutting the conversation short. "I didn't mean anything . . ." he said.

"Just drive," I replied.

Mounted in every serviceable vehicle that we could find, the column was ready to move just before midday. Fósforo led the column from his police car, and very slowly, we began to wind through town towards Highway 23. Well-wishers packed the streets, and our departure was more like a parade than a military movement. I watched from the cab of a Coca Cola delivery truck as Fósforo climbed halfway out the window of his car and sat on the top of the door, gesturing at the crowds. Someone in the crowd handed him a bouquet of flowers, which he waved above his head.

The column picked up speed as we passed the edge of town, though the highway was in such bad repair that every vehicle was forced to weave around potholes and washouts. This was the same route down which we had sent the disgraced guardsmen who refused to join us, but there was no sign of them.

The heat of the day was hard on the guerrillas who were riding in the open backs or on the roofs of our trucks, but we didn't have a plan for where or when to stop to rest in the shade. I leaned out the window to see the front of the column and signal to them. I could see glimpses of the police car through the trees that lined much of the road, but no amount of waving could catch their attention.

"Use your horn," I said to the driver, a young man named Gonzalo who had just joined us in San Jose Guachipilín. He used one hand on the steering wheel while the other held a handkerchief that he constantly used to wipe the sweat from his face.

"Jefe," he said as he gave a long blast.

"Keep doing it," I said, and Gonzalo started to beat out a rhythm with the horn.

"Were you a musician?" I asked.

He looked embarrassed. "No, jefe, I drove this truck for the bottling plant. But I liked to go dancing."

Our honking got Fósforo's attention, and the police car pulled over to the side of the road. When the truck behind him began to stop, they waved it onward, and so the column kept moving. We slowed down as we approached them, and I leaned down out of the truck's high window. Fósforo's face appeared from the back seat of the car. Behind him, I saw Esperanza.

"What is all the noise about?" he asked.

"We need to stop and rest for a moment; the backs of these trucks have no shade."

He looked back at the column, though what he could see from the window of his car, I didn't know.

"I'll find a spot," he said before disappearing back into the car, which sped off to overtake the head of the column again, leaving us choking in his dust. Gonzalo held his handkerchief over his nose and mouth, and I pulled my shirt over mine.

When the dust cleared, Gonzalo struck up an awkward conversation. "How well do you know the Comandante?" he asked.

"I knew him from before all this," I said.

"Forgive me for asking," he said, "but was he always like this?"

I had an answer on the tip of my tongue but checked myself. "Like what?"

"Well," said Gonzalo, "just so, impressive."

"He made an impression on everyone he met, even then," I said.

Gonzalo seemed satisfied with this, and we drove on in silence.

The column eventually stopped on a thickly treed stretch of road, the convoy pulling up nose to tail to take maximum advantage of the shade. Everyone dismounted, and I could see from the beet-red faces of some of the guerrillas that the rest was needed.

I stepped down from the truck and stretched my legs. The guerrillas who rode on top of the supplies piled in the back were clambering down as well. "Check the engine and the tires," I said to Gonzalo. "I'll be back."

I stepped off into the trees beside the road to relieve myself, one of maybe fifty people in a ragged line beside the column who all had the same idea at once. The land beside the road was an abandoned farm, the field full of closely-packed banana trees. The air was sweet with the smell of over-ripe fruit. I went back to the truck, got a machete from one of the guerrillas, and cut a bunch of bananas from the tree that I could carry over one shoulder back to the truck.

"Some of these are still edible," I said as I passed it up to a guerrilla still sitting on the mountain of boxes in the truck bed.

"We'll find them," he said, picking through the fruit with the ease of someone accustomed to it.

"Do you have a tarp or something that you can string up for shade back there?" I asked.

None of the guerrillas answered me. I didn't recognize any of them and saw that none carried a rifle either. I climbed on the back of the truck and started shifting crates of our supplies around to make a sheltered area. "Get up here and help," I said, and the young guerrillas leapt to it. In a few minutes, I helped them build a shaded area where they could all fit, albeit barely.

They mumbled their thanks and then went back to sitting beside the road, waiting for the word to mount up again. I took two bananas that weren't too far gone and brought them to Gonzalo. He stuck one in each pocket and went back to checking the engine.

I knew nothing about such things but watched him with interest. He tugged on the belts to make sure they were snug, and gingerly stuck his hand under the hot engine parts at various places.

When he saw me watching him, he explained. "No fresh leaks," he said. "This truck is fine."

I didn't walk to the head of the column to speak with Fósforo, assuming that he would signal when he was ready for the column to move again. Papi wandered over from his truck farther back, carrying a half-eaten roast chicken under his arm and chewing thoughtfully on a drumstick.

"How did you manage to make that appear?" I asked.

He laughed, bits of chicken in his teeth. "I was waving to the crowds as we drove through San Jose Guachipilín, and a woman passed it up to me from the crowd as gently as if it was a baby."

"Why?" I asked.

Papi shrugged. "Perhaps I'm more charming than I gave myself credit for," he said, chewing thoughtfully. He tore off the second drumstick and passed it to me. "I've been saving this all morning to share with someone over a genteel conversation."

I ate the drumstick, the juices running down my arm.

"And so, as Fósforo's number two, I have a question for you," he said. Gonzalo lingered beside the truck to listen. "What are we getting ourselves into in Hacienda Inocentes?"

"What do you mean?"

"I mean, are we in for a fight or not?"

"There's no permanent garrison there, just a small post at the bridge, but we won't know until we meet up with the escopeteros," I said.

"And what about the guardsmen we let go? Are we going to fight them again at the bridge as well?"

"I don't know," I said, suddenly feeling less sure about the day ahead.

Papi was about to ask another question when the police car turned on its lights and siren. Siki was standing on the roadway waving his arms to get everyone to mount up again, and I could see guerrillas scrambling through the trees of the banana trees to get back. I checked to make sure all of our passengers were aboard and climbed in truck's cab just as Gonzalo began to pull forward. The column was on the move again.

We passed through more countryside filled with fenced pastures and small villages made of shacks clustered by the side of the road. The people we passed all waved at the column, some children running to chase us through the dust. The road curved slowly to the south, and the elevation kept dropping as the plains tilted down towards the sea. In the distance, towering over the plain, was an extinct volcano whose lower slopes were shrouded in vibrant green.

"El Volcán del Santo Sacramento," said Gonzalo, pointing with his chin.

"How do you know that?" I asked.

He gave me a disparaging look. "Everyone knows that," he said.

"Not where I'm from."

Gonzalo's expression could be taken as his judgement on the schools of Managua, but he said nothing further.

The volcano drew closer as we crossed the plains towards Hacienda Inocentes, and a few hours later, when the column stopped again, it stood only a few kilometres from the highway.

"What now?" said Gonzalo.

I checked my watch. "I'm not sure, but we must be close."

We sat together in the truck, waiting, until I saw one of Fósforo's bodyguards run down the side of the column, waving at me. I got down from the truck and followed him.

Tucked into a roadside stand of trees was one of the jeeps we had taken from the Guardia. An escopetero, dressed in civilian clothes and a broad-brimmed hat, with a shotgun over his shoulder, was talking with Fósforo and Esperanza. Behind the wheel of the jeep, also dressed as a civilian, was the guerrilla I knew as Pelón. He gave a little wave when he saw me looking at him, but his expression was dark.

I heard the man in the broad-brimmed hat speaking quickly. "Just follow us," he said, tears filling his eyes.

"What is it?" insisted Fósforo.

The man crossed himself and shook his head. "Just follow," he said again and walked back to his jeep. Pelón started up as he approached, pulled away when he climbed in.

"I don't know what's going on," said Esperanza, "but they can be trusted."

"Let's keep the column here, but go ahead with them ourselves," I said.

Fósforo nodded and climbed in the back of the police car, followed by Esperanza. I got in after her, and another guerrilla after me. Siki and three others sat up front on the bench seat, and when Fósforo waved his hand, the car lurched forward and sped off after the jeep.

It wasn't far to Hacienda Inocentes, but the jeep didn't slow down as it entered the town. We rolled through quickly, it being no bigger than La Trinidad. From every window and signpost hung red and black cloth, some of it bedsheets or carpets, all in an approximation of the Sandinista flag. The colours even adorned the high windows of the small stone convent the town was named after.

"There's not a single person here," observed Esperanza, and as she said it, I knew it to be true. There wasn't even a dog on the street or any other living thing.

Past the town, the trees became thick again, hanging over the highway like a verdant tunnel. I saw the jeep stop up ahead, and the steel girders of the double bridge ahead of them. Neither Pelón nor the other man got out of their seats as we pulled up beside them and got out.

"We think it's everyone," said the escopetero. Pelón sat rigidly, staring straight ahead, his hands gripping the wheel. Fósforo dashed forward, and Esperanza and I followed him until we could see what they meant.

Hanging at even intervals along each side of the bridge were the townspeople of Hacienda Inocentes. The nuns were clustered on the far side of the bridge, some of their black and white habits stained with blood. Closer to us were the smaller bodies of the children. Fósforo kept going, running onto the bridge, and causing a great flock of carrion birds to take off and circle lazily overhead.

"There could still be Guardia," I said. "We should bring up the column."

"To witness this?" said Esperanza.

"It will remind them why they're fighting," I replied.

Esperanza shook her head, at what I'm not sure, and walked forward to stand with Fósforo, one thin arm around his shoulders. Even at a distance, I could see that his body was wracked with sobs. Behind me stood his bodyguards, uncertain as to whether to come any closer to him.

I heaved a sigh, suddenly remembering what Fósforo had said about what motivated every true revolutionary. Love. I walked up slowly behind them, trying not to look too closely at the details of the scene around me. I put my arm around him as well, and for a moment, we stood together, our bodies welded firmly together.

"We need to keep pressing onward," I said. "We'll find justice, on the other side of this bridge."

Fósforo didn't reply, shaking his head.

"This is no place to stop," I said. "This village was celebrating our victory when . . . this happened. We need to keep winning. To find those responsible for this."

Fósforo turned to me. "Don't you see? We're the ones responsible."

"Don't say that," cooed Esperanza. "It's not true."

Fósforo broke away from the two of us, turning to face us instead. "It is true. We gave these people hope. And the prisoners we released? They exacted their revenge, and we did nothing to protect these people."

"It couldn't have been the guardsmen," I said. "There's no way that they've walked this far."

"Well, who else?" said Fósforo. "And who else should have protected these people?"

"The best way to protect them is to keep fighting, to keep the Guardia and the government on their back foot," I said, trying not to sound angry.

Fósforo shook his head. "There are too many civilians with the column now for us to do that. We need to find a place of safety to consider our next move."

"Taking time to think is rarely the wrong answer," said Esperanza.

I wasn't so sure but said nothing.

"Get Juan to find a camp, up above the highway, somewhere that we can defend," said Fósforo. Esperanza looked at me, her eyes pleading.

I nodded and left to find the column.

25

JUAN LAID OUT THE CAMPSITE, much like many others we had inhabited on the slopes of the Serranías. This time, with our numbers swollen again, we stretched much farther across the landscape. He designated an area in the centre of the camp for the headquarters, but Fósforo had selected his own place to sleep. Higher up the slope of the dormant volcano was a small set of ruins—a rough platform of massive stones—and this is where Fósforo pitched his tent. The remainder of the camp spread out below him as if his hammock was a fountainhead.

Fósforo left the day-to-day running of the camp to me, immersing himself in reading what few books we had, and long walks alone. The logistics of feeding and housing these many people were daunting, but I organized the platoons into neighbourhoods and made them responsible for building shelters and defending them. We cooked all of the food centrally and gave it to the platoons to distribute. It felt more like being the mayor than a guerrilla leader, but it needed to be done.

Word had spread far and wide about the massacre at Hacienda Inocentes, though we heard from some campesinos that the government blamed us for the deaths. It seemed that few people in the countryside believed them, even if there were no witnesses alive but the perpetrators. Our presence on the slopes of Santo

Sacramento was too large to conceal, and we began to attract others who sought protection. It seemed as if all the disenfranchised people of the department had decided to throw their lot in with us.

Several weeks passed, but the column didn't move. If Fósforo had a plan, he didn't share it with any of us. Whenever I tried to speak to him about it, he was dismissive.

"We need to keep moving," I insisted. "This isn't safe."

"Safety is exactly what I have in mind. Our first thought needs to be to protect the people who've come to rely on us," he said over and over. "Attacking now is a risk without a reward. The government will still be there to topple when we're ready."

My nervousness continued to grow with the size of the camp, though, admittedly, most of the others were content enough.

"There's nothing wrong with a rest," said Papi, "and besides, Fósforo knows what's right."

Eventually, Fósforo avoided me, or so I thought, until I couldn't stand it anymore. I decided I had to try to convince him, and climbed up the path from the last platoon's camp to where Fósforo was staying. When I arrived, I found a group seated at a long table that had been taken from Hacienda Inocentes and carried up the slope. Fósforo sat at the head of the table, smoking his pipe and reading a book. Siki sat beside him, and the rest of the bodyguards filled benches on either side of the table. Esperanza was ladling out small helpings of sopa de albóndigas to each of them. If not for their filthy fatigues, it was a picture of domesticity.

"Sit down," said Esperanza. "We have enough."

"I've already eaten," I said, but I took a seat close to Fósforo.

"A coffee, at least?" said Esperanza.

"Of course," I replied.

Fósforo put down his book and sent a thick ring rising out of his pipe. The tobacco smelled good, better than that we had become used to. Esperanza picked his pouch up from the table and passed it to me, and I loaded some in my own pipe.

"Siki got it from some people who arrived in camp yesterday," said Esperanza. I tried to picture who that was, but enough people were arriving every day that I didn't meet all of them. "They're from southwest of here, but they came this way when they heard of about our camp," she said.

"Word's spread far," I said. "It must have reached the Guardia by now."

She shrugged. "The Revolution's no secret. And we can't turn people away who need protection."

Fósforo had so far been silent, the steaming bowl of soup sitting in front of him, untouched. He looked thinner and more haggard than I remembered, though his eyes still had the fire that made him stand out from everyone else.

"We need to keep moving," I said. "The longer we stay, the more mouths we will have to feed, and the slower we'll move."

Esperanza sat down on the bench with the bodyguards with her own bowl of soup. "We can't abandon these people."

"Agreed. But we also need to push onwards. The fight isn't won yet," I said.

Esperanza gestured at Siki, who seemed to know what she meant and brought out a map that I hadn't seen before. He rolled it out on the table, everyone lifting their soup bowls to make room.

"The escopeteros have spread out to beyond the river, and one of them brought this back with her. It's all pasture and farmland from the river right to the capital."

I looked at the map and saw that Esperanza had marked it up in pencil, noting where there were garrisons, and in some places, where bridges or roads had been cut.

"There must be other columns operating between here and there," I said. "What news from them? We may need them to coordinate things for us when we move."

Fósforo stood up abruptly, jostling the table and spilling soup onto the map. He turned and walked away, quickly disappearing into the trees above the camp. When no one else moved, I gestured angrily at Siki,

"One of you go with him," I said. "Are you his bodyguards or not?"

"He won't let anyone come with him," said Siki, embarrassed. "And if we try to follow at a distance, he doubles back and sends us away."

"You boys clean up the dishes," said Esperanza, taking me by the arm and leading me back down the trail towards the main camp. When we were out of earshot, she took both my hands.

"He still blames himself for . . . what happened," she began.

"We're all upset," I said, "and devastated and furious and even more convinced of what we must do. But it's not his fault."

"Just give him some more time," she said. "Besides, we received a message this morning that's upset him even more."

"Another massacre?" I asked, my throat tight.

"No, the Sandinista leadership is sending representatives to meet with him."

"That doesn't sound terrible," I said.

"It does if you worry that they're going force you to do something you're not ready to do," she said.

"If they think we should move, then I'd say they're right."

"Then be here for the meeting, as Fósforo's friend. Help him to hear what he needs to hear," she said. "Of everyone here, he trusts you the most."

I let go of her hands. "I don't think that's true anymore," I said.

"It is," she said. "And of everyone, you know him best. He's harder on himself than anyone else." She hesitated for a moment, and then gave me a quick embrace and a peck on the cheek before returning to the headquarters. I walked back down the trail to the main camp, already thinking that I needed to check to ensure that enough rations were being prepared for dinner.

As I walked through each platoon's area, I realized that we must have had as many non-combatants as we did guerrillas in the camp, and unlike before, this wasn't due to a lack of guns. The numbers of very young and very old and the sick and wounded were growing faster than our fighting numbers.

I had a discussion with the cooks about all of this and had started to think about how I might reorganize things again when my head snapped around. From farther away, near the base of the volcano, there were three rifle shots.

People around me screamed, and I saw parents grabbing their children and running away from the noise. I unslung my rifle and listened for a moment, but there were no more shots.

"Be calm, everyone," I said loudly, though no one took heed. I saw Tembo, who commanded the platoon in whose area of the camp I was standing. "Grab as many men as you have, and come with me now."

"For a fight?" he asked.

"I don't think so," I said, "but I can't be sure."

As we walked down to where the shots had been, we were met by a young guerrilla sent to find me.

"You're needed below, Capitán," she said.

"What's happening?"

"More guerrillas," she said.

I saw that our men had spread themselves out behind every piece of cover they could find, in a loose arc around the trees where we had concealed our trucks. Standing in the open facing them was a young man in fatigues, his arms held out to show that he was unarmed.

"What's going on here?" I asked the first guerrilla I saw, a tall man who I knew to be called Flaco. "A group of bandits appeared out of the trees over there, maybe a hundred of them," he answered.

"Bandits?"

"They're neither guardsmen nor us . . ." said Flaco, his voice trailing off.

"Did they shoot back?" I asked.

"No, but that one says he wants to talk to whoever's in charge," he said.

"Madre de Dios," I said under my breath. I slung my weapon over my back and walked out towards the man who stood facing us. He had a long, matted beard and Guardia fatigues. He smiled at me and extended a hand to shake as I approached.

"We look to be in the same business," he said.

I nodded and took his hand, still not sure who or what he was.

"We were operating north of Matagalpa, but we decided to come here when we heard what you were doing."

"And what's that?" I asked.

He seemed surprised. "Clenching a fist to strike a blow," he said. "Not a jab with a single column like a finger in the eye, but a knockout punch."

"How many of you are there?" I asked, scanning the trees behind him.

"One hundred thirty-four of us, man, woman and child," he said. "Maybe more since I've been standing here, some of our women are pregnant." He laughed, and I couldn't help but smile with him as well.

"You're welcome to join us," I said, "and welcome to help us keep everyone fed as well."

"We'll do our part," he said, before sticking both fingers in his mouth and whistling.

On his signal, his column began to gather around him. While our column was a mix of peoples from across the department, this group could all have been cousins, except for their leader.

"This was once a village," he said, as a guerrilla brought over a Tommy gun with an embroidered carrying strap. "Here you go, padre," he said.

"Padre?" I asked.

He pulled aside his beard, and I saw that he wore a priest's collar with his fatigues. "Just Gustavo is fine."

"Paco," I replied, shaking his hand again.

I found what I thought was a good piece of ground for the newcomers to settle on, but when I showed it to Gustavo, he shook his head.

"They won't stay here," he said. He pointed up the hill. "Is that where the ruins are?"

"More or less," I said.

"Then they'll want to be on the other side of that little stream."

"They don't want to be sleeping so close to the rest of us?" I asked.

"No," laughed Gustavo. "These people are Catholic, but they have some Ulua blood. Some of the old beliefs die hard, and to them, those ruins are undoubtedly haunted," he said.

"By something so fierce that the stream will protect them?"

"No, but the spirits of the stream will," said Gustavo.

"That doesn't sound very Catholic to me," I said.

"Even after a few years of living with them, they would never say that it was because of ghosts, but I know they'd have ten other reasons why the ground over there is better than the ground here," he said.

"I'll take your word for it."

He and I took a seat on a rock partially covered in moss, and Gustavo waved his people past us, speaking to them in a dialect so thick that I didn't understand. The man he spoke to replied something agreeable, and his column set out for the ground he had picked for them.

"Are you really a priest?" I asked Gustavo.

"The priests in the seminary in Managua thought so," he said. "Though they sent me to minister to as remote a place as they could find as soon as I was ordained."

"But padre, then how are you leading a column?" I asked, hardly concealing my astonishment.

"Just Gustavo," he said with a wave of his hand. "A better question would be, how could I not?"

"But you already have a calling, unless you've given up your vows?"

"In fact," said Gustavo, "now I am truly living them. In seminary, they taught us orthodoxy—the correct beliefs and rituals of the mother church. The focus was on making sure that we knew the doctrine like the back of our hands."

"Well," I said, "you can't wing it during Mass."

Gustavo laughed. "Indeed, you can't, Paco. But when I started living amongst real people, and away from the eyes of the Bishop, I realized that I was missing something. The village where they sent me was made up of the most honest and generous people I had ever met. They lived communally, sharing the ups and downs of their lives together. And while they were nominally Christians when I arrived, they hadn't had a priest in their church in years. They did it all without any detailed understanding of the beliefs that I held so dear."

"Good people are good people," I said. "That's true everywhere, just as some of the worst people can be found in the first row of pews every Sunday."

"Exactly," said Gustavo, "but how could that be?"

"I don't know," I said, "it seems so obvious that I can't explain it."

"Because it is right there under your nose," he said. "Orthodoxy allows you to know God, but orthopraxis lets you live out his will."

"I don't understand," I said.

Gustavo got up on his feet. "Imagine, everything going on in this country is in some way God's will. The good and the bad. And so, rather than passionately studying and repeating the Word of God, we must get involved in this world God has made for us. We must be as passionate about the lives of the People of this country as we are about scripture, and to live the Word of God in a practical way."

"But who's to say what part of this world you're supposed to live in if it's all God's will?" I asked. "By that theory, a life spent running a whorehouse is as meaningful as running an orphanage. How do you know what life to live?"

"This is good," said Gustavo, laughing. "I haven't had anyone to talk to about this for a long time. In Latin America, everything is screaming one thing at us, every day—the majority of our people are victims of social injustice. They live in poverty that can only provoke a moral reaction from anyone who cares to look. This is God clanging an alarm bell for us—he is showing us where he wants us to be."

I shook my head. "I've never met a priest who talks like this," I said.

"Matthew 10:34," said Gustavo. "Do not think that I have

come to bring peace to the earth. I have not come to bring peace, but a sword." He held up his Tommy gun in one hand. "The source of poverty in our country is sin. Not just the sins of greedy individuals but the sins of the system itself. And there is no way to extirpate that sin but with the sword."

"Amen," I said.

Gustavo clapped me on the shoulder. "Paco, you're like these people when I first met them. A man who lives a good life without even knowing the basis of how he does it. The Revolution needs men like you to lead the way to liberation for others to follow."

I shook my head. "Most days, I'm just trying to survive, and to keep my men alive as well."

"God loves the insignificant, the marginalized, the needy and the defenceless, just as you do," said Gustavo. "We'll have a multitude of columns gathered here like a host of angels before long, and then this rotten, sinful regime's days will be numbered."

Gustavo walked over to tend to his flock, but I stayed sitting on the rock, my mind spinning with new thoughts.

26

GUSTAVO'S PREDICTION turned out to be accurate, as other columns began to seek us out and add to our numbers. Even as our numbers swelled, we managed to find space for everyone. I was amazed at how much like a little city the camp was becoming, with muddy streets leading between platoons, and, for the first time in many months, I was homesick for Managua. Not for my own home, exactly, but for the familiar streets and plazas and parties that were a world away from the present day.

The massacre at Hacienda Inocentes still cast a pall over everyone, and over time, the memory of it only became more menacing. The released guardsmen of San Jose Guachipilín became like a bogeyman to many, and the network of lookouts and guards we set up around the camp kept a watchful eye out for them. The escopeteros ranged widely in the department and farther south as well, but they neither saw any of them nor heard news of where they went. As our presence grew, so did the likelihood of an attack, at least in my mind.

It had become a habit for me to walk through the entire camp each morning, stopping to speak with each of the platoon and column leaders. More often than not, they had nothing of real importance to talk about, but through those chats, I could gauge the temperature of things. The mood of the camp was restless.

Whenever our talk turned to the future, people's eyes would turn towards the old ruins where Fósforo made his camp.

Near the centre of the camp, close to where we had set up the communal kitchen, was a large ocote tree that towered over all the rest. Its resin was so thick that the kitchen quickly collected any branches that fell from it for use in starting fires. The base of the tree was at least three feet thick and covered in memorials to fallen guerrillas and lost family. Two thick black ribbons had been tied around the trunk. All around the tree, scraps of cloth with names embroidered on them or even pieces of paper with names written on them, were stuck into the ribbons, along with braids of grass and flowers and a few odd objects. I don't think that anyone had decided to make a memorial here; it had sprung up seemingly of its own accord. It became the focal point for people from across the camp to pray and remember, and the kitchen started keeping a large pot of tea boiling on an open fire nearby.

I was asking the cooks about the state of our rations when Loba, standing on the other side of the cook pots, caught my eye and gestured for me to come over.

"You have to do something," she said.

"Do I? About what?"

"It's Papi," she said. "He got caught drinking. Not just drinking, but drunk."

"I didn't hear anything about this," I said. "Caught by who?"

"He was stumbling through the brush like a wild animal. One of the sentries challenged him, and they got into a scuffle."

"Where is he now?" I growled.

"That's the problem," she said. "Siki and those boys heard the commotion and came to see what it was about, and when they saw Papi was drunk, they arrested him. He's somewhere uphill with them."

"He can stay there until he sobers up," I said. Loba still looked distraught, so I reassured her. "I'll go check on him shortly."

I had finished my morning rounds and planned to ascend to where Fósforo was camped when there was a commotion down closer to the highway. There were no shots being fired as before, but I could see a small crowd of men, some in suits, ascending towards me, led by a guerrilla. I walked to meet them. The guerrilla was Flaco, who I recognized by his height from far off. He was flustered, waving his arms nervously when he recognized me.

"They wouldn't stop," he said. "Maybe we should have shot them . . ." His voice trailed off, and he looked at me imploringly. One of the men in a suit brushed past him, extending his hand towards me to shake. It took me a moment to identify him, but underneath the heavy jowls and patchy beard, I recognized Jaime Marroquín.

"Paolo!" he said, pumping my hand vigorously.

"Paco," I corrected him. I gestured to the others. "And so, you've brought the leaders of the Revolution with you?"

Marroquín glanced backwards for a moment before laughing. "Hardly, my young man. This is merely my staff and one other advisor." An older man with a neatly trimmed grey goatee and glasses stepped up beside him. This man was dressed in what I imagined tourists would wear on a safari to Africa. Behind him were a half dozen men who looked like factory workers if not for the rifles they carried.

"Let me introduce Doctor Lorca, a professor of Political Economics."

I shook Doctor Lorca's hand as well and then did the same with Marroquín's staff.

"And where will we find the famous revolutionary fighter, Fósforo?" asked Marroquín, eyeing the camp around him.

"I'll take you to him," I said. Turning to Flaco, I jerked my thumb up towards the top of the volcano. "Run ahead and tell Fósforo to expect us."

Flaco nodded and took off at a trot, his long legs carrying him into the trees.

"It's not far," I said, waving Marroquín past me and up the slope.

We slowly ascended the volcano's slope. To my eyes, the trail was well-worn and obvious to follow, even in the dark, but Marroquín could not see it. I soon began to walk ahead of him to ensure that we would reach our destination. Although I walked slowly, Marroquín was quickly winded by the effort. Doctor Lorca sweat through his shirt until it looked like he had been dunked in a river. We paused for a moment so that the visitors could catch their breath.

"Did you design this camp to kill me?" said Marroquín, between breaths.

"I'm not sure anyone 'designed' it at all," I said jokingly, though I couldn't tell if Marroquín laughed or even smiled as he hung his head down towards his shoes.

After a few minutes of rest, I started walking again. "It's not much farther," I said encouragingly.

"Slow down," said Marroquín, "We're not all as nimble as goats." He grabbed at every branch or bush within reach, half walking and half pulling himself along as we climbed. Strung out behind him were Doctor Lorca and the others.

After what seemed like an eternity, we reached Fósforo's camp atop the ruins. Esperanza stood smiling to greet us, and behind her, Fósforo's bodyguards were lined up like anxious schoolboys. Of Fósforo himself, there was no sign.

"Jaime, it has been too long," said Esperanza, putting her hands on Marroquín's shoulders and allowing him to kiss her on both cheeks. "And Doctor Lorca, it is also a pleasure," she said, receiving his kisses as well.

"Quite the little home you've built," said Marroquín, eyeing the sagging canvas and salvaged furniture critically. If she noticed his tone, she didn't react at all, waving everyone graciously to take seats around the long table.

"We have coffee, and I've sent for some bread as well. You must be hungry after your long journey," she said.

"Hungry to meet your leader," said Marroquín. "Where is he?"

"On a patrol," said Esperanza. "He'll be back this afternoon, and we'll make you comfortable until then."

We all gathered around the table, Marroquín sitting at the head without hesitation. I took my pipe out of my pocket and began to stuff the bowl with the rough tobacco to which we'd become accustomed. When Marroquín saw me, he reached deep into his suit jacket. His neck folded over his collar as he strained to reach into his pocket until he pulled out a silver cigar case.

"Would you prefer one of these?" he said, holding it out to me.

I took one and primed a hole in the end with my penknife while Marroquín watched. When I was ready to light it, he held up a heavy American lighter, and I puffed away at it. The cigar tasted light and sweet compared to what I usually smoked.

Siki began to pass out mugs of coffee, and behind him, Esperanza fussed like a housewife. I stood up, making a space on the bench for her. "Come and sit down," I said. "You must have a lot to catch up on."

"We certainly do," said Marroquín, "but that can wait. First, to business."

I looked at Esperanza, who gestured that I should sit back down.

"It was quite the blow, this operation with the Congress," I said.

"Indeed," said Marroquín. "Cero accomplished a masterstroke. But have you heard what followed?"

I shook my head.

"Uprisings in six cities. Managua, Matagalpa, Masaya, León, Chinandega and Estelí. Patriots of all factions, supported by the People."

"Then the Revolution is won," said Siki, slapping his palm on the table excitedly.

"Each one was crushed," said Marroquín. "Thousands of people were killed by the Guardia, and we're left in control of not an inch of ground that we had taken." No one spoke, thinking about how things might have gone differently for us in San Jose Guachipilín had we held our ground.

"The government is stronger than any one group of us. Even within the Sandinista movement, we have had different factions for years. This is why the most practical of us are proposing a third way—the unification of all opposition groups to defeat the Somocistas once and for all. An agreement to fall under a central leadership to achieve our goals."

No one spoke, thinking about what this would mean for our independent column.

"I don't expect that you get the newspapers here, much less the international ones, but can you guess what was on the front pages for days? What the world has been reading about Nicaragua?"

I shrugged.

"The world cries at the injustice of the massacre at Hacienda Inocentes," he said, "even the Yanqui press bemoans the loss of innocent life. A political commission has been created in America to review their support for the Somoza family. And inside this country?"

He paused for a moment, waiting to hear my guess until I shook my head again.

"There is one name on the lips of every person: Fósforo, the brave revolutionary leader, victor in San Jose Guachipilín, and a true son of Nicaragua."

He sat back, satisfied that his news would impress us. No one said anything until Esperanza spoke up.

"All of us owe our lives, and our victories, to Fósforo," she said, "but also to men like Paco, and countless others whose names will never make the newspapers."

"Well, let us get these men and women around the table here, so that they can hear what is happening in other parts of the war, and so that we can listen to them as well. When they understand what is at stake, they'll agree to come back into the fold."

Doctor Lorca had been silent throughout, occasionally scribbling notes in a notebook that he kept in his shirt's breast pocket. He watched me intently as Marroquín spoke, the size of his eyes magnified by the lenses of his glasses.

"Of course," I said, "we'll bring all the leaders together here."

"In the morning," said Esperanza.

"In the morning," I repeated.

I didn't stay to wait for Fósforo to return, but before I left, I took Siki aside to speak about Papi. "What is this about an arrest?" I asked.

"Our leaders can't be drunk in public at a time like this," he said.

"Where is he?" I asked.

"The Novios have him," said Siki. "Until the trial to determine his punishment."

"A real trial would determine his guilt or innocence first," I said. "This doesn't need to be so complex. He's one of my men, I'll put him on guard duty for a month, and that will be the end of it."

Siki shook his head. "Fósforo is going to be the judge. He's already said so."

"Then I'll talk to Fósforo," I said.

Siki shrugged. "He knows what justice looks like."

I walked downhill to the edge of the perimeter, where the Novios were camped and found Jacinto, the man who had replaced Santiago as their leader.

"I want to see Papi," I said without any preamble.

Jacinto stuck out his jaw. "He's our prisoner until Fósforo says otherwise."

"Bring me to him," I said.

Jacinto didn't move his feet but merely flicked his chin towards a shelter built beside a large tree. I walked over to find Papi, lying on his back, with his hands tied together by a long rope tethered to the tree.

"You can sleep anywhere," I said to him, squatting in the dirt beside him.

Papi opened his eyes. "Hold up my crucifix," he said. I lifted the cheap plastic cross, and he kissed it. "I'm glad to see you."

"What is this all about?" I asked.

He rolled slowly into a sitting position, his hands held out in front of him. "I had been making chicha de muko, the same way my mother did, to share some other like-minded folks." I didn't smile, and he hesitated. "With part of our ration of corn, not food that we'd stolen," he said.

"How did I not notice this?" I asked.

Papi smiled sheepishly. "I didn't want to trouble anyone, and so we set ourselves up deeper into the forest."

"And then what happened?"

"When it was about ready, I sampled some. It wasn't quite right, and so I made a few adjustments and sampled it again. I couldn't quite get the flavour right, and before I knew it, I could barely stand," he said.

"What kind of chicha is this?"

"I told you, like my mother made. Not that sweet nothing that you drink in Managua, something with a bit of kick to it." He adjusted his legs uncomfortably. "We hardly drink anymore, I must have lost my tolerance. My grandmother could sit and drink it all day. I'm more embarrassed by the fact that it got me drunk than that I got caught."

"Papi, you need to set an example for the others, especially when times are uncertain," I said. "There's going to be a punishment of some kind, but it's a waste to leave you tied up here."

"Of course," said Papi. "I'm sorry."

"I'm not going to try to fight the Novios and break you out of prison," I said. "I'll be back later on."

Papi looked ashamed, and his voice caught as he spoke. "Thank you."

I ignored Jacinto as I walked back through the camp. Esperanza sent a runner just as the sun set to tell me that Fósforo had returned. She had made Marroquín and their party as comfortable as possible in the upper camp, though I heard later that they complained bitterly at the lack of beds and mattresses. I decided to let Papi stew as a prisoner overnight and to speak to Fósforo in the morning. Perhaps the humiliation of that would be a satisfactory punishment.

I walked through the camp one last time and spoke to each of the column, platoon and section commanders personally to invite them to the meeting tomorrow, and every one of them was eager to discuss what would happen next.

"Fósforo will have a plan for victory," said Juan.

"He always has," agreed Loba.

"Let's hope," I said.

"We have enough of a plan already," replied Juan. "Patria o muerte."

27

WHEN THE MEETING CONVENED, we were sitting three deep around the table in Fósforo's campground. Marroquín had ceded the head of the table to Fósforo but placed himself at his right hand. I likely should have sat there as well, but I was content to sit on the group's fringes, intending to listen rather than to speak.

Before the meeting started, Marroquín offered Fósforo a cigar from his silver case. "These are very good," he said, holding the case open. "Better than that cat shit you smoke up here in the mountains."

Fósforo took out his tobacco pouch and held it open for Marroquín. "Now's no time for us to get soft," he said. "If smoking a pinch of cat shit is all I need to experience pleasure, then my lifelong happiness is practically assured."

Marroquín wasn't sure if Fósforo was joking or not, but he placed a cigar down on the table in front of him and selected one for himself before putting the case away. The cigar on the table sat untouched. Marroquín lit his cigar and then began to speak.

"The time to strike is now," said Marroquín. "The government is on their back foot, but they won't be off balance forever. But to be successful, we must be united."

There was a general murmur of agreement, but no one spoke, waiting for Fósforo, who was blowing a furious column of smoke from his pipe.

"And what of the people of this department?" asked Fósforo. "And the dependants of the guerrillas of the columns who shelter with us? If we leave, they'll be helpless."

"They're helpless if you stay here as well," said Marroquín. Even now, our sources are telling us that the Guardia is planning to send the Batallón de Combate General Somoza to retake San Jose Guachipilín. They won't let this defeat hang over their heads forever."

"They can send a division to try and get across the river," said Huracán. "If we have to, we can hold them at that bridge until Judgement Day."

Marroquín looked at him disdainfully. "Do you think that's the only bridge over the river? They'll be behind you before you know it. And while you sit here, that bridge is undefended."

"Then we move back to protect San Jose Guachipilín," said Loba.

"Do you think that they don't have spies? They know where you are and where you aren't, and they will strike where you least want them to do so," replied Marroquín. "Alone, you are vulnerable, but together we will win."

"Protecting the people of this country needs to be our first priority," said Fósforo. "Without them, this Revolution is nothing."

"This Revolution is so much bigger than any of you realize," said Marroquín. "There is fighting all over the country. I'm asking you to join the Revolution, to stop fighting by yourselves."

"And it's not just the columns in the hills and mountains and swamps, but also the fighting committees of the trade unions and the underground movement in the universities, all working together under the guidance of the movement in a Frente Amplio Opositor," added Doctor Lorca.[12]

Marroquín nodded, taking a moment to mop his brow with a handkerchief before continuing. "Comrades, we're not here to lecture you, but there is much that you are not aware of, which is to be expected given your circumstances. We're here to inform you of the progress of the Revolution throughout the country, and to implore you to strike."

---

[12] *Translator's Note: Frente Amplio Opositor / Broad Opposition Front.*

"No one needs to beg us to act," said Fósforo with a touch of irritation in his voice. "We've acted of our own free will for many months, and have managed to free this department with nothing but words of encouragement from the movement." Marroquín's face began to turn red.

"The hallmark of a true revolutionary is loyalty," said Doctor Lorca.

"I agree," said Fósforo, "but loyalty to what? The movement? To you?"

"To the Revolution," said Marroquín.

"To the emancipation of the People," corrected Fósforo. "Meaning that the People must survive to be free." A lot of the commanders slapped their hands on the table in agreement.

"You're wearing blinkers," said Doctor Lorca. "You can stay here forever, but you're doing nothing more than frittering your strength away at the edges of this conflict. The decisive action will be in the cities, and most of all, in Managua. We need to take your strength and apply it where it will cause the Somocistas to crumble."

"The decisive action is where the people who are most oppressed can be found," said Fósforo. "Emancipating these people, breaking their chains and keeping them broken is what we must not lose sight of. It is the first and only goal of the Revolution."

"You've gone soft," said Doctor Lorca, earning him hard looks from every commander around the table. "The people free themselves, and if they become the grease that keeps the wheels of revolution turning, they do so willingly to emancipate others." He looked around at the other commanders, seeking but not finding anyone willing to agree with him. "Have you already forgotten? Patria o muerte?"

"We have spilled blood for this Revolution, more blood than you've ever seen," said Huracán. But there's no sense winning if all that's left is a smoking ruin."

"If we sacrifice the People, we'll be like fish without an ocean. Even if we're sharks, we need water to swim," added Loba.

"What you are doing here is admirable, but also irrelevant," said Marroquín.

"We need you to strike at the regime's centre, and to do it now when the cities are ripe to answer the call for a general strike," said Doctor Lorca. "The conditions are right for the Revolution to succeed."

"We're making the conditions through our action," said Fósforo. "One doesn't need a degree in economics to see the effect we are having on the mozos jornaleros, and that once every one of them looks to the Revolution for their salvation, we will have won."

"Heresy!" said Doctor Lorca, pulling out his notebook and scribbling furiously.

"Reality!" replied Fósforo, slapping his hand on the table.

We sat in silence for a moment, Marroquín letting the moment pass while he puffed on a cigar. I had said nothing throughout the debate so far. If this was what happened inside universities, I was glad to be uneducated.

Gustavo, his collar still hidden by the length of his beard, had also been listening in silence, but now stood up and addressed the group. His voice was melodious and carried well even without any apparent effort on his part.

"Comrades, we are like the blind men who argue over the elephant," he said. Looking around, he saw little more than blank stares. "Never having seen one, each feels but one part of the elephant and assumes that their limited experience is reflective of the whole. What is missing is knowledge that can bring all of these experiences, true in their own right, together to create a greater truth."

"Indeed, we trust the movement to do so," said Doctor Lorca.

Gustavo turned to him directly. "With respect, professor, I believe that is true to a degree, but only to a degree. What we are missing is the word of God."

"And do you presume to speak for God?" asked Doctor Lorca.

"There is no need for me to do so," said Gustavo, "as we need only reflect on the events around us to see His word in action."

"Marx was right when he called religion the opiate of the masses," said Doctor Lorca.

"I've also read Marx, professor, and I believe that what he wrote was this: Religion is the sigh of the oppressed creature, the heart of a heartless world, and the soul of soulless conditions."

"There is no solution to be found here in duelling footnotes," said Marroquín.

"What I am saying is this: the church has encouraged people to focus less on their troubles in this life in favour of the solace they shall receive in the next one. This is true no longer. We recognize that the source of poverty is sin, the sin of a system built on greed and oppression," said Gustavo.

"None of this is based in the church's teachings," said Doctor Lorca.

"Jeremiah 22:13," said Gustavo. "Woe unto him that builds his house by unrighteousness, and his chambers by wrong; that uses his neighbour's service without wages, and gives him nothing for his work."

"Padre, I suspect that you're both a heretic and a poor scholar," said Doctor Lorca.

"It's no heresy to recognize that to truly know God is to create a just society," said Gustavo.

"This is all well and good," said Marroquín, "but what the movement needs is action. The iron is hot. I ask simply: are you ready to strike?"

I'm not sure what anyone made of the debate that we heard, far removed from anything that we had ever discussed over the past months. With no one knowing what to say, all eyes turned to Fósforo, waiting for his decision.

Fósforo's head was surrounded by a halo of pipe smoke, and he was looking down at the table in front of him. He sent another smoke ring billowing out of his pipe, and it rose up and through the trees before disappearing into the sky. I watched it go as we waited in silence for Fósforo to speak.

"Thank you, everyone, for your thoughts," he finally said, still looking down. "I will take some time to consider." He then stood up and left, heading deeper into the forest where he was accustomed to take his walks.

Without him as its focal point, the meeting broke up, and all the leaders of the columns and platoons wandered back to where their people were camped. I did the same, not wanting to listen anymore to this talk about what we should do.

28

I LAY IN MY HAMMOCK STEWING about that meeting all night, and so, when the rains came in the morning, I got up reluctantly. I untied my hammock, bundled it up on top of my rucksack and pulled a small plastic tarp over it, tucking it in underneath so that it wouldn't blow open.

The rain was just a drizzle, but steady enough that I saw people taking shelter across the camp. Guerrillas were preparing huge pots of food over open fires in the communal kitchen. The pots hissed and steamed as the rain pelted them. I stopped for a moment to chat with the cooks, and one of them handed me a tin cup of broth.

"This is magical soup," said the old woman who was stirring the pot of broth with a tree branch almost as tall as she was.

"How so?" I asked, wondering if she was mad.

"No matter how many mouths there are to feed, there is always enough," she said.

"Are you sure that's not because you're preparing it in the rain?" I asked.

She laughed, but still corrected me. "With Fósforo as our leader, it's like the loaves and the fishes," she said. "Somehow, there is always enough."

"To the soup of victory," I said, raising my cup in a salute. The kitchen staff laughed and went back to preparing the food for the day, and I kept walking.

As I started my rounds, I saw Marroquín and his party coming down the volcano, ignoring the trail and crashing through the brush. They all looked exhausted, and Marroquín's suit was covered in mud. I guessed that he must have fallen a few times on his way down the slope. He stopped to speak to me, even though he was badly winded. The rest of the party carried on past him back towards the highway.

"I've never had a night like that," he said, mopping his brow.

"What happened?"

"What didn't happen? Insects, creatures roaming the bushes, I don't think I slept at all," he said.

"You get used to it," I said.

"Perhaps," he said doubtfully. "But, your leader seems to have more enthusiasm for just living in this wilderness than he does for fighting."

"It's not as simple as that," I said.

"Do you know what he plans to do?" he asked.

"Well, we have a lot of people sheltering with us," I said. "I think he intends to take care of them first."

"This Shangri-La can't last forever," he said. "Next time they'll send more troops than you can imagine, and they'll take care to finish you off. And they'll do the same to every column, every fighting committee, every underground cell in this country, one at a time, unless we can put them out of business first."

"I've tried to talk to him, but he just disappears into the bush without a word," I said.

"Silence is just an argument by other means," said Marroquín. "You need to figure out how to respond so that the Revolution goes forward."

"I'm not sure I can make him understand."

"That's not what I said."

I thought about what Marroquín meant, but before I spoke, he leaned in and poked me in the chest.

"The column needs to move before these rains worsen, and the roads turn to mud from here to the coast."

"I know," I said. He shook my hand and staggered farther down the trail.

I watched him walk away, the back of his suit covered in mud from the collar to his cuffs. I hadn't intended to speak with Fósforo this morning but found myself climbing the volcano to his camp nonetheless. Marroquín's party had worn a more direct path down the slope, and it looked like he wasn't the only one that had traversed part of the route on their backs. Even in the light rain, I didn't find it difficult to make the ascent.

Fósforo was seated at the table atop the stone ruins, and his bodyguards lounged in hammocks all around him. He had Marroquín's cigar clenched between his teeth, puffing away. Esperanza spooned scrambled eggs onto tortillas on a plate in front of him, but he ignored her, reading from a coverless book.

When she saw me, she smiled. "Are you hungry?" she asked.

"For your cooking? Always," I said, sitting down opposite Fósforo and leaning my rifle against the table beside me.

"It's just eggs," she said as she set a plate down in front of me.

"There was a time when we would have climbed over this mountain and down the other side for a fresh egg," I told her as I began to eat.

"I remember," she said, before disappearing into the tent.

Fósforo had not looked up, and the teenagers who surrounded him constantly watched me from their hammocks like bored predators. I finished my eggs before I cleared my throat to get his attention.

"I saw Marroquín as he was leaving," I said.

"Rolling past you down the mountain?" asked Fósforo.

"Something like that," I laughed.

"He asked me if I knew what was next for us."

Now Fósforo set down his book and turned to face me. "And?" he asked.

"I said I didn't know. That your first concern seemed to be taking care of the people who had taken shelter with us."

"Don't you share that concern?" asked Fósforo. From the

corner of my eye, I could see Siki watching me carefully, lying in his hammock and playing with a pistol in both hands.

"Of course," I said, "where we might disagree is how we do that. I hate to say it, but Marroquín's right. We need to keep moving, keep the government on their back foot. We should cooperate with the new Frente."

"We can't take this many people with us, and we can't leave them behind either," said Fósforo.

"And so, we camp here, eating every bit of food in the department and waiting for, what?"

"The escopeteros are looking for opportunities for us, and also watching our back," he said.

"But for how long?" I asked. "The rains have already started, and in a few weeks, the roads will be like soup."

"Have you got so soft that you worry about roads, now?" he asked. "Roads are for the Guardia; we make our own."

"Things are changing," I said. "Marroquín says the country is ready to erupt. It just needs someone to give the government another hard shove . . ."

"And what? It will topple, and Marroquín will step in to lead us?"

"Do you want to revolt against him too now?" I asked.

"I don't want to fight a revolution to get Somocismo without Somoza. What good has Marroquín done us up to this point?" asked Fósforo.

"He got us out of Managua, you might recall. And he says the conditions are ripe."

"We make the conditions ripe ourselves, we don't need to react because he says so, a man who got fat from years of 'leading' the workers towards revolution," said Fósforo dismissively.

"Then why not join the Frente and work to lead it in a different direction?" I asked. "In time, you could be driving this whole thing."

"My place is here," said Fósforo, "leading guerrillas in the field, not scurrying from hiding place to hiding place, living off the labour of others."

"Then lead them," I said. "They're all camped out below waiting for you to lead them, so do it."

"What do you mean?" said Fósforo.

"I mean, stop playing house up here and do something. Someone has to lead us."

Fósforo didn't reply, but I could tell he was furious as he pushed back from the table and walked away. His bodyguards watched him go, but none of them followed him.

Esperanza stood in the doorway of the large tent she shared with Fósforo, looking unimpressed. "He needs encouragement, not whatever that was," she said.

I shook my head. "I just wanted . . ."

She didn't wait for me to finish before disappearing inside again.

I started to walk back down towards the main camp, slipping a bit in the mud. Siki came quickly down the path behind me, pistol still in his hand.

"Paco," he said, "a word."

I turned to face him, his expression making me suddenly regretful that I had slung my rifle across my back.

He pushed his face up to mine, his arms at his sides. "Never, ever, ever threaten the Comandante again," he said, his voice strangled.

"I didn't threaten anyone," I said. "Is no one to ask questions anymore?"

"You heard me," he said.

We stood facing each other for a long moment, my feet sliding out from under me in the mud. It was as we stared at each other that I heard the sound.

"Listen," I said. His eyes broke away from mine and turned skyward.

The sounds of machine-gun fire erupted from below us, first one gun firing tracers into the air, and then more of them, all hammering away madly. Then came the explosions, a line of bombs impacting the mountain not far from camp, and then a second line higher up. We both dropped to the ground, our bodies pressed against each other as we rode out the attack.

My clothes were still stiff with mud when I had finished my rounds of the camp. By some miracle, no one had been killed. A few men on the fringes of the area had been wounded by splinters from the trees, but that was all. The government aircraft had flown too high to be accurate or had not had enough of an idea where we were in the first place. I crossed myself as I thought about the next time they would come.

As I went by the Novio's camp, I stopped and untied Papi.

"What's my punishment?" he asked.

"For now, this was your punishment," I said. "I still have to talk to Fósforo."

Papi looked hesitant, clutching his rosary in one hand. "He didn't say I was free?"

The blood rushed to my face. "This isn't the time to leave competent guerrillas tied to trees. We need you leading your men."

I saw that Jacinto was glaring at me, along with a few of the other Novios, none of whom I knew well. I didn't say anything and ignored them as I walked Papi back to our section of the camp. The platoon cheered when he returned, and he looked chastened. The humiliation of the whole matter was enough to keep him from doing it again, I was sure.

I kept walking around the camp, pausing for a moment in the kitchens to get a mug of tea and then wandered over to look at the memorial tree, where the number of mementoes tucked into the red and black cloth had continued to grow. Tacked to the trunk of the tree, just above the rest, was Rubio's hat. The felt was thin and riddled with holes, and it looked as if it might melt in the rain. I touched it for a moment and thought of Rubio. I must have been lost in the memory because I didn't hear anyone come up behind me.

"Praying?" asked Gustavo.

"No, padre," I said, "just remembering."

"Remembrance is a form of prayer," he said.

"Then I've been praying a lot lately."

I passed him my mug of tea, and he took a sip before returning it to me. We sat down on a fallen tree people had dragged close to the memorial to act as a bench.

"What's caused all of this need for remembrance?" he asked.

"I don't think we had time to remember before," I said. "But now, it feels like that's all I have time to do. Running the camp doesn't occupy enough of my mind."

"And so, you're anxious for action," asked Gustavo.

"For the Revolution to move forward," I corrected. "Not for fighting for its own sake."

"I understand," said Gustavo. "For years our church has preached 'Blessed are the meek, for they shall inherit the earth,' but the truth of the matter is that even the meek will have to act to see that end."

"But maybe that means making a life here, or somewhere in the department, keeping these people safe," I said.

"Man hungers for bread, but also for God. You can give them one of those things, but not the other," said Gustavo.

"I've never claimed to give anything more than bread and a chance to win our liberty," I said.

Gustavo clapped me on the shoulder. "You misunderstand me," he said, "and perhaps misunderstand yourself as well. You heard the professor at the meeting talk about religion being like a drug, yes?"

"I did, but I haven't read the book he was quoting from."

"It doesn't matter what you've read," said Gustavo. "You've lived it. He's not entirely wrong, you know. When the church does nothing but offer salvation in the next life without focusing on the troubles in this life, he's right. Most people are happy to go along, ignoring all the problems in their lives today and focusing instead on the afterlife."

"Isn't that what the church teaches?" I asked.

"It teaches us to love God and hate sin, and the troubles of our people—the needy, the marginalized, the unimportant, the despised and defenceless—all result from the sins of the unjust system. The divine is in every single one of us, and when we lift ourselves up out of poverty, we reveal the Glory of God."

"And so, all of this," I said, as I gestured at the camp around me, "is what we should be doing?"

"All of this, and more," said Gustavo. "We should not rest until every man, woman and child in this country, in all of Central America and the world, are free." He stood to go.

"Is that all?" I asked laughingly. "It's just that I can't see how to get there from here."

Gustavo pulled a prayer card out of his pocket and held it out to me. It was dog-eared and faded, and on the face of it was an image of an angel in armour, his foot on the neck of the devil. "Take this," he said, turning it over to reveal the prayer on the back.

I began to read the first few lines aloud: "Saint Michael the Archangel, defend us in battle, be our protection against the wickedness and snares of the devil . . ."

"We all need help sometimes," he said.

I sat on the log for a while longer, reciting the prayer in my head and thinking about what we needed to do. I thought that I had reached a decision when I got up to walk through the camp again, though the feeling of certainty quickly passed.

As I walked to the farthest platoon to check on them for the second time that day, I spotted one of the escopeteros was walking slowly through the lower camp. He had a shotgun slung over his shoulder and two dead rabbits hanging off his belt. As he came closer, I saw that it was Pelón.

"Good afternoon, Capitán," he said, doffing his hat.

I shook his hand, not sure if he was being sarcastic.

"What news of the outside world?" I asked.

He put a finger beside his nose and quickly looked around. No one was paying any attention to either of us. He leaned closer and spoke quietly to me for a few moments. When he had finished what he had to say, he doffed his hat again and walked away.

29

I DECIDED TO SPEAK with Fósforo again the next morning, leaving my rifle behind this time not to antagonize Siki or the others. In the centre of the camp, Gustavo and his column were gathered together around the memorial tree. Gustavo had a stole around his neck, but rather than saying Mass, he was reciting the Misa Campesina with both hands raised high over his head.

> *I believe in you, comrade,*
> *Christ man, Christ worker,*
> *victor over death.*
> *With your great sacrifice*
> *you made new people*
> *for liberation.*
> *You are risen*
> *in every arm outstretched*
> *to defend the people*
> *against the exploitation of rulers;*
> *you are alive and present in the hut,*
> *in the factory, in the school.*
> *I believe in your ceaseless struggle,*
> *I believe in your resurrection.*

I paused for a moment to listen and murmured "Amen" with his congregation at the end. Gustavo saw me over the head of his people and waved.

I climbed the hill with heavy feet, unsure what exactly I was going to say. Besides dealing with Papi, there were other issues to discuss that would affect us all. When I got to Fósforo's campsite, there was little going on. He was in his hammock, one foot dangling off the side. Esperanza had gone somewhere, probably to wash, and the others were lazing about. Fósforo's expression was friendly until I brought up the subject of Papi.

"Papi is back with my platoon," I said.

"You released him?" demanded Fósforo, sitting up.

"He hasn't gone anywhere," I countered. "He was doing no good tied to a tree while the camp was under attack."

"The Revolution doesn't need leaders like him," said Fósforo.

"You've never been drunk before?"

"I've never stolen food to get drunk," he said.

"Stolen food? What are you talking about?"

"Chicha's made with corn. Where did he get it?" said Fósforo acidly. "Or is your whole platoon hoarding food?"

"He says that he's been saving his rations to make it, and I believe him. There's no proof that he stole anything."

"The punishment for stealing food is death," said Fósforo. "We need to stamp out theft in the camp before it becomes commonplace."

I was stunned. "Death? You're talking about an execution when you don't even have proof of a crime!"

Fósforo practically leapt out of his hammock. "To execute a man, we don't need proof of his guilt, just proof that it's necessary to execute him. It's necessary for discipline."

I didn't know what to say. The silence was broken when Esperanza came back to the tent line, drying her hair. She looked around at all of us, sensing the tension.

"Will you stay for breakfast, Paco?" she asked.

"No, thanks," I said. I had turned around and was ready to

walk back down the hill when I stopped. "One other thing," I said. "We received word that the reporter Passereau is in the area again. He's camped out in Hacienda Inocentes. I assume that you don't want to be disturbed by him."

"Where did you hear that?" asked Esperanza.

"Pelón told me," I said.

"Why didn't he tell me?" she asked.

"He was in a hurry to get back to his post, I think."

"I should go meet him," said Fósforo. "Word of the Revolution needs to spread."

"As you wish." The sleeping area became a hive of activity as the bodyguards began pulling on their gear. Siki went to a crate and began to toss hand grenades to the others.

"This is an interview we're talking about, not a gunfight," I said.

"We'll be ready for both," said Siki.

I waited for Fósforo and walked back down to the bottom of the hill with him and his guard. I tried to talk to Fósforo, idly about small things, but he said little in response. As we passed through the positions of our platoons, arranged in a protective arc, our men watched Fósforo in silence.

"They haven't seen much of you lately," I said. "You should say something."

We stopped near the communal cookfires where a huge pot of beans and rice was being served to a line of runners with smaller pots for each section of the camp. Guerrillas gathered around us, waiting. Fósforo looked at them, hesitating.

"When are we going to advance again?" asked one young guerrilla.

"Soon," said Fósforo. "There are many things to arrange."

"Arrange them as we go," said the young guerrilla. "We're sick of waiting."

"Maybe this one should be the Comandante, he has all the answers," joked Fósforo.

There was a little laughter amongst the men, but the young guerrilla was serious. "I don't want your job; I just want us to fight again."

Fósforo clapped him on the shoulder. "Soon."

And then we were walking again, down the hillside and through the rest of the camp. I hadn't been able to keep to my plan of siting platoons in separate areas, and so the hillside was covered in a carpet of smaller camps. I placed our guerrillas and the other columns who had joined us in a rough circle around the hundreds of civilians who had fled their homes to seek our protection. I sited those civilians in one big mass, more or less. As we passed, people stopped and stared at Fósforo. As word spread that he was there, more and more people gathered to see him.

"That little shit has no idea," said Fósforo to me quietly. His face was lined with worry. I noticed a streak of grey in his beard that had not been there before.

"You used to think like him as well," I said. "Strike or be struck."

"I don't know what I think anymore," said Fósforo, smiling as he waved at the people staring at him. They kept a respectful distance, and we passed through the crowd easily.

At the bottom of the hill, there was a thick stand of trees that concealed our motor pool. A small group of men was guarding them, and they all gathered around when they saw us.

"Comandante," said Flaco.

"All quiet?" asked Fósforo.

"Other than a steady stream of people coming through here to join our camp, yes," said Flaco.

"We need two jeeps," said Fósforo.

Flaco rubbed his chin. "Of course, Comandante, but if I'd known in advance, we would have had them ready."

"We don't need them washed," said Fósforo, "just fuelled up."

"Right away," said Flaco. Siki and the other bodyguards left with Flaco to oversee the preparations. Fósforo and I found some shade in which to sit. Fósforo pulled out one of Marroquín's cigars and carefully sawed it in half with a pocketknife. He tossed one half to me, and I lit it. Fósforo's face was concealed by a cloud of smoke as he blew smoke rings.

"Do you think this reporter will truly understand what happened at Hacienda Inocentes?" asked Fósforo quietly.

"He will if you explain it," I said.

"I mean truly understand. Without the sights or smells . . ."

"You'll have to do your best."

"That's all I have been doing," said Fósforo, looking around, "and this is where it got us."

I looked across at Fósforo and saw him the way that no one else did. He was filthy, and his hair was matted, just like the rest of us, and he'd lost weight while we camped here even while the rest of us had gained it. But with his eyes ringed black with worry, he looked just like he did the night before I'd taken him to the boarding house to sleep. He looked like a man come untethered.

The two open-top jeeps pulled up beside us, the first driven by Siki and the second by Flaco.

"This one's a bit temperamental," said Flaco. "It's best if I drive it."

"We'll be gone a few hours, maybe more," said Fósforo.

"As much as I would prefer to stay here guarding these trucks," said Flaco, "I think a few hours away will be OK." Everyone laughed.

Fósforo jumped in beside Siki. "Get in," he said.

"I have too much to do here in camp," I said. "I spare you most of the details, but this camp doesn't organize itself."

"I insist, you have to come," said Fósforo.

"I have too much to do."

"The Revolution requires sacrifice," said Fósforo. "Do you think that any of us are indispensable?"

"I can't," I said.

Fósforo looked disappointed. "Going out for a drive like this, it'd be like old times," he said.

"Another time," I said.

"We should pack some food," said Fósforo. "Like a picnic. If only I had a flask." Fósforo handed a camera to Siki. "Take a picture of us before we go," he said. Turning to me, he blushed a little. "It was a gift."

Siki walked a few steps away and fumbled with the controls for a moment. Fósforo had to get out and show him how it worked, before getting back into the jeep to pose. Siki finally took several shots of us, each time counting down from three. Through all of this, I couldn't look at the others but just forced myself to smile.

I stepped back from the jeeps and gave Fósforo a wave. "I really do have things I need to organize. Just go."

Whether Fósforo knew then what I was thinking, I can't be sure, but in my heart, I think he did. He gave a wave back and turned to Flaco. "Let's get these things rolling."

Flaco was under the hood of the second jeep, tinkering with something. "Just a few more minutes, jefe."

I turned around and headed back into camp, busying myself with things that probably could have waited. My mind wasn't really on the tasks at hand, as I waited. Perhaps thirty minutes later, it came.

There was the crack of an explosion in the distance, followed by a hail of gunfire, and then silence. People stopped what they were doing and turned to stare in the direction of the noise.

Papi appeared at my side. "Madre de Dios, what was that?" he said.

"Run up the mountain and find Esperanza. Her escopeteros can find out," I said.

Papi's face fell. "I saw her a little while ago. She went with Fósforo . . ." His voice trailed off.

I didn't need to wait for the escopeteros to report. I knew the enormity of what had happened.

And so, I wept, for the Revolution, for my friends, and for myself.

HÉROES Y MÁRTIRES

EPILOGUE

THE CITY WAS SLOW on Sunday afternoons, and so it did not take Rubén long to get from his home in a suburb reserved for Party functionaries to the residencia. He knew that the government plates on his car would allow him to park anywhere without too much trouble, but nonetheless, he found a legitimate spot two blocks away and walked.

The great ironwork portrait of Fósforo on the side of the building wept rust in long streaks down its grey face. The man's bearded face appeared often enough in murals that Rubén almost felt as if he knew him. Looking at it now, he saw that the face was, in fact, a cipher, onto which one could project whatever details one wished.

The orderly at the front desk watched a protest unfold on a tiny television screen, tens of thousands of protesters marching alongside trucks carrying farmers waving banners. Rubén walked by on his way to see Paco. The orderly saw him and quickly came out from behind his desk.

"Comrade Rubén," he said, his eyes wide.

"Yes?" Rubén knew what he was going to say before he even said it.

"The Comandante . . ." The orderly hesitated. ". . . is no longer with us."

Rubén stared at him blankly for a moment.

"He passed away in the night. It was peaceful."

Rubén stood awkwardly in the hallway for a moment, neither wishing to go forward or retreat. The orderly stood with him for a moment before returning to the television. Rubén walked down the hallway to Paco's room. Pushing the door open, he looked inside.

The bed had been stripped, just the bare plastic mattress left sitting on the bedframe. On the side table was a cardboard box. Rubén peered inside, knowing that it was the sum total of what was left of Paco.

There were a few framed pictures that had been on the wall and a couple of books in a stack. On top of the pile was *Pedro Páramo*, and on top of that sat a prayer card. Paco's name card had been taken off the door and thrown in the box as well.

Rubén didn't stay long, walking quickly back down the hall. As he approached him, the orderly turned towards Rubén, gesturing to the television. "You've come from Managua," he said. "What do you think of all this?"

Rubén looked at the commotion playing out on the screen. The crowd was chanting: Ortega! Asesino! The helmets of long rows of riot police could be seen on the far edge of the crowd, rippling as they were pressed by the marchers. "I think that dialogue would be better than this," he said.

"What is there to discuss?" asked the orderly. "The government wants us to pay more taxes and get less in return."

Rubén was about to answer when the crowd dissolved into chaos. Clubs swung over the heads of the police, and the crowd pressed back on itself to get away. Police were pulled from their line and stomped underfoot. Shots were fired. The crowd ran. Blood streaked the pavement behind them.

"Madre de Dios," said the orderly, under his breath. Rubén quietly walked through the doors and onto the street. He wandered away from the residencia and down cracked cement steps to the malecón, sitting on the barrier that separated it from the rocky shore and the sea. An oil tanker slid by to be filled at the refinery.

Rubén knew the history taught in school.

The story began when the many different anti-government organizations in the country coalesced around the Sandinistas. Negotiations between them and the government broke down when it was clear that the Somoza regime had no intention of allowing elections. From that day forward, the Revolution took no prisoners. By June of 1979, the Sandinistas controlled the whole country except the capital.

He knew that the 'Ramón Espinoza de la Fuente Brigade,' composed of a number of different guerrilla columns, led the final drive from the countryside and into the capital, with Paco as its leader. As they approached, Somoza resigned. The fighting that had been intense all the way to the city's gates suddenly ceased, and the government collapsed like the rotten, hollow entity that it was. The country was in ruins, but in that moment, the People were swept to power. Hundreds of thousands of people were lifted from poverty. The socialist government of Nicaragua was a beacon across the Americas.

This was the history that he knew.

A crypt had long been reserved for him and other revolutionary heroes in the Cementerio Oriental in Managua, even though it had been closed to public burials for years. Stacked in vaults a half dozen high, the heroes and martyrs of the Revolution rested together. But Rubén was sure that this wasn't what Paco would have wanted, and so he argued for something different.

Instead, he was buried just outside of Hacienda Inocentes, in a small cemetery that was always on the verge of being overgrown. His remains were placed inside a white cement vault alongside a dozen other fallen guerrillas, but far from the tombs in the capital of exalted heroes like Ramón and Magdalena. Rubén had no influence over what was written on the outside of Paco's crypt, but when he saw it, he knew that it was right.

Comandante Francisco 'Paco' Martínez
"He held the Revolution above all else."

After the funeral, at which Rubén was given a seat near the front row, he took a long walk out to the base of the Volcán del Santo Sacramento by himself. It stood imposing above him, the forest deep and lush, having long since grown over whatever scars were left by the Revolution. He spent hours sitting there, deep in thought, before it was clear what he should do. Rubén reached into his pocket and took out the recording device that he had used in the many sessions with Paco.

Without further hesitation, he flung it into the bush and walked away.

ABOUT THE AUTHOR

Phil Halton has worked in conflict zones around the world as a security consultant and a Canadian Army officer. He is the author of two novels, *This Shall be a House of Peace* (2019) and *Every Arm Outstretched* (2020), as well as a history, *Blood Washing Blood: Afghanistan's Hundred-Year War* (2021). His work has appeared in the *Globe and Mail*, the *Canadian Army Journal* and other publications. He holds a Master of Defence Studies from Royal Military College of Canada and a Master of Arts in Creative and Critical Writing from the University of Gloucestershire.

Would you like to stay in touch?

You can sign up to receive my email newsletter on my website:

www.philhalton.com

I often give opportunities to my subscribers to read advance copies of my books, get invited to special events or receive free swag. It's the best way to stay in touch with me.

Or you can also find me on social media:

Twitter: @phil_halton
Facebook: https://www.facebook.com/philhaltonwriter/
Linkedin: https://www.linkedin.com/in/philhalton/

THIS SHALL BE a HOUSE of PEACE

PHIL HALTON

THIS SHALL BE A HOUSE OF PEACE

After the collapse of Afghanistan's Soviet-backed government, a *mullah* finds himself doing anything to protect his students.

Chaos reigns in the wake of the collapse of Afghanistan's Soviet-backed government. In the rural, warlord-ruled south, a student is badly beaten at a checkpoint run by bandits. His teacher, who leads a madrassa for orphans left behind by Afghanistan's civil war, leads his students back to the checkpoint and forces the bandits out. His actions set in motion a chain of events that will change the balance of power in his country and send shock waves through history.

Amid villagers seeking protection and warlords seeking power, the Mullah's influence grows. Against the backdrop of anarchy dominated by armed factions, he devotes himself to building a house of peace with his students — or, as they are called in Pashto, *taliban*. Part intrigue, part war narrative, and part historical drama, *This Shall Be a House of Peace* charts their breathtaking ambition, transformation, and rise to power.

BLOOD WASHING BLOOD

Afghanistan's Hundred Year War

PHIL HALTON

Blood Washing Blood:
Afghanistan's Hundred-Year War

A clear-eyed view of the conflict in Afghanistan and its century-deep roots.

The war in Afghanistan has consumed vast amounts of blood and treasure, causing the Western powers to seek an exit without achieving victory. Seemingly never-ending, the conflict has become synonymous with a number of issues — global jihad, rampant tribalism, and the narcotics trade — but even though they are cited as the causes of the conflict, they are in fact symptoms.

Rather than beginning after 9/11 or with the Soviet "invasion" in 1979, the current conflict in Afghanistan began with the social reforms imposed by Amanullah Amir in 1919. Western powers have failed to recognize that legitimate grievances are driving the local population to turn to insurgency in Afghanistan. The issues they are willing to fight for have deep roots, forming a hundred-year-long social conflict over questions of secularism, modernity, and centralized power.

The first step toward achieving a "solution" to the Afghanistan "problem" is to have a clear-eyed view of what is really driving it.